ISBN-13: 979-8-9875744-1-6

Cover design and interior illustrations by: Etheric Tales
City and world map by: Ashrale Productions
Printed in the United States of America

To Dad
You told me that all heroes had to have a weakness;
When I set out to prove you wrong
I proved you right
And Daimyn was born

JAGGED EMERALD CITY

~ Obsidian Divide Book One ~

By R.K. Brainerd

World Map

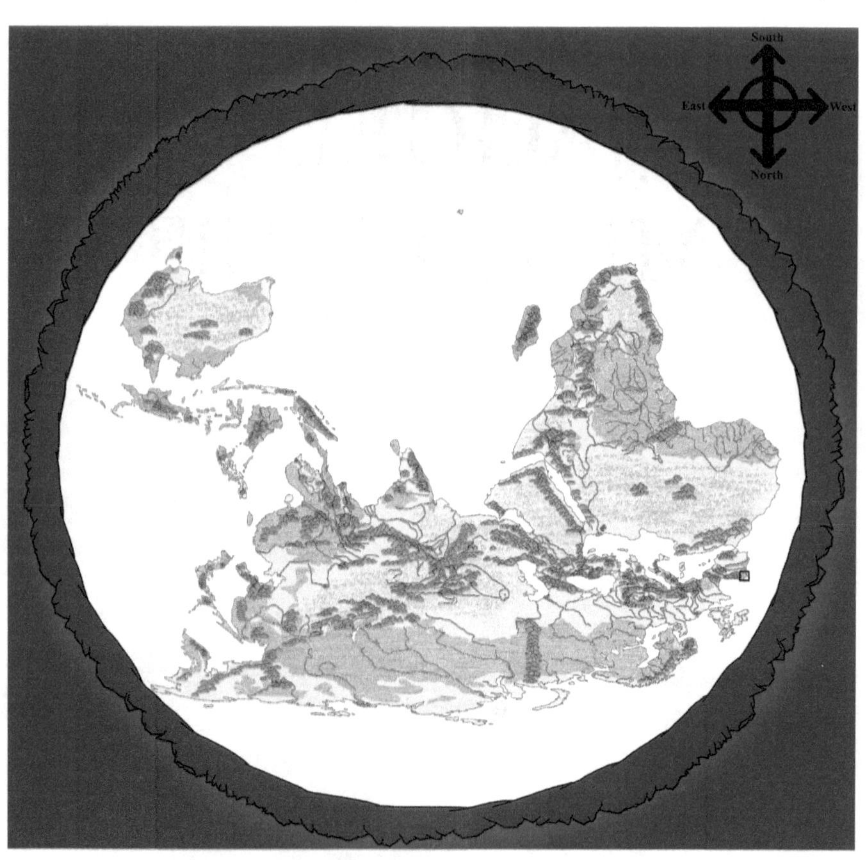

The Independent City of Farfalla

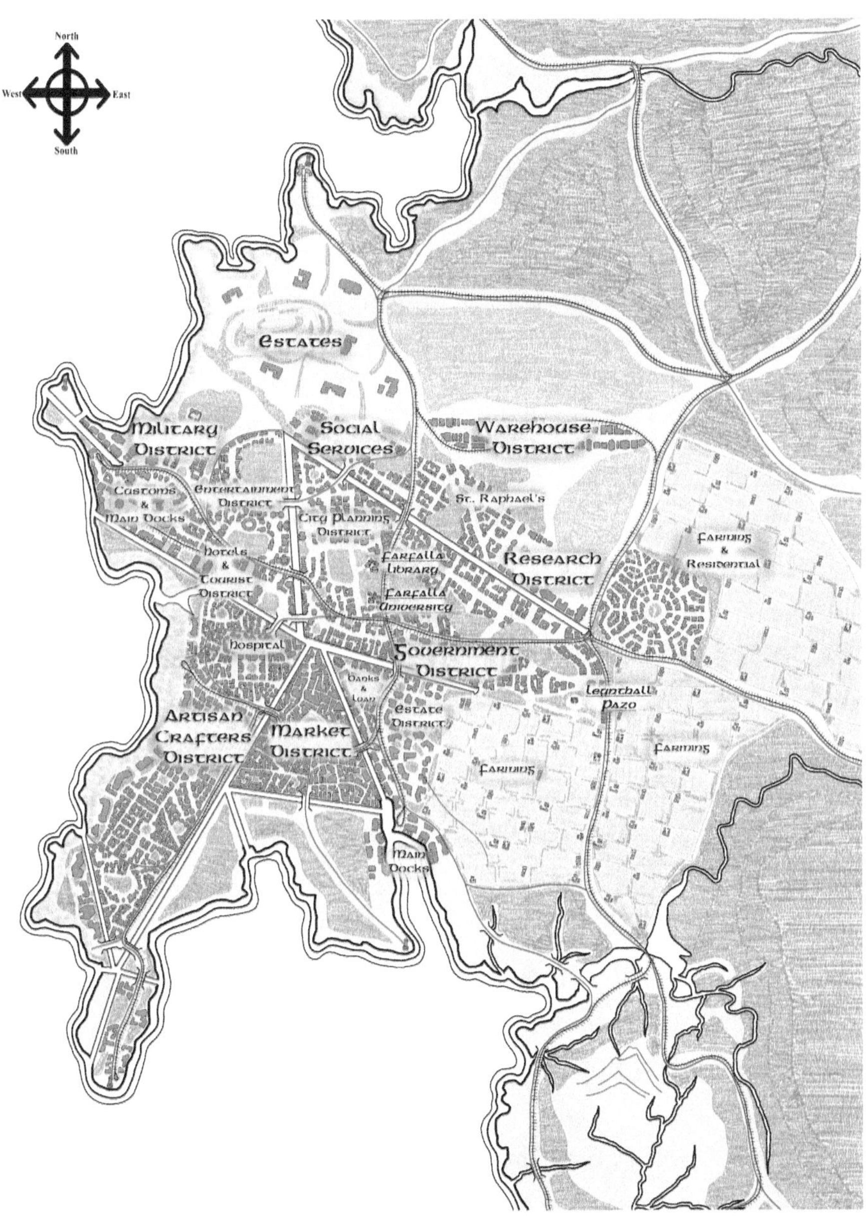

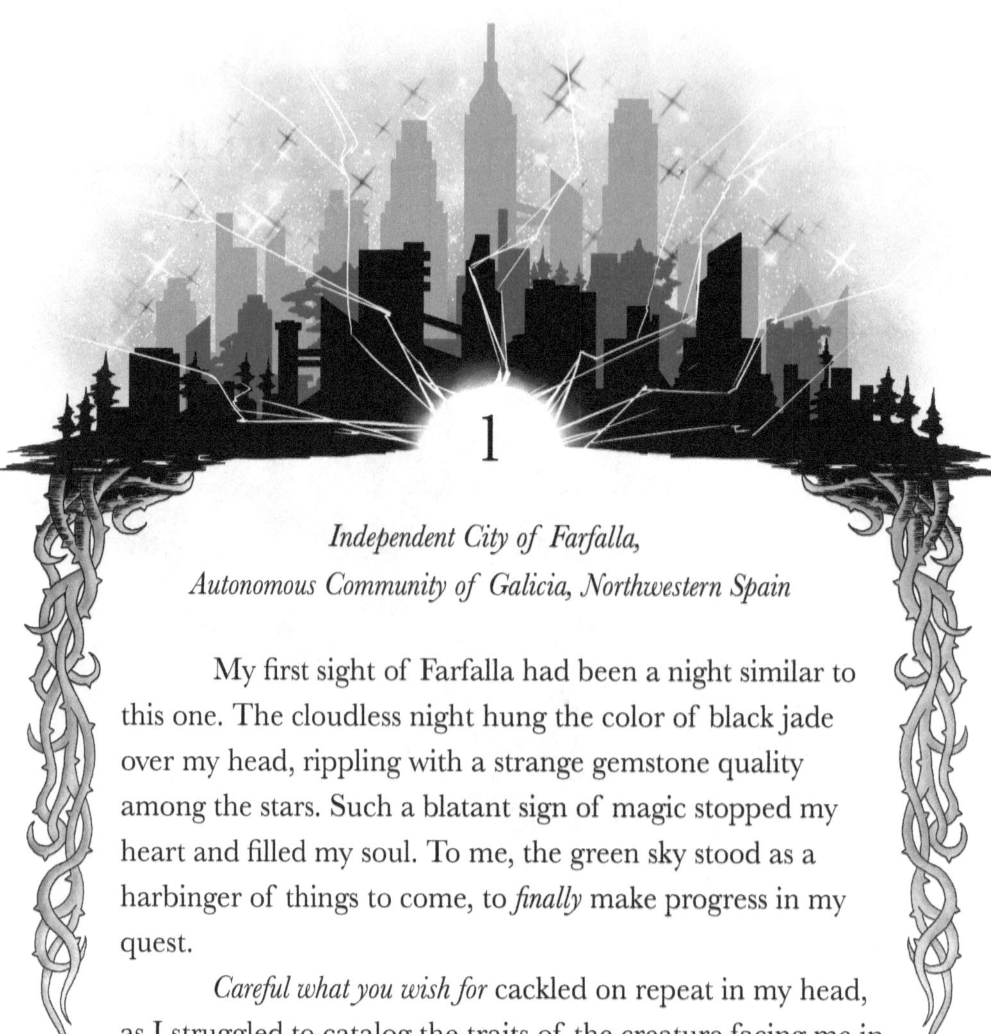

1

My first sight of Farfalla had been a night similar to this one. The cloudless night hung the color of black jade over my head, rippling with a strange gemstone quality among the stars. Such a blatant sign of magic stopped my heart and filled my soul. To me, the green sky stood as a harbinger of things to come, to *finally* make progress in my quest.

Careful what you wish for cackled on repeat in my head, as I struggled to catalog the traits of the creature facing me in the alleyway.

Humanoid. Bleached-bone pale. Twisted features, huge teeth. Milky eyes.

All of it combined into something familiar to me from research, but panic made it impossible to put together. They clutched their upper arm, blood oozing between white fingers.

"Sorry about the stabbing—needed you to let me go." Adrenaline made me sound giddy. "I just want to talk. You're the first I've—"

They—he?—lunged at me. I skittered to the side, avoiding running into the wall. *Don't retreat backwards, you can't see what's there.* The knife in my hand quivered as I brought it up into a better guard position. So much for defense training; I shook like a bloody leaf. Now I regretted forgoing a corset this evening. The extra barrier of boning sounded like a great idea right about now.

"I get you're angry, but you started it."

The hairs on the back of my neck stood on end at the sound that seethed out of the creature. Should I get out onto street with more light, or stay here where they had only one direction to come at me?

"Anything else to say?" My voice shook this time, and my next question came out as a statement. "Or am I talking to myself here."

My stomach sank as they stared with uncomprehending, feverish eyes. Of *course* I wouldn't be able to communicate with the first demon I'd finally tracked down. That just fit with how successful the last seven years had been. If the lead hadn't ended up a dead end, it had been fake. If by some miracle it turned out to be real, the arseholes at the Terra Arcana Security Administration got there first and wiped it clean.

The creature lurched and I darted out of their reach—too easily, really. I frowned at their uncoordinated movements. Whatever I needed to do to communicate with this creature, whatever they needed to be less hostile—I would make happen. I would make dead ends and T.A.S.A.'s coverup crap a thing of the past. I would *make* this the turning point in my quest, damn it.

I lunged to the side again to avoid another manic grab, my feet taking me towards the wider street. Pain sparked in my lip as I chewed on it, just trying to *think*—

The back of my neck buzzed. I stumbled, though I'd experienced this before: the near-artificial alert under my skin that somehow came from outside of me.

Almost simultaneously, the creature halted and twisted to the side, his attention jerking back into the darkness of the alley we'd been moving out of in our slow, bizarre dance. A snap of fabric reached my ears, a muffled thud, and shadow moved against shadow with the tread of booted footsteps.

I shifted my weight back and forth, attention darting between the two points.

Strigoi, my mind suddenly burped up, the absence of the creature's malicious attention giving me some mental breathing room. *Which explains the details in the reports of the attacks.*

Right on the heels of that thought came another: *Strigoi really don't have natural predators.*

My gaze fixed on the shadows.

So who the hell is that?

A tall form in a long coat materialized out of the darkness, and the strigoi let out a bone-melting hiss. Fast as a snake-strike, the creature spun and lunged at me.

I sucked freezing air through my teeth, bracing on instinct with no time to move. The creature snapped backwards in the next second as if yanked, crashing into the alley wall with a sickening crunch. Where they'd just been, the new arrival stood. The broad-shouldered figure planted themselves between me and the strigoi as the creature snarled and righted into a crouch.

"You are safe to run now." The masculine voice broke the air, startling me, the words a twist of gentle, cold, and so very weary. I couldn't identify his accent—it almost changed partway through.

I blinked rapidly, my brain pulled in too many directions. "Uhm, *no*, I don't think so. Do you have any idea how long it's taken for me to find one?"

He turned motionless, the stillness so complete the hair on the back of my neck stood on end. The darkness made only the angle of his jaw visible as he turned his head towards me. Deep in my chest, a Feeling sparked—like something just opened their eyes.

In the face of his continued attention I lifted one eyebrow in an attitude-filled gesture of *"what?"*

"Quen eres?" he murmured. '*Who are you*' in Galician.

"Who are *you?*" I shot back, bewilderment growing.

The strigoi darted straight for me again. The newcomer smoothly stepped to intervene, striking out with a palm and sending the strigoi sprawling backwards.

"Wait—I want to try to talk to them!" I blurted, alarmed that he'd drive the creature off.

He stilled. "Talk to the…" His words came oddly rusty, like he struggled to form them. "… strigoi trying to *eat* you?"

My heart leapt at the confirmation of species even as I winced at the question. "Yeah, well. I'll take anything at this point. Maybe if I get him some food?"

Said out loud, that plan abruptly seemed rickety at best. The strigoi snapped and snarled, finally righting himself again and staring with baleful, uncomprehending eyes.

"Are you… all right?" Words seemed to come easier to the mysterious stranger that time. Only now his accent sounded… Irish?

Before I could answer, the strigoi lunged again—this time right at the newcomer. I blurted sound that didn't quite make it into an actual coherent warning. Smoothly, his arm snapped up, knocking the strigoi off target. Instead of striking his neck, the strigoi latched onto his upper arm. I cringed, stumbling forward an awkward half-step in the want to help.

Mr. Mysterious here reached into his coat with the arm not currently being bitten. He withdrew a slash of red that seared into the dark, which I belatedly recognized as a dagger… that *glowed.*

That's magic, my brain bleated in alarmed joy.

His arm jerked up, and the red glow disappeared. Into the strigoi's chest. The strigoi's whole body jerked, and they let out a terrible gurgling hiss.

Understanding hit like a punch, much too late. "*What!* No, *don't!*"

The strigoi crumpled in disjointed, wrenching pieces—and then all at once, their body practically imploding into dust.

The pounding of my heartbeat filled my ears. Despair rose to choke me.

"What did you just…" The words forced painfully through my tight throat. "Did you not *understand* what I said?"

He slowly straightened. Another Feeling hit: tapping toes across unsteady ground to determine where to place a step. I think that meant confusion. That made Feeling number two off of him in the space of a minute, and I usually got only one bizarre sensation to work with.

"Bloodlust," he said.

"What?"

"That deep into bloodlust…" His accent shifted, now nearly the Queen's own English. "… they no longer make much conversation."

My skin prickled at the tiny scrap of information, the tiny of piece of something *more* that normally took so much time and effort to acquire, which he so easily gave.

"How do you know that?" My words practically sliced the air. *Who is this guy?*

His whole body turned towards me this time. I still couldn't make out much of his features, and I rocked back on my heels to stop myself from following through with the urge to step forward. *What the hell, I should not feel compelled to get closer to Mr. Demon Murderer here.*

"Are you alright?"

My face screwed up at his question. "No! I'm freaking pissed!"

His head tilted to the side. "Your neck," he said in clarification.

Now reminded of it, the throbbing pain along my shoulder and throat became forefront. *Ah, right.* The strigoi had bit me—the reason I'd stabbed them in the first place. I reached up to assess the damage and almost gouged myself in the eye with the knife still in my hand. *Oh.* Probably should put that away.

My attention cut back to the shadowed figure across from me, still holding that ominous glowing dagger. Mr. Demon Murderer looked down and lifted the knife with an odd jerk, like he'd only just noticed he held it. Without a word he smoothly pulled back his coat and sheathed the dagger at his hip.

My hands still shook, so it took a few tries to get my blade back in its sheath. Once finished with that, I patted the other knives on my person, reassuring myself of their presence; iron on the left hip, silver on the right, steel in the sheath on my back.

Then I reached up to my neck and shoulder. My fingertips brushed wet, mangled flesh, and tender pain blared down my arm. Blood coated my fingertips when I pulled them back to look.

Oh, hell. "Thaaat's going to be hard to explain in the morning."

Warmth slid down from my collarbone, quickly chilling in the night air. I pressed my hand over the injury, grimacing. What amount of blood loss could a body take before it turned dangerous? A few pints, right?

I'd need to develop an obsession with fashion scarves for the foreseeable future; thank god for the colder weather right now. Hopefully it healed well. My mother would go mental if I scarred.

"May I assist?"

I narrowed my eyes at him and shifted from one foot to the other. But where suspicion or caution should reside… it didn't. Fear had become a typical part of living in my own skin, so the lack of it while confronted with this imposing, unknown, previously-aggressive person mystified me. His accent stayed distinctly British now, but what had *that* been all about? I tried to summon wariness.

"All right," came out of my mouth instead.

He nodded, and then gestured behind me. "Better light."

Outside the alley, further down on the wide street, a streetlamp was, impressively, still on at this hour. *Must be one of the new ones with the latest solar tech.*

He started towards me, and I belatedly realized he'd need to pass me to get onto the street as I stood in the mouth of the alleyway. Something made me stand my ground instead of moving yet. Each of his steps seemed a little slower and more cautious than the last, the air growing thicker as if the narrowing distance compressed space instead of it simply rearranging.

He passed me—*Christ, be a little taller why don't you*—my skin humming at the proximity. He stalked down to the street lamp and faced me, the glow outlining his form. I moved before I realized I made the decision, each of my own steps oddly loud compared to his.

Once I stood in front of him, squinting at the face-full of light, I dropped my arm and tilted my head to the side to expose the bite. *Yep, just exposing my bleeding neck to a stranger.* Bafflement grew. I'd made *Fear does not dictate my actions* my most sacred mantra, and done everything to stamp it on my personality, my soul, my very DNA. But that mantra didn't create a lack of fear. Except right now. Did I feel vulnerable? Yes. Scared? Nope.

Maybe I'd just used all my adrenaline in the earlier fiasco?

His coat rustled as he moved, hunching over to peer under my chin. His hands slowly lifted, pulling down the collar of my coat. I still couldn't make out his features beyond basic impressions.

"Your artery wasn't hit," he announced.

Well, yeah. If my artery had been hit I'd be a cooling corpse right about now.

A different worry surfaced. "Being bit isn't going to turn me into one of them, right?"

His thumbs gently pressed around the wound and a little shiver spread down my spine at the warmth of his fingers. "No."

Disbelief flared at the answer so easily gained. "So strigoi are born, not created?"

"It depends." A scuff sounded as he adjusted his weight. "You ask a lot of questions."

Yeah, and you actually bloody answer them!

"How common is this bloodlust thing?"

He stilled. "Not common. Usually deliberate. I'll handle it."

He'll handle it. Because, obviously, he somehow had a tie to magic, *knew* about magic. My heart raced so fast it threatened to make me dizzy.

Mr. Rapidly-Becoming-More-Interesting reached into his coat and looked to be searching for something.

Words burst out of me. "Why are you outside at night with a glowing dagger?" *I could have phrased that better.*

"Why are you outside at night inanely wandering around?" he responded promptly.

I grinned. "I'll answer yours if you answer mine."

A breathy sound escaped him, something either a huff or a laugh if there had been more effort. The urge to provoke him into a real laugh seized me. He withdrew a fist from his coat, golden light bleeding between his fingers.

"What is that?"

He applied gentle pressure underneath my chin with his fingertips until I rolled my eyes and tilted my head back again. That hand lifted to my jaw, the side opposite the bite, barely touching skin as his other hand neared the wound. I shivered at the warmth. Silkiness brushed my neck, followed by tingling.

My mysterious caretaker shifted his weight, and it caused the lamp light to slide across half his face. My attention snagged, finally able to see him, the revealed mix of sharp and blunt features fascinating me. He looked younger than I expected, dark hair curled endearingly over his ears and forehead, weariness sitting heavy on his brow. I couldn't make out eye color—though *wow* those eyelashes—with his gaze lowered and his pupils dilated in the dark, making them look black.

Those same eyeballs lifted slowly, meeting my gaze. His pupils contracted as the light hit them, and I jolted. Dilation didn't cause the darkness; his eyes looked black because his irises were that dark.

His eyes echoed the color of the sky right above my head right now.

My mouth dried. I'd been in love with the color since my first step into Farfalla, and that crashed full force into the reality of seeing it reflected in the first person who'd acknowledged magic to my face. All my nerves began to burn. I couldn't look away, even when his eyebrows lifted in question, even as he responded by blatantly staring in return.

As if I wasn't off balance enough, sudden and profound awareness slid down my entire body: the shape of his mouth, his height compared to mine, his fingertips brushing my throat, my torso bare of a corset under my clothes. I swallowed dryly, veins buzzing with *well hello*. His gaze flicked down, following the motion of my throat, then stayed there.

"Do I get to know your name?" he asked, the question almost grudging.

How odd, I wanted to tell him. "Do I get to know yours?"

He hesitated, then straightened and slipped his hand back into his jacket, carrying that golden light with it. "You should be fine now."

No bandages? I cleared my throat and touched my neck, confused that he hadn't—

I froze. Except my heart, which understood before the rest, and slammed itself up against my ribs. My fingertips slid along sticky blood over the smooth, unmarred skin of my throat. I'd felt the punctures, minutes ago. I knew they'd been there.

Process later, ask questions now.

"Okay." I said. "That's new. Can I see? Whatever you just used."

Because he'd definitely used something… gold and magical and WHAT. He hesitated before reaching into his coat again. The fabric moved as if weighted down. I caught impressions of shapes underneath and nearly writhed with curiosity.

Mr. Mysterious pulled out his closed fist again, then opened his hand to reveal a softly glowing gold sphere. My very bones leapt, and I forced my next breath steady. I'd never heard of anything like this. I reached out to touch, and his fingers twitched as if to clamp shut. I shoved down impatience. I understood. We were both strangers to each other.

But I couldn't lose this chance. He knew something. And he spoke to me. Someone actually spoke to me about magic.

Changing tactics, I opened my palm flat next to his and lifted my head to meet his gaze. Vivid dark eyes locked with mine, and my stomach kicked. *What the heck?*

Ignoring myself, I asked: "May I?"

His eyebrows lifted. Seconds stretched. My heart rate did weird things. Wow, holding eye contact was difficult. Not bad; just overwhelming, like staring down the sun. Well, I guess staring at the sun technically had negatives. But whatever, this could be a lead, a clue leading me somewhere—

He tilted his hand, and weight dropped into my palm. My chest squeezed with the victory of his trust. With a deep breath, I looked down. The golden glowing… thing… looked like it should be soft, but rested in my hand with unmistakable hard weight.

Moving slowly, I ran a finger across it. My fingertip slid across a surface I couldn't see, that didn't look substantial enough to be the boundary of physical mass. A thrill spread up my spine.

I'm holding magic.

"What is this?"

"A stone imbued with healing enchantments."

I swallowed repeatedly so I didn't shriek the first excited thing that came to mind, which would have probably been unintelligible. Despite my introduction to larger magic being on the horrifying side of fucked-up, I knew it couldn't all be bad. Having direct proof of something as awesome as a stone that could heal almost made me want to burst into tears.

Eyeing me warily, he extended his open palm out next to mine. I whined inwardly, not wanting to let go… but I really didn't want to strain this fragile trust. I returned the healing stone to him, watching covetously as he slipped it back into his coat.

Urgency seized me with a thought: my Mr. Mysterious here no longer had an immediate reason to stick around. I had to keep him here somehow. Time for some give and take, some trust building.

"Fairian Leynthall," I blurted. "That's my name."

His head tilted to the side slowly. "Leynthall. The steam-engine shipping empire. You're the daughter?"

"The one and only," I said, suppressing the flinch that wanted to follow. Unless he dug for it, he wouldn't know that hadn't always been the case.

Caution threaded through the set of his shoulders. "Why are you out here, Fairian Leynthall?"

I crossed my arms over my chest and gave him a mockingly-haughty look. "You first. I already answered one question."

Maybe the lights flickered, but I swore the corners of his mouth quirk up. Something shifted; I Felt it. *Again! What's with all the Feelings?*

"To answer one of your first questions, I'm out here because I watch the streets for dangerous happenings of the magical inclination."

Giddy excitement crested over my head, even if the sentence didn't really say anything at all. "Which is why you'll be 'handling' the strigoi situation. Wait." Horror filled me. "Are you TASA?"

He snorted with unmistakable distain, fully rendering his opinion on that idea, which sparked a few questions. But he didn't elaborate, only narrowed those dark, vivid eyes on me. "Your turn. What are you doing out here?"

Oh yeah that. I fidgeted. "Right. Okay, so. I heard about the attack at the docks and thought it sounded like something that might be worth checking out." The Farfallan Protective Division regularly put out reports on happenings around the city. I'd been studying them before our move to try to identify what language Farfallans used to disguise something magical had occurred (and thus to be wary). To me, it meant something to look into. "Night is when I usually sleuth around so I can avoid attention and travel without escorts forced upon me."

"Why are you trying to investigate strigoi hunting grounds?"

Oops. Is that what it is?

"Er. I didn't know it was a hunting ground. I just knew it sounded like d-demons." I cursed myself for stuttering over the word, grudgingly glad I managed to not flinch at saying it aloud. Engrained responses to words are a bitch.

His brow furrowed, something almost like confusion. "And what are you looking for?"

He'd gotten to the big question. *Literally anything. The first step. Something that's true. Some guidance on where I'm supposed to go to answer the burning questions in my soul, the questions that don't have words.*

I cleared my throat primly, working to keep things playful. "It's actually my turn to ask a question. I'd like to know why *you're* out here—how did you phrase it?—'watching the streets for dangerous magical inclinations'? Is there a training program to do that or something…?"

He didn't respond for a long moment. I couldn't quite put a word to it, but something changed, like he'd shifted into neutral, into a rote pattern where he was no longer actually present. My heart sank.

"Since you are new here, some advice," Mr. Mysterious said, each word clear and precise. "You're sorely mistaken if you think you won't get hurt gallivanting around these streets. Whatever your reasoning, you should not be out here after dark. This is not the place to run about playing games."

"So it is more dangerous in Farfalla." Maybe the rumors were true on this one. "Is it because of the Divide? Or simply because there's more magic here or… ?"

"You're not listening to me."

Such an obnoxious statement deserved one response: brattiness. I smiled brightly. "I don't do that well."

He stilled for the space of a heartbeat. Then moved, invading my personal space, dark eyes narrowed, unblinking, and glaring down at me. A wave of heat seemed to radiate out of him, charging the minuscule amount of space he'd left between us.

Oh, that inexplicable part of me breathed. *What is this?*

I'd never wanted to further provoke someone so badly before.

"Whatever quest you think you're on, Farfalla will chew you up and spit you out, dead or worse." The hairs along my neck and arms stood up at the change in his voice. At the same time his attempt to be scary just highlighted how everything in him screamed *safe*. "I don't care what your reasons are. You will cease this hunt."

The order struck a match that caught inside of me, wiping out other thought. It briefly occurred to me that I didn't know his identity; challenging him could get me in trouble. The thought evaporated.

"Pfff." I poured as much scorn as I could into the single sound, my chin lifting as I straightened to my (inadequate) full height. "What, I'm supposed to listen to you because you turned on your scary face?"

"We'll start there, and see what it takes." The words pitched soft, like a knife sliding over silk. And I almost laughed. *Why am I so certain I have nothing to fear from him?* It had taken long, excruciating years to learn how to trust these Feelings. I wouldn't doubt them now.

My heart beat quickly against the inside of my ribs, my skin buzzing. "I hate to say it, but your attempt to scare me into compliance is failing."

He blinked. For a second I thought I'd made it through, found him again. Micro-expressions flickered across his face in reaction to some series of thoughts; he had been so still before, the sight fascinated me. Then it all dimmed into resignation that resonated with painful familiarity in my own body.

"If you must be foolish, then your safety is up to me." He waved his hand in front of my face, something tucked into his palm with his thumb.

I glanced without thinking. And immediately regretted it, unable to pull my eyes away. Time warped. His hand moved slower and slower. Darkness spread inwards across my vision.

NOoo sON Of a—

No chance to fight.

I fell down,

down…

… down …

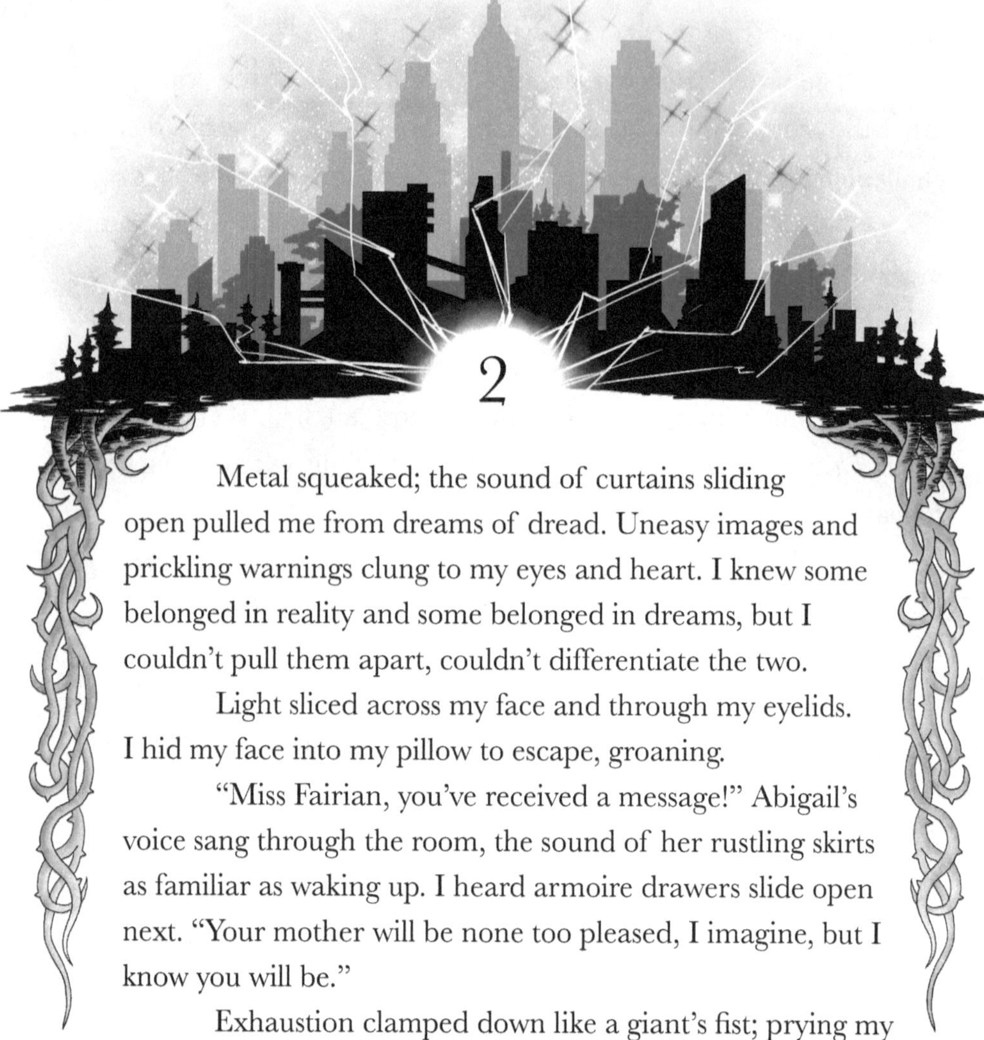

2

Metal squeaked; the sound of curtains sliding open pulled me from dreams of dread. Uneasy images and prickling warnings clung to my eyes and heart. I knew some belonged in reality and some belonged in dreams, but I couldn't pull them apart, couldn't differentiate the two.

Light sliced across my face and through my eyelids. I hid my face into my pillow to escape, groaning.

"Miss Fairian, you've received a message!" Abigail's voice sang through the room, the sound of her rustling skirts as familiar as waking up. I heard armoire drawers slide open next. "Your mother will be none too pleased, I imagine, but I know you will be."

Exhaustion clamped down like a giant's fist; prying my eyelids open became a herculean effort. *When did I go to bed that I felt like this…?* Something urgent built in my chest as the ceiling painstakingly came into focus. My new bedroom ceiling, which hadn't quite taken on the comfort of familiarity after waking up to it a total of three times now.

Then my mind threw open the doors of memory. I sucked in a breath and froze, eyes popping wide as my brain accelerated into wakefulness. I jerked upright. *In my own bed, in my own room.*

How—?

"There she is!" Abigail said, then frowned, her grey eyes trailing down me. I followed her gaze and winced at the sight of my clothes from last night, even as relief nearly assaulted me; that had been real. My heart skipped as I looked up at Abigail for her reaction, but she'd already turned away to fuss with outfits.

Hopefully she didn't recognize the ring of rust along the collar of my shirt. I jerked the garment over my head and shoved it under my pillow, where it would remain until I could deal with it. My fingers bumped into something hard. Frowning, I slid my fingers along it, recognizing my daggers in their sheaths. Relief again blew through me, only then registering their absence on my body, along with my missing boots and coat.

Outrage rose as it finally clicked: my mysterious stranger last night had seriously *sent me unconscious and then carried me back here!?*

Abigail's quiet had gained ominous weight as she pulled out clothes and put them back unnecessarily. I narrowed my eyes at the back of her head, where her rich chestnut hair was pulled into her usual seamless chignon. I didn't know if she had turned away to give me privacy or in hopes I'd incriminate myself so she'd have more details to tattle to my mother.

"You said there's a message for me?" I said, hoping to steer the conversation.

Eyeing the laundry chute and calculating how quickly I could get my breeches there, I jumped out of bed. My feet hit the ground.

"Yes, from a Mr.—"

The world spun. I about hit the floor, my hand slamming into the nightstand as I fought for balance. I clenched my teeth together at the rising flood of nausea. Then everything abruptly righted itself.

"Miss, are you all right?"

I inhaled slowly. *That black stone…* much different from the golden one I'd held, with much different results. And now I stood in front of Abigail in clothing that would undoubtedly catch her attention.

"It seems I stayed up too late and fell asleep in my clothes last night," I said easily. "I am a little sleep deprived."

That would not explain why I wore these clothes instead of nightclothes. I could only hope my eccentrics over the past years had inured her to this strangeness too.

Abigail launched into fretting over my sleeping habits, and I listened with one ear.

How had he even known where to go? How had he gotten past my father's mini-army of security, whilst dragging my unconscious butt along?

My attention snagged: my jacket lay across my desk chair, and my boots were lined up in front of my closet. Not quite where they should be but not so out of place. And my knives, under my pillow out of view. I blinked rapidly, trying to process the mix of overbearing and considerate.

I searched for the alarm I *should* feel, but my usual bizarre giddiness when confronted with unnerving situations overrode it. Last night I'd only gone out because the Farfallan Protection Division had put out several cautionary bulletins about avoiding the area due to "unnatural" violence. I thought I might be able to find clues left behind. Northampton had a similar warning system, but TASA cleaned up too quickly and I'd never found all that much. Certainly not a strigoi, and definitely not an imposing being that so frankly talked about magic.

A shiver spread up my spine, the fingers climbing the column of my throat where the strigoi had bit me. *I had a lead.* After all this time, I had a tangible lead—person—who'd talked to me.

I didn't even get his name.

My grandmother's stories didn't give me any clues to his identity, and neither did any of the scraps of research I'd managed to collect over the years.

Abigail bustled past me to lay out outfits on the bed, jerking me back to the present. Right, my behavior broached suspicious now.

"You said I had a message from a Mr…?" I prompted.

"Kearney. A Mr. Kearney."

I froze. I'd sent three letters to Mr. Kearney, asking if he would consider me as a student. An elusive and highly spoken of martial artist and defense instructor, I hadn't held out too much hope he'd actually respond.

"What does it say?"

"He's agreed to meet with you, and will be here in an hour."

My insides filled with bubbling glee. Two pieces of excellent news before breakfast. Today was going to be fantastic.

Abigail directed me towards the east parlor as soon as I dressed, where my parents apparently had settled to have tea. I huffed as I made my way towards the stairs headed down, trying to expel the butterflies in my stomach. I had three quarters of an hour to revise any arguments to convince Mr. Kearney to teach me. Persuasion somehow always became necessary to convince an instructor to take on a female student, even with my parents' money.

My socks slipped across the surface of the dark wood of the hallway, and inspiration struck. Instead of second guessing myself, too exhilarated by the possibilities of today, I bolted down the hallway.

Right as I hit the top of the stairway, I planted my heels. Then promptly yelped with laughter as I slid, *fast*, right past the top of the stairs, and nearly ate the floor. *They must have waxed it.* I kept my feet by some miracle as I finally pinwheeled to a stop.

Snickering, I eased my way back to the stairs before bouncing down the steps to the first floor. Sunlight slanted through the glass of the front room and spread across the gleaming floors, climbing up the pale walls and dark wood arches delineating the rooms. The foyer arched above my head like a cathedral, but the separate rooms had lower ceilings that encouraged intimacy.

The money needed to bring this 1780s Galician pazo up to environmental standards made most balk, and tracking down who even owned the building in order to actually purchase the property dissuaded others. It had taken my father almost a year to negotiate with the local Farfallan council, but they had been eager to see the estate restored and upgraded with state-of-the-art green tech. Father had made friends due to the lengths he went to implement and support green technology. Farfallans were serious about dispelling the idea of industry and dirty technology being synonymous.

My parents' voices grew audible as I closed in on the east parlor.

"—we've only been here two days and she's already in the rubbish papers." My mother's distressed voice filtered down the hallway. "She can't have been to *that* kind of gathering in this city!"

"Darling, we can't control gossip." My father sounded amused more than anything. "It won't impact her reputation more than it already has."

I paused outside the door to listen.

"She must outgrow this fascination with making herself appear so common." Paper rustled. "Look at this, she's exposed all her skin in these clothes. Nothing left to the imagination for her future husband. And she's with our ward, of course. Ms. Collins' influence, I see it right here."

Aaaand that was my cue to interject. I pushed open the door to the brightly decorated room. My mother and father sat opposite a low table stacked with tea, biscuits, fruit, and dozens of newspapers. For as much as my mother disparaged the rubbish papers, she sure acquired a lot of them.

My father flicked the top of his paper down, revealing his smiling ruddy face. "Good morning, dearest."

My mother beamed. "It's so good to see you up at a reasonable hour! Sit, eat, eat."

I sat down as she poured steaming tea into a cup. People remarked on how similar my mother and I looked: same dark wavy hair, eye shape, angular features, skin that turned ochre at the slightest hint of sun. Our physical similarities deceived.

"Yes, well," I said blandly, ready to rip off this bandage. Maybe if I gave her something more distressing than busybodies taking pictures of my clubbing with Tiff, she'd forget about the rubbish pages. "I just received the most exciting letter from Mr. Kearney."

My mother didn't miss a beat, handing me a cup with a biscuit set on the plate. "And who is that, dearest?"

"A local defense artist." I sipped my tea and eyed my parents under my eyelashes. My father looked up again, met my eyes for a second, and went back to reading.

"And what did Mr. Kearney say?"

"He's agreed to meet with me today." I glanced at the clock. "He'll be here at 11." *Forty minutes to go…*

"Ah," my mother said. "And this is a meeting where he will… teach you."

"This is simply an introduction, to see if he's willing."

"Ah, so it's not a certainty." She laughed lightly, sounding insultingly relieved. "I thought you'd agreed to give up that silly hobby."

"*Mmm.*" I'd never said anything of the sort, but she had strongly, *strongly* suggested Farfalla as the opportunity for a fresh start.

Starting with giving up all the 'silly things' that built my reputation as strange and inelegant back in Northampton.

I had a fresh start in this city alright. But not in her way. I now lived in a place where magic filled the sky, and I had my first live—ha, literally—lead in years. Promise filled the air.

"Have you decided on a dress yet? You've really left it till the last minute," she scolded. Her change in topic was expected. She'd be plotting, but wouldn't do anything unless Mr. Kearney actually agreed to teach me.

"For what?" I asked, even though I knew exactly what she referred to. My mother had been planning a celebration for months to introduce ourselves to the neighborhood. Tomorrow it would all come to fruition.

"The welcome ball, darling."

"Oh, I was thinking about a suit," I said innocently. "That's formal wear."

Behind his paper, my father let out a sound suspiciously like a muffled laugh. My mother shot him a look and then turned her severity on me. I dipped my biscuit in my tea, waited until it almost fell apart, and then quickly transferred it into my mouth.

My mother just watched me.

Two could play this game. I heaped fruit onto a plate and ate each piece with much deliberation. My mother continued to stare. *Damn it, no,* I would not break just because her eyeballs bored a hole into my head.

The silence thickened. My father's eyes appeared above his paper, slowly moving back and forth between us both. Humor glinted there, but I knew who he'd back up in this regard. If I didn't get this over with, she'd just keep doing this.

"Okay!" I burst out. "Yes! I know! It's important to make a good first impression, and Father has possible business contacts coming and so on and so forth."

"It will be our entrance into this community," my mother picked up without missing a beat. "We must welcome people into our home with grace, and make friends with those around us."

Belonging was very important to my mother.

"I guarantee I won't like anyone." I regretted the immature statement immediately.

"I guarantee if you put yourself in that mind-frame, you won't."

We traded scowls.

"I'll pick a bloody dress."

"Language. And if you'd like, I will pick one for you and save you the pain."

"Not a chance." I yanked a random newspaper from the center of the table and snapped it open to hide my face so I didn't have to keep my expression pleasant. "I'd like to wear something semi-reasonable."

I understood why my mother did this. I really did. She had grown up far from this world, and she did everything in her power to fit in now. She'd just ended up with an ungrateful chit of a daughter.

Quiet reigned for several beats. Then:

"Dear, how is the railway project to the east coming along?"

Paper rustled before my father spoke. "Good. Good. I think we'll have it uncovered as soon as next month."

Yes, yes, then it would be repaired and added to my father's endless steam-engine network. I shut the conversation out; I didn't need to hear about it for the thousandth time. I needed to get back upstairs and dress in something presentable for Mr. Kearney's arrival. Talk about needing to make a good first impression.

The headline I'd been staring at without seeing registered.

"Missing Harvey Girls Found; Admitted to Saint Dymphna's for mental care."

Everything inside of me stilled. Familiarity twisted, slowly pulling the ground out from under my feet. I'd seen headlines like this one, over and over, a long time ago. All similar, all implying the same thing.

It couldn't be the same. Of course it wasn't the same.

It's not the same.

I fought to comprehend the article that followed. Two girls had disappeared last week. Then they'd reappeared late yesterday, and after medical treatment, had been admitted to Saint Dymphna's Psychiatric Hospital for trauma and hallucinations. The girls claimed they 'saw their nightmares come to life.'

Chills erupted across my skin. My fingers and lips turned numb as if from a great distance. I remembered what the papers said when Mari and I had been taken seven years ago. I remembered the careful way they phrased everything. I remembered the cover-ups, the vague language, the manipulation of facts.

It was *him.*

My sister's killer. My kidnapper.

In my heart of hearts, in the deep pool buried in my guts, I'd been waiting for this.

He was back. And he was taking people again.

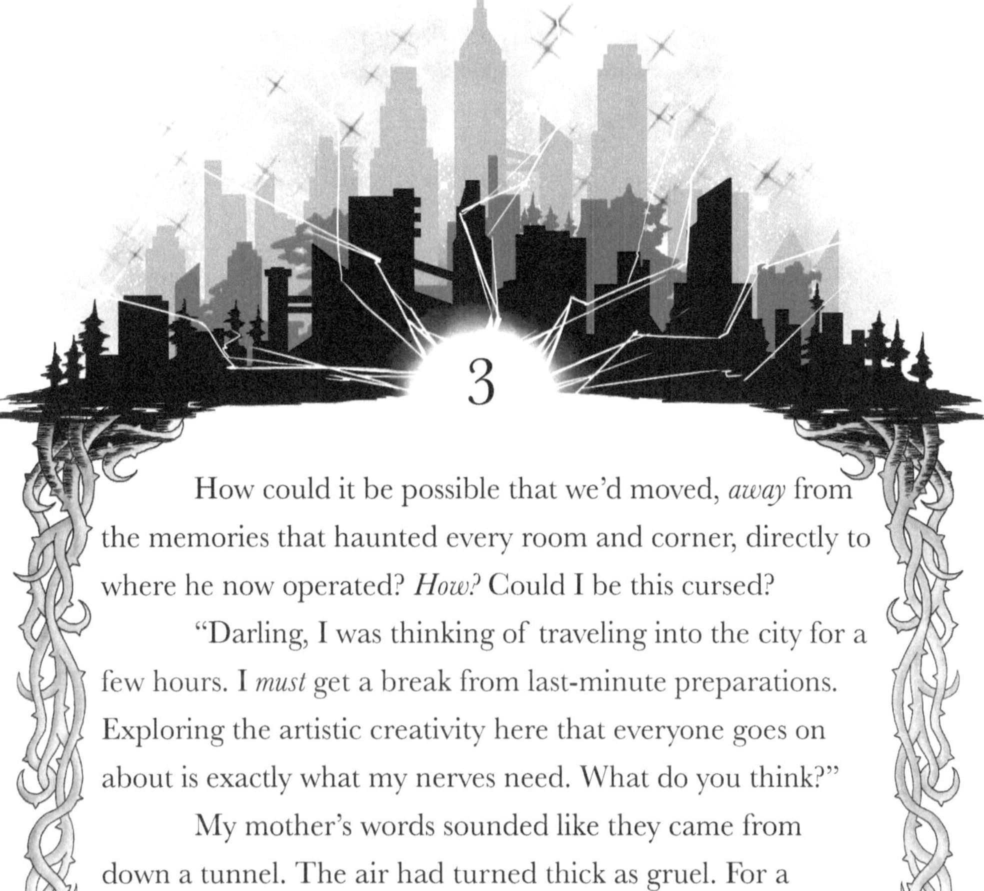

3

How could it be possible that we'd moved, *away* from the memories that haunted every room and corner, directly to where he now operated? *How?* Could I be this cursed?

"Darling, I was thinking of traveling into the city for a few hours. I *must* get a break from last-minute preparations. Exploring the artistic creativity here that everyone goes on about is exactly what my nerves need. What do you think?"

My mother's words sounded like they came from down a tunnel. The air had turned thick as gruel. For a second I almost blurted everything—but my parents hadn't believed me seven years ago. They wouldn't believe me now.

I couldn't let her see me like this. *Deep belly breath in… deep breath out…*

"Don't you have too much to do to prepare for tomorrow?" My words came out shockingly steady. That helped. I sounded fine. I was fine. Everything was fine. I didn't actually know anything yet; I didn't have confirmation. Just a huge… impossible to miss… flag.

Deep breath… hold… slower exhale. My heart slowed in my chest.

Oh hell, my mother had spoken again.

"Apologies, what did you say?" I closed the newspaper and tossed it onto the table between us all, doing my best to exude vague boredom.

My mother pursed her lips. "I said, I need a break. Come shopping with me. We might even find something new and suitable for you to wear."

"I have a meeting with Mr. Kearney in"— I glanced at the clock —"half an hour."

"Then we'll go after. Darling, we need to be seen supporting the local community. We'll explore, see more of the sights, interact with our new neighbors! It will be fun. And the perfect opportunity to approach the disaster of your wardrobe. We can even bring Ms. Collins."

If she kept pressuring me I would freak out for real. I couldn't fight her on this, not while trying to keep my mind together.

"Fine. After my meeting with Mr. Kearney."

My mother smiled tightly. I knew she was just trying to spend time with me. The gap between us had grown wide… but I couldn't focus on that right now.

Breathe, just breathe.

I returned to my room in a daze. *I don't know he's back, I don't know it's him.* And now my meeting with Mr. Kearney took on a whole new importance. I'd been learning self-defense for years, trying to be less helpless. It brought comfort at least. But now, maybe, I needed it more than ever.

Tiffany Collins, my family's ward and my best friend, lay sprawled across my bed as I entered. She faced the door on her stomach, chin resting in her hands, and immediately sprang up when I entered. Corn-silk blonde hair flew out in its usual fury of curls, and hectic pink spots made her particularly rosy-faced today.

"Mom finally let me go from the kitchen," she said, exasperated. "You'd think there'd be *less* cooking with moving."

Tiff's mother had negotiated for my family to take on Tiff as our ward as one of her conditions for working for us, but staunchly believed in keeping her daughter humble.

"Waaa," I told her.

She frowned at me. "What's wrong with your face?"

Bugger. I sidestepped the real answer to her question with a related answer. "Mr. Kearney responded to me. He's going to be here in like twenty minutes."

Tiff sprang to her feet. "Oh hell! I thought you'd written him off. Okay. Uh. Outfit. Not *that*." She waved her hands at me.

With five minutes to spare, we had me in a clingy soft tunic, dark leggings, and messy hair braided back away from my face. While the clothes said wealthy, I didn't look typical daughter-of-a-business-mogul, so it worked well for me. Several pairs of my shoes had gone missing, indicating my mother had raided my footwear again, but I managed to find a plain pair with only a little heel.

Tiff poked at my scalp. "You need a dye. Your grey is coming back again."

I'd been going grey since fourteen years old. I rolled my eyes, and a knock on my door interrupted any need for a response.

"Miss, a Mr. Kearney here to see you. He's been put in the south parlor."

"Thank you," I said, stomach knotting.

Tiff beamed at me. "You got this; what are you looking like that for?" She might not care one whit about self-defense, but she understood its importance to *me*.

"Will you sit with me? As my chaperone?"

Tiff looked down at her clothes and then back up at me with an arched eyebrow. "Warning would have been nice."

Ah, right. My mother made her standards quite clear for how we dressed to receive company, and Tiff wore breeches with holes in the knees and a long sleeve shirt that looked it had shrunk at some point.

"Sorry, I only just thought of it. I'll ask Abigail."

It took only a few minutes to track down Abigail. With her trailing after me, I headed to the parlor where Mr. Kearney had been put. I lifted my hand to knock, and paused. Shut my eyes.

You have to make a good impression, you have to make a good impression, you have to make a good impression.

I knew basic self-defense, but Mr. Kearney had a reputation of being practically an artist in his field. I needed him to teach me. Maybe it didn't make sense—what had hurt me before hadn't been attacks on my physical person but on my sanity itself. But. Sometimes, the idea that I could defend myself in some way was the only thing between me and the abyss.

With a deep breath, I knocked and entered. The gentleman inside turned from the window. He looked about forty. Short black hair, deep olive skin, bold features—and I had the sudden sensation of tremendous power deep underground, like a stirring earthquake. I blinked it away. My Feelings usually came up strange, but that was the most nonsensical one in a while.

I closed the distance to him, only a few steps in the modest room, intentionally extending a hand in greeting instead of curtsying or offering my hand. "Mr. Kearney, I am Ms. Fairian Leynthall."

"It is a pleasure to meet you," he said in a deep and oddly sincere voice, not even blinking before he shook my hand. His attention shifted over my shoulder. "And this is…?"

"Yes, this is Abigail, my lady's maid. She'll be my chaperone for the meeting."

"Pleasure to meet you, sir." Abigail curtsied and headed to a chair in the corner a few paces away. "Don't mind me, I'll just be here reading."

Mr. Kearney's eyebrows lifted. "Will you need a chaperone all the time?"

I slowly lowered myself onto the chaise opposite him. "Never be alone with a gentleman" had always been one of my mother's steadfast rules; with all of her insistence, she made it easy to forget that she didn't make the rules of propriety for the entire world.

"Will you have a problem with our sessions being supervised?" I responded instead, and gestured for him to sit.

Mr. Kearney eyed me and sat. "If you are afraid of me, I will not be a very good teacher."

Oh. "I am not afraid of you, Mr. Kearney. But my mother would have a fit if I was alone with a gentleman for long periods of time."

Understanding dawned on his face. "Ah. Right." He blinked once. "Tell me about your previous training."

I deliberately relaxed my shoulders and walked through my training history. A few years ago I'd worked with an instructor who knew Krav Maga. That had been my most thorough training, until he had suddenly moved to Germany. I imagine my parents had something to do with that. I'd also learned kickboxing for a few months. Everything else had been a mash of whatever I could find.

"… and that's about it." I cleared my throat. Lifted my chin. "You understand, it can be difficult to find someone willing to teach a girl."

"Hmm." Mr. Kearney did not sound particularly impressed by that. "How did you come to be interested in self-defense?"

I forced my hands to relax. "I became interested in being able to defend myself."

No hint of what he thought showed in his expression. "And what does it mean to you? Defending yourself?"

What's with all these questions? Flippant answers sprang to mind, but I didn't think they were appropriate at the moment. Abigail's quiet presence felt like a weight. *Whatever. Bugger it. She can report this to my mother.* "It means safety. It means less of a chance of being disappointed and hurt. It means being less vulnerable and naive."

Mr. Kearney held my gaze. "Is there someplace with enough space for us to move? I would like to see you in action."

My stomach wobbled. *Is he saying yes?* "Right now?"

"Yes." Mr. Kearney rose to his feet. I jumped to mine.

"There is a room," I said quickly. "Though it's not completely outfitted yet. Abigail?"

Abigail rose and darted a glance meaningfully at the low table between Mr. Kearney and I. It took me a second to realize a tray of untouched tea rested there, which I hadn't registered at all, nor offered to my guest.

"I apologize—do you want tea?" I blurted.

Mr. Kearney's cheeks creased in what looked like a repressed smile. "No thank you, but I appreciate the offer."

I suck at being a hostess.

Abigail and Mr. Kearney followed me out of the room, up the stairs, and to the room that my mother called a dance hall but I'd secretly coveted for this very purpose. He didn't seem inclined to speak to fill the silence. Usually I liked that in a person, but something about him made me want to start babbling.

I opened the door to the empty room. Similar to the study, it had large arching windows letting in floods of light. The view consisted mostly of the pine and oak trees bordering Leynthall property. Besides a few boxes remarkably out of place, the room stood empty.

Mr. Kearney took off his jacket and dropped it on the floor next to the door.

"You'll need to pad the floors."

I nodded quickly. "It's in the works." Or it would be, anyway. I kicked off my heels. Thank god I'd worn this outfit; I could move in it. Mr. Kearney scanned me from head to toe, nodded, and then his whole body relaxed. He twisted, head facing me but his torso angled away, giving me the side of his body and making himself a smaller target.

"I will attack," he said. "And we'll see what you can do."

He lunged towards me. I jerked to the side, muscles in my torso seizing. I spun into a guard to—

My leg ripped out from under me. I pinwheeled. Hands gripped my shoulders, set me nearly onto my feet, and I stumbled back to balance. Mr. Kearney spun out of reach, and I stared.

He'd both thrown me and then prevented my head from hitting the floor. In about two seconds. I swallowed. Hard.

"Again," he said.

I barely saw him move.

Sweat broke out along my back, sticking cloth to skin as I twisted, spun, feinted, blocked his hands and his legs flying at my head and stomach and feet, no time to think or breathe or plan, movement all instinct and reaction. I struck, and he stumbled back a step.

"Better."

He lunged, and panic scrambled at my lungs. *Holy hell,* I couldn't keep up; I could barely keep my feet.

"It is unique that a woman of your station would be interested in these activities."

Irritation surged. His palm hit my shoulder, and I spun with it to shed force and momentum—nearly sprawling as he responded by trying to trip me.

"So I'm told."

Mr. Kearney struck my hip, sending me stumbling into the floor on my knees. I popped back onto my feet. Had he just thrown me in a way where it didn't hurt as much when I fell?

"It must have been powerful, whatever convinced you to have this interest."

My throat tightened. I didn't respond, jerking away to avoid having my head knocked off. He tried his nasty ankle-snagging move again and I lithely danced away. He smiled, or smirked, or *something*. I darted to the side to avoid being trapped in the corner.

I'd done nothing to convince him to teach me, I couldn't even hold my ground.

"Did someone you care about get hurt?"

My jaw clenched. "Something like that." I smacked his leg away from me as it came for my midsection. My palm stung.

I had never fought anyone this hard in a setting like this before. Exhilaration and mortification sung in my blood, but I had no time to acknowledge it. I lunged, trying to challenge his steady assault with *anything*. I ducked, lost my balance. He paused a half beat, letting me recover for a millisecond before driving me backwards again.

"You have a lot to learn," Mr. Kearney said.

My face scalded, resignation building between my ribs.

"During an attack on your person, it often comes down to instinct. You must train yourself to react correctly."

His flurry of movement ended with me spinning, scrambling for balance.

"There isn't time to think."

My back hit his chest, my wrists in his hands as he clamped down, pinning me to him. I gasped for breath, lungs constricted by his hold.

He abruptly released me. I danced away, spinning around to face him. He stayed where he stood.

"I can help you train yourself. I cannot promise you will never get hurt or be disappointed, but as you said, perhaps I can help you feel less vulnerable and naive."

Oh. My heart lifted. Hell, my *soul* lifted.

"I will require all of your effort and skill. I have no patience for having my time wasted."

Mr. Kearney didn't cater to my family name, or condescend to my sex. No attempt at flattery, either. What do you know, I stood in front of someone halfway genuine.

"I'm not interested in wasting your time—or mine," I panted. I poured all the truth I possibly could into my voice. "This is not a game to me. It's part of me."

Mr. Kearney nodded. Then walked over to his coat next to the door. I held my breath.

"You're quick on your feet and adapt well. The mistakes I see— well, those are easily worked through. What days would your schedule allow?"

My heart did a summersault. *That was yes. And I* like *this guy.*

"Every day?" I blurted before I could stop it. Then I winced and smiled flippantly to cover it up. "Excuse me. I'm sure you have other clients and duties you must attend to."

"Every day would be acceptable," Mr. Kearney said slowly. "But considering the letter I received from Mrs. Leynthall a few weeks ago, perhaps that is not a good idea."

Someday, I would get used to my mother's underhandedness. My cheeks burned. "Then I must apologize on behalf of my mother."

"It is her behavior, not yours."

I winced. It was still family. And it still affected what few relationships I had.

"Let us start with every other weekday."

I couldn't agree fast enough.

Fighting down disbelief, Mr. Kearney and I discussed times and schedule—after university classes, of course, but not too late, and maybe a day on the weekend as we progressed—and his rate of payment. Which I would be paying out of my *own* pocket money, thank you very much. I'd learned the hard way not to give my mother financial power over things I cared about.

"I will see you next Monday, Ms. Leynthall," he said after I walked him to the door.

I flinched. "Ms. Fairian. Or just Fairian."

Mr. Kearney paused. "Of course, Ms. Fairian. Till then."

He headed down the steps, and the dazed lightness in my chest compressed, tighter and tighter, into a hard, painful lump. All of this might be too little too late.

"It went well, I take it." My father's voice came from behind me.

I spun, fixing a smile on my face. "Yes, quite well. I've learned something about business, after all."

That was the biggest lie ever. I wasn't the one who was good at things like this. The thought of who really should be here hung in the air like bitter smoke. I could see it: the lingering sadness in the corners of my father's eyes, grief touching the lines of his mouth. It had eased in seven years, but never gone.

"Good," he finally said. "As long as it makes you happy."

I wondered how much effort it took for him to say those words.

"Darling!" my mother's voice sang through the hall. "I see you're done. We should go soon, before it gets too hot! This autumn weather is different here…"

Right. Her shopping outing.

I sighed. "Let me change first."

Back upstairs in my room, I found Tiff pretty much exactly where I left her. I frowned. "Did you even move?"

"Yes. Then I came back. Your mother found me—we're going shopping?"

"Oh good." I exhaled. "I was hoping she was serious about inviting you."

"Yes, yes—what happened with Mr. Kearney?"

"Oh. It went good. Really well," I said awkwardly. Sometimes, whenever I tried to be anything but snarky, my intelligence turned off. "He's… really genuine. And he knows his stuff."

"*And?* Is he going to teach you?" She wriggled where she sat, legs tucked under her.

I nodded and smiled.

"See! I told you!" She leapt off the bed and bundled me into a hug. Just as quickly, she jumped back. "Okay. Are we getting you dresses for the party while we're out? I can help you find one that makes you look like you have boobs."

I flipped her off. She laughed. I grinned back, but my face stretched oddly, like I couldn't remember how to do it right. *I need to be normal right now. I neeeeeeeed to be normal right now. You don't even have proof it's really* him…

Tiff's delight faded, her eyes narrowing. I quickly moved to my dresser to find clothing suitable for being outside and moving around in a fall afternoon. I glanced. Tiff still scrutinized me.

"What's wrong?" she said.

I pulled on a shirt, thinking. Could I trust her with this? Tiff knew… the basics. But she also loathed magic. *But* I could also use a level head to help make sure I hadn't made glaring assumptions.

Two steps, and I face-planted on the bed next to her. The mattress jostled as she wriggled into position next to me. After a few seconds of holding my breath as I couldn't breathe through the blankets, I turned my head towards her. She lay on her stomach too, worried eyes roaming my face. She complained her eyes were the color of poop. I thought they looked like wenge wood, textured between dark and light shades, striations of whisky and blackberry jam.

"There was an article in the paper this morning about two missing girls who'd just been found."

Tiff stopped breathing. Two missing girls was all she needed to understand. I swallowed hard. "They were taken to a mental hospital because they claimed they saw their nightmares come to life."

One heartbeat. Two. Three. Four heartbeats before she responded in an exhale: "You think it's him."

My throat closed. We'd never talked about this sober before. This was too bizarre, too surreal, two of my worlds colliding.

"You don't know that, Fair-Fair." She sounded logical, but so gentle.

I nodded.

Her eyes grew fierce. "But you need to know, don't you?"

I nodded again.

"Where do we start?"

4

Tiff and I made a plan. Conveniently, the shopping excursion could be used fit into this plan. After my mother fussed over my outfit, which she said made me look like a street urchin, we took the electric car. To the consternation of the guards with us, I half hung out the window, partially for the view and the fresh air, but mostly to avoid conversation. Tiff situated herself between me and my mother like the best friend she was, and chattered away about fashion and local scenery. No one could talk as much as my mother, but Tiff held her own.

The car slid across cobblestone roads towards the market district, and the sky looked sea-foam green. The salt from the sea mixed with the musky-sweet smell of decomposing leaves in autumn. At first all I could see were stone walls of the buildings clustered tightly together, broken up by trees and vines and narrow alleyways.

Then it all opened up as we neared one of the rivers that criss-crossed Farfalla, revealing the stretch of docks that ran all the way to the sea. Bridges up and down the river arched up into the sky like impenetrable monuments, the daylight glimmering across the recycled steel from the industrial age. Ships moved steadily along the surface, and gondolas traversed into the canals that branched out of it. Cars and carriages moved along the meandering cobblestone roads between bright houses made of red brick or grey stone with white stucco walls. Green exploded from everywhere: trees along the streets, bushes and plants on various roofs, and small gardens and green areas broke up the stone and metal cityscape. Far up the river, the public-owned hydro-power station churned power for official use in places like hospitals and community centers.

The sound of the wheels changed as we moved onto the bridge with a soft *thunk*. This one was smaller, a drawbridge made of crisscrossing steel beams and concrete blocks. Crystal water blanketed either side, the current rushing and still in various places like a rippled patchwork quilt. I couldn't see very far down into the immensity of the river. The reflection of the sky danced across the surface in pale green eddies; the sun was almost directly overhead, the sky broken up by only a smattering of clouds.

My grandfather—father's father—loved to tell stories of what waters used to look like, before and during the Environmental Crisis, when they ran brown and filled with shining chemicals. He used to lament that my generation was bereft of 'real understanding' of the harmful practice of unrestricted industrialization. He'd lived through the last big wave of cleanup projects, where people learned to be *caretakers* of the planet, not users. He often criticized the rise of capitalism ideals in places like Farfalla, with Independent status, and who were unattached to any Confederacy.

When the car reached the highest point of the bridge, I stretched up as high as I could, scanning west, towards the ocean. I didn't know what I thought I'd be able to see; it was only visible if you took a ship quite a ways into the turbulent waters. It, being the Divide. Still, I squinted at the horizon, an odd yearning tugging at my gut.

Buildings rose up to cut off my view as the car descended down the other side of the bridge. With a huff, I relaxed down, wiggling further into the car so I didn't accidentally overbalance and fall out. We hit a bump, the transition point between bridge to street, and my head banged against the top of the window frame. Wincing and muffling curses, I dropped back inside. One of the guards—he was new, a native to Farfalla—had risen half out of his seat, his hands up towards me like he'd been about to yank me back. I grinned brightly, and he gave me a confused smile in response.

My mother, Tiff, our two guards, and I spilled out of the car and onto the street at the first sign of vividly colored market tents. The Market district consisted of a vast span of permanent buildings and temporary structures, and as soon as we left the relative isolation of the car, the roar of hundreds of voices speaking in Galician, Castilian Spanish, and English engulfed us.

Inevitably, my Feelings hit. *Laughter in my throat. A band around my chest. Smoke filling nostrils. Stomach knotted. Cold metal across skin.*

Crowds always brought a wash of them, and still managed to wallop out of nowhere. I winced, my hand flying to my forehead. I quickly scratched my temple to hide the reaction, hyper-aware of my companions. Even after years of trying, I had little control over them. Maybe they would only ever be random. They certainly came and went as they pleased. I'd barely even started to understand what the different sensations *meant*.

The scent of fried seafood made my mouth water. A gust of wind knocked that away, bringing the smell of almonds and sugar, and I looked around to find out where *that* had come from. My mother's voice rose over the din, instructing our driver to return home and wait for a message to come pick us up.

All around us, designers and craftspeople called out from sleek brick and stone buildings with bright cornices, or elegant stalls with vividly colored drapery. Farfalla attracted a lot of master craftspeople, because it was a port city and some other nebulous reason I hadn't pinned down yet. It was rumored to have some of the best apprenticeships available in Europe, and people came from all over to learn. It had been one of my father's biggest reasons for moving us here, to capture the transportation needs of such a growing maker community.

"Oh, darling, look at that!" My mother gripped my arm and pointed at a glass window where a delicate-looking dress draped across hangers.

"Oh the *colors*," Tiff exclaimed, and they dragged me to the window. The front of the building had been sanded and polished until it practically reflected light. But smoothed out gouges covered the surface, turning the surface uneven, almost warped. Two generations ago my grandparents fought disease and pollution and twisted human nature. Now we traipsed through streets worn with age and showing marks from battles we didn't remember.

A prickle ran up my neck, like the point of a knife lightly followed each vertebra in decision of where to strike.

What in the name of—? I twisted, scanning the people around me. In a crowd this large I didn't know if it had been directed *at* me, but my heart beat quickly in my throat.

Tiff opened the door and my mother marched me through the entryway into a cool room decorated in earthy tones. A smartly-dressed young woman with a mass of dark curly hair approached swiftly from the back, where an older gentleman sat at a table working over something. Their gazes flicked over us in quick assessment; the gentleman looked back down in dismissal, and the young woman gave a practiced smile.

"How may I help you?"

"We were just admiring the lovely garment in the window!"

My mother's voice had shifted into full charm mode. These two wouldn't understand the meaning behind her casual arrogance and sugary-sweet voice. But it told me she'd noticed their assessment and following neutral judgement. By the end of the hour she'd have them wrapped around her little finger.

I glanced out the window and searched the crowd again. No more Feelings hit. With a deep breath, I let it go.

Over the next hour and a half, my mother bought something tasteful but expensive from several stores, probably planting some subtext about wealth and sophistication I didn't quite follow.

Tiff and I begged off continuing on up the street, claiming we'd heard about a place we wanted to visit that was further into the district in the opposite direction. My mother let us go with a huff. Tiff and I fast walked from the Market District towards older downtown, where we'd pinpointed the location of Farfalla Central Library. There was a railway around here somewhere that would get us across a different river to where we needed to be.

Tiff kept glancing at me, eyes worried. I didn't have the mental space to reassure her. I needed data and information so dread would stop eating my guts alive.

Farfalla Central library took up almost three city blocks, made of mammoth blocks of stone and Spanish coral with Greek pillars lining the entrance. The road that initially ran through it had been renovated into a pedestrian-only walkway and outdoor sitting area, so the whole thing was rather its own mini-community with safe, easy access between buildings.

Tiff and I ascended the steps of the gigantic 'Public' library, pushed through one of the reinforced wooden doors lining the front, and came to a halt.

"Whoa."

Reference desks and check out stations filled the front room. The smell of leather and paper made me want to sigh out loud. Several rooms branched out from the main area, and three staircases spiraled out, heading upwards and downwards.

During the Collapse and the following anarchic years, millions of books were destroyed, consumed by the desperation for resources of any kind. In response, governments and private interests hoarded and stockpiled books, hiding them away. I could understand the protective measures. It was what happened after I couldn't stand.

Right on cue, two library personnel strode up to us.

"Permits, please," one of them said in a friendly voice.

Applying for access to Farfalla's library had been the first thing I'd done once I knew we were moving here. I handed my permit to the two guards and worked to smile instead of sneer.

"And yours, ma'am?" the other guard said, hand outstretched towards Tiff.

Tiff handed over her papers with a sweeter smile than my own.

In order to 'protect' knowledge and prevent any further loss of information, many European governments or upper class families took over control of these repositories of books. As Europe recovered, libraries returned… with each building outfitted with security measures. Those in control or with a vested interest in keeping knowledge safe had banded together to form the Society of Libraries.

In Britain, due to ruthless years of petitioning and public seething, library restrictions had been altered. Most buildings were now partitioned into 'public' and 'private' sections—public sections holding modern publications as well as 'copies' of older books, and the private spaces only accessible by exclusive permit.

The guard eyed me up and down, scrutinizing my permit line by line. "Leynthall. That wouldn't happen to be Leynthall Industries?"

"Yes, sir," I said, fighting the urge to mock. Right on cue, the guard's shoulders straightened, their posture becoming both more respectful and more friendly.

Farfalla had followed more in the footsteps of Spain. Anyone wanting to access to the library had to apply for a Simple permit declaring an individual's research intentions. It was a quick process and easy to pass. Access to Exclusive sections required a much more intensive and rigorous process. Most were denied.

The first guard handed back my permit with a nod. "Student, huh?"

"We begin at Farfalla College of the Arts tomorrow," I said pleasantly. I'd submitted both our permit petitions under a student status. It had appeared the best option.

"Home Economics or Etiquette?" the guard asked amicably, as if those were the only two options available to me.

I gritted my teeth. *Be nice be nice benicebenicebenice…* "Undeclared."

The second guard still scrutinized Tiff's permit. Her clearance had taken a lot longer than mine, never mind our applications had been near-identical. I'd made absolutely sure Tiff had access to the power of whatever knowledge this library could provide.

I fought not to glare as the second guard handed Tiff's permit back to her. "Looks like everything is in order."

"Would you like a tour?" the first guard asked. "The library can be overwhelming— "

"No thank you!" I said brightly as I linked my elbow with Tiff's and fast-walked away.

"Wow, I am so not used to that…" Tiff muttered.

Towards the back of the entrance hall stood a large kiosk with a map of the building. The Farfallan Central Library looked even bigger on paper than it did from the outside. Large rooms were labeled by subject, with some bookshelves marked as per year or sub-category.

And then there were the sections filled in with grey and no further embellishment, simply labeled EXCLUSIVE RESEARCH FILES. An entire wing of this building was grey. Grey took up nearly half of the smallest building. Another had only a small section.

Those grey sections had always bothered me. Seven years ago, with my brain cracked open to secrets and lies, I'd known I needed to start there. It had taken almost three years and a doddering old man's credentials for me to get access to the small one in Northampton.

Speaking of. I should check in with Sir Lightly.

I'd applied for a transfer of my Exclusive permissions from Northampton, but I hadn't heard back from the Farfallan division of the Society of Libraries yet.

Now I really, really need that clearance.

Dread tunneled in my insides like worms. We should get moving if we were to make any headway. I scanned until I found the news archives section, bumped my hip into Tiff's, and made my way towards it.

We needed to find out how many people had gone missing in a similar way as the article I'd read; additionally, how many times stories disregarded victim's experiences as hallucinations or illusions. We only had an hour or two, which meant we could not be as thorough as I wanted. Tiff and I photocopied every report that mentioned missing persons or "mental instability" for me to study later. I cringed at using paper, but I'd learned years ago not to keep my information digitally.

I'd expected to get some hits, or maybe even none, depending on how well *he* hid his tracks this time.

Yet, our pile grew rapidly. And the hair on the back of my neck stood on end.

After an hour, my Personal Communication Device chirped with a message from my mother, worried about my location. I made excuses to dissuade her alarm and promised to be home soon. Far away, through the fog of my head, I felt bad about leaving her.

But I had to get this done.

It took two hours to go through everything in the past decade with those search terms. The pile was substantial, and one of the librarians frowned when she saw how much paper we'd used. I'd make sure the Leynthalls made a sizable donation later.

One detail stood out from the reports I'd skimmed. If a mental health crisis was mentioned, the people were often admitted to a place called Saint Dymphna's Psychiatric Hospital.

Everything seemed far away, including the choking impatience to pour through the articles. Tiff's surreptitious glances had turned into outright asking if I was okay.

The only thing I remembered about going home was the sound of music; someone sat in a small city square playing a bowl-shaped instrument with a mallet, and the sound made me stop and listen for a while.

My mother scolded me for leaving during supper, but she had plenty of positive things to say about what she'd found and the community connections she'd made.

The meal took forever. Yet it passed in a blink.

Then finally, *finally*, I was alone.

First, I weeded down the news report. Some didn't fit with deeper reading. With what was left, no immediate pattern jumped out at me, so I started organizing them by year. The first report that read similarly to the article this morning was dated seven years ago. Seven years ago, there were a handful of cases.

This year, the incidents came monthly.

St. Dymphna's didn't always get mentioned, but no other hospitals were.

All genders were mentioned in the reports. Single individuals were mentioned as often as pairs. The victims ranged in class, area, age.

He had only taken girls with wealth. It was why everyone explained what happened as 'just a ransoming' turned bad, and made a big fuss about ransoming laws for a while before it drifted away from everyone's minds.

Maybe this was good news. It didn't sound like *him*.

But I didn't know that. I needed to talk to the people in these articles. I needed to hear the story from their own mouths, without the filter of media or covert bullshit.

My Personal Communication Device had a hookup to the Virtual Archive, a collection of information and data uploaded digitally. The search history could be accessed by anyone who asked, and somehow it was monitored for particular terms. I'd had my access shut down the first time I'd naively researched 'demons.'

I didn't think looking into this Saint Dymphna's hospital would send up red flags. According to the vArchive, Saint Dymphna's Psychiatric Hospital was the premier mental hospital in Farfalla. I numbly scrolled through their mission statements and recent medical articles they'd published. In the hospital's 'News' section there was a colorful announcement: they were holding a fundraising gala in a week.

I sat up. My parents were looking for causes to get involved in; our family's generosity and caring for the Farfallan community still had to be proven. It shouldn't be hard to convince them—particularly my father—to seek an invitation to the Gala.

Which meant I had my next step: get inside Saint Dymphna's via this Gala and get more information.

I exhaled, the relief of direction hitting like a punch… and then dragging down further as exhaustion hit like a train. I didn't look at the clock. It would only alarm me how much time had passed without realizing it.

My eyelids threatened to close and never open again as I organized my research into neat piles. There was only one safe place to store it all. Carefully supporting the weight so it wouldn't scrape against the floor, I pulled the heavy wooden chest out from under my bed.

I unlocked the padlock with a startlingly loud *click*, and pushed back the lid. With reverent hands, I gently rearranged the worn books inside. Each of them had been painstaking to find. Their spines were intimately familiar to my fingertips—*Classifications of Demonic Beasts* and *Demonic Creatures and Their Origins* and worn pamphlets and scrolls describing creatures in much harsher terms than any of my grandmother's stories.

Familiar longing bloomed under my ribs; not about these objects in particular, just a nebulous… something. But my head throbbed in warning, and grit filled my eye sockets, so I simply made room for my newest research papers, next to the thick stack of notes I'd been collecting for years, and shut and relocked the chest.

Curled up on my side, buried under enough blankets to crush a horse, my breathing evened. Cool breeze from the open window brushed along my face; that registered. The room still smelled a little musky from all it's years of disuse. There was no fireplace in here as this room had initially been an office, and I missed the smell of smoke and crackle of flames. My room in Northampton had a fireplace. Nevertheless, this room had been *mine* the instant I'd seen it. Through the window was a perfect view of the skyline of Farfalla. Everything above it gleamed green, and I swore the stars glittered more brightly here.

Everything from today blurred, only snapshots with the sound and colors turned up too high.

I'd get some sleep and be better tomorrow. I just had to hold onto my plan: attend the Gala at St. Dymphna's, make connections within the organization, somehow get involved with the hospital to get an in, and track down the patients admitted for 'hallucinations.'

I could do this. *I could do this.*

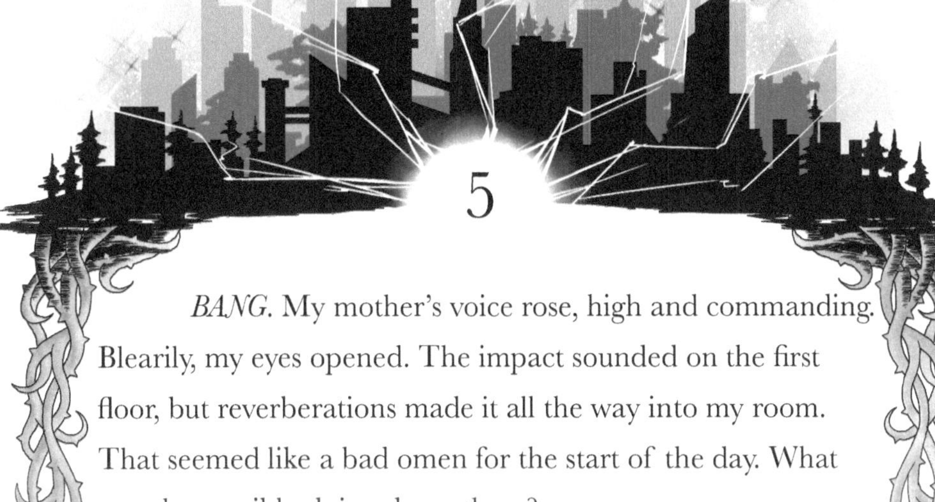

5

BANG. My mother's voice rose, high and commanding. Blearily, my eyes opened. The impact sounded on the first floor, but reverberations made it all the way into my room. That seemed like a bad omen for the start of the day. What was she possibly doing down there?

Wait. *It's Saturday.* I groaned and buried myself further under the covers. There would be a million people in the pazo later for the introduction party. My chest hurt. All my limbs were too heavy. My head throbbed, though mightily lessened from the headache when I'd gone to sleep.

Get up. You've got stuff to do. Not to mention prepare for socialization.

A light knock sounded on my door.

"Miss Fairian?" Abigail asked quietly.

I sighed. "Yeah."

"Your mother has requested your perspective on last minute decorations."

"Yeah."

Half an hour later, with not nearly enough caffeine in my system, I lifted my eyebrows at the transformed foyer.

Skeins of dark blue silk hung in lazy curves from the ceiling, highlighted by chains of white crystal. Those crystals looked to be emitting light; that had to be the new tech my father had been talking about a few nights ago. Lighter blue silk wound up the marble columns, purple irises tucked into the folds.

"What do you think?" My mother said, tapping her lips and scrutinizing the room as well. "And come look at the ballroom."

The ballroom addition had been my mother's condition for moving to Farfalla. I hadn't paid much attention before, but the remodel really blended well into the original build. The same stone and Spanish coral as the original construction gleamed, and similar design detail weaved back into the rest of the pazo.

My mother's tweaks appeared here and there. Like the chandeliers, the large French doors and windows overlooking our small grounds, and the more Greek style marble columns.

The decorations from the foyer spread into the ballroom. The same dark blue silk hung from the ceiling with lighter blue around the marble columns. Groups of hued crystals hung glittering from the ceiling, sending out sparks of light and color. Airy, nearly transparent tablecloths with blue edges laid over tables, with vases of the differing flowers on top. It smelled incredible in here.

Three people I'd never seen before set up a kind of stage in the corner. That had to be what had woken me.

My mother fidgeted as she watched my reaction.

"Stop fussing," I told her. "It looks brilliant."

"Do you think it is too much? Is it too elaborate?" My mother twisted to look back again over the ballroom, skirts swishing with her.

You mean expensive? There was nothing old money disliked more than new money coming in and flaunting. I went over it again, then shook my head. "No. This looks tasteful. Not like an excessive show. The flowers are great."

She beamed at me.

I didn't know how to handle my mother when she wasn't trying to critique me on something. I edged out of the room. "I'm going to go… study."

She blinked, and the mother I knew returned. "Do not forget: your nails and hair needs to be done, and it will take time. Guests are arriving at six. I'd like you to be in the introduction line; this is a wonderful opportunity for you to charm and make friends."

"Sure, okay." *I will absolutely be hiding in a closet for that part.*

"And try not to use *slang*," she protested.

I sped from the room before she remembered to ask about dresses again.

I found my father taking tea in the sunroom. Breakfast biscuits laid out on the low table, but my arms seemed too heavy to justify the effort of reaching for them when I didn't want to eat anyway. He read a business journal, and I scanned the headlines of the papers I could see for more missing or found persons. Nothing jumped out.

I broke the subject as casually as I could. "I think I found a local cause we could get involved in."

He lowered his paper. "Oh?"

"There's a hospital. Saint Dymphna's. They're hosting a Gala next week."

"And what caught your eye about this Saint Dymphna's?"

"They're a psychiatric hospital focusing on holistic health and healing."

The air filled with unspoken words. Once upon a time, my parents had nearly had me committed. It had been a few weeks after *it* had all happened. But they'd worried about my presence in a mental institution being leaked, and the Leynthalls already had the hurdle of a background of little connections. Anything more, and it'd be impossible to move among the level of class my mother had fixed her sights upon.

"This is meaningful to you?" he asked gently.

I'd banked on him assuming I cared about this because of my history with mental health. The manipulation only made guilt bloom a little bit.

"Yes."

"If you put the information on my desk, I'll contact the director today and see if there are available tickets to that Gala."

He lifted his paper back up to read. I tried to summon triumph or relief, but it just sputtered into numbness.

I returned to my room, my gaze falling to the ruffle around my bed as if I could see through it to my secret chest beyond. My very viscera rebelled at the idea of looking through those same reports again. I had more to do: looking through vArchive, for one. Some of the newer news stations uploaded their articles virtually and there might be something there.

Would that even help? Nothing I'd done before prevented *him* from doing anything. What could anyone do, when *he* could warp reality itself?

All I could do was wait. Wait and see.

And for all I knew, my sister's killer waited outside right now.

Saliva flooded my mouth as the world heavily swayed. My body bent, my hands hitting my knees as I sucked in breaths. Deep breaths, over and over, feeling my ribs expand wide and contract. I shut my eyes, focused only on the feeling of air cycling in and out of my nose. Slowly. *Slowly.*

In and out.

I couldn't just stand here stewing in anxiety. Especially as I had to try to be normal this evening for the party. My eyelids slitted open, revealing the pretty wood of my bedroom floor. I needed to do something, something physical, move around and—

Oh hey guess what you have an instructor who gave you some practice material.

Practicing self-defense it was.

Hours later, time fit itself correctly in my head again. Light slanted through the exercise room windows, the autumn sun dipping low. Sweat covered my skin, and my muscles trembled with euphoric fatigue. But my body finally belonged to me.

I definitely should have started my beauty routine already, but it gave me perverse pleasure to be late. I really did the pettiest things sometimes. The buzz of voices from below filled the hall as I crept out of the training room towards my bedroom, and I winced as my mother's voice rose, distinct as she greeted and directed people into the ballroom. Halfway between cringing and snickering, I quietly opened the door to my bedroom.

Abigail turned towards me, her expression very, very patient. "Bath."

My attempt to linger in the shower failed as Abigail yanked me out seconds after I'd finished rinsing off soap. Dressed in my underthings, I headed to the chair set up in the middle of my room and braced myself for the primping.

Pale fabric laid out across my bed, somehow familiar but also wrong. I came to a halt. It took me a second to recognize the shape as a dress, and even longer to consciously understand why my stomach clenched in a vise.

Memory slammed into me. *It's my disguise dress*, Mari would say to me, grinning wickedly as she twirled innocently. *Everyone will think I'm so sweet, and then they underestimate me.*

It couldn't be the same dress, of course. All of Mari's things had been given away or burnt to prevent her spirit from getting stuck, one of my grandmother's traditions. But the style, the fabric, the cut of it was too similar.

"Your mother has requested it for the evening," Abigail said, noticing my stare.

"I'm not wearing that." My voice came out too loud, warping in my throat and in my ears.

"You can speak to her about it later," Abigail said.

Scenarios clicked through my head in quick succession. The choking sensation clamped around my body finally resolved into fuel: fury.

"I think I'll talk to her about it now, actually."

I stalked to the door and yanked it open.

"Ms. Fairian! Guests are here!"

In a second of brief rationality, I snatched my sweaty workout pants from the hamper and yanked them over my bare legs. There, I wasn't dressed *only* in my shift.

The wooden floor cooled my bare feet as I strode towards the stairs leading into the foyer. The room itself was less populated than it sounded; most of the noise came from the ballroom, out of view beyond the Galician-style archway. My mother stood about a meter from the base of the stairs, laughing with two broad-shouldered gentlemen with their backs to me. My father didn't appear to be in the room.

Feelings hit in clusters, and for the first time in years, I shoved them away. *Not the time.*

I didn't let my resolve waver. I didn't care if this was an overreaction. Half-dressed and sweaty pants sticking to my legs, undoubtedly scandalous, I marched down the stairs into the picture-perfect room, half wishing the foyer was *filled* with her guests.

My mother glanced up just as I stepped off the stairs onto the ground floor. Her eyes widened in something akin to horror.

"Fairian," she breathed, resignation and panic bleeding from my name.

I closed in on her. "Mother."

Her half-panicked eyes cut to the two gentlemen she conversed with, and she let out a pleasant laugh that was actually pretty convincing. "Please excuse me. Why don't you head into the ballroom for refreshments?"

She grabbed my arm and turned, probably trying to block view of me with her body. "What are you doing?"

My eyes stung, and nastiness spit out of my heart. "Did you think I would be her if you put me in that dress? Did you think you'd have your perfect daughter back, not the one that's a freak?"

My skin tingled. I ignored the Feeling again.

My mother paled as her lips parted, and she took a second to respond. "Do not call yourself that."

Yeah. Don't remind her about my Feelings, the things that happened to me on the dark moon.

"The dress is of the utmost fashion and will do you good," she continued, pulling her composure around her like a cloak.

Our arguments about clothes were older than bloody dirt, but this reached a new level. I would not, under any circumstances, do anything that substituted me for my sister. I would never be the perfect Leynthall heir.

My skin tingled again, stronger this time—poking at my red-tinged fury, threatening to break it apart. *What the hell?* I refused to look.

"I will wear something presentable." The words tasted vile in my mouth. "But I will not wear *that*."

Arguments built in her eyes, but she nodded once. Only then did I turn towards the stairs.

The *look, look, look* dancing across my skin pounced, yanking all of my focus. The two gentlemen my mother had been speaking to still stood close by, and I knew even before looking that I held the sole focus of their attention. Turning my expression chilly, I flicked my gaze to them for a brief disinterested pass, not about to flinch from their assuredly judgmental—

And stopped abruptly as a gaze the color of the Farfallan night sky met mine.

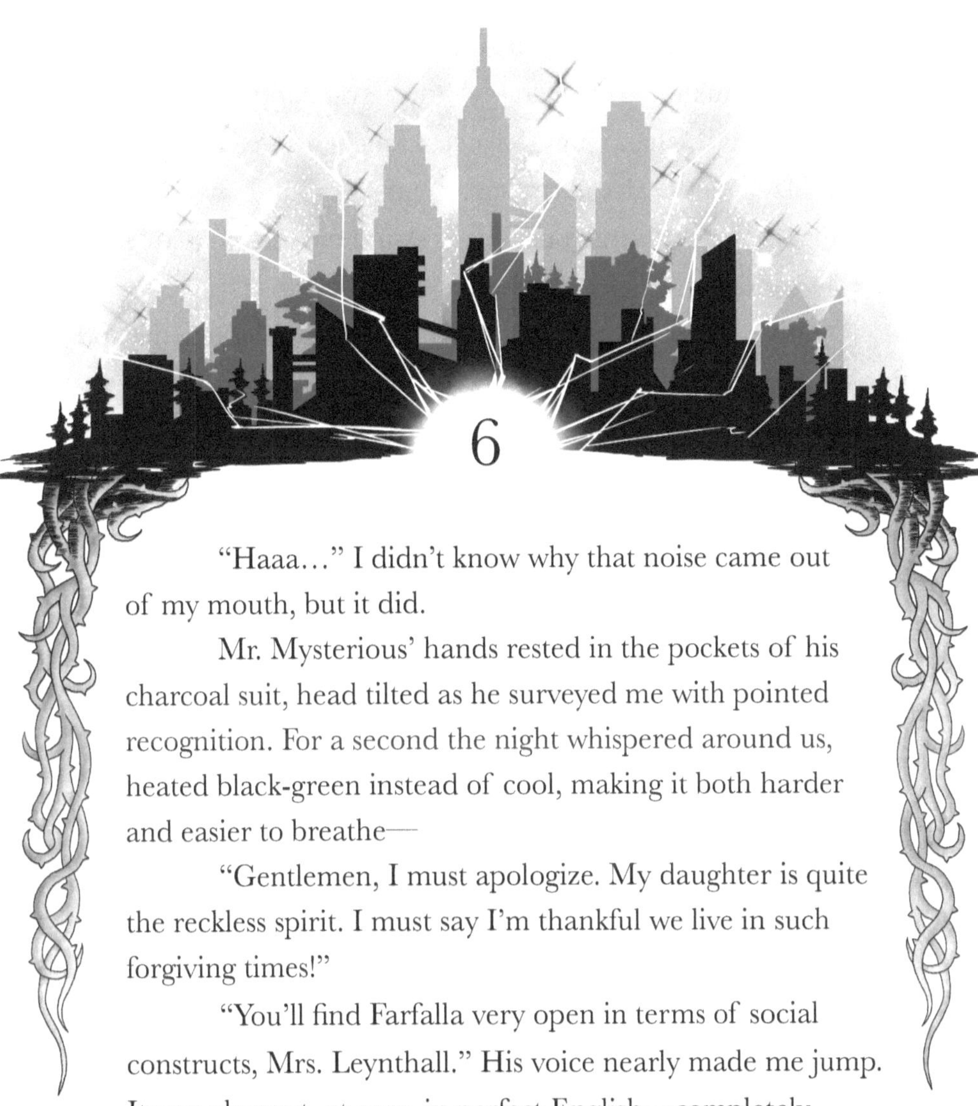

6

"Haaa…" I didn't know why that noise came out of my mouth, but it did.

Mr. Mysterious' hands rested in the pockets of his charcoal suit, head tilted as he surveyed me with pointed recognition. For a second the night whispered around us, heated black-green instead of cool, making it both harder and easier to breathe—

"Gentlemen, I must apologize. My daughter is quite the reckless spirit. I must say I'm thankful we live in such forgiving times!"

"You'll find Farfalla very open in terms of social constructs, Mrs. Leynthall." His voice nearly made me jump. It was pleasant, at ease, in perfect English—completely different than the halting rumble from that night. He stepped forward and extended his hand, gaze still pinned to me. "Daimyn Yillen, at your service."

My stomach flipped and shot up my throat. Daimyn, not Damien—a lilt to his name, an accent I couldn't identify blended perfectly into his English. His last name tugged on my memory. If the Yillens had been invited to my mother's party, they had to be from some sort of social influence.

61

"Ms. Fairian Leynthall. Pleased to meet you," I said, reaching for him. Proper manners dictated my father would introduce him to me, and he'd kiss my hand, not shake it. I fought a smile at his disregard of etiquette. His warm fingers curled around my own, and unidentifiable Feelings surged under my skin then disappeared like a blown out candle.

"This is my brother, Regan Yillen," he said, releasing me and tilting his head to his left.

I reluctantly dragged my gaze off him. It took me a second to comprehend the other figure there. The structure of their faces echoed each other, Regan built leaner, his hair a shade more red than black, and his eyes dark brown close to garnet. Currently, those eyes glanced at his brother, twinkling with repressed humor.

How much did he know about Daimyn's exploits? Was he involved? Would he be less stingy with information?

"How do you do," I managed.

"Well. And yourself?"

"Very well, thank you."

Daimyn studied me with an unnerving perceptiveness, something about it more present than the night we'd met. More… awake, almost. I scrambled for a relevant pleasantry.

"How are you enjoying the party so far?"

"We only just arrived. The foyer is very lovely, I could stay here chatting with you all evening," Regan replied.

My mother tittered. "You're too kind, Mr. Regan. Darling— why don't you go get dressed and then we can continue this conversation?" An edge sharpened her voice.

Paralysis struck. If I left, he might disappear. I didn't understand their presence here in the first place. I'd told him my name the first night, so he couldn't be *avoiding* me, if he'd come here. Daimyn tangled with the magical and dangerous, and then showed up at fancy parties introducing new families to the neighborhood?

At the very least I knew his name now. Unless he lied about his name. Crap, he could have lied about his whole name! No wonder he threw it at me like a gauntlet.

"Excuse us," my mother said pleasantly, her hand clamping down on my elbow. She pushed me towards the stairs, and I broke eye-contact with Daimyn for the first time in… however long that had been.

Heat crept up my neck. Except for when he introduced his brother, I had been staring at him the entire time. It would have been more embarrassing if he hadn't returned the scrutiny in equal measure. I dared one more glance as I was herded up the stairs; both of them still watched me. I felt distinctly… *inspected*.

No, it wasn't an accident they were here.

"That was mortifying, Fairian." My mother's low voice broke me from my thoughts. "Did you think to punish me for trying to dress you well, appearing in your underthings?"

I didn't have the energy to have a real conversation with her about this, not now that my fury-fuel had been doused.

"They seemed to take it in stride."

"That's the kind of gentleman you want to attract—ones interested in seeing you in your underpants?"

Oh. I hadn't considered it from that perspective. It did add a cringe-worthy note to Mr. Daimyn and I staring at each other. Ah, well. I knew it wasn't like that, and that's all that mattered.

My mother and I reached my room. Abigail had called in reinforcements: my mother's maid, Svetica, dug through hair products and nail enhancements.

"I must return to the party," my mother said shortly. "What will you be wearing?"

I heaved a silent sigh. It didn't take long to dig through my closet to find it. The sleeveless bodice shimmered dark blue, with orange and purple zigzag skirts flaring out from a gold waistband. It was bold, vivid, both elegant and modest, and probably the only ballgown I actually liked. Wearing it, I felt a modicum like myself.

My mother's eyes cut to the gown. She called it outdated and garish, and it surprised me she hadn't found a way for it to conveniently disappear yet. After a beat, she nodded. And without another word, she swept from the room.

Abigail and Svetica swarmed. Stockings first, then the corset and dress. Svetica buffed and painted my nails while Abigail curled my hair into an elegant pile partially flowing down my back. I swallowed discomfort as they worked over me. My mother had mastered the art of treating someone as equal while they 'attended' to you; I couldn't get past the feeling of being served. Funny, considering I'd grown up in this life, and my mother had fought her way into it.

The second I had a hand free, I found my PCD and searched "Yillen" in the news database of vArchive. The results loaded.

"A-ha!"

Abigail and Svetica both paused, exchanged glances, then continued.

I *had* recognized the Yillen name. They came from modest old money, mostly known for breeding horses. Several of their horses had gone on to be superb racers, including one who traveled the circuit last year in Britain, which is probably why I recognized it. The family didn't appear very socially active. They did, of course, contribute quite a lot of money to various causes, like all good wealthy families.

It took a while longer to find any photographic evidence of Daimyn's identity. Finally, an article from a few years ago at a fundraising gala for an environmental cleanup project in Germany had a picture. And there he was, looking exactly like he did downstairs.

So he hadn't lied about his name. And Mr. Regan stood beside him. How did he pull off both identities?

"Miss, I'm going to need your eyes for a little while," Svetica said.

I surrendered to the rest of their ministrations. Svetica outlined my eyes with kohl and shadow, and dusted glitter across my face, chest, and hair. After I slipped delicate black heels onto my feet, and white elbow-length gloves, Abigail turned me to the full-length mirror.

"Beautiful," she told me.

I stared impassively at the person in the mirror. Under their ministrations, my face became mature and more elegant. In these clothes and the corset tightly-laced, my body turned into graceful curves, and I actually had cleavage. Elegance personified stared back at me from the mirror and I tried not to grimace. At least I wore *this* dress, the bold colors so like my grandmother it brought a lump to my throat.

Mari used to tell me that beauty was a shield and a tool. If being beautiful brought confidence, use it. If being beautiful disarmed people, use that too. If being beautiful made them underestimate you, or think you shallow, use it to your advantage.

In the few compliments I remembered at social gatherings—because compliments were always necessary at a debut—my appearance had been the only thing commented upon. No one had sought to care about anything else; I'd been too awkward and not enough sweet, too weird and not enough exotic… no one heard when I spoke about anything meaningful to me. So I'd cultured a hatred for surface level attractiveness. I wanted to be *me* before anybody found me attractive. The reality was, I didn't know how to use Mari's advice.

She would have been so powerful.

I swallowed against the soreness that rose in my throat, and with a deep breath in a corset more tightly-laced than usual, I turned with a twirl to exit the room.

My mother had spent a long time deciding the culture of this occasion. Unlike Northampton and it's British etiquette, people from all over the world inhabited this city and even high-society had relaxed social dynamics. One of the differences I appreciated the most was the lack of any kind of announcement as I entered. Being the only living child, my name would be cried as Ms. Leynthall.

That wasn't my name. My sister's name was Ms. Leynthall.

Guests filled the ballroom and spilled out onto the patio on the opposite side from where I entered. Windows and glass doors lined the whole back wall, which had been opened to let people out onto the flower bedecked patio and let fresh air in. The temperature in here made me want to break into a sweat already. Tables lined the right side of the room with refreshments, and on the left side instruments rested in preparation for the band.

A camera rose out from the crowd, pointed towards me. The shutter flicked. *Oh goodie, the news is here.* More cameras appeared, more shutters flicking rapidly. I tried not to freeze like a deer startled by a predator. Mari had been so good at this. She'd make fun of everything alongside me, but she couldn't hide her relish as she worked society politics. She'd flourished in it. A crater existed where she used to be, and I would never be big enough to fill it.

I scanned the crowd for broad shoulders and dark hair, avoiding eye-contact that would inevitably invite conversation. A figure moved towards me through the crowd—my mother. *Crap*. Cutting off to the left would be my best exit.

Then I noticed the gentleman trailing behind her, and stayed put.

"My dear, you look lovely," my mother preened as she reached me, brushing a curl from my face. Daimyn Yillen's attention flicked once over my wardrobe; his expression revealed nothing. At least he'd met me as myself before, in the dark with blood and snark as companions.

"Now that everyone is a little more *presentable*—darling, this is Mr. Daimyn Yillen. Mr. Daimyn, this is my beautiful and headstrong daughter, Ms. Fairian Leynthall."

Eyes locked with mine, Daimyn placed a hand on his waist, executing a perfect gentleman's bow. A strange, weary amusement drove up from my gut. In a snap it disappeared.

That's from him. A bubbly certainty filled me that we both play-acted in this place, putting on a show while a secret only we could see danced above our heads.

"Yillen—you're the family who breeds those wonderful horses," I said, jumping right in, and deliberately not curtsying in return. My mother's disapproval bored into my face.

"That is correct," Daimyn said.

A thrill ran from my head to toe. "I hope to have the chance of seeing them in person. I hear they're something to behold."

"We would be delighted to have the privilege of your company."

I couldn't have looked away from his half-challenging stare even if I wanted to. A rush tingled all the way to my toes.

"How long have you been in Farfalla?" *What is your role here?*

"About five years now." His head tilted. "It is quite the rich collection of people and perspectives, particularly when you least expect it."

What did that even mean? Out of the corner of my eye, my mother's attention flicked back and forth between us; she, surprisingly, did not interject her own thoughts. Usually she'd be full-force by now. Then again, I usually did my best to derail all conversation with gentlemen.

"It is safe to say you've enjoyed your time here, then?" *Have you done the strigoi-stabbing thing the whole time?*

"Undoubtedly, there is no lack of excitement. Though caution is always advised when facing the unfamiliar."

Oh good, another warning. Time to step it up a notch. "Is it true the sky is always green?"

Daimyn stilled—but not like my mother did, in dismay.

"You heard correct," he said, shocking me with truth all over again. His eyes narrowed faintly… and my heart skipped as the air tasted of the same intensity from the other night. But instead of being paired with bewilderment, now only interest lived in his inspection.

My next question came out a lot less playful. "Why is it green, do you think?"

I almost jumped as mother gave a high laugh and grabbed my elbow. "Oh, my Fairian, she does love to rile up the conversation! She might have a bit too much time on her hands. You were saying earlier your father feels ill—not too unwell, I hope?"

Daimyn ignored her, making my eyebrows lift up my forehead. He didn't watch me like everyone else did when I mentioned the unmentionable, like if he stared hard enough he could make me normal. He scrutinized me like I'd handed him a riddle he hadn't seen before and couldn't help but try to figure it out.

I liked it.

His gaze finally flicked to my mother. "Yes, he woke up this morning with a sore throat and chills. He sends his apologies he couldn't make it."

Irritation prickled over me. I wanted to poke at him until I got his attention back. I wanted his interest, so I could find ways to wiggle under his guard and relish in his secrets.

My mother made a sympathetic noise. "And the rest of your family? Are they well?"

"There are just three of us at present. My brother and I are in excellent health, thank you. Our staff are also thriving." His gaze slid to me again.

Maybe I wanted his attention so my own fascination didn't seem so cringe-worthy in return.

Except my mother said next: "Oh! You must excuse us, I see Mrs. Sylvan. I absolutely must introduce my dearest to the family."

My head snapped towards her. "What? No—"

"Of course, Mrs. Lenythall. Thank you for the introduction."

Daimyn inclined his head as my mother dragged me away, and his focus hummed against my back all the way to the other side of the room.

7

My mother steered me (while berating my inappropriate questions) to a middle-aged white woman with bright, intelligent eyes and a heavy northern British accent. And the conversations began. I swallowed frustration and submitted to the inevitable. I would just have to find Mysterious Daimyn Yillen later.

After exchanging pleasantries with this Mrs. Sylvan, my mother moved me from person to person, introducing me to the neighborhood as her beautiful and headstrong daughter. I'd been in the thick of events like these since fourteen, and thrust into the role of the eldest child for the Leynthall empire not long after. And yet, small talk about social gatherings and gossip and business ventures still made me want to crawl out of my skin. It probably meant I was a bad person.

My only insight into the Yillen brothers came from watching their interactions with others. I didn't have a problem tracking Regan, what with the flurry of fans and fluffy hair always surrounding him. Daimyn, conversely, apparently evaporated every fifteen minutes. He moved between conversations quickly, spending only a few minutes with an individual or group before reappearing halfway across the room. After nearly three quarters of an hour, most people had settled into their discussions, which left him to his own devices. *Smart.*

At the precise moment of realization, Daimyn's gaze turned to me, all the way across the room. My heart jumped.

"Darling, what has captured your attention?" my mother passed it off as a joke, but frustration tinged her voice as I ignored the conversation she wanted me to participate in.

Forcing aggravation off my face, I turned back to the people whose names I'd already forgotten.

I'm definitely a terrible person.

Dinner was announced only slightly before I started screaming. Beautiful wooden tables had been set up in the yard, in the fading light of one of the last clear nights of the year. Ornate solar lights circled the tables, creating a golden oasis with the sunset bracketing the whole scene. Fall blooming flowers and plants lay along fixtures and the tables. Soft exclamations of delight and praise rose up, and out of the corner of my eye, my mother's shoulders relaxed a fraction.

As soon as guests sat down, waiters arrived with steaming plates of food. The choreography of it all was impressive. My mother firmly led me to a table before I could escape.

"Behave yourself," she murmured in my ear.

The earlier-met Mrs. Sylvan, along with a similarly-aged gentleman with dark auburn hair streaked with silver, and a younger woman my age who looked like a replica of Mrs. Sylvan, sat with us. A quick glance revealed Daimyn and Regan several tables away, sod it all.

My mother made introductions; the red-haired man as Mr. Sylvan, and the younger woman as their daughter, Clara Sylvan.

"Darling, Clara will also be attending Farfallan College of the Arts soon," my mother said, as if it were the most delightful thing in the world.

Ah, that's what she wanted. To make appropriate friends for me. I mustered up a smile for the sweet-looking Ms. Sylvan, and her whole demeanor brightened.

"What classes are you attending?" Clara asked, voice painfully sweet.

Oh god, why did I hate small-talk so much. Was the night really only halfway over?

In her defense, Clara did seem like a lovely person. Just… perfect in every societal standard possible. I made myself be less short with her, hopefully without letting her think I wanted to be friends. It would go two ways: I'd drive her off with my eccentricities (and I had no interest in being hurt or changing my behavior) or I'd 'taint' her by association (and that was just shitty to do to someone).

Dinner tasted delicious as only Tiff's mom could make it: several different entrées of local dishes with her own flare, consisting of fish, vegetables, and noodle dishes, all in various courses. I noted no octopus. That had been a point of debate for the past few weeks, whether or not Mrs. Collins should try to show her skills with one of foods Galicians held pride in. Apparently that had been tabled for more intimate gatherings so my mother could read the room and create a sense of camaraderie attempting to fit into the culture.

By turning my head slightly, I could see the Yillen brothers a few tables over. It gave me a crick in my neck holding it too long, but whatever. Regan always appeared to be in conversation with someone. I didn't catch Daimyn speaking once, but listening often. Not for one second did I think he didn't track everything around him. Even meters away, intensity bled off of him like a cloud, the subtlest and most pervasive Feeling I'd ever encountered. It kept pulling my attention, even when I didn't intend to look.

Very deliberately, Daimyn turned his head and locked eyes with me, his expression amused.

Crap. I jerked my attention back to my table.

Ms. Sylvan watched me with a peculiar expression. "Have you a prior acquaintance with Mr. Yillen?"

Wow, I'm stellar at this discreet thing. "Ah, of a sort."

"I was surprised to see him attending. They're quite reclusive."

Maybe Clara knows something. "The brothers both? Regan seems to be very charming."

"Oh yes. But he's…" Clara smiled, somewhere between wry and shy. "You know when a gentleman is *actually* interested or only interested in the moment? Regan has never shown interest in the long term."

I glanced towards the table—and Regan watched us.

"So he's a rake," I said.

Regan grinned. I froze. He couldn't actually *hear* me, could he? We were meters apart.

"Oh no!" Clara said. "Nothing like that. He's simply… busy with his own affairs. You know?"

Maybe Regan could read lips. Just in case, I rested my chin in one hand, half hiding my mouth, and focused on Clara. "Tell me about them."

Conversation quieted as the sun set and people no longer fought to be heard over the tinkle of utensils against plates. The mansion turned into a glowing beacon in the dark, even brighter than the solar lamps encircling the tables.

I didn't learn much more about the Yillens than I'd already guessed. Clara had little real information, but she spoke about them with familiarity, with no trepidation or interest belying a mystery. Daimyn had some secret demon-hunting identity, but apparently hid it enough to prevent gossip. Which sent a thrill through my stomach, because if he could do it, I could too.

Notes of music filtered through the glass doors; the band warming up. Dancing would begin soon.

"Oh, I believe it's time for dancing!" my mother exclaimed, as if she hadn't organized this entire thing to every minute detail.

Groups stood up from tables and made their way towards the house, the notes of music a beacon. As Mrs. Sylvan said something that pulled my mother's attention, I took advantage and slipped away into the crowd. Once inside, I darted for one of the pillars lining the two sides of the room and hid from view.

Pressing my back against the cool marble, I shut my eyes and focused on slow breaths. Relief swamped me that I got *away*. Several breaths had my shoulders relaxing their death grip on my ears, and I slid down the marble into a puddle of colored fabric, yanking off my heels with a groan.

Conversation rose and fell as the room collectively tried to be heard over, and then tried to hear, the music. The band warmed up with chords of playful tunes followed by deeply melancholic ones in an ironic fashion that made laughter ripple through the guests.

I peeked around the pillar. Everyone had pulled back to the edges of the room, leaving an open center in preparation for dancing. I didn't see the Yillen brothers. A familiar chord rang out—an English dance—loud in the room. Conversation quieted abruptly. A beat of silence. The band played the same chord again, as if prompting the group, and one of the musicians—an older gentleman with slicked back dark hair and sparkling dark eyes—gave a playfully impatient gesture towards the dance floor. He played an instrument almost like bagpipes, but not quite. Laughter rang out as the entertainer made a big show of getting people onto the dance floor, pairs of people darting into the open space. Then the band burst into song together.

By the second song, I begrudgingly smiled. The group of musicians engaged the room at every turn, played a variety of kinds of dances, and even had *me* paying attention. They looked like a family; a similarly-aged woman with her head covered and dressed in bright colors played what looked like a violin, and two younger women with similar features played a stringed and a percussion instrument. The final one, a much younger boy, played a horned instrument of some sort, his face flushed with effort.

I didn't leave my pillar, though. Even if I went to find the Yillen brothers, I'd be exposed, and no doubt my mother would find me just as I found them. I needed a way to track them down after this event.

"This is such a lovely gathering," said a voice. Older, British-sounding, female—on the other side of my pillar somewhere.

"I must admit I was worried initially." Tittering. "It's really quite difficult to find good taste with new money."

I smirked. When Leynthall Industries first took off, that's all my mother talked about—making sure did not fall into any new money family stereotypes. We would be tasteful, respectful, cultured, intelligent, and generous, until everyone forgot about our bloodline.

"Oh yes, I had low expectations coming in, especially with—well—with the mother's background."

My smirk faded.

"To be fair, it sounds like they don't have contact with that side. Mr. Leynthall has a quite modest and respectable pedigree. He's done wonders with her etiquette, though *I* can still tell. It's incredible sometimes how much a good upbringing changes, don't you think? The daughter, even as dour as she is, has that—how do you say—*air* of better class."

Heat flushed my entire body. Tension crawled up my spine as pain bit into my hands; those long nails Abigail had put on had been a bad idea. *But handy to rip down those ignorant chits faces.*

I flinched at the thought. My grandmother—my *mother's* mother, who these twits dared to insult—would have had a lot of choice words if I'd done something like that. Somehow, the things said about her, which I'd witnessed as my mother had brought us further and further into this circle, never seemed to affect her. At most it only seemed to amuse her.

But Grandmother wasn't here. I forced my fingers straight, old and familiar hurt tightening around my chest. I hadn't seen her in seven years. She'd found me only a few nights after returning from the horror of *him*, still smelling of dust from the road as she fervently reassured me that she believed me when I said my kidnappers had been magic. But when my mother overheard, she barred Grandmother from the house.

Sometimes her absence hurt almost as much as Mari's.

The group of arseface women moved away to dance, removing my opening to confront them before I could recover my breath. I didn't even know what I could do except spit fury at them. I let my head fall back against the pillar with a thud that made me wince.

What am I even doing here?

A welling sense of *not belonging* rose, startling me with its strength, coming on too fast for me to fight. I swallowed at the ache in my throat, muscles tightening in the desire to run and get out of here.

Out of the corner of my eye, movement—I jolted as Daimyn leaned back against the pillar to my right, arms crossing as he scanned over the crowd. His head tilted, his eyes meeting mine for a second for flicking back. My chest squeezed as something charged the air, something too quiet and calm for the cacophony of music, dancing, and laughter that filled the ballroom to bursting.

Then I saw it, and couldn't unsee it: we both ill-fit here, lonely in this place filled with people. That charge grew searing, as if part of me resonated on the same frequency as him and now rebounded, growing in strength. I swallowed hard, tensing with the urge to run away and towards him at the same time.

Then two young women approached, snapping the *sameness* tension: Clara and another girl with curly dark hair and warm skin. Daimyn's smile was practiced as the dark-haired girl spoke; I couldn't quite hear over the din. Then he nodded, offering his arm to her. His attention flicked to me for a second, and then he walked towards the dance floor.

The ballroom floor leeched cold into my bare feet and sound roared back to consciousness. I shut my eyes briefly before I stood and slipped my heels back on. I peered around the pillar and then quickly strode out from behind it, heading towards the exit without any real hope of escape.

"Fairian, darling!"

I closed my eyes. *That has to be a record.* I forced my feet to stop and turned towards the sound of her voice.

"Let me introduce Mr. Silverstein!"

A gentleman hovered at my mother's elbow: late 20s, dark blonde, blue eyes and prominent cheekbones. He smiled broadly when he caught my gaze. My stomach tightened as if in threat. It came as no surprise my mother pushed me into the path of eligible men at every opportunity.

"It's a true pleasure to meet you, Ms. Leynthall. May I have this dance?"

I offered my hand, because the sooner I got this over with…

Abigail loosened the corset and I gasped dramatically as I shook off the thing so it flopped to the floor. Like the mature adult I was, I then face-planted on my bed. *I can smell myself.* Being around endless amounts of people certainly made me sweat buckets. My feet cramped, and I couldn't help my groan as I wiggled my toes. I was not used to those bloody shoes, and my mother had me dance with what felt like the entire room.

Abigail rustled around behind me as she no doubt put the corset away and everything else I'd haphazardly thrown around.

The Yillen brothers had left not long after the dancing started. So I drank a lot of champagne to deal with the social situation, which only gave me a headache, and then drank water, which just made me need to pee constantly. I'd finally been able to leave after Mrs. Sylvan remarked about my pale color. Final introductions and farewells had taken at least an hour.

"Here are your bedclothes, Ms. Fairian," Abigail said. "Do you need anything else?"

"No I'm good," I mumbled, and then yawned. "Thank you for helping me. You didn't need to stay up this late."

Abigail laughed softly. "Goodnight, miss."

The door clicked shut. I relaxed with a sigh, finally alone. Bless'ed quiet.

Wait. *Alone.* My eyes snapped open and my gaze drifted towards my open window, where the curtains rustled softly with the wind. The sky rippled black overhead, broken up by hints of dark green, like my own personal siren call.

My heartbeat picked up. The party wouldn't be over for a while; chaos made the perfect opportunity to sneak out. My parents wouldn't bother me until morning. I didn't have any particular reason to jaunt around Farfalla, unlike last time with the strigoi and my nebulous-at-best plan of showing up where there'd been reports of attacks. I could still go out and see what stirred. I'd found the strigoi on my first attempt in this city, after all. And even if I didn't find anything, nothing compared to seeing a city in the dark.

But it was possible my sister's killer was out there.

My ribs contracted around my heart, dropping dread into my guts. I slid instantly back into a familiar headspace, fear sliding along pathways and hooking into places that had grown wide from use.

I shouldn't go outside. Not if *he* was out there.

The sharp edges of me violently rebelled.

No. NO. I would not make decisions based on fear. It shocked me how quickly I'd fallen into that headspace again. *Fear does not control me.* I remembered being a mindless creature controlled by terror, and never again. *Never* again.

Now that I knew I was afraid, I absolutely *had* to go out, a legitimate reason be damned. Teeth gritted, I pushed myself off the bed and got dressed in warm clothes I could move in.

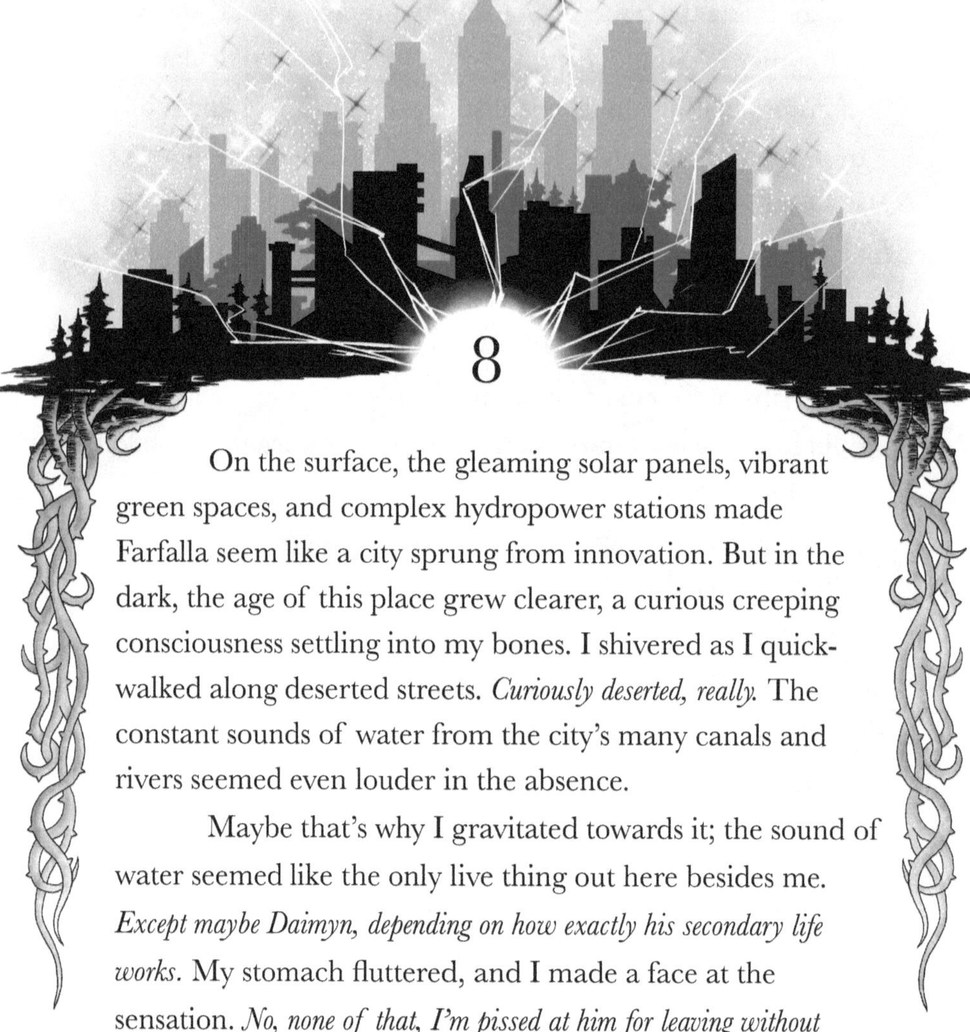

8

On the surface, the gleaming solar panels, vibrant green spaces, and complex hydropower stations made Farfalla seem like a city sprung from innovation. But in the dark, the age of this place grew clearer, a curious creeping consciousness settling into my bones. I shivered as I quick-walked along deserted streets. *Curiously deserted, really.* The constant sounds of water from the city's many canals and rivers seemed even louder in the absence.

Maybe that's why I gravitated towards it; the sound of water seemed like the only live thing out here besides me. *Except maybe Daimyn, depending on how exactly his secondary life works.* My stomach fluttered, and I made a face at the sensation. *No, none of that, I'm pissed at him for leaving without saying goodbye.*

Wait! No I'm not. I don't care. I don't.

I meandered along the boardwalk that ran the length of one of the rivers partitioning Farfalla. Solar tiles set along the aging wood glowed softly, highlighting the outline of the walking path. The reflection of the waning moon rippled across the black water, reminding me I needed to look at the date for the next new moon. I'd lost track in the hustle of moving.

It'll be the first Episode since moving to Farfalla. That ought to be interesting.

Something pulled my gaze down. I blinked, unsure how why I stared so hard at one spot. But a tickle in my head… and the water shifted, barely-not-quite hinting at a shape and movement under the surface. My breath caught.

I stared, unable to look away. Water rippled. Even though I *knew* something lay under the water, I jumped when two wide nostrils appeared, flaring wide once it breached water. A grin split my face as more surfaced: an equine nose, face, ears. Their eyes emerged, murky and pale, yet somehow burning. Something hungry and predatory. Goosebumps prickled across my skin.

The equine face became a powerful neck, a barrel chest and slender torso as the creature leapt out of the river onto the dock. Their hooves made hollow *thunks* against the weathered wood. Breath heaved out of me, my cheeks hurting I smiled so wide. Their dark tail flowed all the way to the ground in rippling waves, their mane tumbling almost to their knees. They shook themselves, spraying water and hair in all sorts of directions. Then they stilled, watching me.

"Hi," I breathed.

The creature's head slowly cocked to one side, farther than anatomy should allow. Adrenaline flooded my veins. Wow, that was a deeply buried instinct I'd been unaware of until this moment.

The creature slowly turned, revealing a long pale-colored furry back, head tilting again as they watched me. Waiting. A breathless laugh escaped me. I definitely knew what they were.

Water horse in English. Ceffyl Dwr in Wales. Kelpie in Scotland. Bäckahäst in Scandinavia.

"No, I'm not going to get on your back," I said. "I'm not interested in being dinner."

The water horse snorted, then shook their head again. I hugged my arms around myself, tilting back on my heels to remember not to close the distance. The water's edge lay right there, a few meters away. Any closer and it would be an easy topple and watery death.

"Thank you for showing yourself to me," I whispered, my eyes stinging. "I've only ever read about you."

I'd only ever read about most things.

See, this is why we don't cower in fear. Because you go out and confront life and see THIS.

The kelpie stirred and turned back around, facing me again with pricked ears. Then they slid forward a few steps, away from the water. Maybe I should back up, but instead I lifted my hands, fingers trembling.

The moment stretched until it seemed it would go on forever. Then a damp, furry nose hit my palm, and the kelpie huffed, sending slightly-warmer air down my arm. Disbelief flooded me in a whole-body shiver. They *thunked* forward a few more steps, my hand slipping off their face as they lowered their head and sniffed at my belt.

No, sniffing the dagger on my hip. The iron one. They snorted and abruptly pulled up their head, until the hungry, murky eye glared level with mine.

"Hello," I breathed again.

Nearly holding my breath, I pressed a hand against the tangled mess of their mane, over their neck. The flesh quivered under my palm, then relaxed. Something fizzed against the back of my neck… not quite the danger-prickles I knew, more hiccoughing, like the sparking of a machine unable to start. I swallowed carefully. I probably should get out of here soon, and calmly noted my escape route and that the water horse didn't like the iron dagger should I need either of those things.

The creature slowly circled around me, their long tail dragging across the dock behind them. I tensed, preparing to throw myself clear at the first sign of aggression. Snuffling ran across my hair, down my back. It tickled. I giggled, then twisted around and hesitantly put a hand on their furred side.

Bone stood up sharply against my hand under cooler flesh. I traced each rib with careful strokes, my smile fading.

"Are you built like this? Or starving?" I murmured.

They stilled and watched me with a single eye. A burning, nearly colorless… *intelligent*… eye. My heart gave a hard thump against my ribs.

"If I get you food, will you promise not to eat me?" I whispered.

Look at me, trying to feed everything I come across.

Nostrils flared, their head tossing in a decidedly equine way. It scrambled my brain, the horse mannerism familiar but somehow *off*.

"Fairian." The voice erupted out from behind me. "Back towards me. Slowly."

The water horse froze. The next second, their head lowered and posture shifted in a way I couldn't describe, and the Feeling sparking against my neck grew crawling and constant. *Oh, hell.*

"Daimyn," I said incredibly calmly, torn between aggravation he interrupted my moment here and the giddy satisfaction of his name rolling off my tongue. "You're not helping."

"I am not jesting," he continued firmly. "Back up. Now."

The water horse's lips peeled back from their very sharp, very meant-for-flesh-tearing teeth. My stomach dropped.

"You're making it wor-rrrrrrrse." I said, sing-song. "How about *you* back up."

The lightest scuff of sound came from behind me. The kelpie's head blurred and teeth clamped around my thigh.

"Shit—"

The kelpie ripped my leg out from under me and flung me like a rag doll. My head and limbs snapped backwards from the momentum, sharp pain blaring down my spine. The wooden boardwalk flew past, dark water abruptly looming under me. *But I'd been meters from the edge!* I crashed into freezing cold that swallowed me whole and formed ice in my blood. I kicked, disoriented, nauseated with how quickly I lost direction in the world.

Oh, fucksticks.

Something yanked the back of my coat, then hauled me sideways. Water rushed past my ears and fingertips, fast and growing faster. The temperature dropped shockingly quickly, burrowing into my flesh and stealing all warmth from my bones. I writhed, fighting the pressure of the water to reach over my head and figure out what had me.

Except I knew what had me.

I whimpered, and the sound echoed back at me. I fumbled for the handle of a knife along my back with fingers numb from cold, almost losing it. Once I had it, my heart a tiny bird in the restricting space of my ribcage, I reached over my head again. Thick, sharp hairs tangle in my fingers. Farther up, the skeletal face, their teeth embedded in the hood of my jacket.

I struggled to aim up over my head, fighting the current. Measuring it with my free hand to make sure I wouldn't hit their eyes or anything that could mean permanent damage…

Sorry, water horse…

… I stabbed down with the knife. It skittered across bone. A shriek burst my ears, my movement through the water abruptly jerking. I pinwheeled in the dark.

Up, up, which way is up?

My lungs began to burn. Heart rate accelerating, I let air trickle out of my mouth. It ran sideways across my face. Any second now I'd be grabbed again and—

Wheeling in nothingness. Disoriented. Danger existing just out of sight, never knowing where it might appear or strike.

True panic sprouted in my chest. I twisted in the water, trying to follow where the little bubbles out of my mouth led. My stomach roiled with disorientation. The bubbles churned. Did that really lead towards the surface?

Heat flared in the dark, and pressure clamped down on my arms. I spasmed, barely controlling my gasp. *Fingers.* I knew the sensation of fingers. They pushed me—towards the direction I'd discerned as up, then releasing. My heart hammered, hammered in the freezing cold.

I kicked hard. Something braced against my foot and *shoved*, sending me hurtling towards what I really hoped was upwards. My lungs ached with a new acidic fire, tantalizing me with the idea of opening my mouth and sucking down anything just to breathe. I lunged with every fiber of my being.

Water jolted and rushed. I kicked harder, my arms leaden. *Surface, where is the surface, how far am I down?* The knife in my hand did bollocks; I stabbed it into my coat, my fingers too numb to put it away properly. Then I utilized both arms, straining upwards as hard as I could. Ice turned my joints frozen, my fingers to my wrists to my shoulders.

Water beat at me, surging in fits and starts unrelated to my own movement. A shriek exploded right in my ear. I jolted. Pressure threatened to cave my chest in.

Not like this not like this—

I whimpered, loud in the water, my panic broadcasted all around. I clamped one of my hands over my mouth and nose, the urge to inhale a scream coming to life.

Fighting weakness, I lifted a hand… and it broke the surface of the water and smacked back down. I groaned, tipping my head back as I broke into the air.

My inhale sounded obscene. Shards of ice slammed into my lungs, the air hurting almost worse than the lack of it. I coughed, gasped, spluttering for breath, shaking and trying to stay afloat as the gentle rocking of the river threatened to send me under again.

Everything felt sideways. After being in the directionless water, the entire world had gone off kilter. The sky flipped, the river defied gravity and stuck to the side, and I hung weightless in the middle. Everything in my stomach tried to turn with it, crawling up my throat.

Eerie quiet filled the space beyond my own noise.

"Daimyn?" I croaked.

My heart sprinted in a new rush of panic.

"Daimyn!"

Water erupted in a screaming fountain a meter to my left. I yelped, almost submerging again. The churning mass crashed back down, hooves thrashing and human legs clamped around an equine torso. Water splat across my face.

"Daimyn!"

I swam towards where they'd disappeared again, limbs heavy and frozen. There—a flash of something pale. My skin crawled, legs tucking under me instinctively before I nearly submerged again, as I needed them to stay afloat.

A rhythmic splashing jerked my attention to the right. A humanoid figure swam towards me, arms churning with powerful strokes. Oh, hell, they moved fast. No way I could out-swim that. I scrambled for the knife I'd jammed in my coat earlier—

No! It was gone! I'd lost one of my knives!

I fought not to wail. No time, no time; I fought for one at my hip, biting back a whimper as cold water surged against my unprotected belly. My numb and slow-responding fingers barely had it—

Their head popped up a meter away from me, revealing a face. Regan Yillen.

I sagged in relief and almost sunk again.

"Hey, lady," Regan said, breathing heavily and grinning. "Had enough adventure for the night?"

"Daimyn," I blurted. "He's under the water—"

"Yes, he's trying to get the kelpie under control. Let's get you home."

Fury surged, a burst of heat in my blood. "Stop trying to bloody send me home!"

My voice cracked across the river like a shot. Regan blinked.

"He needs h-help, I d-don't know how long he's been under —" Teeth chattering, I scanned the water around me uselessly. I could see nothing.

"He's just fine." Regan eyeballed me. "We should go to shore."

"If you're not going to help then go away," I spat. My whole body shuddered in protest of my words as my limbs slowly numbed to uselessness.

"Fairian Leynthall," Regan said. "I think you're smart enough to realize Daimyn is not typical, and I promise you he's got this handled."

I swallowed. It wasn't like I really knew, was it? "Are you sh-sure?"

Regan let out a surprised—or maybe delighted—bark of laughter. "I am absolutely sure."

My limbs grew heavier by the second. The water surged, briefly submerging me, and I came up sputtering.

I caught the tail-end of Regan's dive before he appeared next to me, one of his arms wrapping around my waist and pulling me firmly head-above-water and against his side. His skin blazed warmth into me, and I shuddered involuntarily. Without another word, he turned and side-stroked towards the shore. Each powerful pull of his arm brought a crest of water over my shoulder and down my shirt.

The distance of the shore, the realization of how far the kelpie had pulled me along, startled me. Another wave of disorientation threatened to send all the contents of my stomach up my throat. I swallowed and craned my head around, searching for Daimyn and the kelpie. Nothing.

Hauling another person and only utilizing one arm made Regan's progress slow. As adrenaline faded, my strength seemed to go with it, my eyes growing thick and heavy.

I made a face and struggled to free myself from Regan's grasp. "I got it now. I've had a rest."

Regan's eyebrows lifted, but he released me. I pushed through cold and weak limbs with all my strength, aiming for the shore.

We reached the boardwalk a million years later. My arms shook as I reached for the edge to haul myself up, my feet searching for something to brace against. A chuckle sounded behind me. Regan seized the back of my jacket and tossed me halfway onto the boardwalk. Scowling, I flopped myself the rest of the way out of the river not unlike a waterlogged seal.

Curling into a ball on my side to preserve warmth, I panted for breath and fixed my eyes back out across the water. The wood of the boardwalk bit into my cheek, the glow from a solar-tile glaring right into my eyeball. I shifted my head so it didn't blind me.

Regan leveraged himself up next to me, eyes glinting garnet as they caught reflections of light.

"Maybe not home, but we need to get you somewhere before you catch your death."

Refusal tightened all my limbs. I didn't bother to voice it out loud. I just gathered strength, tension gripping all my insides. I hadn't seen Daimyn surface in minutes, unless I missed something. How long could he hold his breath? What if the kelpie ate him?

Oh god, this was my fault.

I told him it was fine! If he'd just backed off!

"Hey, let's not go into shock…" Regan's voice came, overly-gentle. "Let's get you up, okay?"

I scowled, sitting up fast enough to make me dizzy, and glared. "I'm not going into shock. I'm watching the water. And I'm not bloody moving until I see him."

His head tilted, interest soaking his expression. "Ohhhkay."

Regan leaned back on his hands, smiling as he looked out over the river, both of us dripping water onto the boardwalk.

Minutes stretched. A fist gripped my stomach and began to twist. Even if Daimyn had gotten air at some point that I'd missed on the swim over here, now it had been too long. But Regan just smiled, glancing at me occasionally with increasing amusement. If he wasn't worried, it had to be okay, right?

But I didn't know Regan. He could be cruel or playing a game and wanted his brother dead for some reason—

"What?" I demanded, after the millionth glance.

The arseclown grinned at me. "You know kelpies go for the most gullible or naive for their prey, right? That one went right for you."

I tucked that information away, ignoring gratefulness that Regan had given me information about demons. "I was doing just fine until—"

Water thrashed a few meters to my right. My heart surged into my throat and yanked me onto my feet. Daimyn's head rose out of the churning river like some kind of primordial water god, and relief turned my joints into jelly.

He scanned me once with vivid, dark eyes. I stilled in the face of another *difference*. The mild-mannered gentleman who'd been at the Leynthall pazo earlier tonight had been shed like a cloak, and now the near-feral intensity of his attention created its own kind of gravity.

His shoulder and arm rose out of the water with something like twine twisted in his fingers. The water bulged to his right—and he effortlessly hauled the entire kelpie onto the boardwalk, nearly at my feet. The kelpie hissed and writhed on the deck, their feet bound together with something.

"Now do you see this is dangerous?" Daimyn's voice cut through the dark.

Relief still crashed into the sucking emptiness that terror and dread had left behind, a heady cocktail.

"I was *fine* until you showed up." My voice shook.

Daimyn lifted one eyebrow. "Excuse me?"

I curled my hands into fists. "I was *just fine* until *you showed up* and ruined *everything* all *over again*."

Daimyn stared at me incredulously. *Hey at least that's familiar.*

"First you kill the strigoi. Before I could ask *anything*. Now *this*. Showing up exactly as I finally *find*—" I froze as something occurred to me. "Oh," I groaned, gripping my hair. If he had the covert organization from hell covering his tracks, no wonder he could have two lives. And why would he have been truthful the first time we met? "You *are* a part of TASA."

Regan's laughter burst out behind me, making me jump and swivel around. He sounded so genuinely surprised and delighted I faltered.

"Oh, Fairian, you are a treat. We are definitely *not* a part of that sad excuse for an institution." He looked back at Daimyn, eyes twinkling. "You got this? I'll get the truck."

Regan spun on his heels and jaunted off. I blinked as he disappeared rapidly into the shadows.

Water splat, and I turned as Daimyn hauled himself onto the boardwalk, shedding sheets of water. He wore only breeches and a long-sleeve shirt, which currently molded to his entire body like a second skin. My focus hiccoughed.

Daimyn stilled under my staring, expression wary.

"They're thin," I croaked.

"What?"

"The water horse."

I looked at the creature in question, who laid there heaving deep breaths that seemed to expand and retract their entire body, eyes riveted to me. My fingers tingled to touch them again, but I didn't. It was one thing to touch when they were unbound and could object. Quite another to force myself on them while tied up.

"We need to take them home," I said, attempting to put thoughts together. "And feed them. Is it normal for kelpies to be here? In Farfalla? Aren't they farther north? I mean, according to their legends." Bollocks, maybe I didn't know what I was talking about. Who was I kidding, of course I didn't know what I was talking about. "Or are they everywhere?"

Daimyn pressed water out of his hair with one hand, and curls bounced back, sticking out in all directions. "Farfalla does attract water types, but… yes," he murmured, frowning. "They look hungry."

"Should we feed them? Before taking them home, I mean."

He eyed me. "You do realize *you* were almost dinner."

"We had an understanding."

Both eyebrows winged upwards. "A what?"

"An understanding. I was going to track down food and they wouldn't eat me," I declared. Okay, that stretched things a bit. But that Feeling on the back of my neck hadn't turned to *real* danger-prickles until Daimyn had shown up with all his ordering.

He scrubbed a hand down his face. "What is it you are looking for?"

"What?"

"Right now. In general. Why are you out here?"

I fidgeted. Didn't we cover this? "I want to find magic and demons."

"Yes and *why?*"

His eyes fixed on me, every bit of his attention pulling at me for an answer. *Oh.* He actually wanted to know what I would say. I almost didn't know what to do with that.

I lifted my chin, swallowing, and gave a response out of my heart, even if it sounded trite: "I want the truth. About magic, how it actually is. The world is huge and complex, and I can't just ignore part of it because people decided it's scary or dangerous or something to bury. I want the truth and I don't care what it costs me to find it."

"'The truth'? Something in specific, or are you speaking of all the secrets of the world?" he said dryly.

"I don't know," I said through gritted teeth. "I'll stop when I feel like it. Maybe it will be all the secrets of the world."

His eyes slowly narrowed. "No, that's not it. People don't wake up one day and decide to throw their lives away on a nebulous quest." He paused. "You're looking for something specific. Some*one* specific, perhaps."

My stomach lurched. "You are, in fact, incorrect."

Maybe at the beginning I'd wanted some kind of revenge or justice. But finding *him* wasn't going to bring her back. I may not be able to put an exact finger on *what* I wanted, but it wasn't that.

"Sure, maybe I didn't wake up one morning and decide to do this," I amended. "Everyone has a path from somewhere. But I've always…" I flapped my hands around, trying to summon the right words. "I've always been interested in things other people avoid. Maybe there was a catalyst. But that doesn't change anything."

I'd be damned if her death meant nothing. But more than that, her death had stripped all my blinders, and I had no interest in other people's truths anymore.

Daimyn inspected me from head to toe. A lump formed in my throat, because he seemed to actually consider my words.

"Fairian," he began. A little shiver slid down my spine when he said my name. "Whatever you have in your head about what you're going to find here, this isn't something you can play around with for fun and come back unscathed."

"I'm not looking for the *thrill*," I retorted, though I guessed what he meant. When I'd first discovered others also looking to learn about demons, I'd been exhilarated. It hadn't taken me long to realize most people just liked to feel rebellious and talk about magic without doing anything real.

Daimyn's eyes glittered. "You cannot do this and expect just to go back to normal life. At some point there is no return."

My lungs filled with heat. "Good, I don't want to get out."

I wanted to be stuck. I wanted to be incapable of escaping. I wanted to know glorious terrible things and I wanted to be changed, again, into something even more powerful, and when it scared me, it wouldn't matter, because I wouldn't be able to stop it.

Did it make sense? No. Did that fact dampen the restless, sourceless, endless hunger in my soul? Not even slightly.

"It's not your responsibility to keep me safe," I said. "Just in case you have that misconception. I'm going to be out here whether you like it or not." I swept a hand out towards the city, and remembered the end of our first encounter. "You can knock me out with bloody stones all you want, I'll just come back."

Something behind his eyes seemed to… go blank. "I understand."

My heart quickened, protesting through yet another dose of adrenaline. He'd stopped arguing. Not to concede my point, but to shut down.

"Speaking of weird knock-out stones," I blurted, latching onto the first thing that came to mind to provoke him. "Were you having a power trip when you decided to send me unconscious, or did you just wimp out because I was winning our argument? What was even the point of that? I mean, congratulations I guess, you have physical power over me." I bowed dramatically, fluent in snark as a body language.

Daimyn's mouth quirked into an almost-smile. His gaze shifted to the street behind me. "I thought I might scare you into making some basic self-preservation decisions."

I snorted.

"But here we are," he said. "And you're not even a little afraid of me."

Odd statement. "Am I supposed to be afraid of you?"

The tell-tale hush of tires over ground reached me. I spun, alarmed that someone approached. The water horse lay there in full view! But Daimyn didn't look alarmed at all as a small covered truck slid rapidly towards us and came to a halt. *What should I do?*

Then Regan jumped out of the driver's seat, and I felt like a nitwit. He strode to the back and pulled open the doors into the bed, just as Daimyn walked past me… with the entire bloody water horse in his arms.

Uhm?

They growled, writhing and apparently not straining Daimyn's grip in the slightest. They all disappeared into the back of the truck— which sank down significantly on its wheels. My eyebrows shot up. With a loud bang and a shriek, the truck rocked briefly.

Daimyn's emerged—kelpie-less—and shut the doors, the banging growing in volume and strength as the vehicle creaked and rocked more violently on its springs. Daimyn and Regan exchanged looks. Then Regan headed for the cab of the truck, spinning the keys around one finger. He hopped into the cab and started up the engine with a soft hum, winking at me while he did so.

"Do try not to get eaten. It would be sad."

Then he pulled away, traveling down a narrow street before disappearing around a corner. *Okay well just bye then.*

Daimyn's arms braced across his chest when I looked at him, eyes flat. My throat tightened.

"All right, so obviously that was much too orchestrated for you to not have done it before," I barreled forward, his departure like a bad smell in the air. "You both just—knew what to do."

'I watch the streets for happenings of magical inclination,' he'd said, that first night we met.

"That truck has not been sitting in the garage collecting dust and you…" I hesitated. "You're strong." *Yes, very eloquent.* "Certainly stronger than…"

"Someone human?" he asked softly.

My stomach did a terrific flip. *Duh*, my brain said. Then Daimyn inhaled, lips parting like he would speak, probably to make some excuse to leave—

"Why were you at my family's party tonight?" I blurted.

He studied me for long enough I wondered if he would answer.

"We had to make sure you were who you said you were. I couldn't reconcile your behavior to some privileged human girl. I thought perhaps you were…" That odd, weary smile played on his lips. "Something else, pretending to be Fairian."

I delighted at the round of questions *that* sparked.

"Enough," Daimyn said, cutting me off before I could ask any of them. "I may not be able to force you to care about your safety. But I will not contribute to your quest to get yourself killed. You are alone in this."

His words hit with quiet devastation, like a knife between the ribs. The shock of him finding a mark froze me solid. *I care what he thinks.*

No, no, no. I couldn't care. Caring meant that when I inevitably drove him off, a piece of me would be ripped out. I shouldn't feel this way; I'd known Daimyn all of two seconds! In the next minute, he would walk away—I knew it, I could Feel it. No matter how much I wanted to believe that someday, maybe, there would be someone who would stay. Those who who stayed around me now just didn't know the whole story.

It was always me against the world, forever alone. I couldn't do it again—I *wouldn't* watch him leave.

My lips peeled back from my teeth, grinning widely and without an ounce of humor. "Nothing new there, Daimyn. I've always been alone."

I spun on my heel and walked away. I did it before he could.

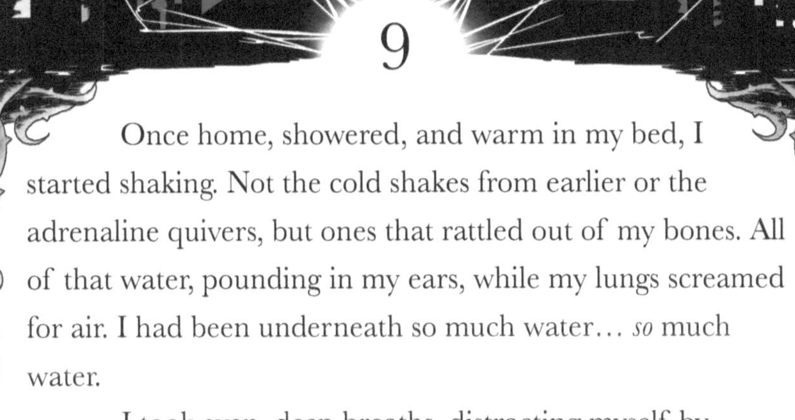

9

Once home, showered, and warm in my bed, I started shaking. Not the cold shakes from earlier or the adrenaline quivers, but ones that rattled out of my bones. All of that water, pounding in my ears, while my lungs screamed for air. I had been underneath so much water… *so* much water.

I took even, deep breaths, distracting myself by running through facts about water horses and mysterious arseface strangers who wouldn't share. I'd found someone who knew about magic—probably *was* magic—and he wanted nothing to do with me. Just perfect.

I pulled the blankets up around my head, but sickening disorientation flooded through me. I flung back the covers, gasping even though I knew there was enough air, trying to stop shivering for just one second. My clothes stuck to me with sweat.

There had been one guy—James something—I'd found over a year ago, who might have been someone with real info. Then he'd disappeared for a few months, and refused to talk to me when I'd finally tracked him down again. Possibly TASA's interference again. He'd been a lot less sure of himself than Daimyn, though, and I'd had a lot less proof he'd known something. Why couldn't I find one damn person who wanted to talk?

So much water… I'd been sightless in that place. I could only just swim and wait to be yanked down again—

Stop.

I filled my lungs as far as they could go, focusing on the softness of the blankets, the feeling of the mattress under my back…

If only Daimyn could see me now. I choked on a bitter laugh. Maybe he was right and I couldn't handle the reality of this. Never mind that for those bare moments I'd touched the water horse, my restlessness finally quieted. Never mind that for the entire encounter, my mind had stopped suffocating in its constant desire for *something*.

Never mind that entire time I'd been with him, I'd felt like someone I actually wanted to be, instead of the person I really was.

Tiff and my first day at Farfalla College of the Arts dawned overcast and cloudy, the sky the color of basil. Or maybe a pickle. Tiff and I walked onto campus fully fed, primped, and—well, this was just me—absolutely not ready to seize the day. The black tea in my hand did very little to improve my sleep-deprivation.

FCA consisted of several clustered buildings broken up by clover lawns, sculptures from various students over the years, and fruit trees. Pollinator-friendly flowers peaked over the edges of most of the roofs. The cafeteria building at the center of campus, an old-style Spanish brick and clay style not unlike the Leynthall pazo, had a full-on garden up there. People strolled or quick-walked from place to place, dressed in all kinds of styles and colors.

I sighed.

"You look like you're expecting to be tortured," Tiff said wryly.

"I'm so tired of college," I muttered.

That wasn't exactly true. I was tired of feeling like I *had* to be in college. Because as soon as I finished, my mother would ramp up her efforts to parade me in front of eligible men. She took pride in her daughter getting a college education when she herself hadn't had the same privileges, but her priority lay in establishing Leynthall as an important family. That meant I needed to make baby Leynthalls. ASAP.

"It's just senior-itis," Tiff said. "You'll be able to finish up this year."

My stomach cramped. *Not if I have anything to say about it.* I couldn't fail all my classes my first semester, because getting kicked out of college would *also* ramp up my mother's matchmaking efforts, but failing a class or two over the next year would drag this out another semester. Or year, if I could manage it.

That won't work forever.

I ignored that persistent truth.

Tiff bumped her hip into mine, getting my attention. "Come on, Farfalla is a completely different city and culture. And before you say all people suck, remember you are in fact a member of the human race, despite trying to convince everyone otherwise with your wanker-y."

I muttered insults into my tea, and Tiff laughed. When she linked her arm with mine and tucked me close, I rested my head on her shoulder, grateful she'd inserted herself as my friend all those years ago when I had been drowning in the absence of Mari.

Classes at FCA were, unsurprisingly, not that different from classes back at Northampton. After we finished for the day and we picked up our books from the bookstore, Tiff and I sprawled in the grass to wait for our driver. It was a pretty nice afternoon; a little cold and breezy, and the sky had turned closer to a shamrock shade, with mint-colored patchy clouds.

Students scattered across the clover lawn, enjoying the sun, which probably wouldn't be around for long. Nearest us, three men kneeled on beautifully colored blankets, facing away as they lowered their torso with straight backs. On the other end of the open space, tucked under some trees, two women in hijabi were side by side as they gracefully observed their own prayer. Mid-afternoon *salat*, then.

Tiff chewed a fingernail as she skimmed her literature book. No doubt she'd be studying before there was even a first assignment.

My geography class book was the only thing interesting in my stack. Bigger than my head, it had a stylized, full color depiction of the five known continents of the world on the cover: Europe, Asia, Africa, Australia, and Antarctica.

I traced a path from memory up the Atlantic ocean: off the coastline of Africa, cutting close to Senegal, then Galicia, Ireland, the U.K., Norway, and then Russia. There was no depiction of the Divide— there wouldn't be on any popular map—but something inside of me settled as I outlined its location to myself.

People didn't just build gigantic walls for no reason. Particularly walls that—supposedly—defied gravity and completely encircled the globe. Popular opinion dismissed the Divide as some ancient civilization construction built as defense against the violent storms that often came out of the ocean, and completely ignored the magical component. I'd read one singular article that only acknowledged the obvious demonic influence, dismissing it as from 'barbaric' and 'uncivilized' times. Damn could humanity tell the biggest tales when we didn't want to acknowledge uncomfortable questions or truths.

I craned my head upwards and studied the sky again. Maybe I'd put together a ship and find a way past the Divide. If there really was *nothing* on the other side of it, maybe I'd study ocean currents or something. If we survived the giant storms that either sank or drove off all adventurers who ventured there. No one had ever made it past the Divide. No one that had ever returned, anyway.

"You're looking melancholy again," Tiff said, snapping her book shut. "Soooo. Should we talk about your weird reaction to those Yillen brothers in the foyer last night?"

I choked on my own saliva. "*What?*"

Delight spread across Tiff's face. "Oh my god you're turning the color of currant. I'm right, aren't I?"

"What the hell, were you hiding under the *tables?*"

Tiff hadn't been at the party. She'd be invited to less-formal events as the Leynthall ward.

She laughed like an arse. "No, but Annie caught the whole thing, and the staff is talking about you staring at Yillen brothers while in your skivvies."

My mouth opened a few seconds before words came out: "I had trousers on."

Yeah, that didn't do anything helpful.

Tiff's eyes narrowed, smile turning decidedly more evil. "Don't tell me, you actually found someone you're attracted to."

I guffawed entirely too loudly. "Oh dear god."

And then the memory of Daimyn standing on the boardwalk, soaked clothes molded to every line of him, popped up with obnoxious clarity. My face heated. Okay, his face and body were nice, whatever.

And he moved in ways that made it impossible not to watch. And my breathing did fool things when he looked at me with all of that intensity he carried around.

And none of that mattered since he'd written me off anyway.

"I was just caught off guard. Confronting my mother, then I… thought I recognized him."

My ability to lie had apparently left the building.

Tiff's grin widened. "Him? The eldest."

I growled under my breath.

"Recognition is not why you stared at Mr. Daimyn Yillen for a full five minutes." Tiff bounced up and down on her butt. "Or why he stared at you, for that matter. Tell me the truth."

"It was not five minutes."

"Okay, sure, with Annie's love of exaggeration, it was probably two. You know if you stare in someone's eyes for a full minute you can create feelings of love? That was twice as much time as you needed."

I huffed, staying *far* away from her last statement. I couldn't tell Tiff anything close to the truth. One, she'd freak. Tiff and magic weren't just oil and water, they were oil and a river on fire. I didn't make a habit of bringing up my interests to people anyway, but the few times I'd tried to ease my way into talking to her about magic, she'd shut down the conversation instantly.

As much as I didn't like her current line of thinking, it would be worse to implicate him with anything demonic. Which led to reason two not to tell her anything: outing Daimyn's magic-dealing nightlife would be a betrayal. If any sort of relationship existed after his declaration two nights ago, that would definitely ruin it.

I inwardly groaned. The best choice was letting her think my reaction was due to attraction.

"I… he was… *is*… very nice to look at."

Tiff stayed shockingly silent while her expression screamed triumph. She cleared her throat delicately while she laced her fingers and stretched them out in front of her before tucking them under her chin in a deceptively sweet pose.

"I'm telling you right now, with your history of actually being attracted to people who could be nice for your future… you need to jump on that. In whatever way you want to take it."

I rubbed my face with a hand. "Tiffany. How did we get to matchmaking?"

"Hey, with as little as you give me for making sure your future doesn't suck, I've got to work with what I have."

This conversation had my hair standing on end. She was the one without the 'good name,' who'd need to marry well to build a life more comfortable than the one her mother had. We didn't need to talk about this.

A familiar electrical car pulled into view and stopped by the curb at the end of the lawn.

I lunged to my feet, yanking my stuff up with me. "Renald is here!" *Thank god.*

"The fact that you're so squirmy with this conversation means I'm right."

I made a face as I hurried to the car.

"Good afternoon, Ms. Leynthall and Ms. Collins," Renald said, stepping out of the car. Salt and pepper hair slicked back, his grey suit impeccable, he looked debonair as usual.

"Good afternoon, Renald," Tiff and I said in unison.

He opened the boot and we piled our bags in.

"And how were your classes, young conquerers?"

I grunted, fighting a smile. Renald was one of the only members of our staff who had been around when my sister and I were taken. I tried not to get close to the staff anymore—after everything following my sister's death—but Renald had been there before I'd decided to wall up my affections. He'd never made me feel uncomfortable or like I had to explain myself.

"Fair-Fair looked about ready to melt into boredom, but I thought they were very promising," Tiff declared.

"So, the usual then," Renald said, and opened the door to the back seat for us to enter. He still opened the damn door even after I told him he didn't need to a hundred times.

Pressure brushed the back of my neck. Not the real kind, the Felt kind. Distracted, my gaze swung back to the clover lawn. Several meters away, lying in the grass, a young masculine-presenting person with sandy-blonde hair stared at me intently. He quickly looked back down to a book in his hands. I frowned and got into the car.

"So have you looked up his family yet?" Tiff asked the instant we were settled.

I stared at her blankly. Renald got to the driver's side and slid behind the wheel.

"Daimyn Yillen," Tiff said, using way too much lip and tongue to enunciate his name.

Great, apparently we were still having this conversation. "Not really."

Tiff poked me in the side. "Where's your PCD, we're researching this. Mine doesn't have a V-Hookup yet."

Damn it, that was a good idea. About a decade ago, there'd been a big push (mostly by historians) to upload ancestry information to the vArchive. It was an easy way to check people out, and I should have thought of it sooner.

Tiff poked me increasingly harder when I didn't move. Sighing heavily, I pulled out my device and navigated to the Family Histories and Ancestry database, secretly grateful she pushed me into this. Tiff snuggled into my side and rested her chin on my shoulder to look.

My heartbeat skipped as "Yillen" populated. At the top of the screen, a message appeared:

"Rudimentary documentation has been found on the Yillen family. Known facts, provided with permission of the family, are as follows:"

"Huh," Tiff said.

I decided I was utterly unsurprised.

Records started at the present. Daimyn's name scrawled across the top with Regan's—and their father, Markus Yillen, one below. I scrolled, scanning new names that meant nothing to me. Concrete information only went back a century, and it was—as warned at the onset—sketchy at best. The farther back in time, the fewer descriptions and names. There were no pictures, only basic sketches of faces or places where the Yillen's had lived. No Peerages or family offshoots of any sort had been listed.

While male names were badly recorded, the female Yillens were worse. Each generation in the past couple centuries comprised one or two boys, and beyond that a lot of question marks. All women, if mentioned, married into the family—and no names, beyond Daimyn's grandmother and mother. His mother's name was Ariana: she'd died, two decades ago. It didn't say why.

The Yillens also apparently moved around a lot. Britain, Germany, Sweden—about once every decade or two, in fact. That was a lot of time and resources to move an establishment of horses. It was one thing to have multiple homes, but quite another to uproot every decade.

I blew out a noisy breath.

"Well that was unhelpful," Tiff grouched.

The sound of the tires changed as we shifted from public streets onto the private drive of the Lenythall pazo. The lower light of autumn cast golden outlines across the grounds as we approached, and the deciduous trees had just barely started dropping their red and orange leaves. It really was a beautiful place. No wonder my father had fought so hard for it.

Tiff and I thanked Renald and juggled our various items up into the pazo. My mother swept in from the nearby sitting room immediately as we entered the foyer.

"Darling!" she sang.

Crapsticks, it was an ambush. She had an agenda.

"Hello, Mother," I said quickly. "I was thinking of heading to the library to study, I—"

"I'm so glad you're in a studious frame of mind! I have a surprise for you!"

This is not going to be good.

"Just leave your books, Abigail will get them. Goodness, they're heavy. I hope you didn't strain yourself."

Linking her arm in mine, my mother pulled me towards the stairs. Tiff and I exchanged looks; she blinked cluelessly. With no time to chew my arm off to get out of my mother's grip, she led me to one of the smaller sitting rooms towards the back which had been fashioned into a kind of study. When she opened the door, a stoic-looking gentleman rose to his feet, inclining his head stiffly. He looked plain and almost unassuming, but something unpleasant rushed over my skin.

"Darling, this is Mr. Frederickson. We've hired him on to tutor you!"

I slowly turned my head to look at her.

"With how much you've struggled to focus on your studies, now is the perfect opportunity to start fresh and earn the excellent marks I know you're capable of! Mr. Frederickson will help you regain your good studying habits. He's agreed to see you after classes every day."

"It's a pleasure to meet you, Ms. Leynthall."

I twitched. *That is not my name.*

"You did *what?*" I finally managed to demand of my mother. *I'm sorry, how old am I?*

"None of that now." Her voice made me falter, her tone completely free of her constant faux emotion or drama. "Let's get you freshened up."

How long had she been planning this?

"I look forward to our time together, Ms. Leynthall," my new tutor said.

My stomach cramped into a vice, my heart scrabbling against the inside of my ribs trying to get free.

Half an hour later, my new "tutor" slowly circled me as I sat at the desk designated for these sessions. Apparently, we'd all gone back in time, and I needed to be treated like a child.

"Your mother tells me you have quite a few diverting hobbies," Tutor said. "I think it's best we start by going over those and deciding what is priority in your education moving forward. What distractions can be discarded for more productive tasks."

I guffawed. "Um, *hell* no. That is my business."

Yes, my parents knew I had 'unnatural interests,' but I worked hard to keep specifics out of sight. They couldn't know—

Thwack. Pain seared up my fingers. I gasped, clutching them to my chest in confusion. Abigail, reading quietly in the corner, looked up in alarm.

Tutor calmly held a ruler. The one he'd just brought down on my knuckles.

"I've been tasked with correcting your behavior in several regards," he said. "I will implement many tools at my disposal, but it will be more pleasant for you if you try to cooperate."

I absorbed each one of his words calmly, slowly cycling air in and out of my lungs. I would not let this man make me feel like a child. *I would not let this man make me feel like a child.*

"Is that understood?" he asked, and it took all of my willpower not to lunge out of my seat.

I turned my head slowly, meeting his gaze. "If you hit me again, I will break your nose."

They'd never done this before. They'd never had someone use *pain* on me before. Something inside of me shriveled up and died, and I didn't know if I'd ever get it back.

Fear does not control me.

I had to reach deep to find the strength from my mantra.

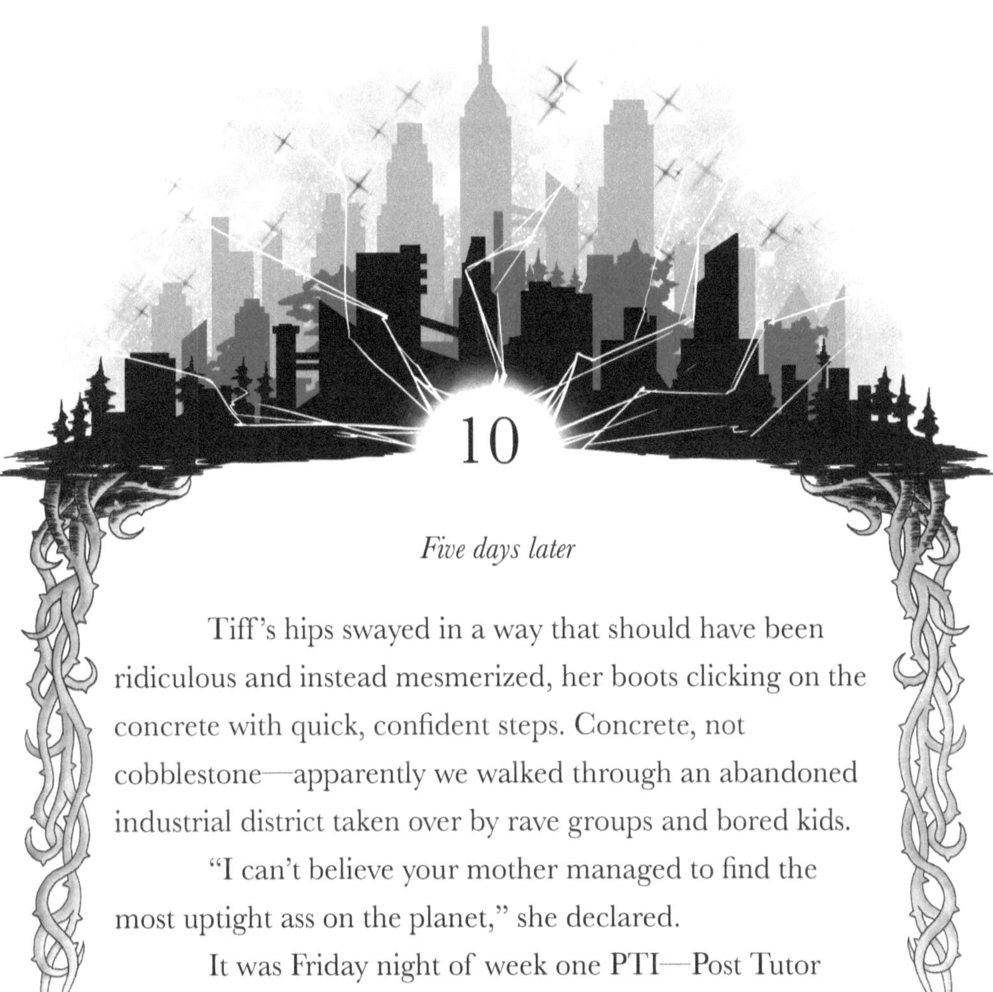

10

Tiff's hips swayed in a way that should have been ridiculous and instead mesmerized, her boots clicking on the concrete with quick, confident steps. Concrete, not cobblestone—apparently we walked through an abandoned industrial district taken over by rave groups and bored kids.

"I can't believe your mother managed to find the most uptight ass on the planet," she declared.

It was Friday night of week one PTI—Post Tutor Invasion—and Tiff had shown up at my door after supper with skimpy outfits and wouldn't hear a single excuse about us not going out. She'd originally planned this as a celebration for completing our first week at FCA, but it had become more than that. Now it was a blatant need to bugger off when the entire week had been an exercise in various forms of routine hell. Tiff, being Tiff, had weaseled out the locations of some of the best clubs in the city.

The back of my neck prickled—*again*—and I shivered violently. Between it and the cold, goosebumps covered every centimeter of my flesh.

Is it real or am I imagining it is it real or am I imagining it…

Tutor hadn't been the only problem that cropped up this week. I had not missed the sensation of being watched. I had not missed it at all.

He's back he's back HE'S BACK—

I coughed loudly, shaking myself, stamping my feet. Jolts of pain up my legs and vigorous movement kept me in my body.

"You good?" Tiff asked archly.

I hadn't told her about the new eyeballs on me. She'd freak, and I would panic, and we'd blow everything out of proportion. I didn't have proof it was *him*. I had barely made any progress figuring out what happened with the people who'd been taken and claimed hallucinations. My father hadn't heard back from Saint Dymphna's.

"It's bloody freezing," I said instead. "Why are we walking here again?"

She sighed dramatically. "I told you. Apparently this club only meets once a month and it's incredible. And apparently the rail doesn't come out here this late. Are you seriously not going to bitch with me about the new wanker in your life?"

I rubbed my forehead. Tutor was the least of my problems. But he made it ten times more difficult to do anything about anything else, that was true.

"There's not much to say. Welcome to my new reality."

My neck prickled again. *If it's you, just do something!* If *he* was really in Farfalla, what was the hold up? Our pazo wasn't nearly as fortified as our home in Northampton. I attended university every day this week. Maybe the presence of those around me dissuaded him? Or maybe he didn't know it was me, and this was something else?

I hated returning to the headspace of just *waiting* for something bad to happen. I'd wasted too many years because of it. It was like being frozen with all my insides exposed and vulnerable.

"If you do better in classes you won't need a tutor," Tiff near blurted, as if she couldn't keep the words in any longer.

For a second I didn't comprehend her words. Then heat filled my eyes. "I have had literally *everyone, all week* tell me what I bloody need to do, so I'd appreciate it if I didn't hear it from you too."

Tiff gaze dropped to the ground. I winced; that had been harsh.

"I know you feel you need to do these things," Tiff said before I could think of how to backpedal. "But there's got to be a better way to be rebellious that doesn't endanger your future—"

I whipped towards her, stopping in my tracks. *'Another way to be rebellious,' as if this is some bloody joke.*

"You seriously think anyone is going to care about my grades once I have a degree? Or that anyone will even care if I have a degree? As the only living child of the Leynthall-bloody-empire, my job is to marry well and pop out babies! My education increases my *prospects* for a *husband*. If I found one now, I'd be expected to drop out and start making a home!" Panic tightened over my heart at the words out loud. My lungs refused to expand.

Tiff wrapped her arms around her torso. "You don't know that. Your parents won't *force* you—"

"Oh, sure, they'll make it look like I have control. They'll make it a decision between impossible choices, and tell me I have free will."

Tiff swallowed, and she stared at the ground, rocking back and forth on her heels. "You're so smart. It'd only be a little effort and then they'd get off your back…" Her voice softened. "Maybe if you gave them just a little of what they wanted, they'll give you more of what you want in return."

I shut my eyes, reminding myself Tiff was just trying to help. And maybe she was right. If I bent just a little for my parents, kept my 'eccentricities' out of the public light, if I did well in classes, if I looked to be interested in eligible men, if I kept partying to a minimum and never, ever said anything about demons, maybe I'd have more choices. So many things I could do to make my life 'easier,' all within the constraints of appropriate behavior.

But there was only so much more time left to be *me*. My parents would ramp up the pressure to find me a suitable match before long, and I didn't know what I would do. The idea of their predetermined path for me filled my soul with dread. But walking away meant disownment, and yeah, the lack of having financial support gave me *pause* because my privileged arse didn't have any bloody skills really worth anything. It also meant leaving *everything* I knew behind and my parents completely childless.

Unless *he* showed up… that'd be a quick way to escape a life of marriage and babies.

"You're not helping, Tiff."

She nodded quickly. "I'm sorry. I'll stop."

I lifted my hand to rub my eyes and aborted the movement at the last second, remembering my face full of makeup.

"Come on."

I opened my eyes to see her reaching for my hand. Our fingers linked together and she tugged me forward.

"We need this. We need to have some fun."

Tiff skipped—in bloody heels, how did she do that—grinning at me. I reluctantly smiled. Then she tripped, abruptly quitting her skipping routine. I sniggered. She stuck her tongue out at me.

Aaaand there was the sodding prickle on the back of my neck again. Humor dying a quick death, I clamped my jaw, tilting my head back to stare at the sky. Black with highlights of the darkest emerald glittered back at me. Despite everything, it gave me a tiny gasp of peace.

"Wait, I think this is it!"

Tiff took off ahead of me. She reached the corner of a building, peering around the steel-supported concrete structure with her fingertips lightly touching the wall. Then, tossing me a grin over her shoulder, she disappeared around the corner. My stomach lurched as soon as she was out of eyesight.

I bolted around the corner, nearly twisting my ankle. Tiff strode briskly towards an old metal door set into the concrete wall.

Tiff is fine… chill.

Faint humming trembled through the wall and ground. As I drew closer, I realized it was music, muffled through the layers of the building. Tiff hesitated before yanking open the giant metal door. Sound burst out at us in a wave.

Through the door, a metal staircase led down to the huge sunken dance floor, where maybe a hundred people were writhing or talking in groups or lined up at the bar. I'd expected the smell of all those bodies. Instead I got peppermint and stone.

A bar ran along one wall, packed with people trying to get the attention of two younger women darting back and forth. The shelves behind it were filled with shining bottles of liquor. The bartenders snatched bottles off shelves as quickly as they replaced them, drinks tossed and handed over amongst the cacophony of noise. Opposite the bar, a makeshift stage sat with sound equipment and instruments. Pre-recorded music blared through the speakers at the moment, though Tiff has said a live band would be playing tonight.

My gaze lifted to the ceiling as Tiff and I trounced down the stairs. Dozens of recessed lights hung alongside spotlights and colored lights, along with a few more speakers.

How in the crap did they power this place? It had to have an official hookup to the hydro-station. Unless they had a huge battery set-up and soaked up solar during the day…

Well, Tiff had mentioned this place wasn't open often. Maybe whoever owned this place stocked up on juice and then opened once they could. It would explain the hours of operation, and turned the place into a novelty. Which also might explain the crush of people here.

We reached the ground floor and Tiff signaled to follow her to the bar. As we made our way through the throng of people—

Butterflies.

Screaming euphoria bursting in every one of my veins.

A slow pulse, down my spine, blooming in my hips.

I cringed, the assault of Feelings flickering out as fast as they'd come. They acted like a check-in, there and then gone.

Tiff leaned over the bar to get the server's attention. I eased up next to her, trying not to brush up against anyone inadvertently. I needed alcohol before I could relax.

Someone bumped into me. I fought the hostile expression off my face, and a cute boy with tawny skin and slicked back dark hair shot me a grin of apology. He paused for a second, eyes searching mine, and then his buddy pulled on his shoulder. He turned and went with.

"He's cute," Tiff purred in my ear. "Dancing and make-out partner for the evening?"

I rolled my eyes.

The cute person in question glanced over his shoulder. I lifted a hand and wiggled my fingers, but I don't know if he saw before getting lost in the throng of people.

Tiff pursed her lips, her eyes scanning. "What about her? She's gorgeous."

She gestured at a pale girl with big eyes and curves to die for. Not that either of us knew if she swung that way.

"Sometimes, you are a guy."

"Hey! I'm just trying to make sure you enjoy your evening."

Tiff was all sexual being in a way I… well, it wasn't so much that I *wanted* to be. I just wanted to be *able* to be that way. Usually my insides just squirmed and I burst out into inappropriate laughter, or my brain left planet earth thinking about all the better things I could be doing with my time. Tiff had taken it upon herself to try to set me up with positive experiences, which was only annoying sometimes. It wasn't like I was shy. I *wanted* to, I just… honestly, I'd started to wonder if I was asexual or something. But I still wanted to know what it felt like to actually enjoy something like that.

One of the bartenders shouted to us, and we ordered. Tiff and I leaned back against the counter as she prepared the drinks, and my skin prickled with sweat; it was stifling in here.

The door to the club opened across the room, another group of people trundling down the stairs. Cool air wafted across the room for a second of relief. Sandy-Blonde hair caught my attention. Not so much the hair as the style. And not so much the style as the fact I recognized it instantly.

It was the same kid who'd stared at me getting into the car on the first day at FCA.

Tension crawled up my spine into my shoulders. Over the past several days, I'd caught Sandy-Blonde lingering outside my classes at FCA, and a few tables away in the dining hall. That shouldn't be alarming; a college usually had, you know, students. Maybe he had a similar schedule to mine. I'd never caught him looking at me directly since the first day.

But distasteful familiarity wormed in my head. It reminded me too much of times before, the same person following me in the depths of research, when leads—and then the person—suddenly disappeared.

Sandy-Blonde kid… young man… student… whatever—I took a breath. *Check the paranoia.* TASA had no reason to watch me. I did things subtler now. Seven years ago I'd been loud and angry and I understood why I'd gotten their attention, but I'd fixed that. I was no threat. There was no reason for Sandy-Blonde to be TASA.

"Hey… you okay?" Tiff nudged me with an elbow.

"What? Oh yeah, fine." I jerked my attention back to her, latching onto the drink Tiff shoved at me.

"Hurry up with that one, I wanna dance."

Yes ma'am.

Lithe figures slid onto the stage about half an hour later, and the whole room erupted into cheers. I laughed and covered my ears. A second later, light faded until pitch black encompassed the entire room. The cheers fell with the lights, softening into silence.

For a long moment, quiet and darkness ruled. Anticipation crackled in the spaces of nothingness.

Then a single note whispered out softly, lingering and then growing. Until another note rose, and another. They intertwined, playing off and then against each other, building into something almost classical sounding. But instead of playing in rhythm, each instrument followed the next with a millisecond pause, and each note echoed, built on each other, pulsed into one another. Something about it made the hairs on my body stand on end.

I blinked hard as it *changed*. Reality tilted. Those weren't instruments, those were heartbeats. A hundred heartbeats harmonizing. My own heart fluttered, compelling to respond. Faint, nearly indiscernible light rose, and as it traced impressions of the crowd around me, I'd never been more aware of everyone around me in my life. Not just a mass of collective noise and sweat; each individual, intricate soul. Heads turned, and people stared at each other as if they'd never seen each other before.

What the absolute—?

Another sound rose, emerging out of heartbeats like it had been born from them. It sank through my skin, pulsed in my viscera, fitting into my bones. A clear, feminine voice began to sing. Shock rippled through me, through the crowd, like we'd been struck all at once. My flesh pebbled with goosebumps. Her words spoke directly to every single person in this room, hitting every worry, every terror, every joy. She tore into the heart of all of us, hit upon the things we only *dared* to speak of, turned complexity and confusion to beauty, made you hope even as you bared your teeth.

I couldn't tell you a single actual word she said.

Her voice tunneled into my mind, spread down to my toes, and clamped down on every vulnerable part of me. Relentlessly, she smoothed away the twisted ball anchored in my gut, until I could breathe, and just me remained. *I could breathe.*

I danced. I danced, because if I didn't move through the aching understanding pulled from every single note, I would shatter all over the floor. Every person around me *surged*; they understood, were being understood, yanked mercilessly into everything they needed in this place.

Minutes—hours—later, the song ended. I gasped for breath, lightheaded and fragile. Tears streamed down my face.

"You look like you're high," Tiff laughed through a choked voice.

"I feel high," I mumbled.

That voice rose again. This time, light and playful, filling the space with mischief and fun. Tiff and I danced with all the ridiculous fervor in our souls. One song turned into the next, turned into the next, creating a bubble of safety and vulnerability that no one dared shatter.

The cute guy from before approached me with a shy grin. I let myself get pulled closer by gentle hands and kind eyes, everything too loud for actual conversation. My skin tingled when he touched me. Tiff turned all her charm on his friend. Sweat layered my body and my throat was sore with laughing and multiple shots of orujo, and I felt… okay. For the first time in a long time, I was okay.

11

Monday arrived with a cloud cover that made the whole sky look like split pea soup. The wind bit at anyone who dared go outside, and campus grounds stayed fairly vacant all day. Classes settled into the first hints of routine, which made me want to cry only a little. But the gloom couldn't touch me, because I had my first defense instruction from Mr. Kearney.   I was beyond ready to get started.

"Has Mr. Kearney arrived yet?" I asked my father's butler, Mr. Greaving, shedding my bag and coat in the foyer. I bounced lightly on my heels, still riding the high from the near-spiritual experience from the other night. I had no proof, and I understood that concerts could induce feelings of euphoria, but I would bet money that the singer had been a siren.

"Dearest," my mother's voice rose behind me. "I called Mr. Kearney and let him know we won't be needing his services today."

I froze.

"After discussing things with Mr. Frederickson, we've decided three days a week is quite a lot of time when your attention is better spent elsewhere."

My fingers curled into fists, nails digging into my palms.

"I let him know to arrive tomorrow, and perhaps Friday, as long as your marks improve and you behave in your tutoring sessions."

My grandmother used to tell me the tale of the Too Good Mother. The mother in the tale was so worried about her child's success and safety that she ended up entirely stifling them. I'm sure my grandmother was implying my own mother had the best of intentions, and that was all well and good.

But good god, I *suffocated*.

I should have attended a boarding college. But I didn't want to be separated from Tiff, and the places my parents found acceptable had rigid rules I worried would be worse. With the move to Farfalla, part of me had believed that things would be different.

I stalked past my mother with only a bare idea of my destination. She didn't say a word. It made something inside of me lurch violently, because she had at least some clue about how this hurt. I strode up the stairs, down the hall, to my father's study. With no real plan, I rapped on the door.

"Come in." His words filtered through the door, distracted.

I walked in using all the calm-breathing skills I possessed. "Father."

"Sweetheart," he said, rising to his feet as I approached. "It's good to see you. Oh, I have something for you. But how was your day?"

He kissed me on the cheek, sitting down on the short lounge and pulling me down with him.

"It was pleasant enough," I replied, forcing myself to relax my hands and shoulders. "I came home to discover Mr. Kearney will not be arriving this afternoon."

His brow furrowed. Hope sparked.

"Yes, we decided it was best to limit his time with you, instead of your previously agreed upon three times a week."

The last of the joy I'd been carrying around from the concert faded like wisps of smoke. "And you know Mr. Frederickson meets with me, nearly every day." *Do you know what it's like, being trapped in that room with him for hours?*

"Yes." He said gently. "But you know why we're doing this, darling. We have tried and tried to speak to you about your behavior and your… interests."

I gritted my teeth, horrified as my eyes started to burn.

"I know it doesn't seem fair, and like your whole world is going to be ruined. But my father had to bring me to heel too, about your age. It's just your turn. You must learn to be successful in the ways things are, and your mother and I… we need to be sure you're prepared for the future."

Breathe in. And breathe out.

I hadn't spoken to my father about my new 'tutoring' before now. Maybe because I knew the conversation would go something like this.

I fought to keep my voice even. "Is my future not my own? Do I not get a say?"

He nodded, slowly. "Your future is yours to shape. But you were headed down a dangerous path, and it's our responsibility to protect you from that."

"What, it's so dangerous to know how to defend myself?"

"You know what I am speaking of, darling."

It threw me that he went there. My parents had been there when I'd told Ransom Recovery everything after I'd been rescued, already too late for my sister. They were the ones who got me out of jail weeks later, when I'd gone to the wrong people for answers and been arrested for involvement with 'unnatural organizations.' They were the ones who found odd things in my room and destroyed them. But we never quite addressed it.

The honesty of what he'd said made truth rise in my own throat. "I can't just pretend it didn't happen. You *know* what happened when—"

"Fairian, *stop*." My father rarely raised his voice and it froze everything inside of me. "She's *gone*. There's nothing more to do about it."

I flinched at the grief ripping through his voice, my stomach contracting as if punched. "So your answer is to make sure every moment of my life is controlled and orchestrated. So I can't *harm* myself."

"If that's what it takes."

Silence thickened the air. My father's next words were quiet.

"Farfalla is giving us an opportunity to get *away* from our past. We can do good things here, and move on. You can be a new person here."

I fought my expression blank. Whereas he wanted me to become an acceptable kind of person, I walked towards the fully realized version of what Mari's death had taught me: a seeker of uncomfortable truths.

"This place… is good. We can be good here. We can leave all of that behind."

My father didn't realize what this city was. He didn't realize magic filled every breath here. Somehow, he couldn't see it. I almost asked *how* exactly he explained the green sky, but that would turn into an argument that would do nothing to change his mind. I shut my mouth, defeat filling my throat.

"I do have something for you," he said, almost apologetically. "It came today."

I looked at him, mostly so he'd continue without me having to say anything. He rose and strode over to his desk, where he retrieved an envelope and walked back to hand it to me. I vaguely recognized the symbol on the front. Numbly, I took it and pulled out the thick paper from inside, blinking a few times before it made sense.

An invitation to the annual Gala of Saint Dymphna's Psychiatric Hospital scrawled down the page. That managed to penetrate.

"You see?" My father said after whatever expression had crossed my face. "We're not complete monsters. We like that you're interested in this, dearest. Medicine of the mind is something we can all get behind."

I swallowed thickly. Yes, because my father thought my interest lay in St. Dymphna's mission, not who or what might be inside.

"The director was thrilled to send us a last minute invitation. It's tomorrow, so I imagine your mother is off arranging your wardrobe. She was a little peeved at the late notice." He was trying to joke with me. I didn't rise to the bait.

"She's not coming?"

"No, this will be just you and me." He sat down and bumped me with his shoulder. "What do you think? Want to be my date for the evening?"

My skin numbed. Father used to take Mari to galas and events, just the two of them. It had even been a joke; the dangerous duo, father and prodigy, Mari even more dangerous because people underestimated her. It had made me jealous. I couldn't wait to be old enough to go to the parties and be important too. But not long after I came of age, Mari was dead, my father was too broken to be seen in public for a long time, and I didn't care about society anymore.

Now we would go to an event, just the two of us. And I gained a new understanding of the word *heartsick*.

"I'll be ready tomorrow, looking respectable," I said.

He shifted on the lounge. "We'll need to leave half past six. And I checked, it will be over in time for us to get home. Before midnight."

I blinked, not understanding. Midnight? Why—oh. Crapsticks. Tomorrow was the dark moon. Great. Just great. I had *that* to look forward to along with everything else. I'd have to work quickly before my brain fritzed out in its monthly melodrama.

I smiled at my father, trying to ease over the last of the tension of this conversation. My insides felt peculiar. After his big speech about getting me away from danger, I'd tricked him into helping me with my quest. Something bubbled up, something that almost turned into guilt. I crushed it. I was getting into Saint Dymphna's. And somehow, I'd figure out if the people being sent there were *his* victims.

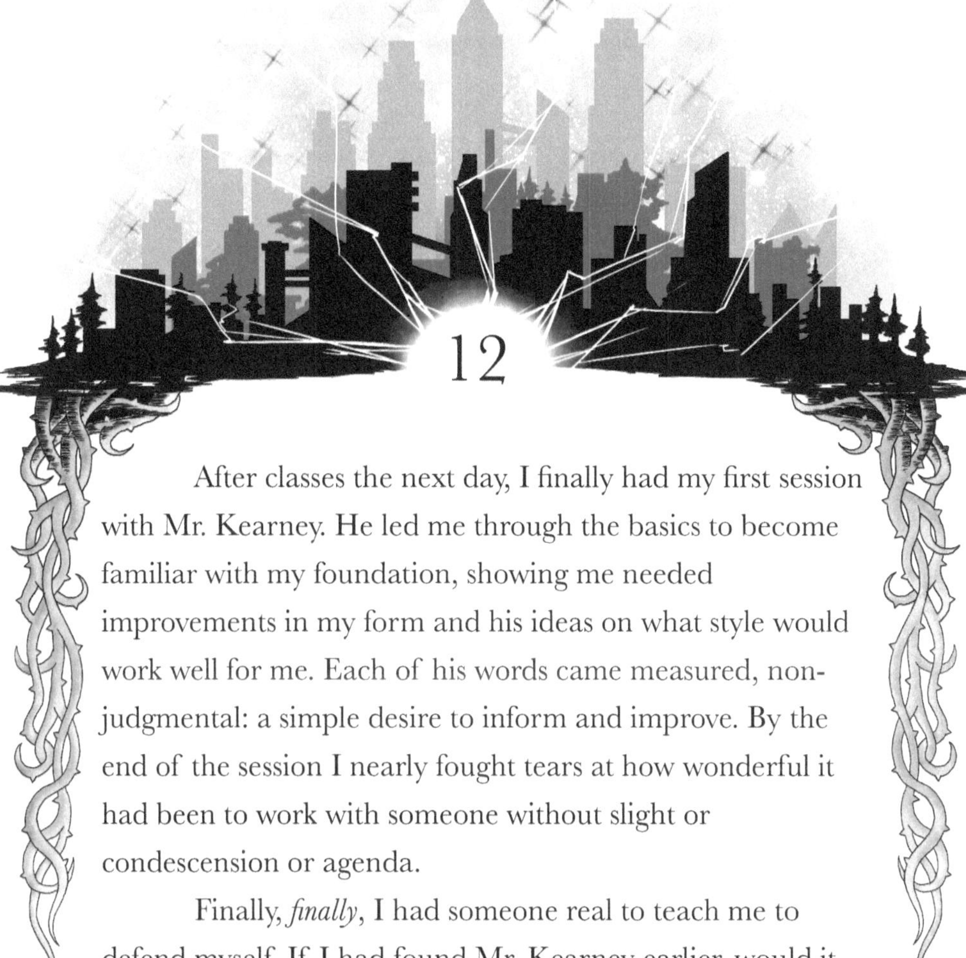

12

After classes the next day, I finally had my first session with Mr. Kearney. He led me through the basics to become familiar with my foundation, showing me needed improvements in my form and his ideas on what style would work well for me. Each of his words came measured, non-judgmental: a simple desire to inform and improve. By the end of the session I nearly fought tears at how wonderful it had been to work with someone without slight or condescension or agenda.

Finally, *finally*, I had someone real to teach me to defend myself. If I had found Mr. Kearney earlier, would it have made a difference? To anything that had happened or I'd done?

The session brought another highlight: I only had to endure Tutor for an hour before I left to prepare for St. Dymphna's Gala. Abigail assisted me into a fashionable pale yellow-almost-gold gown. While elegant and beautiful, all of it —from my shoes to my hair—looked alien on me. It felt like a costume; I played a particular role tonight, and it meant looking the part.

My father waited in the foyer as I glided down the stairs, looking quite dashing in his suit. His hair was made up with something that brought out the grey; he'd been doing that a lot lately. I wondered then… he'd been comparatively very young when he turned Leynthall Industries into such a success… maybe my father had been made to feel inferior in the circles he traveled.

"Father, you make quite the escort."

He spun towards me, grinning broadly at my entrance. "You look lovely."

My mother swept in from the sitting room at his pronouncement. "I knew this gown would suit you—you look like an angel."

Ew.

She beamed as she touched my hair, the collar of my gown, the top of the long gloves on my arms, with featherlight brushes. My father approached and kissed my cheek, his smile wry. Then he tucked my arm in his.

"Shall we go conquer the night?" he asked.

My mother's smile faded slightly. "Be sure to be back in time."

Thanks for the reminder, mother.

"Come now, Fairian looks enchanting and we must show her off —lets go before we're late!" My father leaned down and planted a firm kiss on my mother, who tried to look stern and failed. He sounded almost… happy. Excited, with careless humor so rare from him the past years.

Our car slowed as we reached a tall, intimidating concrete and steel building located near the ex-industrial side of Farfalla. Brightly colored decorations and wooden additions softened the severity of it, and a field of trees swept out behind it into the darkness. It had to be a cleanup site: all the trees were relatively small and exactly the same height. Despite the lack of occupied buildings in the area, the street was bright and clean.

A line of electric cars and carved wooden carriages led up to the front steps, which were bathed in the golden light that spilled out of the windows and doors of the lower level. Our car came to a halt at the entrance and the door opened, letting in the buzz of conversation and laughter. My father exited with a skip in his step. I muffled my sigh and allowed the footman to 'help' me out of the car. After all, I was on my best behavior tonight.

The edges of my vision blurred for the second and I made a face. The sodding moon would make tonight difficult.

Walking up the steps into the gala was like sliding into an old skin. Familiar, but outgrown, too small. In Northampton, the Leynthalls had been a regular sight at any fundraiser, particularly supporting environmental cleanup projects. Springing from either personal mission or determination we fit into upper class society, my mother had made sure we'd been involved in *everything*.

There were only a few major cleanup projects left in Europe. Many scientists estimated most ecosystems would be recovering by the end of my generation. Nevermind the toxic storage plants no one knew what to do with, housing by-gone era chemicals and materials and what scientists had managed to pull out of the earth and sky. Or the ecosystems that needed careful replantation so as to not incite a return of furious toxic growth that had nearly taken over towards the end of the Collapse.

It would still be centuries until everything *really* recovered.

We entered the building and I stuck close to my father. I didn't know anyone here, and while Farfalla might be relaxed on social norms such as needing proper introductions, I needed more information to effectively navigate this social sphere.

Within the first hour, my eyes nearly crossed with the effort of trying to pay attention to the details of conversations. A few faces I recognized from my family's welcome party, and I utterly blanked on their names. Even now most names fell out of my head as quickly as I shoved them in. Bugger, even when I actually *tried…*

Then an older figure approached, masculine with big blue eyes, porcelain skin, and salt and pepper hair.

"Director Decker, it's a pleasure to meet you in person," my father said, voice exuberant. He extended his hand, and the older gentleman took it with a wide smile.

"Mr. Leynthall, the pleasure is mine. I'm glad you reached out to me with your interest. I'd only just heard of your family's move to our wonderful city."

The Director's eyes slid to me. My father didn't miss a beat, stepping back and placing his hands lightly on my shoulders. "This is my daughter, Ms. Fairian Leynthall."

The introduction sent a twist through my heart. He'd introduced me how I wanted—Ms. Fairian Leynthall, instead of Ms. Leynthall—but Mari's absence throbbed like a hole in my being.

Would it ever stop?

I curtsied to the director. *I am demure and sweet I am demure and sweet.*

"I understand you have an interest in mental health medicine, Ms. Fairian," the Director said.

"I do." I smiled—not too widely, not too small. "I've been looking for opportunities in the area since our move, and stumbled upon your event announcement. I absolutely begged Father to go."

The Director smiled warmly. "Well, we're so delighted you came! Can I interest you both in a tour? We won't disturb the tenants, of course, but I can show you what we do here."

Excellent.

Director Decker escorted out of the main room and down a hallway, launching into the history of the place. I enjoyed history as a rule anyway, but the passion in Decker's story turned it from interesting to enthralling. Decker himself had started this institution twenty years ago after seeing how Geel in Belgium built around those with psychiatric disabilities. He came to Farfalla to build a community where neurodivergent people and those with mental illness could thrive.

"I didn't want a hospital, despite the name," he said. "Emergency care is important, yes, but I wanted more than that. A home for those who needed it."

This building had been a mess of crumbling infrastructure when he'd scraped enough together to buy it. The renovations had taken years, but during that time, he'd gathered benefactors and donations, building a following of people who believed in his mission.

"People still want everyone to fit a particular idea of 'normal,' which is harder for some more than others. It's probably harkening back to when we needed to be similar to survive." He winked at me. "I built this place to be a home and respite from being forced into a mold, to both teach and learn."

He loved this place. That fact dripped from every word. As we moved from the front hall and recreational areas to the offices and classrooms, Decker's lecture moved from history to their current mission and methodology.

"Unfortunately, most struggle with understanding what neurodivergent people need, especially in raising children. A majority of what we do here is just give people space to be themselves and the tools to understand."

Soft chairs and pillows with bright colors filled most of the classrooms. Many rooms had specific purposes: anxiety relief, stimulation, anger management, sensory deprivation chambers, and 'happy rooms,' with lamps designed to help with depression.

For those who wanted, they were also taught skills—or encouraged to expand upon what they already knew—that would help them be independent or add to the community of St. Dymphna's. Many of the people here eventually left to return to their families or start their own, Decker said, though some had been tenants for almost a decade. Those who left regularly returned, either for therapy or to volunteer, and the bonds of this community criss-crossed the entirety of Farfalla. Some who had left had gathered into their own smaller communities, living close with the friends they'd made, helping each other utilize the tools they'd gathered.

"And you take on emergency cases, as well," I said, wrangling my brain back to the reason I was here in the first place. "I read in the paper about the two girls who'd disappeared. It's how I originally heard of you."

I saw it only because I watched for it: the slightest twitch around his eyes. "Oh, yes," he said. "Many of our cases are emergent. We're not taught how to take care of ourselves, not until we're at the breaking point."

"And are they all right? The girls."

Decker smiled. "We have a strict confidentiality policy here."

"Of course, of course, my apologies," I said, and dropped it.

We headed down a long, nearly bare hallway with windows on one side and stone on the other. Names were carved into the stonework, arranged in patterns and near-artful scatterings. Several names of powerful families in Farfalla, Galicia, and even greater Spain jumped out at me.

"These must be your benefactors," I said.

"Yes, the wealthy extended family," Decker said dryly.

Then a name on the wall grabbed my attention like a beacon.

YILLEN

I nearly tripped. There it was, Daimyn's last name, written in big ol' letters along the top. My scalp prickled. Was this significant? His family had wealth, of course they were donating to causes of all kinds. St. Dymphna's was in their backyard.

"Director, I do wonder something," my father said. He'd been listening intently up until now, smiling at me as he watched. "How do you handle those with more… violent tendencies? Those you cannot communicate with?"

"Ah. We address everyone with the philosophy that *we* must learn how to speak their language, that violence is often a symptom of fear or…"

A rush of dizziness crested over my head, my hearing cutting out for several whining seconds. I took a deep, slow breath, careful not to overreact and send myself crashing to the ground. *Midnight approaches.* I needed to move this conversation along before it got worse.

"There is a misconception that mental illness and neurodivergence makes people violent, turns them into criminals." I flinched as Decker's voice returned with a vengeance. "But we find that with space given and communication established, everyone becomes much happier."

My father glanced at me, then tried to repress his double take at whatever he saw on my face. I quickly blanked my expression.

"I do hope we can support and become involved in your mission." *Whoops.* I tried to turn my assumption of my father's support into a joke, smiling wryly: "Well, *I* hope I can, anyway."

Director Decker offered his elbow to me. "We must return to the hall as the auction will start soon, but let's keep talking, Ms. Fairian. I'm sure we can find a place for your passion."

An hour later, the auction ended, and alcohol and finger food flowed freely. Voices rose and fell without comprehension, like someone turned the volume up and down randomly. Lights hurt. No one here apparently believed in clocks, but I knew it grew closer. The room blurred around the edges, my tongue fit strangely in my mouth. My heart beat like a war drum. Whether regular ol' anxiety or the preternatural bullshit about to ensue this evening affected me, it was anyone's guess.

The last half hour before we left stretched into hours. Then, finally, we headed out of the mammoth building. My vision tunneled down to only directly in front of me. I tried hard to be normal as my father and I slipped into the car to return home.

"—believe the things that come out of his mouth." My father chuckled. "But you! You were absolutely charming. Director Decker really took a shine to you."

I knew I smiled a beat too late. "I only follow your example."

"Hmmm, I don't have quite your charm. It's unique… no pretense. People will be attracted to it, that genuineness." He paused. "Though many will try to take advantage of it too."

Was he lecturing or sharing? "I'm pretty sure more people are off-put than enjoy my attitude."

I looked out the window. My head throbbed in a beat too slow to be my pulse. Colors… brightened, even in the now-dark.

My father said something. *Crap.* My mind whined as it coughed up comprehension of what he'd said:

"Only when you throw it in their face. A lot of people *like* difference and rebelliousness, my dear, but you have to give them a moment."

"I don't… want to be anything less than I am. If I have to *restrain* myself to even… get people to *like* me…" I answered.

Looking at my father was very strange, like two people superimposed on top of each other, but slightly off. I shut my eyes tightly as reality edged slightly off kilter. It betrayed me, but my thoughts fuzzed, mashing together into gibberish.

"What is it you were looking for in coming here?"

My heart jangled in my chest in alarm.

"It's been a long time since I've seen you this interested in… something like this." Something appropriate, he meant. "I can't imagine you were just looking for causes for us to support."

Now he sounded wry. And he was prying. Either he really wanted to know, or he was trying to keep me talking while my brain frizzed out.

"I was thinking more along the lines of an internship," I said, too scrambled to pretend coy. An internship would give me some valid access to the place while I gathered information. It sounded manipulative even in my own head—but I wouldn't hurt anyone. That was the absolute last thing I would do.

My father hummed. "I'll talk to the director."

I smiled widely, and his eyes twinkled.

Dizziness surged, and I lost breath and the feeling of my skin as the world tilted violently. My hands slammed into the seat on either side of my hips, orienting myself. Nausea twisted through me as I heaved for breath.

"I'm all right," I said before my father could speak, addressing the elephant in the room. Well. In the carriage.

My father reached out and so very carefully took my hand.

"Your mother is looking into any local physicians who—"

I yanked out of his hold. "No more doctors. I'm fine, father… I'm always fine. We just need to get home."

Time stretched forever, and then minutes snapped into seconds. The car halted and my father held me steady by the elbow and the huge doors to the pazo loomed in front of us. The night spun gloriously above my head, sharp and beautiful—but looking at it made the sky open a great maw that made me want to crawl along the ground so I didn't get sucked into it.

"You should go lie down," my father said as we shed our outerwear.

"Yes, father."

Cement blocks inexplicably glued themselves to my feet as I walked to the stairs. I gripped the railing hard to keep vertical as I ascended. The house was silent, no sign of staff as my footfalls whispered down the hallway. The late hour could have explained the absence, but it was always like this on the dark moon.

Half of my body abruptly numbed, disconnected from the rest of me; I touched the side of my face to make sure it was still there. I fought through the final steps to my door, and relief coated me as I shut it, finally alone, away from the noise and lights and expectations of acting. My skin gave a sickening lurch, and my body felt whole again… though now distinctly off, like it had been assembled differently.

Cloth lay out on the foot of my made bed, soft sleeping clothes of some sort. I kicked off my heels and checked the clock in my room. Quarter of an hour until midnight. My heart raced already, my thoughts humming insects repeatedly smashing into each other. I padded across the floor to my window. The fabric of the dress turned chilly against my skin once I neared the less-insulated pane of glass. I curled up on the window seat, resting my forehead against the cold.

My "episodes," as my parents called them when they actually spoke of it, had occurred every month since I could remember. Some of the doctors my mother brought in called them seizures. Other said migraines. I doubted both of those. They happened every month, on the night of the dark moon, exactly at midnight. Did that sound natural?

The distant tolling bell shattered my thoughts. I'd lost time again. *Midnight.* My heart throbbed hard, mimicking the deep, hard tones. My vision warped: everything tunneled farther and magnified in the same moment. When I shut my eyes, the outlines of everything reverberated on the backs of my lids to an inaudible pulse.

My stomach dipped, like I'd just dropped off a cliff. Adrenaline flooded me up to my eyeballs. The pulsing grew faster and harder, each impact striking the center of my chest and my brain. My skin crawled with sensation like it tried to writhe off my body—

Don't scream, don't bite your tongue, don't dig your nails into yourself—

The spaces to breathe between each pulse narrowed. Then disappeared. All of it combined, gathered into a continuous wave, and slammed into me.

The city of Farfalla exploded into my head.

Hours had passed, and only seconds. I laid on the floor in a pile of chilly fabric and sweating skin, trying to stop hyperventilating. My body seized and trembled like electricity had hold of all my limbs. I hurt. I hurt everywhere. My head ached like it had been torn apart and put back together again by a toddler.

Everything was so… simple.

My eyes opened. I stared at the shadowed gap underneath my dresser, my cheek pressed against the dark wooden floor. One real inhale managed to make it into my seizing lungs. My throat felt raw. I swallowed and heard a click.

Ow.

I winced. Bracing myself, I fought my thoughts into line. *Think thoughts. Think. Think think.* Something important eluded me. Something had been different this time. Instinct demanded I shy away from *anything* about the raging chaos I'd just had in my mind, all of everything screaming for attention. But instinct and I had a love-hate relationship.

I shifted upright. It was like struggling through molasses as my equilibrium settled. I moaned as I deliberately thought back to the cacophony of what had just inhabited my head. But I reached for it, forcing myself to remember, because—

—Incandescent colors; forms made of light and music; the beat of butterfly wings like drums in my head. Everything was connected and the same, almost indistinguishable from each other as separate from the roiling, seething, entangled mass of life and stardust—

My eyes widened. *Oh my god.*

There were demons *everywhere*. Walking and living and breathing throughout every *centimeter* of this city.

I rose to my feet, steadier already as I walked to my nightstand to down the glass of water dutifully set there. I'd known this city was different the second I'd arrived, but I'd vastly underestimated on how many demonic forces resided here. Giddiness burbled up inside me, a smile trembling onto lips that didn't want to obey me yet. How had I not run into more of them? They overwhelmed this city, teemed with magic and life.

I pressed my thumbs hard to the corner of my eyes on either side of my nose. The pressure sent relief through my skull.

There's something else. For a second I almost… and then it slipped through. *Damn it.*

Come on. Remember what you saw. There's something else.

Panic seized muscles tight. I inhaled as slowly and deeply as possible. *Come on… it's okay… it's just fine…*

—three white holes of power; beacons in the chaos; they walked and magic grew around them; ancient, lonely, mad, powerful—

A blinding headache split across my head. I caught myself on the side of the bed before I hit the floor. Okay. *Okay.* I'd *never* felt anything like *that* before. Usually I couldn't differentiate individuals in the mass of overwhelm, but those… beings… *required* attention. Not Seeing them had been impossible.

Familiarity snagged at my thoughts, pulling at frayed brain matter. I think my neurons whimpered. One of them, *one of those beings—* I struggled to connect it, mind stretched and thin. As soon as it hit me, I exhaled hard. *Of course.*

Daimyn Yillen, why do you Feel like that?

There'd been hints and he'd implied things, but nothing like *that.* I could barely comprehend what I'd just Felt off him, except *Really Bloody Magical BEWARE.* It should be terrifying… except for my bizarre inability to be afraid of him.

Something else occurred to me. The silk of my dress whispered over ground as I drew to my window, chewing on my lip, staring out towards the northwest. *I know Daimyn's location, right at this moment.*

It wasn't even that far. It wouldn't take me long to get there.

13

Daimyn had made his opinion of my quest clear. He refused to help me, his reasons all probably logical and fully of crappy rationality. But if my encounters with him gave any indication, magic happened around him. He *was* magical. Maybe he wouldn't help intentionally, but it wasn't like leads on magic had been dropping out of the sky.

The streets were filled with demons…

Fear and delight stroked a corpse-cold finger down my heart. I bared my teeth. *Fear does not control me.* Maybe I'd meet more demons I could communicate with and wouldn't have to dodge Daimyn's heels for scraps of information. The more I saw, the more I'd understand, the more I'd know where I could go to learn.

I stripped out of the pale golden gown and my sweat-soaked undergarments, yanking out my usual night-expedition wear—boots, thick breeches and coat, knives—from the back of my closet. Then paused and grabbed one of my sturdier corsets for some kind of protection, only loose-lacing myself into it.

For all intents and purposes, I was the plague tonight. No one would bother me. After dozens of hush-hush doctors couldn't explain my episodes, the consensus of the household was to ignore it. Mari used to hold me through them, long ago. Listen to me as I told her about everything. But Mari wasn't here anymore.

Redressed and buckling my knives to my hips—I still needed to replace the steel one I'd lost in the river, damn it—I strode to my window. Daimyn hadn't been moving during my brain-explosion, but I couldn't exactly trust my judgement in the chaos. I'd have to be fast.

Instead of sneaking out of the house down and out through the kitchens, which held too many dangers of people seeing, I pressed open my window silently. Lattice attached below my window all the way to the ground, something I'd requested from the landscapers under the guise of wanting flowering vines. My window (and the lattice) was situated along one of the two corner turrets where the wall curved and hid most of it from view. If I could get down it fast enough, and across the open clover lawn, then I could get to the trees ringing Leynthall grounds and be free.

Under normal circumstances this would probably be difficult, but the night practically spoke, whispering the movement of the world to me. Two guards made their rounds on this side, their torch beams panning the clearing between the house and the trees that ringed Leynthall grounds, turning wisps of mist and fog opaque for half-seconds.

Chilly air skid across my face and down the back of my neck. I shivered. Farfalla appeared so still and sleepy. Such a facade.

When the guards moved far enough away, I swung my leg over the stonework windowsill and fit my toes into the lattice, heart immediately pounding. *Let's see how much of a bad idea this is.* Carefully, I eased my weight down and weaved my fingers into the wood… then leaned back until my hands held my weight and stepped down, fitting the toe of my boot into another slot.

Each tiny creak of the wood made me cringe, though the sound of the wind masked the noise. The air smelled cold and sweet, hinted with salt from the ocean and pine from the trees, and turned the sweat gathering on my back and under my arms chilly. My knives bumped my ribs with each step.

And then, what felt like a year later, with my pulse thudding in my ears, my toes touched ground. I pressed my back against the stone of the mansion walls, now partially concealed by the curve of the tower, and blinked rapidly. One part down, one to go.

One guard walked out of view to the back of the mansion; another came into view towards the front. Another returned to the guardhouse. Now only one guards was close enough to see me, and—

They turned away. Every muscle in my body tensed.

Yes, now. I didn't doubt the sudden certainty; I bolted.

My feet hit soundless in the noise of rustling trees. My heart seemed to stop beating in the effort to be silent. The night itself held its breath—and then I'd crossed the clearing and slid into the shadows of the trees. Panting silently, I peeked around a trunk back towards where I'd come. The black on black form of the guard, and his torchlight, continued their inspection. Away from me. With a grin, I turned and raced away.

The aftereffects of my episode clung to the inside of my skull, the face of the city pulling back to reveal the dizzying array of layers. The strange, misaligned alleyways and twisting streets were arteries of a breathing giant. Life sprouted through the cracks of cobblestones, arched high into the sky, clustered on rooftops and inside buildings.

My blood sang in tune with all of it, bubbling into my head like champagne. No, self-preservation was not my strongest instinct. I'd probably broken it, because glee took over at the whispering of magic over my skin. *Technically I'm heading* towards *safety*, my not-at-all intoxicated thoughts rationalized. I'd be sure to yell loud enough for him to hear if something happened.

I drew close to where I'd Seen Daimyn, which turned out to be a heavily grown green space in the center of one of the residential districts, more wild than tended, with gazebos and covered areas swallowed by vines and trees. Blood rushed in my ears as the wind rustled the trees, making it hard to hear. I entered the gloom and fought to see anything, ears pricked for any new sound. At least this place would make it easy to hide. Daimyn didn't want anything to do with me, and showing up may be obnoxious, but who cared what he thought. I *would not care* what he thought. I rounded a bend in a path, which led to a blocky covered area—

Hell. I darted back out of view. Barely illuminated by a weak solar light attached to a gazebo, Daimyn leaned up against one of the supports of the covered area with his arms over his chest and one heel braced against the column. He remained so still, I never would have seen him if I wasn't post-Episode-high. A giddy surge buzzed along my veins. I squashed it viciously.

Heat seemed to thread through the trees, then disappeared, leaving the uncomfortable sensation that something stalked in the trees. Pulling a deep, silent breath, I peeked around a tree towards him. He'd turned his head. *Looking this direction.* And straightened off the pillar as soon as I came into view.

I jolted back, entirely too late, cringing. *Okay so wow I am useless at this.*

Footsteps rapidly crunched over dried leaves, growing louder. I huffed, then stepped out from behind the tree like a normal, rational person.

"How did you even *find* me?" he instantly said.

I locked my knees at his swift—okay, intimidating—approach, a jarring wave of unease hitting me in the gut. Fear and I had grown to be intimate friends, but this wouldn't fit in my head, like it was—

It evaporated. *Oh.* That came from him. His hands wrapped around my elbows before I could blink, his body close, entirely into my personal space like he tried to blanket me from sight.

"You have the absolute worst timing," he breathed. "Your presence will not be appreciated in what's about to start. You must leave."

I swallowed, staring into intensity of the darkest green. My stomach was in the slowest free-fall known to man. Heat rippled off of him in waves and seemed to *pull* something awake inside of me, something previously numb. I wondered if I'd been lying to myself about why I'd come out tonight. *Of course I did. I'm good at that.*

"But I just found you," I said, then cringed. Wow, that didn't sound needy or anything. "I mean—magical things happen around you. You're the only real lead I have, and I don't care that you don't care, I'm not letting you just *disappear.*"

His voice lowered. "As I recall, you walked away last time."
I blinked. *What?*

Daimyn froze, head cocking to the side. A second later I heard it too: hushing, breathy noises, too loud and too rhythmic to be the psithurism of the trees. My eyes widened, skin prickling with goosebumps in time with the rise and fall of that... hissing.

Daimyn gripped my arms right above the elbow and lifted me right off the ground. I muffled a squeak as the world lunged, twisted, and stopped. We stood in the shadow of two trees now, and Daimyn carefully set me on the roots of the one behind me. A little dizzy, I looked up—and closed my mouth at the finger pressed against his lips in the universal sign for quiet.

I had to respect someone who didn't *force* me to be quiet.

Daimyn leaned to the side, scanning the dark beyond the tree. The hissing came from beyond, almost a whispering, and closed in quickly. The air thickened alongside it, goosebumps prickling across my skin in awareness of something in the night. Something*s*.

Daimyn clasped my elbows again and tugged down, pulling me into a crouch along with him. He leaned forward, crowding me, pressing a hand against the tree behind me. His head lowered towards mine—*ohmygod, what is he* doing—and at the last possible second put his mouth right next to my ear.

He spoke, the warmth of his breath skating over my ear. Comprehension of his words took a few beats longer than normal.

"I can't get you away without attracting notice. What will it take for you to stay here and not make a sound?"

I swallowed hard. There was really only one answer to that. I followed his example and spoke directly into his ear: "Answer my questions."

Hair tickled along my cheekbone and nose. His shoulders rose and fell as he exhaled soundlessly, heat skating down my neck. I clamped down on the shiver threatening to break out across my whole body.

"You get one question. And I have veto power over subjects."

I knew I should negotiate. Instead I croaked: "Deal."

"Stay. Do not make a sound."

I rolled my eyes. *Woof woof.*

Daimyn rose, the heat of him swirling away. The light that managed to filter through the lush darkness silhouetted his form as he moved swiftly towards the hissing. His footsteps didn't make any noise this time. *Huh.*

"Greetings," his voice broke out calmly, and much farther away from me than expected.

A hissing response chattered through the dark. The hairs on the back of my neck stood on end and I struggled to fully fill my lungs.

"The greetings without death is appreciated," said a new voice. "But what can you do that we have not already tried?"

"I need to understand what has been happening," Daimyn said, the words easy and patient.

That other voice rose again—but not in English. I blinked. Was that Latin?

A thrill ran down my spine. Latin was… discouraged in most circles. Considering how many texts about magic were written in Latin, I didn't have to try too hard for a guess. I'd heard only very high level language experts were allowed to use or translate. Because consolidating power in a few people was *definitely* the way to go about it.

Lucky for me, my uncle on my father's side had been a bit of a language connoisseur back in his day. Argus Leynthall had been delighted to break rules and supply me with the tools to teach myself. I wasn't exactly fluent, but…

The Latin ended, and snapping hisses rose in the trees. My whole body shuddered. It came to a halt, and the other voice spoke again, in English:

"You know what has been happening, or you would not be here. The deaths of our own were not enough to motivate you, but apparently now that it's *anyone else* you are here."

"The depth of your situation was only revealed to me recently," Daimyn said. "I am here now to provide assistance."

The voice rose again in Latin. It almost sounded like they were translating Daimyn's words, but very badly. Or I was rustier than I thought.

Snapping hisses rose again, sparking in my diaphragm like acid bubbles.

"Not revealed to you, or were you *not paying attention, Deathless?*"

I stilled, something about those words echoing as a taunt.

"No matter," the other voice continued before Daimyn responded. "They say this is an internal problem and you are not welcome."

"The problem isn't internal when people outside the issue are killed," Daimyn said.

And there they were speaking Latin again. I rubbed my eyebrow. I was definitely missing something. The new voice seemed to say Daimyn believed 'all they did was his domain,' or something.

As quietly as humanly possible, my heart a frantic beat in my throat, I eased to my feet, and peered around the tree. Something slid along my skin, cool, trailing down my arm. Christ, that almost felt real. What was that?

More hissing. My lungs barely inflated at this point.

"They say…" Other voice, English again. "That it is still not your business."

I squinted. A faint impression of another humanoid figure stood shadowed beyond the gazebo, standing under the bows of a larger tree. Daimyn stood a meter to my left, turned mostly away with a sliver of his profile visible, facing… the trees apparently. Everything about him held preternaturally still. His hands braced on each bicep, his feet planted, and I was weirdly convinced nothing in the world would be able to move him without his permission.

"If I have to solve this myself, I will. But I'd rather be of help. I promise you won't like my version of cleaning up."

Yikes. His voice turned arctic at the end. And I thought he'd been cold with me before.

The other voice rose again, once again in Latin. *Wait.* I was pretty sure they said Daimyn would kill one of them for every new death. I had to be translating wrong. Right? But how could I be *that* wrong?

The trees thrashed, violently. I ducked and swallowed my heart back down into my chest. In the branches, there… whatever they were, there were a lot of them.

The other voice rose again. "They do not agree."

Daimyn's quiet practically became its own entity. "Offer a mediation between parties with me present. This has to end, and I would prefer not to resort to violence."

Latin, again, from that other voice in the trees. Wait. That was totally wrong—there was a much better way to translate that sentence. This dude made it sound like Daimyn said he would end their differences with force, no mention of the offer to mediate.

I inhaled to speak—then froze as I remembered I wasn't really supposed to be here.

Son of a turd.

Shadows slid down from the treetops. My heart convulsed as my vision seemed to reorient. The trees were *bloody filled with whatever made that hissing sound.* The prickling on my skin turned crawling, up my spine, down my arms, over my head. The air ripped from my lungs as if a giant had inhaled all the oxygen in the world in preparation for unleashing violence—

Goddamn it.

I launched out from behind the tree. "He's lying!"

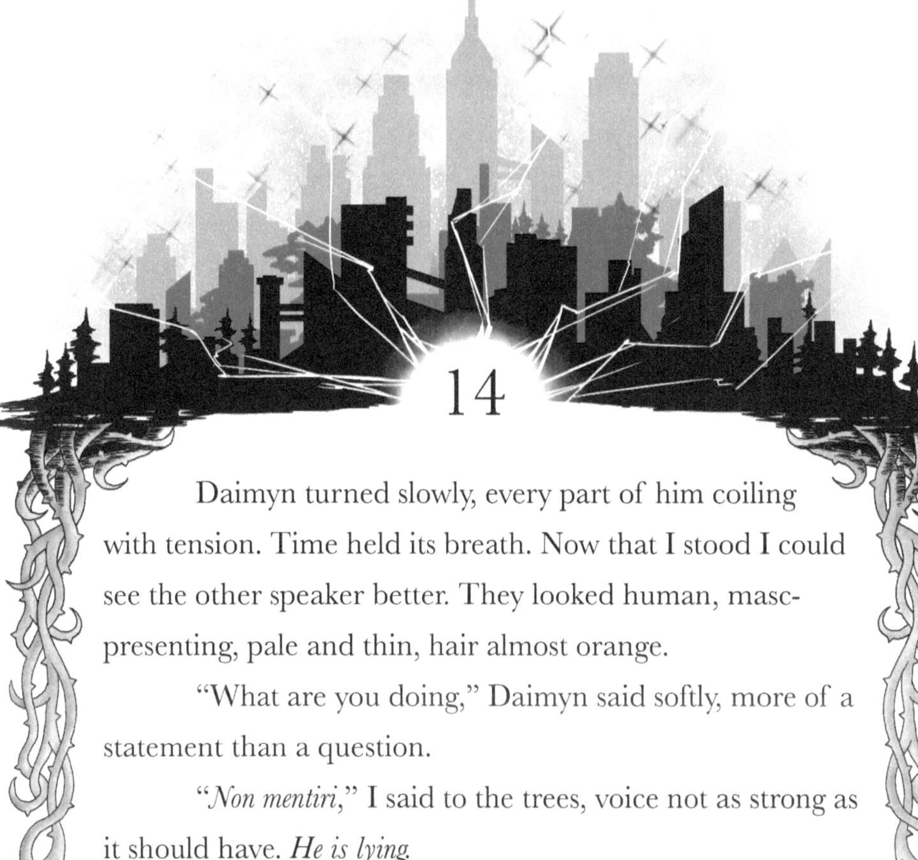

14

Daimyn turned slowly, every part of him coiling with tension. Time held its breath. Now that I stood I could see the other speaker better. They looked human, masc-presenting, pale and thin, hair almost orange.

"What are you doing," Daimyn said softly, more of a statement than a question.

"*Non mentiri*," I said to the trees, voice not as strong as it should have. *He is lying.*

"Who is this?" Orange-Hair by the tree demanded.

I took a half-step forward, another, under what felt like boulders resting on my shoulders. Boulders about to explode, anyway.

"Care to explain how I am lying?" Daimyn asked, his words cutting gashes in the air.

"Not *you*." I fought for the right words in Latin, since apparently that's what the creatures in the trees understood. I gestured at Daimyn, nervous to focus on one spot in the trees too long. "*…Dicunt his verbis non fecit…?*" *'He did not say those words.' I think I said that right.* I gestured obviously at Orange-Hair. "Non mentiri."

"What is this? You brought a shitty Latin speaker—an *outsider*?"

"Well your translations are blatantly wrong," I retorted, and turned to Daimyn, repressing a flinch at the light in his eyes. *Ohhh he's mad.* "He's telling them you want to lock them away—"

Orange-Hair laughed, loudly. "You speak the true language like shit, and you want to lecture me? I do not believe you *know* what I say."

My skin heated, and I bit my tongue to hold back a retort.

Daimyn stared at me for a heartbeat. Two. Three. "Is that true, Alwin?"

Relief suffused my whole body.

Orange-Hair—Alwin?—made an incredulous noise. "Who *is* this? You doubt me off of—what?"

Daimyn turned his head back to him. "A private interest. Are you translating my words correctly?"

Chattering rose in the trees. I exhaled slowly in an attempt to calm my racing heart.

"I am *Speaker*," Alwin spat. "I translate perfectly for the needs and desires of my people."

Then he barked something in Latin: *She's an enemy on the side of death.*

This wanker—!

"Non mentiri! *Non sum hostium*," I said hastily. *He lies! I am not the enemy.* "Um… veritatis et quasi?" *I like the truth.* I blanked on how to explain more eloquently. Hopefully that made sense to everyone.

The chattering in the trees doubled in volume. Alwin's cold eyes locked with mine before turning away, murmuring too low for me to hear. The chattering quieted, but I could not hear what Alwin said.

"Damn it," I muttered.

The hiss-chattering rose and fell as if in conversation. Charging forward to break it up would probably be a step too far. I'd already barged into the conversation. But my feet itched—what was Alwin saying?

Daimyn slid closer, his arm nearly brushing mine. "Tell me, did you consider the danger when you barged into a meeting you don't know the first thing about?"

I swallowed. "His translations were making you sound really bad—"

"Where did you learn Latin?"

I blinked at the question and forced myself not to fidget. If I told him I was self-taught, he'd probably doubt me. Hell, maybe he should doubt me. Did I honestly know what I was doing?

A slow lick slid down my spine. Daimyn turned motionless. Turning my head slowly, I barely breathed as liquid shadows slid down a tree trunk near me, looping and coiling down between branches. Daimyn's hand closed lightly around my bicep, barely there but undeniably ready.

Scales were the only thing I could make out on the sleek darkness wrapped around the tree. Part of it lifted away… in the dim light, I made out a huge, wedged head drifting towards me. The eyes shimmered gold, without reflection, barely visible in the dark.

All the hair on my body stood on end. Should I look down? Refuse to look away? Alwin barked something out in Latin. The snake-like head stilled. I didn't understand the phrase—Trust is truth? Trust the truth? *What?*

A forked tongue flickered out of the shadowy coils next to me. Once. Twice. Three times. Then they slid fully from the tree, pooling on the ground across tree roots even as their head barely moved position, tongue still tasting the air. Alwin said something about me being untrustworthy and fictitious and out for my own gains. I scowled, shooting him a glare. The shadow-snake-creature-person hissed softly, shifting closer. Daimyn's grip tightened. The snake didn't like my attention off them. Or on Alwin. One or the other.

"*Quam pulchra es,*" I told the scary creature. *You are beautiful.* Which wasn't a lie, despite my attempt at flattery. What I could see from the dim gloom was striking. Like liquid gem-shadows.

"Your pronunciation is awful." Alwin sounded condescending and amused. I twitched.

A soft croon from the creature, and… around their head a ruff flared outwards, framing their face. It was lined with near-glowing veins of pale gold, breaking through the darkness like a glittering, lightning starscape.

"Yeah, that's beautiful too," I said, letting out a breathless laugh, and then fumbled through it in Latin.

"What are they doing?" Daimyn muttered in my ear.

"Hell if I know. But I said they were beautiful and now there's preening. I think."

Their head tilted towards Daimyn. Then back to me. Then the head tilted back, up towards the trees, and rising cadences of their voices rose again.

Alwin spoke rapidly in Latin again. He denied something… saying he was their trusted something—I didn't know that word—he was their loyal—again that word—something about eternity and—

The snake-creature turned back towards me, and bared fangs the size of my finger.

Daimyn's arm cinched hard around my waist. My head thunked back against his chest as we abruptly stopped, two meters back from where we had been. *Whoa.* The snake creature shut their mouth, head lowered. The treetops rustled, all the hair on my body standing on end.

"Yes, I'd recommend getting out of here. They don't like interference," Alwin said neutrally.

"Because we're going to believe what *you* say," I retorted. *Maybe I need to shut up.*

The coiled giant of a creature retracted… but no, slid across the ground towards us. Then paused. They moved again. Then paused. Were they trying to show they weren't going to hurt us?

The head rose again, veined-gold ruff framing their wedged head, fangs delicately bared. I tensed against Daimyn's grip, preparing to be yanked backwards again. Their fangs gleamed, and down one of them something dripped. Dark, dark gold.

"Oh, for fuck's sake," Daimyn muttered. "What is it about you?"

"*No!*" Alwin shouted. He strode forward, and Daimyn swiftly shifted our positions so he stood between Alwin and I. But Alwin tripped, wheeling for balance; a shadowed form slowly wound around his legs, sliding up his body. Alwin didn't look afraid—he looked furious, his hands clenched at his sides, glaring murder at me.

"What's happening?"

One tick. Two. "They have a venom that allows someone to understand them."

Oh. "They want me to translate."

Daimyn exhaled slowly, his breath tickling my ear. The creature near me slid closer, that drop of venom wobbling at the tip.

"Uh. What should I do?"

"You started this," Daimyn said mildly.

I huffed.

"I advise against this, in case you care."

"But you're not stopping me."

He didn't say anything.

Oh come on! Like I'm going to turn down being a temporary diplomat for freaking magical snakes!?

I paused. "Wait, why don't they just give you the venom? Then you can just talk directly."

"Their venom doesn't work on me."

"Oh." I chewed on my lip. "Long term effects?"

"With repeated exposure it can start degrading certain organs. Speakers' lifespans are significantly shortened. For a single exposure, you might feel sick tomorrow."

Stomach bubbling with nerves, I lifted my hand. "What do I… do?"

"They're going to bite you." Daimyn's arm flexed around my torso. "It'll probably hurt."

I made a face, fully extending my arm towards the lithe shadowy form. "This is probably a bad—"

The snakehead blurred, and pain exploded in my hand. Staying silent wasn't an option. Formless sound burst out of my throat, every muscle in my body turning rigid. I writhed back into Daimyn's arms even as I fought not to yank my arm back. Fangs pierced my hand with what felt like pure fucking fire. I slammed my heel into the ground once, twice, trying to keep my knees under me. The fingers of Daimyn's free hand dug into my shoulder. It grounded me, forced me to think about something else.

My arm shook. More pressure around my hand, and a pulse of *something*. The snake delicately pulled their fang out, and I gasped.

"Ah…" I cradled my shaking arm to my chest, feeling a bit like I would vomit. My whole body flushed with heat, my clothes sticking uncomfortably to my back and under my arms.

"Are you all right?" Daimyn said tightly.

"Might hurl."

Hissing chatters filled the air, tunneling into my ears until my head rang with it. The sound changed. A splitting headache crested over my skull…

Oh, this was a bad idea.

My brain churned sideways, and—

"*—too much? Not enough?*"

"*I'll bite her again, whatever,*" the one nearest me said. The hissing-chatter underlay each word, as if the sound itself were not the language, but carried on them like a vessel.

"Oh good," I groaned. "I'm going to vomit, but I can understand."

"What are they saying?" Daimyn said.

Haltingly, in Latin, I told the snakes I could understand them. Crapsticks, this headache did not help matters. Daimyn held me on my feet, and I probably would have fallen if he let go, but I couldn't muster enough of me to care.

"*She speaks.*"

"*And she understands us.*"

"*Good job.*"

"*Excellent idea.*"

The one nearest me grew closer; their presence pressed on me like a second skin, though they were still about a meter away.

"*Tell us what Deathless said.*"

"Who is this you speak of?" I mumbled in Latin.

"*Holding onto you.*"

I blinked, then slowly looked at Daimyn.

"What?" he asked.

"They wanna know what you said," I said in English.

"Well, let's start from the beginning again and be really clear this time," he muttered, barely audible. Then his voice slid into cool professionalism: "Tell them I'm concerned about the deaths with the markings of their clan. The war with the Sheshaki is spreading to innocents and—"

"Wait, wait, I can only translate so fast."

Alwin snorted with utter distain. I made a face but didn't look at him. I'd almost forgotten about him. With painstaking care—as much as I could—I translated each sentence Daimyn fed me. Apparently there was a snake-war going on, and bodies were piling up.

Alwin snorted. "The language you use… like a child."

I ignored him. Daimyn ignored him. Even the snakes seemed to ignore him.

"Your clan is powerful," I continued, Daimyn's words. "There is no need for blood if you want the power of the Sheshaki."

"*We do not want power*," one said, who I was pretty sure spoke most often. "*We do not want blood. But the Sheshaki will not stop.*"

"That doesn't make sense," Daimyn responded, after I told him what they'd said. "The Sheshaki are running scared. Why would they provoke continued violence when they're clearly losing?"

"Even the venom does not work on your feeble mind—you are translating it all wrong!" Alwin laughed.

I swallowed down my twisting stomach.

"Just ignore him. He's trying to throw you off because he thinks his position as Speaker is being threatened," Daimyn murmured, the vibration of his voice rumbling against my back.

I gave a short nod, taking comfort from his words as my body temperature seemed to spike again.

"*How do we know? They show love for bloodshed like a human, hiding away and striking just when we think they're done… we must end this in the only way they seem to understand*," the creatures in the trees responded to my earlier statement from Daimyn.

"Have you talked with them about this?"

"*We try. They won't come. But deny everything.*"

Daimyn's brow furrowed. "Does that seem like them, lying about something they did?"

The trees thrashed briefly after I turned the words into Latin. Alwin said something else disparaging.

"*Nothing they do seems like them.*"

Daimyn shifted, the arm around my waist light as he held me to his side. He scrubbed his face with his free hand when I finished translating.

"The Sheshaki say *you* started this…" Daimyn murmured. "They looked like your kills."

"*We explain this to them. Not our kills.*"

Daimyn's eyes narrowed, his head tilting to the side. "Are you sure the Sheshaki are actually the ones doing this? At the beginning— the first deaths. Could it be possible they were made to look like their kills, but not? Like your kills looked like, but not."

Silence stretched through the trees as I relayed the last of his words. I could feel Daimyn's heartbeat against my shoulder, his face tilted upwards as he searched the trees.

"Is it possible you are being set up? By someone close enough to know how to mimic your kills?"

"*Why? What could possibly be gained? These tricks are of a human nature—*"

I swallowed, relaying the words. "—and then they cut themselves off."

My eyes caught on Alwin, still in the grip of one of the shadow-snakes, his arms crossed and scowling at the ground.

Daimyn shifted, and his voice came out painfully polite: "I understand that… the natures of others can be hard to understand. But even your people can be seduced by an idea. Do you know of anyone who would benefit from chaos between your clans?"

My eyes narrowed on Alwin as I translated. I *knew* I mixed up conjunctions and tenses this time, and he said nothing. He caught my stare and sneered, averting his eyes.

"You don't seem to have a lot to say anymore."

Alwin blinked as he realized I spoke to him, then his eyes narrowed. "Nothing to say. This is all ridiculous."

"You think it's ridiculous that someone is provoking a war?"

"The idea that someone is manipulating the peoples of Denashkesh is ridiculous."

I turned to watch Daimyn's reaction, wondering if he would come to the same conclusion, in time to catch something downright predatory rise in his eyes. I repressed a shiver... not afraid, exactly. But something in that look didn't resemble anything I'd seen before.

"You've always been an ambitious one," Daimyn said. "The Sheshaki didn't accept your proposal for Speaker, did they? Yes—I remember you now."

"*What does Deathless say?*" I flinched at the hissing voice right next to me, having forgotten about them for a second while too busy staring at the angles of Daimyn's face.

"I don't know what you're talking about," Alwin said flatly.

Stumbling through the words, I tried to translate while still tracking the ongoing conversation. My tongue seemed too big for my mouth.

Daimyn's head tilted. "It seems unconscionable, doesn't it? The Denashkesh are the more physically powerful group, yet they defer to the Sheshaki's judgement on... so many things. The Sheshaki's Speaker is requested so often for diplomatic meetings. And very highly regarded."

Okay, too many big words to translate. I did my best.

"It is ludicrous what you are implying," Alwin said.

"It is," Daimyn said, and his voice lowered. "Because even if the Denashkesh take over, that would not have guaranteed you'd be Speaker, or that they would be even as remotely involved in external affairs as the Sheshaki."

Alwin's lips pressed into a hard line. I finished translating the best I could... and the trees grew quiet. *Oh, something is definitely about to go down.*

The hair on the back of my neck rose, prickled, *hard*, like the air was filling with electricity, warning blaring under my skin, stealing my breath. The creature already half-wound around Alwin slid up, twining to his shoulders and around his neck. Alwin turned ghost-white, eyes nearly feverish. His eyes rolled back even before the wedged head struck, fangs driven into his shoulder. He staggered, knees buckling, and the large form wrapped around his body cushioned the fall, taking him gently to the ground.

"We will find out the truth about this," the voice said near me.

I nodded. Then said belatedly to Daimyn, "They said they'll figure out the truth."

Daimyn only stared at Alwin, his mouth a flat line. "I probably just sentenced him to death."

I didn't think I was supposed to translate that for the snakes.

The large creature nearest us moved, suddenly up close. I tensed, Daimyn's arm tightening around my waist again. The giant wedged head rose up until it was barely half a meter away. Their tongue began to flicker again.

"She did good," said a voice from the trees.

"This one lied. We should keep her instead," said another.

"Uh," I said, leaning back against Daimyn.

The one in front of me edged closer. It tasted the air around me, the fluttering disturbance brushing against my cheek. *"Let me tell you about what we could offer…"*

Daimyn let go of me and crouched. Startled, I looked down—as he took my knees out from under me.

"Gah!" I thumped bodily against his chest, one of his arms under my knees and the other behind my back.

"Tell them goodbye and I will be watching," he said, without explaining his actions whatsoever.

"Ominous," I muttered.

Daimyn turned and strode away, breaking through underbrush onto the pathway that led out of the green area.

"Shit—*dicit vale*! Uh—" and I did my best to yell back his final words. The one who'd been nearest us didn't move, large form still coiled on the ground as they watched us leave. They were hunting-still, but light or… something, caught across their face, and briefly lit up the golden, slitted-pupil eyes.

Behind them, shadows converged on the helpless form of Alwin on the ground. They cradled him, lifting him into the trees almost tenderly. Except every hair on my body stood on end. The entire area grew heavier, like the very mass of the creatures increased. After a few seconds there was nothing to see but shadow.

Daimyn rounded a bend, and trees cut off my view.

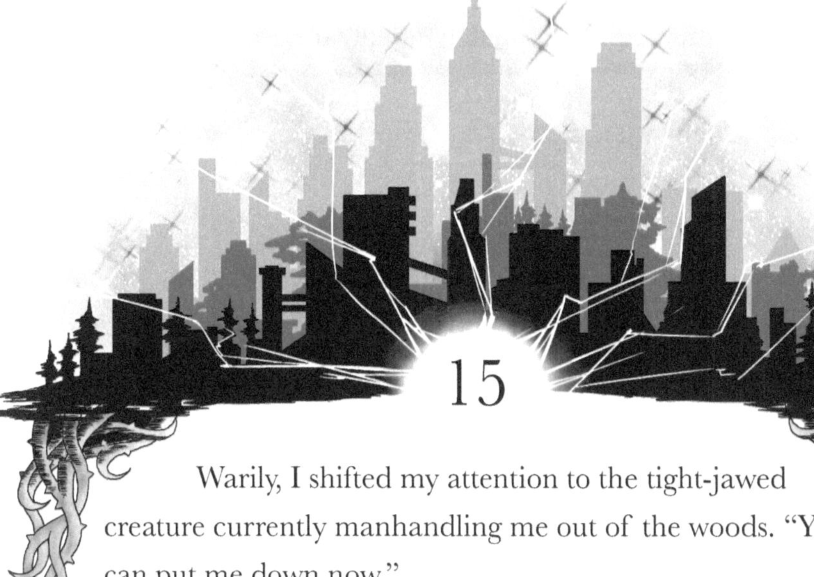

15

Warily, I shifted my attention to the tight-jawed creature currently manhandling me out of the woods. "You can put me down now."

"*Mmm.*"

I contemplated struggling. Decided to better use my time. "Sooooo what was that?" I asked brightly.

Daimyn's lips thinned. "I'm only telling you this because you single-handedly turned that entire meeting around."

I grinned, unrepentant and now entirely high on his compliment, even if muttered in annoyance.

"Two factions are at the point of war. Innocents have already died. I've called meetings to stop it. Apparently, it was all a setup."

"Yeah, I got all that already. What's a Speaker?"

"It's a translator for the Umbra Serpentibus." *The shadows of snakes"?* "Speakers act as translators with other species. Diplomats of a kind."

"But they know *Latin*? Why is that?"

Daimyn glanced at me, a sharp dart of black-green attention. "Is that the question you are requesting of me in our deal?"

I blinked. Remembered what he was talking about. Made a face. "What was this about me single-handedly turning that meeting around?"

"Yes," Daimyn said slowly. "After breaking our agreement you were not to make a sound."

I froze, heart rate picking up in apprehension. Was he serious?

Daimyn broke out of the trees onto the street, and my feet met the cobblestone. He steadied me, then one hand slid down my arm to wrap around my wrist. He pulled it up and inspected the palm of my hand. The bite wasn't nearly as bad as it had felt in the moment.

Daimyn nodded. "Keep it clean."

Then he took a half a step back. It hit me that not once during that whole man-handling process, from when he'd grabbed me initially in the woods to inspecting my palm, had I ever felt trapped or uncomfortable. Interesting.

He exhaled hard, raking a hand through his hair. "You barreled in there with no understanding of consequences—"

"Don't give me that," I bit out. "That Speaker-whatever was deliberately mistranslating your words and it could have gone *badly*—it *was* going badly. Do *not* spin this."

Daimyn's eyes shut. "I know. But you are so reckless, Fairian."

"It wasn't recklessness."

His eyes opened to glare.

"It wasn't!"

"And what would you have done if they'd attacked? Hm? How were you planning on getting out alive?"

"They were already going to attack!" I threw up my arms. "Alwin was saying you were going to eat their babies or something!"

"Yes, attack *me*."

"And you expected me to just stand there and do nothing?" I said scathingly.

His eyes narrowed, and he blinked once. Twice. *That was exactly what he had thought.* He thought I'd just hide in the bushes while shadow snake things attacked.

I reared back in offense. "I know we don't know each other, but seriously?"

"You were trying to protect me," he said slowly, half a question.

"What the hell did you think I was doing?"

"Inserting yourself in a situation in the hopes of gaining leverage," he responded easily.

My face screwed up, even as some part of me went *oh actually that's smart.* "That's the conclusion you jumped to? Not that I'd help you, but that I wanted influence?"

He gave me a flat look. "You've made your enthusiasm of getting involved in the magical community quite clear, even if your agenda is not."

I crossed my arms over my chest. "Okay. Sure. But you need better friends if that's the first place you went."

Daimyn stared. I lifted an eyebrow in response. He continued to stare, almost like he wasn't aware of how much he was staring. Heat rose in my cheeks and I fought not to do something belligerent.

"Let us walk," Daimyn said abruptly, striding past me. "What is the question you want me to answer?"

My stomach flipped, and I jumped to his side in an instant, though I had to move fast to keep up with his long legs. *Okay. We're doing this.* I took a deep breath to settle myself.

I had this one question, one question from the mysterious gentleman who mediated demon conflicts and obviously knew stuff. My gaze lifted to the vivid sky, the blanket of the darkest gemstone glittering and holding the world together, exhaling night and stars. A bitter pang followed. I couldn't ask why the sky was green. If I only had one question, I had to ask about my sister's killer. Because that was the priority right now; not the hidden secrets in my heart, but how to keep myself out of the hands of danger. I ripped my attention down to the ground.

"I'm trying to identify a particular demon," I began slowly, trying to work out how I would ask this question without revealing too much.

Daimyn cleared his throat. "I'm going to interrupt with some free information, for as you said, your intervention did greatly help."

I blinked at him.

"Magical beings are not 'demons.'" He glanced at me. "Demons are beings from another plane, a word used as propaganda by religious institutions during the crusades to justify the hunting and extermination of magical creatures. When you use that word, be aware of its history."

I blinked. *Oh. It's a slur.* "Thank you."

He glanced at me again. Then his pace slowed, and it grew easier to keep up with him.

"You're trying to identify a particular magical creature," he prodded.

"Right." I curled my hands into fists against my sides. "Are there…" I could do this. "The de—magical creatures I mean. There are magical beings who can…" I stopped as it occurred to me I could ask a more general question that would both give me more info *and* reveal less to him.

"I'm trying to identify a particular creature," I restarted. "And I need more resources on how to find out information. Where can I find more information on magical beings?"

Daimyn's attention prickled along the side of my face and I resolutely didn't look at him.

"If I had more specifics about what you're looking for I might have a better answer."

I pursed my lips. "But is there a place in general?"

Daimyn didn't respond for three steps. Our steps had matched up, and the synchrony of our movements briefly fascinated me.

"The Exclusive Section in the library holds most information on magic in Farfalla," Daimyn said. "But I imagine you already know this."

I fought a sinking stomach. I *did* already know of that. I'd been waiting for my credentials for weeks.

"Private individuals may have libraries of their own, but it would be hit or miss whether or not they had what you wanted, and getting an invite would take a deep friendship."

Frustration writhed through me and the restless movement broke up the pattern of my footfalls, breaking our synchronized steps.

"Why is it so important you identify this creature?" Daimyn asked.

I looked away, my stomach cramping into a knot.

Daimyn's arm brushed my shoulder, lightly enough I didn't know if it had been by accident or not. "If you answer my question, I'll answer another one of yours."

My head snapped towards him, steps faltering. "What?"

One side of his mouth kicked up. "I'm allowed to be curious too."

"You already know everything," I said crossly. "More than me, anyway."

Mischief glinted in his eyes. "I don't know about you, though."

If I didn't know any better, I would have said he was flirting. I almost rolled my eyes. The unexpected playfulness tugged at something in my chest, easing the pressure. My stomach quivered. I wanted another answer, but I really didn't want to answer Daimyn's question.

But to gain trust, you had to give a little trust.

"I…" I licked my lips, thinking over his question. "It's important to me because information is power. Protection."

Daimyn's eyebrows twitched upwards when I didn't elaborate further. "And you're feeling powerless?"

"Is that another question?"

He rolled his eyes. "Fine. Yes."

A lump formed in my throat. I hated, *hated* the answer to his question. "Yes, I feel powerless," I forced out. "*You* keep going on about danger, this should make sense to you. I need to know how to protect myself."

My words hit the air and his head turned, the full weight of his attention locked on me. It practically turned the air solid.

"Protect yourself from what?"

I winced. *Yeah, I knew that would snag his attention.*

"It's my turn for questions," I said brusquely, barreling past the subject. "And I get a big one because that was two questions." I stabbed my finger at the sky. "Why is the sky green? Wait—that's not my question." *Focus, nitwit.* "Why is there so much magic in Farfalla— evidenced by the sky and how many magical creatures are here?"

Daimyn blinked at me and then slowly looked up, as if shifting his attention took effort. My heart raced as I scrutinized his expression. Did my question even make sense?

He ran one of his hands down the bottom half of his face. "The short answer is 'because of the Divide.'"

My stomach somersaulted.

"The longer answer is… the Divide has supernatural influence on the land nearest it. There are a range of things that happen, including Flux situations, and, as you mentioned, the green sky."

Shock strangled my brain. Ironically, I could barely hear his words over the roar of disbelief, the ease of just *getting an answer*.

"This influence makes it easier for magical beings to hide, versus inland, where overt magic may be less common. It attracts a lot of beings here, especially the ones who have a harder time blending with humans." Daimyn glanced at me. "Farfalla also has historical significance to the magical community, which is another subject altogether."

I stared, lips parted. My chest hurt, as if this illumination dug into a bruise. It made me ravenous, parched for more.

"What do you mean, historical significance? How many are here? And what's a Flux situation?"

"Nope, my turn." His eyes flicked to mine. "Are you in danger?"

Ugh. "Haven't you been telling me that all along?"

"You answered a question with a question, that doesn't count. You know what I mean. You specifically brought up needing to protect yourself, and yet you've made the lack of consideration for your own life *quite* clear in our previous interactions. Is someone threatening you?"

I growled with frustration under my breath, panic beating alongside my heart. In truth, I didn't know if *he* was really here. There was just the article and my nebulous Feelings I couldn't even talk about in the first place. I was not going to open myself up to ridicule and scorn, not again. Daimyn obviously acted as some kind of protective force but how could I possibly explain—

In that place in my head that always churned, something clicked.

"That's why you're here," I said slowly. "In Farfalla. You're here because of all the dem—sorry. Magical creatures. And this is your… job or something."

Daimyn's lips quirked. "Job or something." He shook his head once.

"Well?" I challenged. "Is it?"

He watched me out of the corner of his eye and smirked. "I believe that's another question, and you haven't answered mine yet. Come on, we're almost having a conversation with give and take like normal people."

I huffed and repressed an urge to kick the ground. "Ask a different question instead."

His head tilted. "No, I think I like this question. Why can't you answer simply yes or no?"

I could Feel how hard he tried to keep this light and teasing, like he knew if he got serious I would bolt. Instead of panicking, I lunged at the opening he'd given me.

"Because it's complicated and I don't know if I can trust you. There, I answered a question, answer mine now."

A laugh coughed out of him, the sound startled and rusty, like it didn't know how to form correctly. When was the last time he laughed for real?

"Ah, Fairian, what am I going to do with you," he murmured, sounding aggravated and amused and soft and sad all at once.

I liked the way he said my name, and I knew he meant his words rhetorically, but my mouth opened anyway: "Take me with you. Show me what you do."

The smile slid off his face. My chest constricted, reminding me that for some sodding reason, I cared about his opinion. He made a frustrated noise, steps quickening. "This is not a world you can just recklessly barge into."

"I literally just did, and it was fine." *Come on already.* "Maybe it's easy for someone like you, who works with this every day, to shut other people out."

The muscles in Daimyn's jaw flexed. His posture straightened as his movements took on grace and aggression that I only now registered had softened over the last however-many minutes. Almost as if he'd been intentionally making himself less threatening.

"I *just* helped you—I'm not bloody useless." I *hated* how desperate I sounded. "I'd stay out of your way and do my best not to get hurt. I'm not helpless, despite what you think."

Daimyn inhaled, held his breath, and let it out. Then he disappeared out of the corner of my vision as he halted. I tripped to a stop and spun to face him.

"I have certain abilities, right? You've seen me."

"Yes…" I drew out the word.

His hand cut through the air. "I'm not just anybody who decided to take this on."

"Someone is forcing you?" I blurted. "I know all about being forced into a life you don't want. I'll trade with you. You can play the courtly gentleman who cares about polite society, and I'll hang out with magical beings."

He huffed that almost-laugh again, a fracture in his intensity. "What happened that made you like this?"

I stiffened, all of my hackles rising. "Nothing *made* me. *I* made me." *Get that out of your bloody head right now.*

He studied me for a long moment. Then he shook his head, shifting his weight restlessly. "I can't trade my life for yours, even if I wanted to. You can get hurt—you're…" He waved his hand as if searching for the word. "Vulnerable."

"Of course I am," I said, exasperated. "So is everyone. You do your best, then you die. You say that like you *can't* get hur…" My eyes widened. "Wait."

The evidence stacked up quickly. Daimyn Felt like nothing I'd ever encountered. His strength. The night of the kelpie, he had been under the water for far longer than anyone could conceivably hold their breath. Earlier tonight, he hadn't been angry with me putting *him* in danger… he'd been angry I put *myself* in danger. And the final hammering fact that clicked only just now: the shadow-snakes had called him Deathless.

Daimyn watched me with heavy resignation, as if he braced himself.

"What *are* you?" I breathed in wonder.

I instantly regretted it. *'What' he is, you arseface? As if he's not a person?*

Daimyn's expression flattened. "There isn't a word for what I am. I don't fit into your classifications."

My heart lunged at his answer, but mortification demanded I fix my thoughtless question first. "I wasn't trying to *classify*—no—that's—that wasn't what I meant. That came out wrong."

Black eyebrows lifted, the rest of his expression unchanging.

My hands curled into fists. *Fix this!* "I'm sorry. I—"

Urgency blew out of nowhere. Our little bubble of conversation popped in a blink. Daimyn's head turned sharply to the side, eyes unfocused, and then went motionless.

I opened my mouth to say—*something*, then slowly frowned. He didn't even seem to be breathing. I edged closer, trying to read anything off of the tension in his face.

He refocused on me so fast I jumped.

"I need to go."

Denial swelled in my throat. "What?"

Daimyn glanced over his shoulder, everything about him restrained like he fought not to bolt. "I don't have time—I have to go."

Nooooo. What is happening?

His eyes locked with mine, filled with something weary and endless. That same profound awareness from the night we'd met rose up to swallow me: our proximity, the subtle exchange of reactions between his body and mine, the unspoken language of eye-contact and heartbeats.

"Keep in mind that you'll never get answers to anything if you get yourself killed," he murmured.

Then he shot towards the nearest building. And I mean *shot*. I barely turned my head fast enough to see him *leap* a meter from the wall, grab the edge of the roof, and flip himself up on top of it. He raced across the rooftop in a blink, onto the next building before my eyebrows even shot up, and disappeared from view before I finished taking a breath. I stumbled forward a few useless steps, already knowing I couldn't catch up to him, or even hope to follow.

My mouth hung open at the blatant display of… well, *that*.

What had just *happened* to him?

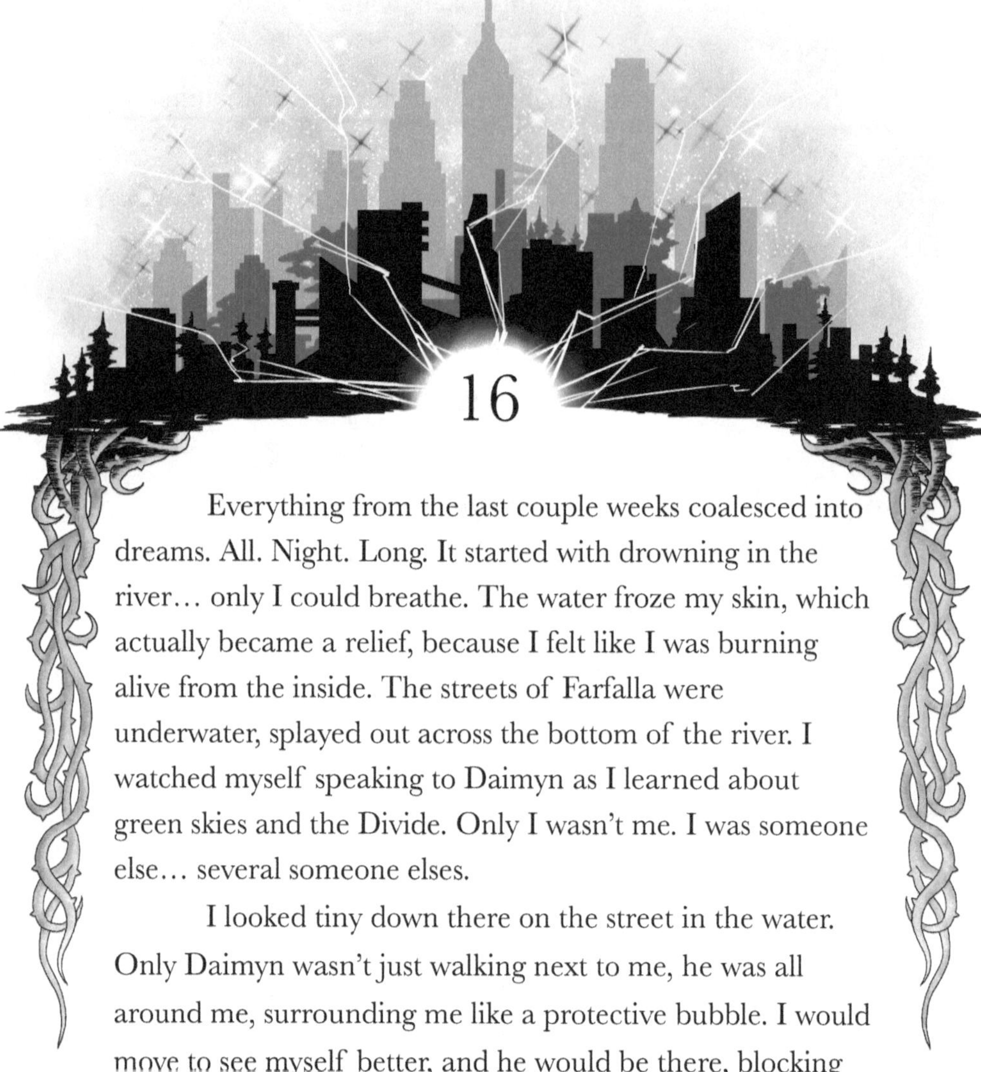

16

Everything from the last couple weeks coalesced into dreams. All. Night. Long. It started with drowning in the river… only I could breathe. The water froze my skin, which actually became a relief, because I felt like I was burning alive from the inside. The streets of Farfalla were underwater, splayed out across the bottom of the river. I watched myself speaking to Daimyn as I learned about green skies and the Divide. Only I wasn't me. I was someone else… several someone elses.

I looked tiny down there on the street in the water. Only Daimyn wasn't just walking next to me, he was all around me, surrounding me like a protective bubble. I would move to see myself better, and he would be there, blocking my sight. And I was thrilled. I was absolutely delighted Daimyn kept shielding me, keeping Me from reaching myself down there with him. In the dream, I knew Daimyn wasn't aware he protected me from view, and that was even more exciting.

His voice echoed words about skies and magical beings, only it was different this time. He was soft, warm, kind —telling me everything I wanted to know, even if dream-me couldn't quite hear what he was saying. I tried to get closer, and Daimyn was there to block me.

Something very bad would happen when I caught myself. Dream-me kept trying to test him, to try to get at me, just to see what would happen. There was no relief when Daimyn blocked the attempt, because the glee I felt from his actions made it seem like he was doing exactly what dream-me wanted.

Something bad wasn't going to happen; it was already happening.

I woke drenched in sweat and boiling under the covers. I bolted from the bed, dawn only just lightening the sky outside my window. Great shitgibbons, I hated dark-moon dreams. This one had been worse than usual, deja vu crawling up my throat. I cringed and flicked my hands back and forth, trying to get rid of the dread curdling in my stomach.

I jumped into a cold shower, instantly relieved as my skin cooled.

It was only perturbing because of everything that had happened with Daimyn last night. Why my subconscious had decided to latch onto him was anyone's guess. Probably because he was impossible to ignore. That protectiveness exuding from him…

For a second, I wondered what it would be like to be that girl in my dream. The one who had the focus of Daimyn's protection, the person he talked with. The idea hit too hard and too fast for me to pretend it didn't fill me with yearning.

Come back to reality, Fairian. He wasn't going to save me. The only person who could save me was myself. I was not going to be seduced by the idea of some dream-Daimyn.

Another missing person had been found claiming they saw their worst fears become real. Admitted to St. Dymphna's, again. This one was a young man, someone who'd been visiting from out of town. There were bare details beyond that, and I read over the same words again and again in frustration.

Tiff plunked into the cafeteria seat opposite me, carrying a waxed-paper package and wearing a shite-eating grin. I lifted an eyebrow.

"What's that?"

"Pimientos de Patrón," she declared. "Some of the last of the season."

My eyes narrowed into slits. "Those *are* what I think they are."

"*Yes*, the Russian roulette of peppers," she said gleefully, and unwrapped the paper to reveal a dozen or so smallish green peppers, lightly fried and sprinkled with salt. "*Os pementos de Padrón, uns pican e outros non.*"

"*Padrón peppers, some are hot, some are not*" was a local point of pride. Padrón peppers normally had a mild, sweet, almost tart flavor—except for something like 15%, which were the fires of hell. There was no true way of knowing until you ate them; it was up to chance and courage to see what you got.

I picked one up before I even made the decision. I'd nearly forgotten Tiff and I had talked about trying these months ago. I popped almost the whole thing in my mouth before I thought twice. Tiff's eyebrows shot up.

We waited...

Waited...

"Okay, that's really tasty," I said. "My taste buds are still intact."

Tiff actually looked disappointed and made a great show of picking out her pepper. Then she tentatively put it in her mouth, cringing as she bit down.

"Look at you being all cowardly," I scoffed.

Her eyes lit up, and she stuck her tongue at me—with bits of chewed pepper, ew. "No fires of hell!"

We laughed and ate another each. Both of which were mild and honestly very tasty.

"What were you looking at so intently when I came up?" Tiff asked, gesturing at my PCD with her chin.

"Oh. Uhm. More reports about people admitted to St. Dymphna's."

Her eyes sharpened. "With hallucinations?"

"Seems like it."

"Have you figured out it's… if it's proof?"

I shook my head once.

Tiff methodically licked salt off her fingers, a furrow forming between her eyes as she stared down at the table. "You know, if you haven't found proof… there's no reason to put yourself in danger with that kind of business unless absolutely necessary."

I swallowed and carefully responded. "I know. It shouldn't be too much longer."

It was habit to reassure her and move on from a conversation touching on magic. I wish she'd talk to me about whatever made her react the way she did. It's not like I wouldn't understand. Then again, maybe I *wouldn't*—I refused to believe magic was inherently bad, and Tiff's reactions made me think she did.

My PCD buzzed with a message.

"Renald's here," I said.

Tiff and I swept up our bags and our peppers and headed outside. I'd only been inside for a few minutes, but the formerly-clear sky had taken a turn for the worst.

"My spicy babies!" Tiff exclaimed, hunching over them to protect them from the drizzle.

Rolling my eyes, we scampered across the lawn and threw ourselves into the waiting car.

"Renald," Tiff said. "Would you like a pepper?"

He looked at us in the rear-view and laughed. "Oh Ms. Collins, I'm not sure I need that much excitement in my life."

"Oh, come on. There's three left! That way it's even."

He chuckled. "Leave the last one for me when I'm not driving."

The car jostled lightly as it ascended onto the bridge. The water below swirled dark and murky with the rain. I smiled out the window at the green clouds and greenish fog that cloaked the city.

Paper rustled, and a pepper appeared under my nose.

"Last one."

I smirked and turned. We locked eyes as we simultaneously lifted our peppers to our mouths and bit down. I winked, crunching through the sweet-tart—

I froze.

Tiff's face flushed scarlet, and panic flashed in her eyes.

"Oh no," I mumbled.

I swallowed hard, trying to get it over with. Which just made it ten times worse as *utter bloody lava* slid down my throat. My eyes filled with tears, my vision blurring. Saliva abruptly pooled in my mouth. The burning crept up into my nose.

"Oh *fuck*," I gasped, sucking in rapid breaths to keep cool air flowing over the charred-feeling parts of my mouth.

Tiff frantically fanned her mouth. "Thish ish bad, ohmagahd!"

From the front, Renald let out a bark of laughter and the car turned onto another street.

"Thish is your shtupi' idea!"

Renald started laughing harder.

"I know I'm sharry!"

We had barely collected ourselves when we turned onto the long driveway up to the pazo.

"My sinuses have never been so clear in my life," I said thickly.

"There we go. Positives." Red blotches still covered her face. "That was fun. Do it again next week?"

"You are ridiculous."

Renald slowed the car to a crawl. I knew his driving patterns at this point, and the difference pinged in my head. I looked up—a sleek black vehicle sat in front of the pazo, "Farfallan Detective Division" written across the side. I stilled.

"That's weird," Tiff muttered.

"Have you a wish to go anywhere else, ma'am?" Renald asked, his serious eyes meeting mine in the rear-view mirror. Fondness surged in me. But also, wow, he just assumed this was about me, huh? This was the problem with having staff around who remembered me from years ago with all the trouble I'd gotten into.

"No, it's all right. Let's see what they want."

This couldn't have anything to do with me.

With a nod, Renald eased the vehicle forward again, coasting down the final distance and parking in our usual spot. Tiff and I took out time getting out of the car.

"It's probably just them welcoming us to the neighborhood or something," I said, and rolled my eyes at myself. *Really? That's what I come up with?*

Tiff arched an eyebrow and didn't bother addressing that comment.

Not even halfway to the front door, it opened to reveal my father's butler. His deep blue eyes met mine for only a second, but it felt like an endless meaningful beat before he smiled, pale cheeks creasing.

"Welcome home, Ms. Fairian. Ms. Collins. There are officers here from the Detective Division here who are asking some questions about a case."

"Thank you, Mr. Greaving." I reached the doorway and walked through. "Do you know what they are asking in particular?"

"My apologies, I do not, Ms. Fairian."

He took my pack in the foyer and handed it to Abigail, who nodded to me and headed up the stairs towards my room. I met Tiff's eyes and subtly jerked my chin at the stairwell that headed towards her room. She nodded and scurried away.

I heard a door open down the hall, and looked up to see a light-haired, light-skinned, masc-presenting individual wearing a uniform striding towards me.

"You must be Ms. Fairian, I'm delighted to meet your acquaintance."

My father stepped out of the same room the officer had been in.

"And you are?" I said austerely, making a split second decision to hide behind etiquette and act like a proper British brat, despite Farfalla's more lax social etiquette.

"Darling, this is Detective Kent," my father said easily when he reached me, gesturing towards the younger gentleman standing in front of me.

I scanned my father's face. His expression: smooth and pleasant, polite and formal, but not rigidly so. I recognized it, and a little tension eased from my shoulders.

"What's going on?"

"Kent here would like to ask you a few questions about a case they're working on," my father said.

"I apologize for the intrusion, Ms. Leynthall."

I breathed carefully through my nose at the address. "What is all this about?"

"All will be explained," Officer Kent said easily, giving me a big smile. "We shouldn't take too much of your time."

Down the hall, another door opened, the sitting room with huge glass windows. My mother stepped out, her chin lifted and posture perfect. A figure followed closely behind her, another masc in a uniform, but a different kind, something about it almost… military. He looked probably later thirties in age, his hair a shade lighter than my father's, and his bright blue eyes landed on me. Uneasiness shifted through my limbs.

"Thank you for your time, Mrs. Leynthall," I heard him murmur.

My mother curtsied pleasantly, and her head lifted to see me.

"Darling, you're home!" Her skirts rustled as she strode down the hall to my side. "It seems these lovely officers need our help on a case of theirs. They're trying to track down a group of ransomers"—she gave a heavy sigh for emphasis on the tragedy—"and would like our help seeing if we recognize some of the details."

My mother's dramatics: high, which meant her discomfort probably matched. Where she'd grown up, law enforcement was not an organization of safety and comfort. This had to feel like an outright invasion.

Also, why are detectives looking into ransom cases? That's Ransom Recovery's jurisdiction.

"We will only take a few minutes of your time," Detective Kent repeated. "Is it alright to use the sitting room again, sir?"

The blue-eyed gentleman grew closer, and uneasiness hardened closer to dread as he watched me.

"Of course," my father said, his eyes on me.

"Yes, let's see what we can do to help," my mother said, starting to lead me down the hall.

"Ah, madam, if you don't mind, I'll speak with you briefly while Andrews speaks to Ms. Leynthall. You know how it is, kids sometimes not wanting to say things in front of their parents… "

My mother and I turned almost in unison to stare at him. How old did he think I was?

My mother's hand tightened on my arm. "Oh, I'm sure there's nothing she can't say in front of me."

"My mother is right—I have nothing to hide." And the more I thought about it, the more I liked the idea of my mother in the room with me.

"All the same…" Kent's smile didn't waver.

An awkward beat followed. My mother slowly let me go. Protesting probably wouldn't be viewed favorably. I touched my mother's arm in reassurance and walked out of her grasp, down the hall to the room she'd just come out of. I heard murmuring behind me, and footsteps followed. The hair on the back of my neck rose.

I entered the room and spun, chin lifted. As I'd been afraid of, the blue-eyed gentleman followed, carrying a slim briefcase, and shut the door quietly.

"There are some excellent tea and biscuits just brought up, if you'd like." His voice was somber but oddly pleasant.

I smiled in reflex and sank into one of the chairs.

"What can I help you with, Detective?" I said, voice crisp and polite, and fiddled with some tea, though I wasn't sure I actually wanted to drink it.

"Lieutenant Andrews, at your service." He inclined his head, and then walked over to the chair across from me and sat down.

That answered my military question. I didn't recognize any determining characteristics on his uniform. Suspicion rose even higher; mixing military with citizen protection divisions was never a good idea.

An awkward beat followed before he inhaled to speak.

"Ms. Leynthall," he said, and I twitched, sick of being called by the wrong name.

My sister is Ms. Leynthall, I am Ms. FAIRIAN Leynthall—

"I'll get right to the point, as I have no desire to waste your time. I am a representative of the Terra Arcana Security Administration. I believe you may know us as TASA."

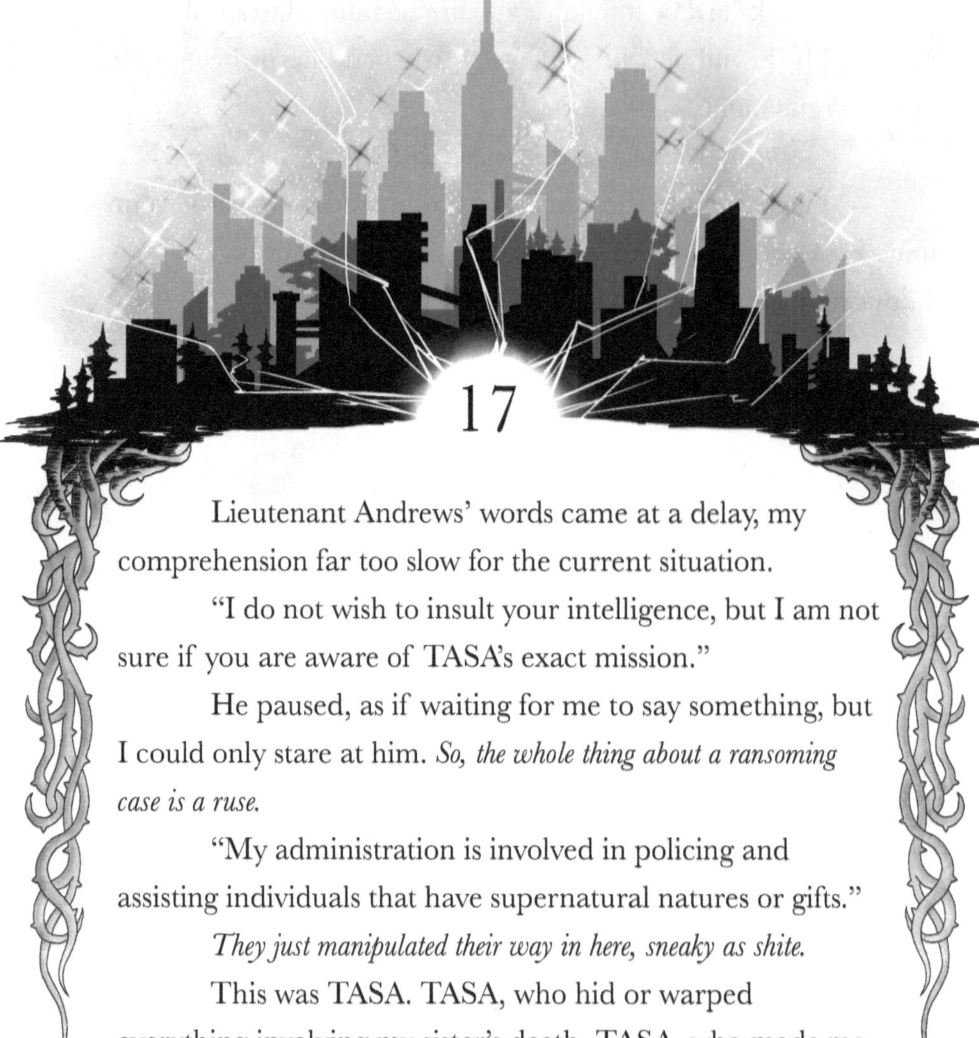

17

Lieutenant Andrews' words came at a delay, my comprehension far too slow for the current situation.

"I do not wish to insult your intelligence, but I am not sure if you are aware of TASA's exact mission."

He paused, as if waiting for me to say something, but I could only stare at him. *So, the whole thing about a ransoming case is a ruse.*

"My administration is involved in policing and assisting individuals that have supernatural natures or gifts."

They just manipulated their way in here, sneaky as shite.

This was TASA. TASA, who hid or warped everything involving my sister's death. TASA, who made me think I was losing my mind. TASA, who made every inch of ground gained feel like a mile up a cliff.

"We have recently become aware of a relationship between yourself and a particular gentleman we have a great interest in. Someone who is a security risk in all senses of the word. Our main objective is to be able to protect everyone, Ms. Leynthall, and this individual challenges that responsibility at every turn. Do you know who I am talking about?"

180

Deep breath in. Deep breath out. "Who?"

"You know him as Mr. Daimyn Yillen."

I breathed through any reaction. "Who?"

His eyes held on mine for several beats. Then he turned to the briefcase he'd set to the side and pulled out a folder. Flipping it open, he spread three large glossy photos across the low tea-table.

"I'd appreciate if you gave me the courtesy of not insulting my intelligence either, Ms. Leynthall."

All three photos were dark and slightly blurry, as if taken at night from far away. In the first one, Daimyn was walking along a street, half of his body hazy from motion. The person he carried— one arm behind their knees and the other behind their back—was in full focus, and looked to be asleep.

And with a wrenching jolt, I recognized me, my head tucked onto his shoulder. But it couldn't be. I had no recollection of this event. Hilarity bubbled in my throat; TASA strikes again, making me feel like I was losing my mind.

The next picture, Daimyn and I faced each other. The perspective came from over Daimyn's shoulder but farther away, only a sliver of his profile visible. My hair and clothes were plastered to my body, the river behind me, my expression sharp as I glared up into Daimyn's face. Daimyn's hands loosely fisted at his side, his clothes and hair drenched, his legs and shoulders tense and braced.

The final picture showed both of us in motion, walking side by side along a wide street. We looked at each other. He had one hand lifted, as if starting to run it through his hair. And something about his expression…

My dream, that disturbing dark moon dream. Me but not me, staring down as Daimyn and I talked. As if something watched us. Deja vu, as if it wasn't the first time.

"Now that we have established you indeed know the gentleman in question, may we speak?"

My gaze lifted. Heat surged from my gut into my chest, burning my lungs with each breath. My legs felt like jelly, and thank god I was sitting. My mouth curled into a wide grin, too bright, that probably made me look manic.

"Sure. Let's speak."

Lieutenant Andrews looked decidedly more cautious. "I am not sure how much you are aware of this individual's history and abilities, but the things he can do are astronomical. They are also dangerous."

I barely listened. That first photo, Daimyn carrying me—that had to be the first night I met him, after he knocked me out. They'd been following me since the bloody start! How? *Why?*

"We have reached out many times over the past decades to form a partnership, and he has rejected all attempts. We have also tried to rein in his dangerous abilities, but our methods have had only little success."

"What does this have to do with me," I said flatly.

Keep your composure.

Lieutenant Andrews nodded and shifted in his seat, lacing his fingers together in front of his torso. Usually I enjoyed staring down people for uncomfortably long moments as silence unnerved most. This time, heat built up behind my eyes until I could barely see.

"We have attempted to get someone close to any of the Yillens in the past. The family is paranoid and secluded, and often impossible to reason with. Yet Daimyn has taken an interest in you, and that gives us an opportunity."

I barked a laugh. "Well you're wrong already. He wants nothing to do with me. He made that abundantly clear."

Lieutenant Andrews' chin dipped. "We have been studying this creature for a long time, Ms. Leynthall." He leaned forward a fraction. "His kind crave connection, even need it, and form intense bonds. Trust me on this, the time and attention Daimyn has paid you is unprecedented."

I fought a cackle. *Trust* them? And Daimyn's *kind*? God knew I wouldn't ask this wanker what that meant. Even the thought of asking, learning about Daimyn from *this* person, made me want to vomit all over Andrews and his pristine uniform.

Actually, maybe doing that would get him to shut up and leave.

Andrews shifted. "Time is also a factor here. That family is often ruled by their darker nature, but it appears that the elder brother has become conscious, and possibly could be reasoned with or form attachments. But we don't know for how long."

Annoyance joined the riot in my chest. I hated when people used "dark" as a synonym for "bad."

"We need to get close him, to find a way to rein in his dangerous excesses while we can keep his attention."

Oh. I understand now.

He studied my face carefully. "We would not ask for anything dangerous, or to act against someone of such power, simply—"

"No." The word practically broke my throat at the force of its exit.

Lieutenant Andrews paused, regarding me for a beat. "You haven't heard our offer for your help, Ms. Leynthall."

My face felt numb. "I don't care."

He blinked, incredulity briefly alighting on his features. "Has he inspired such loyalty in you already?"

"It has nothing to do with loyalty. I just have no interest in acting a spy to your bloody organization." I tried to stop, but it came spilling out of me: "Do you have any idea what it's like, having a sibling die in your arms and *every* answer is ripped from you?"

My throat clamped shut, preventing me from saying any more.

"Then let's call this a path to making amends. I understand what we've done, and how you must view this, but you must know we did it for your safety and the safety of the world. In this,"—he tapped the photo nearest him, the one where Daimyn and I glared at each other soaking wet—"I think we can find a mutual way to help each other. Support us in this way, and we will start by giving you the information we have on your sister's death. All of it."

My breath shuddered out. The possibilities sprinted out in front of me before I could stop it. Here was the organization that covered up everything—if anyone knew the truth, or something that could lead me to answers of *why*, it would be them. And if they were to be believed, they'd give it to me, just by doing something I already wanted: get close to Daimyn.

Daimyn, who saved me. Daimyn, who didn't want anything to do with me. Daimyn, who practically drowned me in questions, who was unlike anything I'd never encountered before, who listened and treated me like I mattered.

"No," I said softly. My chest began ripping in two, excruciatingly slowly. "No, I won't do it."

Andrews sat back in his chair, eyebrows twitching upwards. "You realize that information on your sister is not the only knowledge we possess. As the primary organization handling magical beings, we have access to an endless amount of data, and as one of our valued informants, much of it would be yours as well."

I really *would* vomit all over these pictures. "My answer is still no."

A muscle ticked in Andrews' jaw. He held eye contact for a long moment, and despite how much I wanted to howl, relief trickled through my veins. This would be over soon. Once he realized I meant my words, he would have to leave.

Andrews turned to his briefcase again, rifling through it briefly. Pulling another folder out, he handed it to me this time. I cautiously took it, a horrible, cloying sense of premonition rising with it.

I opened the folder. It contained another glossy photo.

Only Tiff was the star of this one.

I barely recognized her, her face so much younger. Even once I did, the rest of the photo didn't make sense. It would not compute. It would not fit together in my head.

There was no way that this was my best friend, sitting in the center of a circle of runes, covered in blood, staring up at the camera with eyes as wide as saucers, as she clutched a body in her lap that looked like it had been ripped open from the inside out.

"How…?"

How long ago was this? How did he have this? How have I never known?

"It's our understanding that Ms. Collins' paramour at the time was meddling with very dangerous magics, and he pulled her into a ritual of some kind. We did not arrive in time to stop it, and it went badly, as you can tell. We forgave her naiveté in being involved for the names of the others, who fled right before this was taken."

My ribs compressed so tightly my heart could barely beat. "You're apparently good at that. Not arriving in time."

They hadn't arrived in time for Mari, either.

Andrews shifted. "We can't win all of them. But we *can* do more. With your help."

My help. Right. Because that's what this was all about.

"Why are you showing me this picture?" I asked, avoiding the sinking dread of understanding.

"I don't think I have to explain what the consequences would be to your young friend's future if this were to come to light."

My face turned numb, and I couldn't form words for a long, drug out minute.

"Why would you do this?" I hated myself for sounding so young. "What did she ever do to you?"

His head tilted. "You know why. Based on our observations, threatening your own future would not be nearly as effective as threatening hers." He paused. "I really did want to do this nicely, Ms. Leynthall. But you must understand the danger the Yillens present to the world. We cannot let this opportunity to learn about such a creature go unheeded."

Words stumbled in my mouth. "And you just came here all prepared to… was this just *lying around*, waiting for you to use? What the hell."

Andrews smiled slightly, and made no move to reply. Just waiting. Frustration and helplessness rose and choked me. I tore my eyes away and stared at the wall, struggling to think of a way out of this. To just *think*. But the choice was obvious: I wouldn't do anything to hurt Tiff's future, so I gave myself the space of a few heartbeats to scream silently in my head.

"What exactly is it you're looking for me to do." At least I sounded calm.

"We would like you to earn his trust, and then learn about him and his movements. There will be an initial stage, to allow you time to bond. Then we'd like to see if you can gather specific information."

I need to hide as much real information on him as I can. The thought came loud, clear, and shocked my brain back on. Just because choices were taken away from me *yet again* didn't mean I had to roll over and die. They thought they had me; they thought they had me backed into a corner.

I'd been wiggling my way out of tight spaces that didn't fit me since I'd been born.

I kept my voice subdued. "And what is it you really want to know?"

"Unfortunately, we are in the dark about much regarding that family. You will help us fill those gaps in information to find a way to exert control of their movements and capabilities."

They wanted to *control* him. They wanted to control Daimyn, like he was some sort of—of—

"I understand this seems harsh, Ms. Leynthall, and heavy handed. But willingly or not, you will be helping us make this planet a safer place for everyone."

It probably wasn't a good idea to meet Andrews' eyes. But I couldn't stop from meeting his gaze and promising, silently, they all would pay for this.

~ PART TWO ~

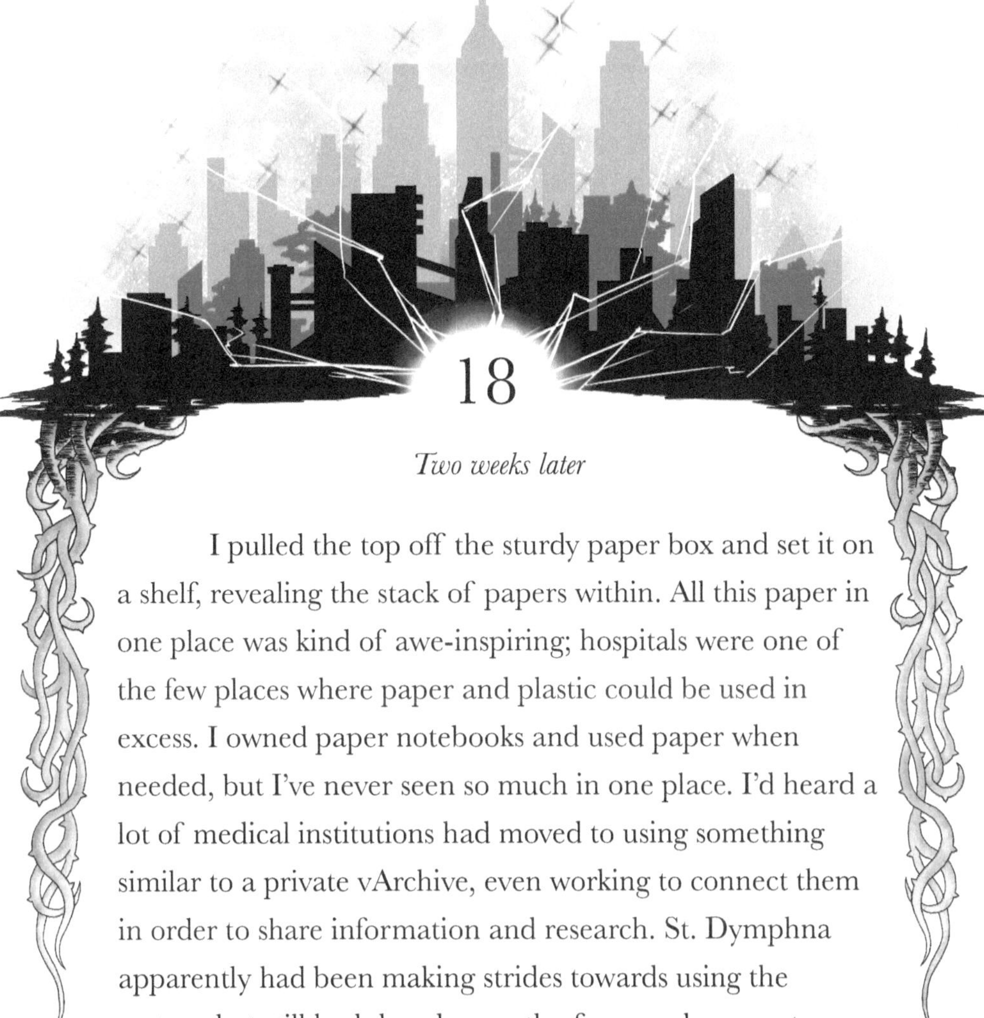

18

Two weeks later

I pulled the top off the sturdy paper box and set it on a shelf, revealing the stack of papers within. All this paper in one place was kind of awe-inspiring; hospitals were one of the few places where paper and plastic could be used in excess. I owned paper notebooks and used paper when needed, but I've never seen so much in one place. I'd heard a lot of medical institutions had moved to using something similar to a private vArchive, even working to connect them in order to share information and research. St. Dymphna apparently had been making strides towards using the system, but still had decades worth of paper documents.

The top sheet of paper looked like a copy of a prescription for medication. For a *Louise Harold.* Paper in hand, I started down the long row of shelves until I reached the 'H's, pulled out the correct bin, and flipped through the files until I found them. Slipping the paper into her file, I returned the file to the bin, and put it back in its spot on the shelf.

My internship at St. Dymphna's Psychiatric Hospital had started a week and a half ago. Decker originally wanted to utilize me in a way more suited to my name: publicity and fundraising. I'd told him that I wanted a true taste of what it was like to be here, and to put me to work where needed. I did it mostly because A) I sucked at publicity and fundraising, and B) I needed to actually be on the ground in order to find the location of the people "suffering from hallucinations."

Decker had taken my request as a challenge. I'd assisted the nurses one day, helped teach a class for another, and now sorted documents into patient files (after a very rigorous and intense confidentiality discussion). St. Dymphna was meticulous about their details, and generated a document for everything.

This morning, I'd been delighted by the idea of sorting through their information. It meant me, by myself in a dimly lit room, left alone with what I could put together. Unfortunately, I barely understood what I was reading. They had a complicated coding shorthand that baffled me, and used metaphors and numbers like they'd created their own language. I knew confidentiality was important, and this was all very clever… it also selfishly made it very difficult to do anything.

I stifled a yawn, and took a second to rub my eyes before scanning the next paper.

… Patient Daniel Nicholson given CRF for panic episodes…

I sorted that document, then had to double check I did it correctly when I immediately forgot what I'd just done.

… Patient Renni Andreź given X5234 for Nightmare-caused PTSD…

I stopped. Nightmares? With a capital N? It had to be another one of their metaphors. But it got my attention. I fast-walked to the 'A' bins and found the correct patient file. Then hesitated, glancing towards the door of their filing room to double check I was alone.

According to her file, Andreź entered the hospital two months ago, directly admitted into 'ThFl R Ward.' Which I guessed meant

Third Floor Right Ward. During my initial tour, they'd labeled the different levels and areas of the place with boring obvious names. Each ward was a small community, set up as a home with privacy, living spaces, etc.

I wasn't sure what this gave me. I placed the new document in the file, and returned back to my bin. I got through several more patients before I saw it again.

… Patient Briar Harvey given X5234 for Nightmare-caused PTSD…

I nearly ran to the 'H's bin. Briar Harvey, also admitted to 'ThFl R Ward,' about four weeks ago. I exhaled silently.

Next to Ms. Briar's file was another Harvey, a 'Felicity Harvey.' And it turned out, flipping through her information, that they were admitted at the same time, to the same ward, with the same shorthand notations I couldn't decode as their admittance reason. They had to be related maybe or—

The girls. The ones I'd read about weeks ago. This was them. Chills spread down my spine. Did I have a clue? *Finally?*

ThFl R Ward.

Third Floor Right Ward. Those with "Nightmares" appeared to be there. I took a deep breath, shutting my eyes. I finally had my next step.

Hours later, I blinked dry eyes and tried to pay attention to Ms. Clara Sylvan. The golden lighting of the dinner hall gleamed against platters and utensils and glasses, little distractions making it even more difficult to concentrate. Seated on the other side of Ms. Sylvan, Tiff did a much better job of… well, being awake. I was very glad Tiff had been invited to this dinner with the Sylvans for more than one reason. My brain felt like sludge.

My father and Mr. Sylvan were next-closest to me, deep in discussion about the reports of coral growth just off the coast of Farfalla. Mr. Sylvan was apparently an amateur oceanic scientist deeply invested in the revitalization of the coral ecosystem along the coastline. Care-taking the ocean ecosystem was one of the main missions of the Farfallan Labs up to the North. Coral colonies and marine life still recovered from the ocean toxicity during the Collapse, and according to the snippets I overheard, this was made worse by some sort of cataclysmic event during the middle ages that had damaged the ocean floor and caused issues even today.

My mother and Mrs. Sylvan were discussing the winter-controlled burns. It was one of the measures to prevent wildfires, control invasive species and pests, and promote forest and wildlife growth. Apparently, in Farfalla, all of this was kicked off by a conference highlighting the health of the land and forests in and around the city. Part fundraiser, part party, part debate, it would set fire-breaks and water-breaks, determine what land would be used for what environmental service, pinpoint special-needs areas (such as soil erosion), establish guidelines for agricultural land for that year, and many, many other things. This was all accomplished democratically. My mother remained riveted to Mrs. Sylvan's gossipy insider details.

Tiff, Clara, and I had been dutifully discussing the winterizing changes in the city. Then we'd somehow gotten onto the subject of inner-city transportation, then horses, the lamenting lack of horse racing in Farfalla, and now Spanish horse bloodlines. Tiff thankfully carried a lot of the conversation.

"Oh!" Ms. Clara Sylvan suddenly blurted. "I cannot believe I haven't brought it up before: how much do you know about the Yillen family's Arabians?"

My stomach flipped at the reminder. I muscled the reaction off my face. Tiff lifted one eyebrow at me; damn it, she'd seen it.

"Only the basics," I responded, because Ms. Clara looked at me for an answer.

"Oh, they are *exquisite*. We should seek an invitation to go see them together!" Clara smiled widely, eyes shining, and I tried to be annoyed with her. Her happiness was just so sodding genuine.

"Ah, yes, that would be delightful," I responded by rote. Inwardly, I cringed. *Do not do it, Fairian. Do not touch this with a ten foot pole. You will not be a bloody TASA pawn.*

"The horses have such care, and so much land to roam," Clara continued. "They are so kind to them—Mr. Daimyn says that is why they are so gentle. But they have so much spirit, as well! I do not know how they do it…"

"So you and Mr. Daimyn are close," Tiff said, leaning forward and giving me a look. "To have spoken with him thus about his horses."

I ignored her. Now, more than ever, I could not entertain Tiff's matchmaking attempt.

"Oh, I wouldn't say that. They are just very kind." She grinned, even her attempt at mischief sickeningly sweet. "I suppose they are not unlike their horses: gentle, but with such spirit."

I managed to stop myself from snorting.

"Oh, and their estate is very interesting, too. It was built several centuries ago by the first Yillen, and apparently it fell out of the family's hands for centuries. They only recently acquired it back."

Interesting. Maybe that was why their family had only been in Farfalla for five years? They had a habit of moving around according to the vArchive—

Stop it.

"What about their mother?" Tiff asked.

"Oh," Clara said softly. "Ariana Yillen passed away a long time ago. The Yillen family has been without a female complement for a while."

I knew that, but I didn't know why, and my mouth did things without my consent: "That's right, I heard she was gone."

I'm just learning information that everyone else knows… this isn't a betrayal of anybody.

Clara's voice lowered. "Oh, yes. Poor Ariana—and those poor boys!"

Tiff and I both leaned in close, and Clara rightly took that as a sign to continue.

"It was almost two decades ago, when Mr. Daimyn and Regan were young. A group of thieves broke into the house when Ariana was there alone." Her voice dropped even lower. "She tried to stop them and they… *killed* her."

Tiff made a sympathetic murmur, her hand lightly covering her mouth. Clara blinked rapidly, her big eyes shining. I inwardly sighed, because those weren't crocodile tears.

"That's awful," I said quietly. *Thieves killed Ariana Yillen? Or something else?*

Maybe that was part of the reason Daimyn was so obsessed with safety.

"Oh, gossiping about murder, our daughters *do* know how to have a conversation!" Mrs. Sylvan's voice nearly made me jump.

"I apologize, mother, that was a morbid topic of discussion," Ms. Clara said softly.

I scowled, unable to keep my face muscles under control. My mother's eyes flashed in warning.

"Those Yillen brothers, though…" Mrs. Sylvan said. "So very handsome, and such manners."

"Oh?" my mother queried.

"Though I am quite put out that they make no advances in finding wives. They're both of age to do so, but their father seems to take no interest in securing the next generation. And with an absent mother, well."

Mrs. Sylvan glanced at Clara, and I wondered if she'd tried to proposition one or both with Clara's hand at some point.

"Perhaps they are bachelors at heart," Ms. Clara said.

Or big secrets at heart.

"It is not good for a man to be without a wife," Mrs. Sylvan said. She glanced at her husband, who was busy discussing the finer points of… ocean salt content? "It would be awfully lonely, and with such an estate, they would benefit from a good wife managing affairs."

I wondered if I should point out that 'insistent bachelor' usually meant gay, and maybe they weren't interested in women. Or maybe they plain didn't want partners. I certainly didn't want to get married.

By the time I managed to drag my mind back to the present, they'd moved on in the conversation.

"Oh yes, we promised Clara a gelding when her riding improves," Mrs. Sylvan was saying. "She needs practice."

Ms. Clara smiled bashfully.

"Oh, but my Fairian is a beautiful rider," my mother said. "They could ride together!"

Mrs. Sylvan looked delighted. "We could take you to some of our favorite riding trails before the weather turns!"

My mother turned towards me expectantly. Clara straightened, eyes big and excited.

"I would love to, mother, but you forget: I have tutoring on the weekend." With my time being split between school, martial arts, interning at St. Dymphna's, and other 'appropriate' duties my mother was handing out, Tutor was quite miffed at his lack of time. He'd spoken with my parents, and now the wanker took up time on my weekends.

My mother must be excited about developing a relationship with Ms. Clara if she forgot that. It gave me a little pleasure to ruin her friendship matchmaking plans with another of her schemes.

"She's such a studious young lady," my mother said offhand to Mrs. Sylvan. "Darling, I think you can skip tutoring once in a while! With your marks coming back so nicely, you deserve a day off." She smiled at me, the message behind this clear.

I smiled back blandly. "That sounds great, mother."

Clara clasped her hands in excitement next to me. "Oh, Ms. Fairian! This is so exciting. It will be so much fun!"

So I got time off for appropriate activities when I played nice. Great.

Tiff accompanied me back up to my room after the Sylvans departed.

"Well, I think that went splendidly," I said. Was I slurring? I think I slurred there. My vision also blurred a bit. And I really didn't know if the evening went splendidly, because I couldn't really remember the last part of it.

"Fair-Fair, when was the last time you slept?"

"I slept last night," I muttered. For about 2 hours, when the sunrise forced me back inside before anyone discovered I'd snuck out to pace the streets of Farfalla until my brain finally shut up. *How can I sleep when every minute of my day is so structured I can't breathe, when even my free time is restricted to a list of acceptable places? How can I possibly sleep when I can feel the clock ticking, a fist in my gut twisting tighter and tighter? How can I possibly sleep when something is wrong, and more and more I think it's just all in my head?*

"You look awful," Tiff said.

I snorted, pushed open the door to my room, and dropped face-first into bed. My brain spun around my skull until it bruised.

Tiff tugged at my dress. I groaned and got up to help her out of her corset, too. I stumbled and almost ate the floor trying to get into my bed clothes. Tiff stared at me like I was an alien, then pushed me onto the bed and yanked the covers over me.

"I don't know what's up with you, but you need to sleep."

"Yes, mother."

Tiff flicked me on the nose. I grumbled at her, but she already shut off the lights and closed the door as she exited my room. My eyelids grew heavier, a blissful dark seeping into my head and slowing my thoughts. *Oh, maybe I can sleep tonight.*

Out of the corner of my eye, a small light flashed. My PCD sat there on my nightstand, blinking with a new message. Blearily, I reached out and flicked on the screen to read it.

From *[User Named]* "Terra Arcana Scheming Arsewipes": *Report*

My stomach lurched. After a beat, I slid it closer and my numb fingers typed: *No interactions.*

Instead of chucking my PCD into the wall like I wanted, I tossed it in a drawer, curled up under the covers, and stared out my window. Darkness enveloped the world, and the sky hung like a curtain of gemstones, and… my mind stretched thin, winding up and down, up and down. Frantically chattering nonsense sounds. Going absolutely nowhere.

Daimyn had followed through on his promise not to help, and disappeared like smoke. I'd predicted this weeks ago, I couldn't be surprised. Hell, maybe he even knew about the blackmail.

My eyes prickled.

Take that, TASA. You bet on the wrong horse.

I pinched myself until my eyes stopped stinging. It was actually a good thing he'd disappeared. If Daimyn wasn't around, Andrews' blackmail meant bugger-all. All of my ridiculous emotions stemmed from sleep deprivation. It would be better tomorrow.

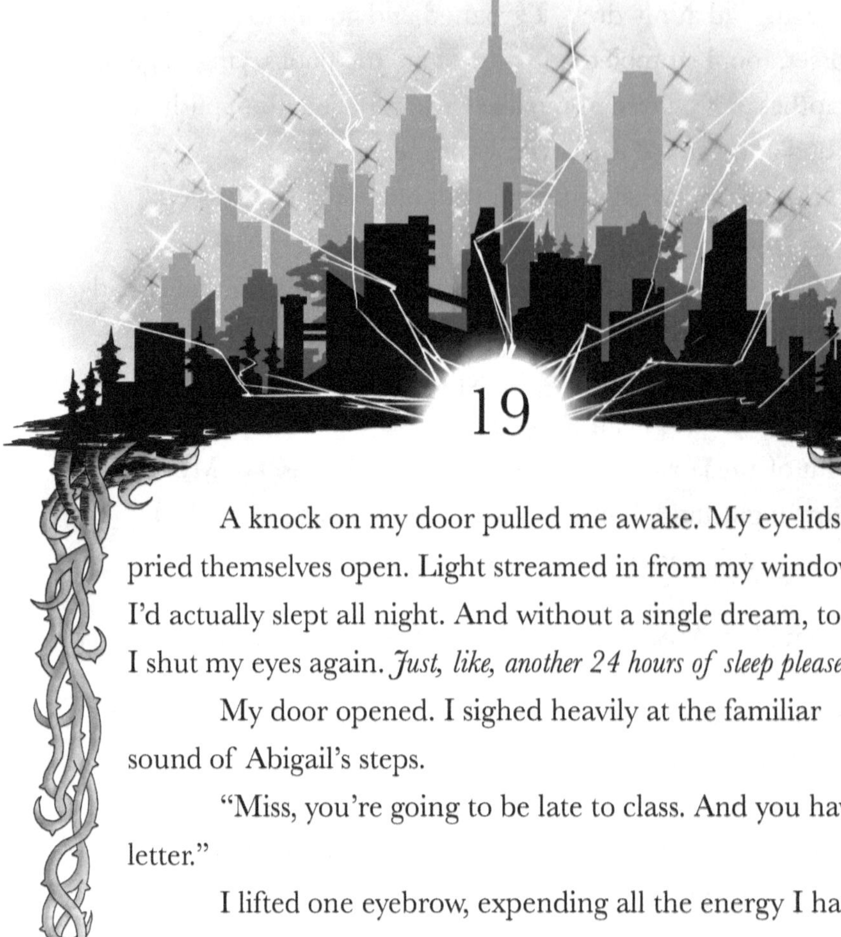

19

A knock on my door pulled me awake. My eyelids
pried themselves open. Light streamed in from my window;
I'd actually slept all night. And without a single dream, too.
I shut my eyes again. *Just, like, another 24 hours of sleep please…*

My door opened. I sighed heavily at the familiar
sound of Abigail's steps.

"Miss, you're going to be late to class. And you have a
letter."

I lifted one eyebrow, expending all the energy I had
for lifting anything. "Who's it from?"

"The Society of Libraries."

It took two seconds for that to register. I lunged
upright. "I'll take that please."

She handed the letter to me with raised eyebrows. "I'll
help with your outfit. Ms. Collins has already breakfasted and
is ready to go."

Ignoring her, I tore the letter from the envelope and
read feverishly. Once I finally managed to comprehend what
was in front me, my face split into a grin. My Exclusive
Section permissions were here.

Okay, so they weren't *my* permissions per se. Years ago I'd met Sir Lightly, a very kind old man with a giant private library. I'd made contact with him in the beginning days of my research, expressing an interest in his collection after hearing rumor of its extensiveness. He'd granted access, but he hadn't exactly left me alone while I perused. He became my personal shadow as I read. I think I brought out his protect-and-educate old man instincts.

While at first very annoying, I grew fond of him. After closeness brought about part of a confession, he'd added me to his library Exclusive Section credentials as a "research assistant." He didn't know the depths of my interests of course, but he liked my ferocious curiosity, and shared views that everything in a library should be open to everyone.

There had been a lot of paperwork to get his credentials transferred to Farfalla and assign myself a delegate for his research affairs here. But it had worked. A shiny new pass allowing me into Farfalla's Exclusive Section rested in my hand. Now, I could look into magic and the Divide and whatever else my heart desired.

After arriving on campus, I made like I headed towards my first class—and at the last minute turned and marched off FCA grounds. The library pass burned a hole in my pocket and my brain sparked with possibility. Tiff would be miffed when she found out, but I wanted to check out the ES alone first. I'd been able to sneak her into the ES in Northampton before, but I didn't know how Farfalla's library worked yet, and I needed to scope out the obviousness of magical information before deciding to bring her. Tiff would probably freak out more than my parents if she saw my real research goals.

The air felt brisk, fortifying. After only a few minutes of walking, I darted up the front steps of the library, showed my Simple pass to the guards at the front doors, and headed directly to the security area leading to the Exclusive Section.

The two minders of the door looked up as I approached: a pale 20-something person with curly black hair (and no obviously presented gender), and a middle-aged masculine-presenting person with russet skin and an impeccably groomed beard. They stood behind a tall desk with two giant computers, and the heavy, ornate door to research heaven lay behind them. My mouth practically salivated.

Curly-hair turned to me expectantly. I handed them my Exclusive pass.

"Good morning!" *Yeesh, tone down the glee.* "My name is Fairian Leynthall, I've just received my Exclusive permit, transferred to Farfalla on behalf of Sir Lightly, as a research assistant."

The masc returned to studying his computer screen, reading something with a mild frown. Curly-hair scanned the pass under a small device next to the keyboard, eyes darting across the screen in front of them as they clicked through and read whatever popped up.

I forced myself to remain still instead of hopping from foot to foot.

They clicked a few more times, a furrow appearing between their eyebrows. Impatience bubbled in my stomach. I mentally tallied all my limbs to keep them still and not fidgeting too much.

"I'm sorry, but this pass has been declined." Curly-hair turned and handed the pass back to me.

"What?" I let out an awkward laugh, slowly reaching for the card. "I literally just got it in the mail this morning."

"Regardless, this access is denied."

Something swelled jittery and sharp, making it hard to breathe. "May I know the reasons for why it is denied?"

Their attention drifted back to the screen and then back to me. "It appears your… benefactor has died. And as your clearance is tied to his, yours is now revoked as well."

The world narrowed starkly. "… What?"

Their crisp expression softened. "Did you not know?"

"No, the… last time I talked to him was weeks ago." Horrifyingly, my eyes suddenly burned.

"I'm sorry," they said, looking a bit awkward. "Were you close?"

I cleared my throat. *We used to spend hours in each other's company, but I haven't talked to him in months, but he never knew the truth about me, but I didn't let him in, but he helped me so much.* "You could say that."

He'd been fine the last time I'd seen him!

"I'm sorry you had to learn this way."

I blinked rapidly, forcing my voice to remain steady. "Me too."

How would I get inside? I had to get inside. I'd been waiting for this clearance so that I could better teach myself, better prepare myself, better protect myself.

"I still want to continue his research," I said. "I have to. It was— it was important. I can't just quit."

Cooler professionalism slid over their expression. "You'll have to apply through the Library Society and gain approval through them."

That would never happen.

Move. I skittered to the left, moving before the thought turned conscious, and a pallid hand missed in its descent towards my shoulder. I spun to face a very masc-presenting person in a guard's uniform, instantly hostile. He recovered and shifted his weight like he would honest-to-god tackle me.

"Is there a problem?" he said, sounding very British.

"No, sir," Curly-hair said. "We were simply discussing the process of gaining access to the Exclusive Section."

"All of that information is available at the vArchive," he said.

His weight shifted towards me again. Heat boiled up inside of me.

"Your assistance is not needed," I said, in the coldest, most austere, British upper class voice I could muster.

"Those not entering or exiting the Exclusive Section are not permitted in this hallway," he responded promptly.

Asshole Guard there wasn't about to let me stay here. And the other two weren't about to let me in. Staying here would accomplish nothing except make me memorable and make them less inclined to even talk to me. Every cell in my body wailed in protest.

"Thank you for your help," I said calmly to Curly-hair.

Then I spun on my heel and stalked away. Attention prickled along my back, but I didn't look, didn't do anything but stare forward as I left the hallway, left the front lobby, left the whole library.

"Well I might as well just go to bloody class then," I muttered to myself. "No point in being here."

I pivoted sharply on my heel as I reached the sidewalk. My pack bounced against my hip from my brisk pace back towards campus.

Halfway down the block I realized I'd lost control over my breathing. A small street ran along the back of the library, a narrow cobblestone pathway currently deserted. I turned down it, stalked several paces, and came to an abrupt halt. For several seconds I panted.

Then it burst out of me.

"What the fuck WAS THAT?" I howled at the sky. "What WAS that! Just a big ol' *fuck you*? A 'here, let's dangle it allllll in front of you, but nope, FUCK YOU'?"

My nails bit into my palms, each of my breaths like sandpaper in my lungs. The fire in my chest sputtered, and strength left me in a rush. My chin dropped to my chest.

"You all right, spitfire?" a voice called.

I glanced over my shoulder: several meters away, a nicely dressed, femme-presenting, older person with dark hair and warm-bronze skin leaned on a beautifully carved cane, watching with some alarm.

"Yeah," I croaked. "Sorry to disturb you."

I turned and continued back to class. My eyes burned something awful. *It's just sleep deprivation making everything hard, it's just sleep deprivation.*

I messaged Tiff with a simple question: *Any good clubs open tonight?*

The next morning, I gingerly made my way down the steps, doing my utmost to not remind my stomach or head how much alcohol I'd drank last night. After letting off steam, I no longer felt like murdering something, but… *wow* too much alcohol.

I made it to Tiff's room without seeing anyone. Some anxious part of me needed to confirm she was safe and sound. I didn't remember much about us getting home, only the constant feeling of prickles up and down my neck. The alcohol haze could be to blame, but the prickles had been particularly bad last night. The disturbing part was they were so consistent now, I sometimes forgot they were there.

I needed to confirm Tiff was in her room.

No light came from under her door. I tried the handle, and then eased it open. The telltale lump under the covers shifted.

"How are you upright," the lump muttered.

My shoulders relaxed at the sound of her voice. "Need some water?"

A heavy sigh. "Please."

A few of the staff were cleaning up and preparing things in the kitchen as I walked in. I waved cheerfully, as if I didn't look haggard, finding a container closer to a pitcher in size to fill up with water.

Tiff sat up when I returned, hair going everywhere and her makeup only half cleaned off her face.

"Are you really deciding to be up at this hour?" she said groggily, after downing half the pitcher.

"I'm heading back to bed. I just wanted to check on you. And shower."

"Oh my god, shower." She face-planted in her bed. "Maybe later."

I rolled my eyes—which kind of hurt—and heaved myself to my feet. "Okay. Wellness check complete. I am sleeping the rest of the day away."

"It's Saturday, right," came her muffled voice.

"Yes dear."

She grunted. I shook my head as I opened the door and slipped out. I looked up—and my mother glided down the stairs towards me. Her frown deepened as she scanned me. "Darling, what are you doing? We need to depart for the Sylvans within the hour."

I froze. I had totally forgotten about riding with Clara. *Oh, crapsticks.*

"Ah, right. I was just on my way to get ready."

My mother's frown deepened. "What did you do to yourself? You do not look well."

Wow. Not "are you okay?" but "what did you do to yourself?"

"I have a gift for you back in your room," she said after I didn't respond.

With a deep breath for sanity, I followed her up the stairs. We'd just reached the second floor when she said stiffly: "You look like you've been on a bender."

I winced. "I'll be fine after a shower. Promise."

She didn't respond to that.

Back to my room, Abigail arranged navy blue and brown fabrics across the base of my bed. My mother turned and smiled, though it looked a tad forced.

"I bought you a new riding outfit," she said. "Ms. Sylvan is such an elegant, accomplished young lady. It would suit you to have her friendship."

My eyebrows slowly drew together, not liking the tone in her voice.

"Come, come, come!" she said. "Try it on."

I slowly undressed, really wishing I had showered before this. My mother didn't speak for a worrying long minute.

"Did you hear that Ms. Erath just returned from her ransom?" she said suddenly.

I blinked. "Oh?"

The name was vaguely familiar. I think she was a debutante back in Northampton who'd been loosely in the circle of my acquaintances. I hadn't even known she'd been taken.

"They asked for an obscene amount of money," she clucked, pulling at the buttons at the front of the outfit, nodding to herself as she looked over how it fit me. "It turns out Mrs. Erath had an unexpected business windfall they hadn't disclosed." She chuckled softly. "How they manage to know…"

Then she fell silent again. Trepidation prickled over me.

"It suits you," she finally said, guiding me to the mirror. The riding outfit hung elegantly on my frame, and fit snugly. It also *wasn't* the usual pastel color she tried to force on me. I didn't hate it, how about that.

"Did Ms. Collins accompany you in your… activities last night?"

I stilled. She had to be worried about me being alone in suspicious company. "Yes, I had a chaperone."

My mother pulled on the collar of my jacket, repositioning it along my neck. She made no comment for another long moment. "As we grow older, we tend to grow into new and different friendships. It's perfectly natural to outgrow old ones as we mature into new versions of ourselves."

I narrowed my eyes. My mother fussed with the riding jacket's collar, and then the skirts, which were shorter at my front, about mid-thigh over the dark brown breeches, but longer in the back nearly to my knees.

"I am not sure young Tiffany is the best influence for you."

"For doing what exactly?"

"The gossip papers have pictures of you both again," she said tersely.

I waved her words away. "That's just because someone is bored and doesn't know what to write about. I'm an easy target." She already knew this.

Her mouth firmed. "You have taken to wearing those terrible clothes, which I know you learned from her. You're even mimicking her behaviors. I am trying to establish friendships in this community for both of us, but you make it incredibly difficult when you act like this. I was happy to take in the Collins family, and her mother is a gem. But Tiffany is not entitled to the treatment we give her if her influence on you is unacceptable."

"*What?*"

My mother's gaze met mine calmly, but steeled now. My heart pounded like a war drum.

"Be clear, mother. What are you saying?"

She lifted her chin. "I am saying that I've allowed certain behaviors, but that time has come to an end. If Tiffany continues to be a negative influence, I will separate you. For your benefit."

I snorted, exuding skepticism by force of habit. "How would you even do that? Assign a guard to make sure we don't get within touching distance?"

"Tiffany is not *entitled* to the gifts we give her. She doesn't have to live here."

Unsteady heat rose in my gut. *Calm. Be calm.* "Mrs. Collins' work here is contingent on Tiff's place in our household."

"We can find another cook," my mother said, disparagement coloring her tone.

I curled my fingers into my palm to keep them steady. I wasn't completely daft. I understood what she was saying. "So what kinds of behavior will provoke this response? Any clubbing, of course, you've made that perfectly clear. If I speak out of turn, will that be Tiffany's bad influence? If I don't obey every level of etiquette, will that be because of Tiffany's *horrible* influence? One wrong step, and you'll kick them out?"

I nearly shouted by the end.

"You make it sound so cruel. They're employees, Fairian. With excellent benefits. But they're not *entitled*."

She sounded so bloody *calm*. How could she use this as a threat when she *knew* the reality of impoverishment, the need to claw a way into a better life? And now she wanted to deny the Collins' a chance because of *me*?

"Tiffany is the reason I do well in school at all, mother." I fought to make my voice audible, or not to scream, I couldn't tell. "She urges me to keep up my grades, to act a lady, to be rebellious in a way that doesn't harm myself. She's done more than you or your *bloody tutors* ever will." I sucked in air, running out of oxygen.

I faced towards the mirror, refusing to look at her. My too-pale face stared back at me, hectic flushed spots on my cheeks. "I don't know yet what exactly I'll do if you throw Tiff and her mother out, but it won't be pretty."

"There's no need for such dramatics," she said with a sigh.

Of course she was calm. My threats didn't mean anything. If I had to throw a fit, it wouldn't change the fact my mother had kicked them out. She wouldn't reverse her position because I acted worse. My actions wouldn't matter then. They mattered now.

God, I need to sleep. My mother had put Tiffany's future in my hands. And that was more effective than anything else she could have done.

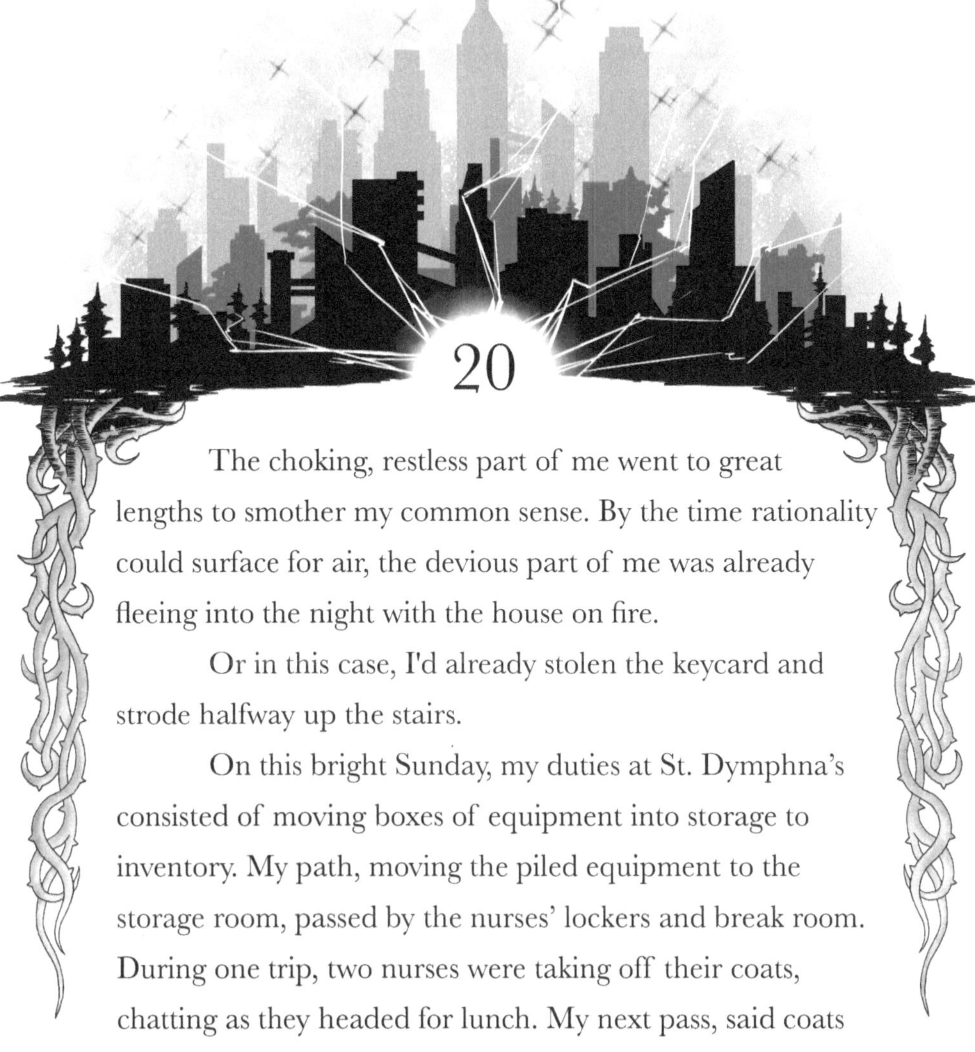

20

The choking, restless part of me went to great lengths to smother my common sense. By the time rationality could surface for air, the devious part of me was already fleeing into the night with the house on fire.

Or in this case, I'd already stolen the keycard and strode halfway up the stairs.

On this bright Sunday, my duties at St. Dymphna's consisted of moving boxes of equipment into storage to inventory. My path, moving the piled equipment to the storage room, passed by the nurses' lockers and break room. During one trip, two nurses were taking off their coats, chatting as they headed for lunch. My next pass, said coats were hung up on hooks next to their lockers, the two nurses gone.

A keycard dangled out of one of the pockets.

In order to get into the ward housing those with "Nightmares," I expected I'd need one of those keycards, like the other secured wards on that floor. I made two more passes as that keycard seemed to gather all the gravity in a square kilometer. Then, without my permission, my feet veered into the break room. I was alone. I had the keycard in my hand and fled out the door.

Nerves ate through my stomach. I should be waiting to figure out a safer way to scope around. Gather more information before taking the leap. To start with, I had no idea how long they'd be out for lunch.

Still time to sneak back down and replace the keycard…

I headed towards the third floor, the stolen badge hooked to my waist but face-down, so the picture wasn't visible.

What am I doing. My own voice in my own head even sounded exasperated with me.

Another nurse came down the stairs, making my heart jackhammer. I threw on an easy smile, meeting her gaze firmly for a second before looking away. She blinked at me once but smiled in return, her eyes flicking briefly to the badge at my waist.

What if someone got close enough to read it? What the hell was I doing?

Escalating my quest, that's what I was doing. It had nothing to do with sleep deprivation making me irrational. Asking the staff here about the people mentioned in the papers hadn't led anywhere. My subtle prodding had made one nurse tight-lipped already. I'd had to back off that tactic immediately. What else could I do?

I made it to the third floor, and my hand froze on the door handle out of the stairs.

I am so getting fired.

Not that they paid me in the first place. Ahhh, the privilege of wealth: the ability to donate time without getting compensated for it.

I had to make this count. I doubted I'd get out of this with my internship intact, so this would be my only chance. I had to find those people who'd come here claiming their nightmares came to life.

With a deep breath and a faint smile just in case, I opened the door and eased through it, keeping mostly hidden in the alcove that housed the stairway door.

To the right, down the hall, a nurse's station oversaw the floor. To the left, another hallway, and lots of rooms. I needed to go past the nurse's station to get to the door leading into the ward on the right. I bit my lip. There were two nurses there now, looking to be sorting through papers of some sort. Bits of their conversation filtered down the hall towards me.

Could I make a distraction? Ask one of the patients to make a ruckus? Charm my way past them?

I made a face. Then peered around the corner to get another idea of the layout.

Oh. Both nurses were walking away now, still in conversation. The area was clear. *Shite.* I strode out into the hallway, walking on my toes so my steps were quiet, keeping my eyes unfocused and the nurses in my periphery. My heart beat hard in my throat, nerves burrowing into my stomach-lining.

I am so getting caught.

I turned the corner and headed towards *ThFl R Ward.* There was another short hallway before a single door. I sped towards it, snatching the keycard up from my waist and praying fervently this worked.

And there was no keypad.

Son of a—how did this door open? This would all be for nothing. Could I sneak back downstairs without being seen? I reached out anyway, grasping the handle with frustration. I pushed uselessly on—

The door came open.

Ohmygod.

There's no way it's this easy.

I thrust the door open the whole way, cringing as it hit me there might be an alarm. No alarm sounded. I peered into the room and saw a short hallway, soft warm lighting, but no people. I slipped through the door, glancing behind to make sure no one had caught me entering. It closed with a soft *sssnik*. My heart thudded in my ears for several beats. No voices. I breathed out softly.

The short hall stretched out before expanding into a larger room that disappeared out of view. I crept forward. Nice lounges peaked around the edge of what I could see. A bookshelf lined one of the walls and a softly glowing lamp sat on top of a warm wooden table.

The usual hospital layout had been gutted, turned into a larger living space. I'd seen other wards that looked like this too. Closed doors lined the hall farther down. The door closest to me was open, the tinkling of water and the rattle of… someone was washing dishes.

I stepped forward, and an older femme in a recliner came into view on my right. She looked up from a book, eyes widening as she froze.

"Jared," she said sharply.

I cringed. Before I could even think of what to say, the rattle from the other room ceased, and an older masc with deep bronze skin strode in, wearing nice slacks and a button down, sleeves rolled up to his elbows as he dried his hands on a towel. His movements slowed as he saw me.

"H-hello…" I said.

"And you are?" he asked, and I wondered about his occupation, because I instantly got the impression I wasted his time and he was already bored.

"My name is Fairian—I came here to speak to you…" I trailed as another figure entered the room behind him. A chestnut-haired younger femme in soft, loose clothing. That made three. The older woman sitting in the chair tried to surreptitiously reach under a table, moving too slowly for it to be any good.

"Please don't," I said, shifting backwards with my hands out. "I promise, I mean you no harm—of any kind."

"Then why are you here?" the man asked.

A door clicked open down the hall, beyond the living-room-looking-area. Two heads peaked out, wary expressions on young faces. They had to be the Harvey girls. I lifted a hand and gave them a small wave, trying to seem unthreatening.

"I'm looking for information," I said, addressing the older woman. "I'm afraid—I'm afraid that what happened to you is connected to what happened to me. And my sister."

I managed to get the words out smoothly, right before my throat clamped down viciously. Surreality overwhelmed me for a second. The man and the woman with the towel shifted their weight, glancing at each other. The edge in the room softened. Just a little.

"And what is it you think happened to us?" Bored-man said.

I fought not to fidget. I needed to give as much detail as I could, but I also didn't know if *his* tactics had changed or what his bloody motivation even was, then or now.

"I don't know how things might have changed—what happened to me was seven years ago." The words had to be forced out this time.

His eyebrows drew together.

"You were kidnapped, or maybe it happened to you at home, I don't know. But you saw things. Things that weren't real, but were— they were far from hallucinations, but everyone c-calls them that. You might have been… hurt. A lot." I swallowed. "Things chasing you, just to make you afraid."

I studied their faces, trying to catch recognition or anything that told me I was on the right track.

"Were you in Farfalla? This thing that happened to you, seven years ago," the man said.

I blinked. "No, Northampton."

The man nodded brusquely. "Then we can't help you."

"What? No—please." I took a steadying breath. "Did he take you? Was there someone—someone not quite *human*—"

"Ms. Fairian," the man said, his tone broaching no argument. "I am sincerely sorry for whatever happened to you and your sister. But I can promise you it's not the same."

"How? How do you know—"

"Now you need to leave."

My throat locked down, and something pitiful trembled in my gut. I had no right to push. I had promised myself I would not hurt or upset anyone.

"All right," I said, fighting my voice calm. "Thank you for your time. If you change your mind later and feel up to talking—I would appreciate any assistance you can provide—you can find my PCD number in vArchive. Fairian Leynthall."

No one said a word. Just stared with stoic, wary expressions.

Not knowing what else to do, I edged backwards and exited the strange living space hospital ward, back out into the main hospital hallway. The light blinded out here after being in the warmly-lit room.

"Ms. Fairian?"

Hope soared. But the voice hadn't come from behind me. It was Dr. Decker, standing beside the nurse's station only a few meters away, staring at me with increasing alarm.

Ah, crapsticks.

Dr. Decker paced in front of me as I sat on the small couch in his office.

"I cannot fathom how you would get the impression it would be acceptable to wander around this facility unaccompanied, or risk the health and stability of everyone around you. I told you from the very beginning, the safety and comfort of the tenants are my number one concern—and you violated the trust of everyone here."

Decker wasn't wrong, which made it worse. Our driver headed this way to pick me up, which is why I had to sit here and listen to him. I stared at the tile of the floor. I really just wanted to walk or take the light rail home, but Decker insisted I wait and so far hadn't let me out of his eyesight.

"I apologize, again, for violating their sense of safety," I said quietly. I'd been apologizing for about half an hour now.

"I still don't understand *why*," he said, almost like he wasn't speaking to me.

I swallowed. Decker understood something about having a mission in life. I had no doubt I'd never be allowed back, but maybe there was a scrap to be saved. Maybe I could prevent this from utterly blowing up in my face. Everything seemed a little fuzzy, distant; I couldn't quite get my head around the dread of what consequences this would have.

And all for nothing.

"Do you really want to know?"

Decker looked at me, anger thinly coated in exasperation. "Yes, that would be greatly appreciated."

Surreality rose as my lips parted, disbelief nearly choking me as I inhaled to speak. *This? Here? Now? Why would I talk about it now, when I've been silent for so long?*

A great distance swelled as I felt my lips move and heard the words. "Do you know I had a sister?"

His brow slowly furrowed. "I did not."

"She was taken. Killed." The simple statement felt wrong, not enough and too much. "The people inside that room… I thought… I thought they were hurt by the same person who hurt her." *I thought…* "I had to know. If it was h-him."

The stutter of my voice seemed to jerk me halfway back inside my body.

"That does not excuse your behavior," Decker finally said quietly after a silence had filled the room.

I swallowed, my lips tingling like blood flow returned to them. "I know. But I had to be sure."

Decker stilled for a beat, arms braced across his chest. Then he gestured sharply with one hand. "And you decided that… coming here under false pretenses was better than being direct."

"And how would that conversation have gone? 'Hello, Director Decker, I'm here to ask about *magic*?'"

Catharsis rushed at saying the word out loud. He flinched.

Yeah, I thought so.

My eyes roamed the room without really seeing, struggling to put together a connection he could relate to and understand. "You built this place… you built it when no one believed a place like this could exist, that it was ill-conceived or at very least a fantasy. You must understand what it is to fight for something that doesn't make sense to the rest of the world, a nebulous idea that isn't quite fully formed." I swallowed, and my voice came out hard: "I have to know if my sister's killer is here."

Decker stared hard at the wall above my head. A muscle twitched in his jaw, but I couldn't read anything else. I was afraid if I kept talking I'd only make it worse. *This would be a great time for some Feelings to pop up and hint at what he's thinking.*

A knock sounded on the door, and one of the nurses stuck his head in.

"Mrs. Leynthall is here, sir."

My stomach seized. My mother had come? I'd sent a message directly to Renald for only him to come. I needed space for damage control, away from whatever Decker would say. She'd said she was busy today. If she was here, she'd find out what I'd done.

Reality rushed in an almost audible pop.

Oh god. Her warning about my behavior and Tiff.

Dr. Decker studied me. As soon as I met his eyes, he rose and headed for the door. Legs like lead weight, I followed him out of the small office. The hallway stretched long to the front entrance, every step constricting my chest. My mother rose to her feet as she caught sight of us.

"Darling—Director Decker—is everything all right? I was concerned when I saw the message."

Oh god, this would land on Tiff. It would be all my fault. It would be all my fault *again*. My heart battered in my chest like a bird in a cage.

"Mrs. Leynthall… I apologize for the alarm." Next to me, Decker let out a slow exhale. "We've had a tragedy in the hospital. I cannot go into details, but the intern program has been suspended until further notice. I am sorry to lose your daughter's assistance, her intelligence and passion does her service."

I swallowed convulsively, staring at the ground.

"I do hope this won't impact the relationship with your lovely family," he continued.

"Oh, of course not," my mother rushed to reassure. "I do hope everything is all right."

"It's a disappointing development… but some things are what they are."

I winced. He managed to make me feel even worse, even as I nearly swayed with heady relief.

"Now, do you need anything before you're on your way?"

"Oh, no, we'll get out of your hair. I know my daughter will be sad not to return. She's always looking forward to her time here."

My mother hesitated briefly, then offered her hand to Decker. He shook it firmly, and then started us towards the front doors. My legs wobbled underneath me. The bomb would drop here at some point, right?

"Goodbye, Mrs. Leynthall, Ms. Fairian," Decker said, at the top step.

My mother dipped in a small curtsy, and started towards the car.

I hesitated at the top step. "For what it's worth, I do admire what you've built here."

Decker looked at me with flat eyes. I winced. Yeah, time to go.

"Did you find it?"

About to take a step, I almost fell over as I abruptly aborted the movement. "What? Find what?"

"What you were looking for."

No.

My stomach knotted at the instinctive response, even as my mind spun rationalizations on why this didn't mean a dead-end. "I found… something."

I'd found just more questions.

21

A change rolled towards me. I could feel the shift, the end of something, like a gathering storm cloud. Despite Director Decker saving face in front of my mother, my parents eyes lingered too long, their conversations a little too pointed. Tiff's future had been thrust in my hands. And I had absolutely no evidence my sister's killer was actually here. A horrible realization dawned, but I couldn't think about it. I couldn't think about it, because sleep deprivation made it a black hole to even go there.

I was so tired.

So tired of fighting for every little thing. Something had to give, and maybe it meant my surrender, but at least it was for the right reasons. I had a boundary—*don't do anything to harm Tiff's future*—and I could understand that. My mother wanted good behavior. So that's what I had to work with.

Tuesday morning, three days after my mother and my conversation about Tiff, I made my first move.

"I will spend an extra hour every day with Mr. Fredrickson if I'm allowed to spend Saturdays in the library," I tossed at my mother over breakfast.

My father had already left for an early meeting of some sort. My mother looked up, eyes locking with mine. Maybe I'd pushed too soon.

"My marks have been returning excellent," I said calmly, for once thankful about that. "And I have no plans to change that."

She spooned more warm cereal into her bowl. I let the seconds tick by in silence, instinct demanding I keep still as I waited for her response.

"And what happens if you are not on your best behavior?"

It took a second to force the words out. "Then I lose my library privileges. For a time you determine fit." *Because I exist as a child in this place…*

Another long silence pervaded the room as she prepared her cereal with milk and some sugar. "We will have a trial period to see if we can make this work."

My heart leapt. "Is that a yes?"

She held my eyes for a beat longer, then nodded. Good god, had that worked?

My second move came that evening: actually get sleep. I tried. I really, really tried. The clock ticked softly across the room, darkness blanketing my room. Exhaustion ached in all my joints, my eyes bruised in their sockets.

The back of my neck prickled. And again. I fisted my blankets and wanted to do violence. Was it getting worse? It seemed worse tonight. The sensation ebbed and flowed, but never stopped.

It wasn't real. It wasn't *real*. It *wasn't* real.

I'm never going to be able to sleep unless I figure out what this IS.

I flung my blankets off. Disregarding a corset or anything restrictive, I dressed in a dark tunic and breeches, strapped on my knives, and slipped out the window minutes later.

The back of my neck practically buzzed in alarm. *What is this, goddamn it?*

Once I escaped Leynthall grounds, I headed to the water. I walked along the edge, looking for movement under the surface. I moved through the darkest shadows in alleyways, with nothing but my breathing as a companion. I crunched through the dried underbrush of trees in the green areas, listening.

The night greeted me, pleasant and quiet. Except for the prickling turning to chills down my spine. Something was happening. Nothing was happening, but something was happening, and I would start screaming any second now and never stop.

This must be what losing your mind feels like.

Out of ideas, I meandered, my path turning aimless, mind numb as I trudged forward because I didn't know what else to *do*. I found myself over one of Farfalla's larger bridges, its gleaming steel a testament to industrial times. The water churned in a dark maw below me, the bridge supports cutting the water's path and sending synchronized Vs surging into each other. It was hypnotic.

God I need sleep.

Another prickling surge; I ignored it. Then another—that pulled my scalp taut and stole my breath, shuddering into my gut. I lifted my head and slowly turned. Cold sweat rushed down my body; mechanical, outside my control, and coming from absolutely nowhere.

"Come out, come out, wherever you are," I whispered.

I scanned the dark, trying to see *anything* that would explain the shivers racing up my spine.

Movement. My breath sucked in. Across the bridge, on the opposite side from me. My spine sagged in relief as every part of me understood: *there it is.*

A bulk of muscle and sinew, something *wrong*. Finally, finally, finally something actually *here*. My relief lasted about the length of a heartbeat. Because whatever approached was not alive, yet hunted. I knew it instantly and instinctively. It vaguely resembled a huge dog, but no kind of dog I had ever seen. Almost the size of a pony, it's flesh hung almost melted and grey. It's feet were long, talons curving over top of nails, it's joints overextended so it was hunched close to the ground. It's head was huge, broad, too big for it's body, with a muzzle taking up most of its face while ridiculously huge fangs dripped saliva onto the ground. Where eyes should have been, there were only sockets.

It picked speed to a trot, aimed right at me. I stopped breathing. It started to lope. I stumbled back two steps, and it burst into a run.

Well. I wanted something real!

I bolted the opposite direction. Each second slowed to a crawl of flinching anticipation. My breathing drowned out my ability to hear how far away it was, how much ground it gained. Prickles radiated down my back in waves. My legs already burned as I hit the slope where the bridge met the street, my breaths coming as gasps. I could hear it now, claws clicking and the thud of weight hitting ground. I chanced a glance behind me—

It was barely a meter away. I twisted around a corner of a building, trying to put something between me and *whatever the hell that was*. I turned another corner, diving into the gloom of a narrow alleyway, then into the weak light of a streetlamp.

A freezing gust up my spine. I dropped and darted sideways. *Snap*, right where my head had been. I kicked hard at one of its legs, the impact making it stumble. It lashed out with a clawed paw. I didn't pull back fast enough. Sound exploded out of my throat as pain seared up my leg.

I lurched sharply into another alleyway, my leg trying to buckle underneath me. The thing crashed into the wall as it didn't quite make the corner. I tore down the space, looking for something, anything solid to put between it and me. Broken broom handle, glass bottles, and various piles of rubbish—

Crunch, behind me. I picked up a glass bottle, spun and threw. The glass bounced off it's thick forehead. It stalked forward another step. I threw another bottle, missed, and another, the glass shattering across its massive skull. Something dark trickled down it's face. My nose burned with something sharp, sweet, and acrid.

My hand searched for another bottle and found nothing. My knives were too close range for this. Pressure built in my throat.

Don't panic, don't panic, think, think, think!

It lunged. I threw myself to the side and felt my coat snag. Fabric ripped. My toe clipped my heel, and I fell. Hard. Crashing onto my side, I rolled, *too far*, scrambling away like a crab on my back. His jaw parted as it prepared to snap at me again. I kicked and made contact with its nose.

It lashed out with one huge-clawed paw. I twisted. *Not fast enough.* Talons slammed right above my hips, hooked into clothing and skin, and yanked.

Fire sliced across my torso. A scream ripped out of me, like part of my soul fled. I scrambled backwards, twisting away in animal-panic, unable to stop. I couldn't control myself. I couldn't *think*.

My hand hit something hard and cylindrical. It rolled and my hand shot out with it, my back smacking into the ground. The monster in front of me crouched down with all its bulk, its hind end swaying back and forth like a cat's—

My fingers curled around the cylindrical pole I'd slipped on. I yanked it up. *Broom handle.* The creature lunged, mouth wide, a thousand fangs headed towards my face. My wrist readjusted on its own, aiming, honed in on the massive chest barreling towards me.

The monster hit the handle first, driving it into the ground next to my side. Weight slammed into me. It's head whipped back, a flesh-tearing sound burst out of it. Acid burned into my nose, searing up into my eyes. The creature convulsed, the weight of it crushing down, harder and harder.

Stars danced in chaotic spirals in front of my eyes. My ears rang like church bells. Pain. Pain. Waiting for pain.

Tick.

I couldn't *breathe*.

Tock.

Weight ground me into the cobblestone.

Tick.

My eyes streamed with tears, the smell curdling up into my brain.

Tock.

But no new pain.

Tick.

No new pain.

Tock.

The creature didn't move. Something cold and sticky ran down my hand, fingers aching from gripping the makeshift weapon. The cold soaked into my sleeve, began to drip onto my chest.

I hit it.

I tried to push. Nothing. I wriggled, trying to scoot upwards, then heaved upwards with all the strength I had left… and shifted some of the weight off my chest. Air surged into my lungs with a horrible sound. Relief—no, that didn't encompass the entirety of this, the word *relief*—burned in the ends of my nerves. A sob ripped out of me into the cold night, the sound too loud, trying to breathe.

A flush of heat spread up my arms; unreal, near-artificial.

Something else approached. And I was trapped.

"No, no, no…"

The joints in my legs ground together under the weight, throbbing in warning. I bucked—all it did was leave me breathless and threaten to pop my ankle out of its socket. My breathing gasped, conspicuously loud, but I couldn't stop wheezing.

The night abruptly held its breath.

The body of the monster jerked off of me.

Blood surged back into my legs, bringing pounding pain. I shrieked—and swallowed it halfway through. Daimyn stood to my left, his body half-twisted away but all of his attention on me, face ashen.

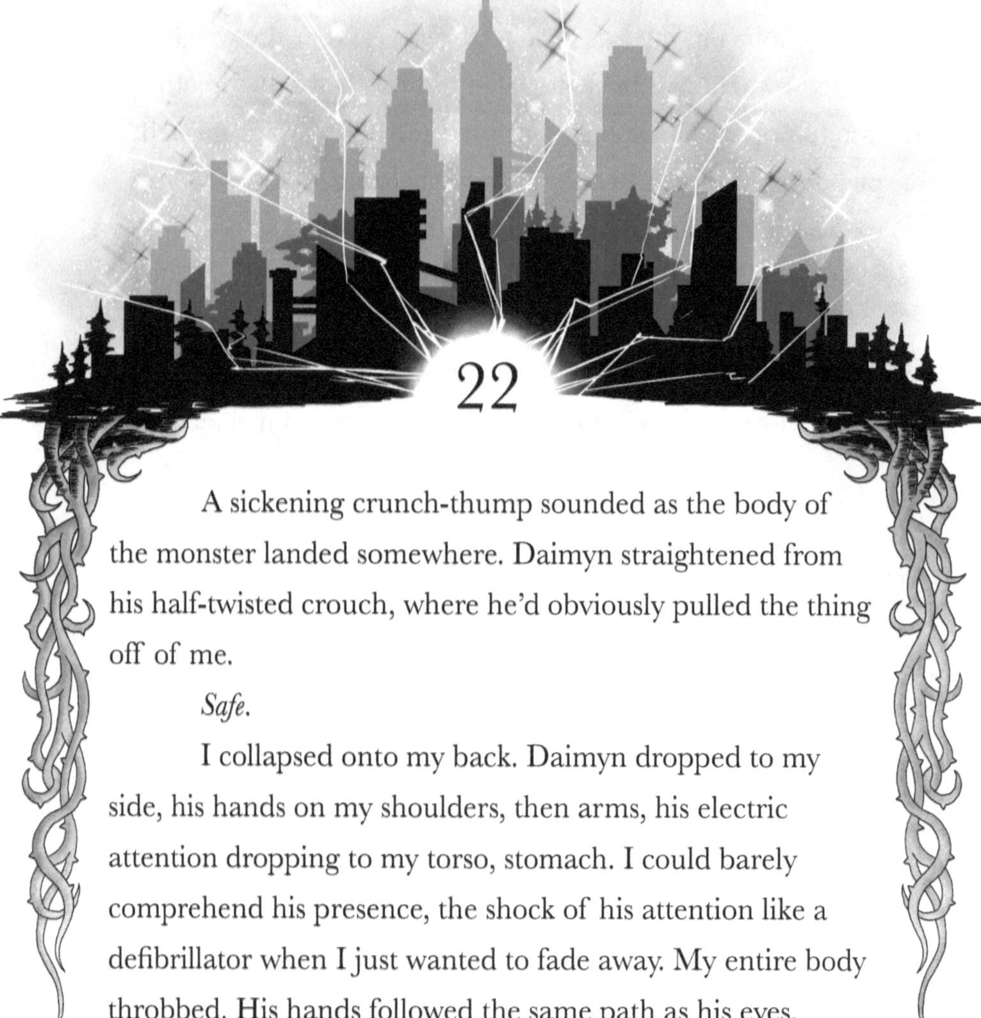

22

A sickening crunch-thump sounded as the body of the monster landed somewhere. Daimyn straightened from his half-twisted crouch, where he'd obviously pulled the thing off of me.

Safe.

I collapsed onto my back. Daimyn dropped to my side, his hands on my shoulders, then arms, his electric attention dropping to my torso, stomach. I could barely comprehend his presence, the shock of his attention like a defibrillator when I just wanted to fade away. My entire body throbbed. His hands followed the same path as his eyes, pulling at my clothes over tearing, scaring places. Each one of my breaths caught halfway through.

Daimyn touched my hip and it *burned*. I lashed out, slamming my fist into his arm. His shoulder rolled with the hit, but he leaned away from me. I collapsed onto the stone again, shivering. The relief of space filled my mouth, my chest.

"Where are you hurt?" Every word tore out of him.

I shifted, wanting to twist onto my side and curl into a ball. My stomach and thigh screamed at the slight movement. *Bad plan.*

My teeth chattered. "What was—what was *that*—"

"Necromantic minion. *Are you hurt.*"

I managed a nod. Tears burned my eyes at the admission. Where was my *fear doesn't control me* now? My mantra stripped away like the lie it was. Bravery meant fighting fear, and there was no bravery left in me. Because all I wanted was to never *ever* feel like this again.

"Fairian, I need to see." His icy chill cracked. "*Please.*"

He hovered on his knees, half over me, every part of him restrained. Vulnerability right now felt like shearing off my skin. But this wasn't the first time I'd been vulnerable with him. I swallowed thickly and nodded.

Daimyn reached out, and the trust I gave him balanced painfully on a knife's edge, monumental and fragile. I wasn't sure I'd survive it's destruction. He unzipped my coat. Fabric stuck to my skin as he pulled it away, cold air turning sticky wet into ice. I watched Daimyn's face for the verdict, relieved not to be alone to face it. He looked over my torso, my side, then noticed my thigh and leaned over, hands carefully hovering.

With a slow exhale, he sat back.

"I stop watching you for *one second…*" His voice shook. "I have a safe house not far from here. We need to clean this up."

I licked my lips, trying to put everything in comprehensible order. "In a minute." I just needed a minute. Just a few minutes. I'd get adrenaline under control and be able to act normal again and—

His arms slid under my knees and back and stood, the ground disappearing from under me. The movement pulled at my split flesh, pain tearing across my body. I gasped, violence surging. Then heat and teeth-numbing protectiveness rose out of him like its own being and practically smothered me. The Feeling left no room for me to doubt it.

Daimyn cradled me to his chest and strode forward. I sucked in unsteady breaths as he moved swiftly over the cobblestone, his strides lengthening as he seemed to stick to patches of shadow and avoid the lit streetlamps. I tried to keep still, but no position spared me from the throbbing burn. Weakness leeched into all my limbs as shivering broke out along my skin, in my bones. My brain slid into neutral, thoughts impossible to put together.

Movement ceased. I jolted, heart lurching into pounding. My eyes opened to see the column of his throat, the dark collar of his jacket, the side of a small grey residential-looking building beyond. Daimyn crouched, one of his arms shifting under me to reach down. He tugged at something, and metal clicked. Then he straightened. I turned my head to see him push a key into the doorknob of a small wooden door, a mat half turned over at his feet.

"That's a terrible hiding place," I managed.

Daimyn's head turned towards me; heat and pressure brushed against my brow. My breathing hitched. Then the door opened, and he stepped into the dark building. With a click, the light burst on.

I made an unintelligible noise and pressed my face against his neck again. He kicked the door shut and moved further into the building. It smelled stale in here.

"Can you stand?"

My fingers tightened instinctively on his clothes. But my brain struggled back from its offline status, and my behavior since Daimyn had shown up… my face heated. He had to think of me as some kind of helpless thing.

I wrenched my head up, nodding to his question. My eyes adjusted more easily in the slightly darker room. Daimyn lowered me into a chair, and I grabbed onto it, cringing, as movement tore fire across my torso again.

An island counter stood to my left. Daimyn strode around it and crossed the room in two steps. The walls were bright yellow, the floor patterned with colorful inlays. Daimyn yanked open the doors of the dark cabinets, pulling down boxes and containers.

I took a deep breath. My spine shuddered, and some of my trembling eased.

To my right, a chair and couch sparsely furnished an open darkened room. Almost directly in front of me a hallway disappeared further into the house. I could barely make out the shape of another door.

Daimyn returned with small boxes and containers piled in his arms, dropping all of it on the island next to me. He shook his shoulders, shrugging, and his coat slid unceremoniously off him and hit the floor with a heavy *thump*. A harness with pouches and knife sheathes and pockets criss-crossed his torso over a dark shirt. On his right hip was a *scabbard and sword*, on his left hip a dagger sheath.

He crouched in front of me and carefully pulled the fabric away from my torso. I cringed. Then smacked his hand, more intentionally and less reactionary this time. Daimyn lifted his hands.

"Explain what you're doing," I insisted.

His lips parted to speak, but it took a beat longer for his teeth to unclench. "I need to see how deep it is." His chest expanded tight under his shirt as he took a breath. "Necromantic creatures carry diseases. It *hit* you."

I paused. "Okay."

"Was that a yes?"

I blinked. "Yes."

Daimyn lifted the fabric up my torso again, and I took it from him and held it out of the way.

Black-grey ichor soaked my clothes, smeared across my stomach. Trails of rust and red weaved into the color—and four vivid gashes of split flesh ran from ribs to hip. Well. At least I didn't see my own organs? Two shallower gashes angled across my thigh. I stared in numb fascination at the layers of skin and viscera and muscle.

Oh good, I was definitely in some sort of shock.

Daimyn's eyebrows pulled together tightly on his forehead, his focus nearly physical.

"You should shower first." His voice sounded like gravel. "The thing's guts all over you will not help."

My knees quaked at the idea. But I nodded anyway. He rose, lifting me off the chair and ignoring my weak protests as he strode down the dark hallway opposite the front door we'd come through. He halted partway down, and another light flicked on, revealing a small bathroom. Daimyn shouldered through the door and set me on the lid of the toilet.

"I will find you something to change into."

He left before I comprehended his words. I wrapped my arms around myself, wincing as my elbow hit my split side. White and blue walls surrounded me, and maybe would have been charming any other time, but it smelled like death in here. *I* smelled like death.

You did kinda ask for this. You asked for proof, and a rotting monster from hell answered.

The walls… moved. Subtly tilted, unevenly expanded, and then retracted again, like I sat inside a giant breathing beast. I shut my eyes tightly. *Not real, not real. Just my imagination.* Dizziness rushed my head, and my eyes popped back open. The walls moved again, worse.

I'd been here before. Panic clawed up my throat—and Daimyn appeared in the doorway with a bundle of dark clothing. The walls snapped back into place and I exhaled a shudder. He set the bundle on the counter of the sink and crouched in front of me again, meeting my gaze as his hands bled warmth into the sides of my knees.

"Do you think you can shower?" His face set in stone, but his voice was so gentle.

I swallowed, unsure how to tell him I might crumble if I moved right now.

"Let me know when you're ready."

His patience built the ground beneath my feet. I shut my eyes. "Alright. Alright."

Daimyn nodded, and rose to fiddle with the faucets over the tub. Water gurgled and hissed. He set something at the corner of the basin. Soap, it looked like.

"I will be right outside."

Daimyn rose and left, pulling the door behind him. But not all the way shut. A sliver existed between the door and its frame, letting in the gloom of the hallway. I stared at that sliver of darkness until it became my anchor. The bathroom walls stayed still.

The water warmed, and my legs shook as I stepped inside the spray without removing my clothes. I wasn't sure if the clothes could be salvaged, but I wanted the ick out of them at least. I pulled off my tunic with weak arms, my face twisting in pain. But I didn't make a sound. It made it more real, if I made a sound.

Once undressed, I soaked and wrung out my clothes as best as possible. The water stung on my split skin, and I gritted my teeth, giving up on my clothes to wipe away the gross from my body instead. As soon as I started, I couldn't get it off of me fast enough. If I never had to smell the sickly-sweet tang of rot again, it would be too soon.

Reaching to get the soap off the edge of the tub hurt. I managed to lather it across my chest, and it was a relief, such a relief to get clean. I carefully avoided the gashes, soaping everything else, even my feet and neck and hair. Soap suds slid down my front. I didn't think about it until too late—

Pain lit like gasoline as soap hit split flesh. I choked, whipping around towards the water to rinse it off, clenching sound behind my teeth.

"Fairian. Are you—"

"It's fine." My voice broke.

I shut off the water, eyes stinging.

"There's a towel next to the clothes."

The chilly air felt even worse, like someone threw liquid nitrogen across me. I jerked on the clothes set on the counter, biting my lip hard. The simple shirt and pants were grey, about two sizes too large, and very soft. My entire body shook by the time I finished.

I stared at the handle to the bathroom door and shut my eyes tightly, breathing deeply to get a grip on myself. It barely did anything. I wasn't going to be normal anytime soon. With one last breath, I pulled open the bathroom door.

Daimyn leaned against the wall directly across from me, arms crossed, expression tight. "Better?"

I nodded, and he straightened off the wall, gesturing back towards the kitchen with his chin. I followed him back down the hall, wincing as each step pulled painfully on my torso and hip. Once back to the kitchen chair, I sat slowly. Daimyn pulled small containers out of the bigger boxes he'd originally grabbed from the cabinets.

Then he turned towards me, holding a small cloth and a bottle of a faintly blue liquid. "Will you lift your shirt?"

I bundled up the soft grey fabric under my breasts, holding it tightly to my diaphragm. He kneeled before me again, his face close to my exposed torso. The action hit differently without the ick making me disgusting. Heat crept up my neck and I swallowed. His eyes flicked to mine in a brief flash of intensity.

Wetting the cloth with the blueish liquid, he gently dabbed it across the gashes. I sucked my lips between my teeth. It stung, but numbness followed in its wake, and my shoulders relaxed away from my ears.

"It's a bloody miracle these aren't deeper," he muttered. "You were almost fucking disemboweled, Fairian."

"That's a bad way to go," I croaked.

Daimyn stilled. Shut his eyes for a beat. Then opened them to continue. His ministration grew certain, and despite the pain, despite the ripples of something heated and dense coming off of him, my eyelids grew heavier with each blink. Why did he have to feel so bloody safe?

"I'm going to push up this pant leg."

I pried my eyes open and nodded, and Daimyn bundled up the fabric up my calf, over my knee, up my thigh… I placed my hands next to my hips and lifted my butt off the seat, wincing, so I could trap the fabric under my thigh and out of his way. Daimyn applied more liquid to the gashes there.

"Are those… ah, creatures, very common?" I asked softly.

A muscle ticked in Daimyn's jaw. "Necromantic creatures like that, the ones who have been altered into unnatural forms, the ones so intent on their quarry, are usually controlled by Mortis Mercators."

I blinked.

"Mortis Mercators, professional dead-raisers, create them for assassinations. Their creatures consume their victims and then can be quickly disposed of themselves, so it's… 'clean.'"

I'd turned into a sponge, absorbing information without knowing how to react to it.

"Mercators tend to be political creatures. They follow their own set of laws—their own code of ethics, you could say. They don't accept just any contract." He paused. "They have a particular abhorrence of me."

I made a face. "Why?" I meant why they didn't like him, but another thought tripped over the last: he was being verbose. Why was he being verbose?

His glance didn't quite connect with mine. "They view me as unnatural."

I squinted. "*You're* unnatural and they're the ones raising the dead?"

"Dogma generally has glaring errors in logic." Daimyn pulled a cylindrical container off the counter. He opened it and dipped his fingers inside; they came out covered in white goo. He gently applied it on the gashes with barely-there brushes of his fingers. The heat along my neck crept up into my face.

"A Mercator sending minions after you means someone is paying for your death."

"Oh." The hell? "Why?"

Daimyn stood and pulled open one of the small pouches on the harness across his torso. He palmed something into his fist that glowed gold between his fingers… I smiled even as he opened his hand in front of me, revealing a familiar sight. The golden stone from the first time I'd met him shone back at me.

"Hey, I know this one."

"This will seal the skin, which will aid with healing, exposure to infection, and it should also take care of disease that thing was carrying. It will also prevent scarring."

Well wasn't he just prepared.

"But it doesn't penetrate very deeply; you need to watch for bruising that gets worse, tender pain, or a fever." His eyebrows furrowed together tightly. "And if you feel ill, you need to alert me immediately. This is not the time for being tough. Understood?"

I nodded, eyebrows raised. He held my gaze for a beat, and kneeled again. He murmured something under his breath as he brought the glowing stone closer, and it brightened. Warmth spread across my stomach, followed by a strange tingling.

Daimyn passed the stone over the lacerations, his other hand gently pushing the edges of my skin together. Tingles spread across my skin; the sensation grew to prickling, and my eyes widened as the edges of my skin came together and sealed. I hadn't seen it happen last time.

"That's incredible," I whispered.

He finished with my torso, then moved to my thigh. My skin remained flushed and swollen, but besides a few blood smears, everything looked normal. It ached, but not even close to the same intensity. I traced one of them along my stomach and jerked my hand back. *Sensitive.*

A wave of exhaustion hit me right in the eyes and limbs, weighing them down, right as my stomach hollowed with sudden, gripping hunger.

I winced, leaning forward. "Whoa."

Daimyn nodded. "You're going to want to get extra sleep and food tonight. Magical healing has some side effects."

I dropped the fabric of the shirt to cover up my stomach again, fighting to keep my eyelids open. Daimyn sat back on his heels, hands dropping to his thighs. Light pulsed once between his fingers, and then the stone dimmed—almost completely dark. He looked down at it, expression grim, but the distance in his gaze made me think he wasn't actually seeing it.

"Why does someone want you dead?" he asked quietly.

I blinked grimy eyes rapidly. "I don't know."

Daimyn nodded once. "I don't think this is about you."

What the? "Funny, it felt a lot about me."

"I think someone has noticed I watch over you."

I squinted. "… Uhhh, what?" I huffed a laugh. "No you don't."

The muscles along his jaw flexed. "Death merchants only take assignments with power and clout and… connections. You are a nobody in the magical community—except for your run-ins with me."

I stiffened as that hit a little too close to home. "And you've just assumed I'm this nobody, huh."

He focused on me. "It's an educated guess. If you had the kind of connections that warranted a Death Merchant contract, you would at least know who I am and what I do."

Daimyn stood and tucked the gold orb back into his harness. Then he moved back to the island counter and shuffled around the supplies without seeming to do anything with them.

Indignation bubbled up, despite the fact that he was right. "You really think—you don't know—you don't know me, you arse."

Daimyn pressed his palms against the edge of the counter and leaned heavily on his arms. "All right. Perhaps my conclusion is too hasty. What are you mixed up in where *Mercators* are targeting you?"

I opened my mouth. Shut it. Hell, *did* I have a plausible reason for being the target of assassination? The only magical people I really knew were Daimyn and—

The blood drained from my face.

Daimyn's eyes narrowed. "What was that."

Ah, crapsticks.

"Maybe I pissed off someone I don't know about," I mumbled. "I get in trouble all the time."

"Something more specific." His attention moved over me like a physical touch, his whole body hunting-still. "If there is a *chance* the magical community isn't coming down on your head because of me, that is far preferable."

I flung my hands up. "Seriously, who are you? Why would anyone give a shite about a girl you've met like three times?"

Daimyn stared at me like he hadn't heard me. "There's something else you think, something specific," he said slowly. "And I'm going to hazard a guess that it's related to the danger you didn't want to tell me about before."

Maybe I really did need to come clean. But would *he* really do this? Would he go to this level? *Why?* And Daimyn just watched me. Waiting.

Exhaustion made it easy for recklessness and frustration to take over, and I spoke before I fully thought it through. "Okay, fine. Let's try this then." My heart lurched, bravado trying to die a quick death. "I had a sister. We were kidnapped, she died, and I didn't." At least I sounded bland. "He might be here. The person that took us. You want to know a reason I'd be a target? Maybe to finish the job."

Finish the job. Whatever it was.

Daimyn's eyebrows slowly drew down and together. "Why do you think your kidnapper is here?"

A band tightened around my chest, making it impossible to draw full breaths. Haltingly, I told him about the article with the two girls, and how *he* had made us see things—

"That's not what's happening to them."

"What?"

He hesitated. "What you're referring to is a phenomenon of this city due to its proximity to the Divide. St. Dymphna's—and now I understand why you were sneaking around there—has a dedicated ward where people are housed until recovered and safe."

Fight bled out of me slowly… and then evaporated all at once. *How does he know…?* Any of that. How did he know any of that?

Daimyn's studied me, his weight shifting restlessly. "Would there be any other reason for the Mercators to target you?"

I stared at him. Swallowed. Tried to focus on what he was talking about. But how could I focus on something as inanely named as "death merchants" when my entire reason for thinking *he'd* returned had just been blown away?

Have I been chasing ghosts for the past month?

Did I jump to conclusions and believe myself in danger for no reason?

Am I even capable of judging danger correctly anymore?

I just shook my head in answer.

Daimyn shut his eyes. "This is bad. Their attacks will be pointed, organized, and endless, if my enemies think they can get to me through you."

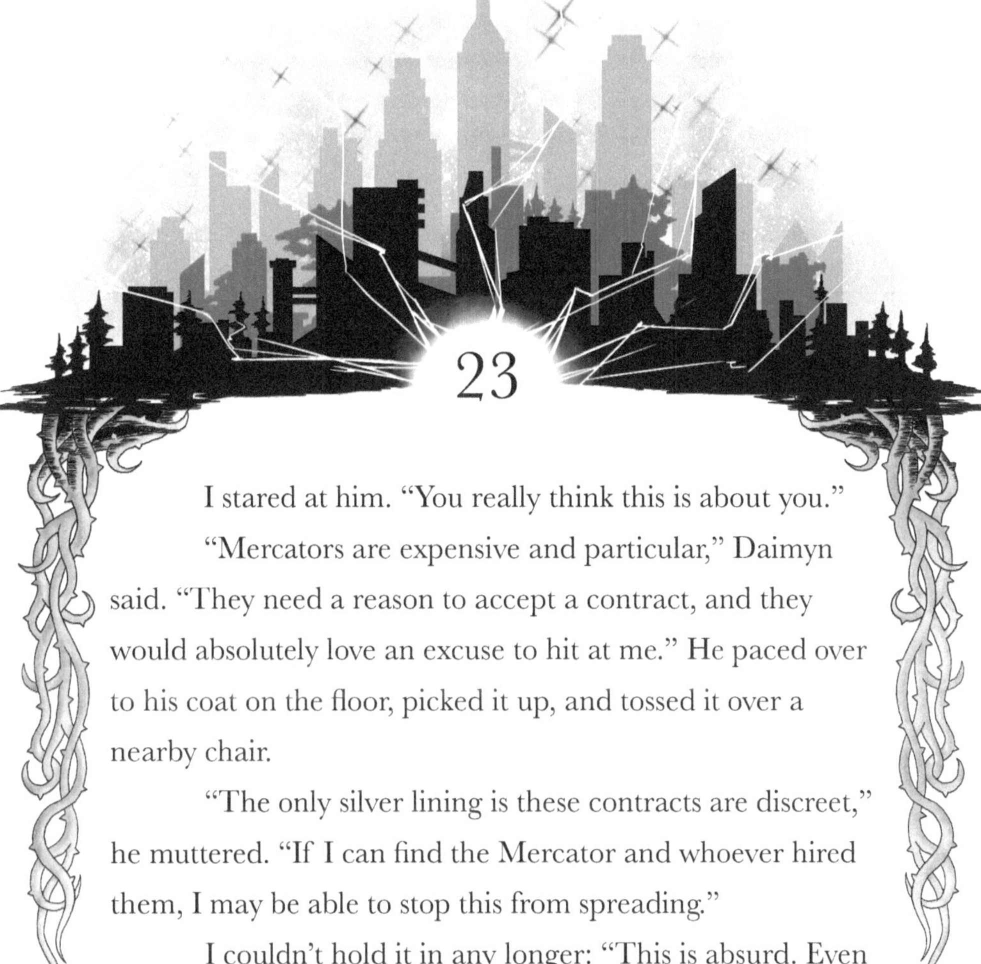

23

I stared at him. "You really think this is about you."

"Mercators are expensive and particular," Daimyn said. "They need a reason to accept a contract, and they would absolutely love an excuse to hit at me." He paced over to his coat on the floor, picked it up, and tossed it over a nearby chair.

"The only silver lining is these contracts are discreet," he muttered. "If I can find the Mercator and whoever hired them, I may be able to stop this from spreading."

I couldn't hold it in any longer: "This is absurd. Even if I accept that this is somehow about you, why in the hell would murdering me be the answer?"

"A variety of reasons. That's irrelevant." His gaze pinned me in place. "You will need to be guarded at all times. No more night excursions—"

Giddy fury inflated sharply inside of me. "No."

"Damn it, Fairian—" He stopped, jerking a hand up into his hair as frustration tightened his features. His chest expanded as he took a deep breath, then carefully exhaled. A deep rumble filled the air, the containers on the counter rattling in response. Daimyn winced, and the sound abruptly cut off.

Did he just… *growl?*

Daimyn gripped his hair in a fist, staring hard at something over my head. "That wasn't at you."

Pressure bubbled up my throat and came out as a giggle. I clapped a hand over my mouth. His gaze slid to me, one eyebrow arched. I clamped down harder with my hand. That was probably not the correct response to anything that had just happened.

Focus. We needed to have this conversation, even if all I wanted to do was rock back and forth in the corner. This real danger—and the fake danger I'd apparently made up—would not force me to play it safe.

I cleared my throat and dropped my hand. "So. Okay. You're saying that someone hired the… merca-whatevers, to come after me because that would affect you somehow."

"Yes."

"Why do they think hurting me hurts you?" That part didn't make sense.

Then I remembered Andrews' conviction that Daimyn treated me differently. Maybe it wasn't so absurd.

The reminder of TASA made acid fill my chest. No doubt they'd want a report on this whole evening. Unless—they hadn't intervened when I'd been attacked. Had they not seen this?

Focus. Daimyn still had one hand fisted in his hair, unmoving.

"Is this really because you defended me a few times?" Now I wanted this answered for two reasons. "Isn't your job to protect people?"

"Yes."

"Okay," I said slowly. "Then why is this such a big deal?"

Daimyn's hand dropped. "Alwin has been running his mouth, which started an unhealthy interest in you the past couple weeks. I've been heading off anything sniffing around. I thought I had been quiet about it, but maybe not."

"Wait. The Speaker? He's alive?" I blinked as the rest of his statement registered. "But you haven't been around," I said, and cut off before the rest: *for over two weeks.*

He ran a hand down his face. "Just because you didn't see me doesn't mean I didn't see you."

My mouth opened. Then shut. *Well, okay.* I didn't know whether to be flattered or just annoyed.

Both. I'd be both.

"That still doesn't make sense," I said, returning to the original point. "Just because you—"

Wait. An explanation popped to mind.

I consistently put myself in danger. Daimyn defended me— apparently more than I realized—and since he was some big shot, people noticed. It mirrored the situation when I'd spent a lot of time at Sir Lightly's house and some rubbish paper ran a story about me being his underage mistress. This became a question of quantity, not quality.

"Just because I what?"

"My decisions to get in trouble are not your fault," I began slowly. "You really should just let me deal with the consequences."

I mean, I had technically killed the undead thing tonight before he'd shown up.

Daimyn's head slowly turned towards me, eyes glittering. Nerves jittered through my stomach.

"You said before that I wasn't your problem," I remembered. "Let's just—"

"I know what I said."

"Okay… well. Good. That means the trouble I create is my own, and—"

"No."

I blinked. "No?"

"I know what I said, forget I said it."

My face screwed up in confusion. "Wha—"

"What are we going to do about you becoming a target, Fairian?"

I stared at him. Decided I really liked it when he said my name. He stared back, expectant; the question hadn't been rhetorical.

I latched onto the first thing that popped to mind. "Why don't we use me as bait?"

Daimyn exhaled and pinched the bridge of his nose, eyes squeezed shut.

"No, wait, I'm liking this plan," I said, grinning like a snot. "We'll parade me around, wait for them to attack, find clues, and confront whoever hired the death people! We'll be a team."

Daimyn started massaging the center of his brow in circular movements.

Giddiness burbled in my brain. "You know…" *What the hell, this whole evening is a disaster anyway.* "The best way to protect someone from scary, powerful threats might be to directly watch over them. And let them in on, I don't know"—I coughed into my fist, staring hard at his expression—"your supernatural adventures."

His eyes opened, expression carefully neutral, hand dropping to his side.

Intuition sparked. "You've already thought of that."

A muscle flexed in his jaw.

Glee erupted in my chest, a grin spreading across my face. *If this has already crossed his mind, what had he decided?* The glee died just as quickly. His neutral expression told me nothing. My tongue welded to the top of my mouth as air grew heavy, not with a Feeling, just an instinct. I didn't know what to say, if I could convince him, how to even start convincing him.

"Considering your proficiency at flirting with danger, you're giving me little other choice," he began, voice quiet and logical, almost inflectionless. "But if we're seen together, it would bring further attention. We may take care of this Mercator problem only to have six more similar situations. It may be safer for this moment if you were near me, but navigating through this without repercussions will be incredibly difficult."

Oh, son of a turd, he was serious. "You're considering it." It came out more of a wheeze.

"Are you listening to me?" Emotion surged back into every word. "Do you not understand how dangerous this could be to you?"

"I'm listening," I insisted. "But I've told you from the beginning I don't care about that."

His gaze flicked down my body and back up, mouth a tight line. I realized I had my hand pressed against my abdomen, but I didn't remove it. That just made it seem like I denied I'd gotten hurt.

"I accept the danger willingly. I understand and accept it," I said, careful to keep my voice level and serious. "But you'll let me come along with you—while this is going on? I can help, you know."

I couldn't read anything from his expression or body posture.

Words built in my throat until I couldn't hold them in. "I get you don't understand me, and you think I should stay safe. But I'm not interested in safe. I want to be *me*. Me has to mean something, and this is what I've chosen."

Why couldn't I just clearly articulate what I wanted? Why couldn't I even explain it to myself?

Daimyn stood eerily still again. Conflict touched his eyes, thoughts moving in dense circuits where I couldn't interpret. We stared at each other, frozen and assessing each other, for what felt like forever.

His throat moved once as he swallowed, right before he spoke, voice soft with surrender: "This is a very bad idea."

My heart and stomach flipped places. "I think it's a fantastic idea."

"That's because you have no self-preservation instinct."

My pulse hammered in my throat. "Let's start now. What do we need to do to figure this out?"

Daimyn huffed. "You were just attacked and now you want to go gallivanting across the city?"

"You may change your mind later. Or think it would be better just to keep an eye on me instead. Or anything else, really."

Had I seriously misunderstood something, or were we really talking about this?

"I've tried that. You're a damn magnet for trouble, so picking off whatever is following you is even productive. But that method is now unacceptable."

He pushed off the counter, putting the medical supplies back in their boxes and bundling up the waste.

"You need to—" He stopped, eyes turning skyward briefly. "I would like it, if, after this, you returned home. Get some rest. And we'll start tomorrow night."

I narrowed my eyes, disbelief soaring through me. "I'll be out here tomorrow, whether you like it or not. Magnet for trouble, blah, blah, blah."

"And I will bring you along, for better or worse. Since you seem intent on bringing about your death."

I deliberated. If I couldn't trust him to keep his word, this wasn't going to work anyway. Plus, he had definitely stopped himself from ordering me around right there. "Okay."

"Gods, it's like pulling teeth to get you to agree on anything," he muttered.

I stuck my tongue at him. *Pot, meet kettle.*

Daimyn rolled his eyes, picked up the now-organized medical supplies resting on the island, and placed them back into one of the cupboards. The kitchen had returned to looking spotless and barely-used.

And I hadn't helped at all during this whole process. I hadn't even said—

"Thank you." Yikes, I was awkward. "For taking care of… wounds. Me."

He inclined his head, the movement oddly formal, but off somehow. "Let's get you home."

He picked his coat up off the chair and flung it around his shoulders, covering his harness with a million interesting things. I wanted to ask about them, but exhaustion rose again to smear coherence into incomprehension.

Daimyn ushered me out the door and locked up the house behind us. The cold stung my face and burrowed into my borrowed clothes, shocking me a little more awake. He glanced at me then placed the key underneath a large stone off to the side of the door. With another glance, he stepped out onto the street.

We walked, Daimyn close enough that the fabric of his jacket brushed against my arm. His presence took up more space than his actual physical body, the heat bleeding off of him half enveloping me. *Here we are in my damn dream again.* I didn't want to be any sort of damsel in distress, but I'd suck it up until I knew how to navigate this. Since apparently I had attention.

… Attention that wasn't really about me. Unsteady mirth rose: my watched-Feelings over the past few weeks really *had* been warning me—but I'd misinterpreted everything, from the article to the Feelings so similar to the ones after my sister's death. The warnings *had* been real. I'd just misconstrued the meaning.

My eyes cut to Daimyn. It had been about him, from the very impetus of our acquaintance. TASA had those damn pictures from the very start. I wanted to start laughing, maybe a little hysterically.

"What?" Daimyn murmured without looking. Apparently he didn't need to actually use his eyeballs to know what I did.

"Just finding the humor in this situation," I said lightly.

He made an aggrieved huff and shook his head. I didn't bother suppressing a smile that time.

Could I really trust this? This fragile thing growing in that space where Daimyn nearly touched me, that might actually be mine, because I was able to choose it?

My smile faded as a sickening realization dawned. No. No, I couldn't trust it.

Because I'd made a partnership with Daimyn—however tentative—and hadn't considered TASA's hold over me. My stomach sank with heavy, dreaded weight. In doing what *I* wanted, I'd done exactly what TASA wanted. Maybe they hadn't seen the events of this evening, but I wouldn't be able to avoid their sodding eyeballs forever. I could stall. But only for so long.

Working in close proximity to Daimyn, I would inevitably see things about him. My chest tightened until I could barely breathe. The consequences of my choices landed on more than just me now, and I was a fool for forgetting it.

~ PART THREE ~

As I walked out of class, a familiar creeping sensation tickled up my neck. Eyes narrowed, I turned—and there he stood, staring at me. Sandy-Blonde. The usually vague friendliness on his face had disappeared, replaced by somber focus, the difference so stark I stopped in my tracks.

He jerked his head behind him as he turned, a signal to follow. Adrenaline flooded my mouth. I spun around, lunging down the hall. Slamming through the doors into the biting wind outside, I fast-walked, barely resisting breaking into a run. Technically my next class didn't start for another half an hour, but sometimes students showed up early. If I sat near someone, maybe Sandy-Blonde would leave me alone. Or would the cafeteria be better?

"Ms. Leynthall," he called behind me.

Nope nope nope. I should have headed towards the cafeteria, at least there'd be more people outside since it was at the center of campus.

"This won't solve anything, Ms. Leynthall."

Stop bloody calling me that! At least he didn't sound so composed, a little breathless as he jogged to catch up with me. The blinding urge to break into a run nearly tripped me up.

"Have you changed your mind in regards to Ms. Collins' future?"

I shut my eyes, my pace slowing. Sandy-Blonde caught up, his eyeballs prickling over my skin like a disease. The urge to stuff something in his mouth so he couldn't speak nearly overwhelmed me.

"I bloody knew it." I swallowed until I could control my voice. "This is the first time *you've* approached. What changed?"

"You failed to report an interaction."

My stomach cramped. *So they did see it.* "Piss off. You want something, come and get it. But don't act like I'm a willing participant in this situation."

"The reporting rules are very clear."

I bit my cheek until I tasted metal. *Tiff. You have to think of Tiff.*

"Next time, you will contact us upon any interaction."

"Or what?" The words shot out of my mouth.

Sandy-Blonde's eyebrows rose. But he wasn't nearly as intimidating as Andrews.

"Have you forgotten that we hold Ms. Collin's future—?"

"Here's what I know." My voice was dead-even. *Thank god.* "You have only one shot with that. Once you spend it, it's gone. No more Fairian getting info on the big-bad Daimyn. You're not going to spend it on something as little as me not checking in at the appropriate time."

Sandy-Blonde's eyes narrowed a hair.

"God knows I can't refuse you, but don't pretend for one second I'll contentedly play along."

My pulse beat hard in my abdomen and throat, and my knees slowly turned to jelly.

Sandy-Blonde looked to struggle for a few moments before finally speaking. "Lieutenant Andrews is waiting just outside the grounds for your report."

I have to do this I have to do this I have to do this.

"Lead the way," I said, sugar-sweet.

Sandy-Blonde turned, making sure I followed, and then set off across FCA grounds. I did follow, doubting everything about myself.

Over the past several hours I'd gone through all the stages of grief at least a few times. In the wee hours of this morning, staring at my ceiling with the comfort of darkness all around me, I had seriously considered telling Daimyn I'd changed my mind on the whole working together thing. That, *never mind, I was scared, and would just stay inside.*

Then I couldn't be a pawn in TASA's schemes.

Everything would just… go back to normal. I'd go to school. Avoid parents. Squeak as much freedom out of a life that grew heavier every year.

Daimyn would probably update me once he solved the question of who targeted me, then slip back into the shadows. The thought had sent panic blistering through my lungs. I wasn't ready. I couldn't give him up—not yet. Not when it felt like I'd finally found a bubble of air as I slowly drowned.

By the time the sun rose, anger had taken over. Would I really allow TASA to take this—*him*—from me? *I'd* found him. *I'd* chosen him. Daimyn didn't even want me—*I'd* made this happen, and goddamn it if I would let another of my choices get yanked away.

My shoes sank into the clover lawn as we left the circle of buildings of FCA, and I focused on slow, even breaths. I was smart. I was *smart.* I could navigate this.

Everything would have to be played close to my chest. I had to give them information to keep them content, but I would avoid any subject related to Daimyn to limit my exposure to his secrets, and bury information that might hurt him. Maybe I could even give them false information…

Sandy-Blonde walked off the grass and onto the sidewalk, turning left. My knees weakened.

Give them false information? Who was I kidding? I didn't even know what they already knew about Daimyn. I'd probably clue them into my manipulation immediately and they'd plaster Tiff's blood-soaked picture all over town.

Sandy-Blonde slowed, then grasped the door handle of a big van parked in the shelter of a tree, remarkably out of sight for being in the open. He pulled open the door. Andrews and another individual looked up at me from inside.

My side and thigh throbbed, more heat than pain, but a very loud reminder of last night. I filled my lungs until they hurt. *I can do this*. I could get through this without hurting either Tiff or Daimyn.

"We won't be taking you anywhere," Andrews said in what he probably meant to be a reassuring voice.

Swallowing, I forced myself to bend over and step into the vehicle. I barely slid in enough to get the door closed, and Sandy-Blonde shut it without getting in himself. *Don't get in cars with strangers*, I wanted to cackle. I put my hand on the handle.

"This is Dr. Manning," Andrews said. "I brought him along to look at any injuries you sustained last night."

"May I see?" the other man asked politely. He looked about the same age as my father, lighter hair and gruffer features, his expression professional. "I understand you encountered a necromantic minion, which is a rather nasty creature."

"You were there? You saw what happened?" I needed to establish a timeline of what all he'd seen. And distract them from this medical path.

Andrews nodded. "We observed most of the encounter, except for the hour in the house."

My heart sank. I'd really been hoping they'd missed *something*. I easily conjured fury, though not for the reason I expressed: "You were there the whole time and you didn't try to stop it? You just *let* that thing try to kill me?"

"By the time we realized the direness of the situation, it was too late to bring in someone who could handle a beast like that. We knew Daimyn was approaching. Considering your mission, we thought it best to let it play out. Are you all right?"

"Let it play out?" *What was it he'd said in our first meeting about not asking dangerous tasks from me?* "You told me this wasn't dangerous! I was almost eviscerated!"

Andrews watched me calmly, somehow everything and nothing in his expression. Expectant, without being desperate. Calm, without being detached. I gritted my teeth.

Andrews let out a quiet breath, broke eye contact, and reached into the door of the van next to him, pulling out a notepad and pencil. "To our knowledge, Daimyn has never personally taken care of someone's medical needs before. Usually he takes victims to hospitals if they are in need to care. This is a good sign; he's attached to you."

Dr. Manning piped up. "I have supplies with me, if I could take a look—"

There is no way in hell this dude is touching me. "I can't do this if you're just going to recklessly risk my life."

"Let's not play more games, Ms. Leynthall. You've been placing yourself in danger since you were 14. We are asking you to do no more than you already aim to do."

I nearly erupted like a volcano.

MY choice! Those are MY choices! This is NOT MINE!

I swallowed and breathed over and over until I didn't fear bursting into flames. Finally, I forced out words in an even voice.

"What is it you want exactly?"

"A debrief," Andrews said patiently.

My jaw started to ache around clenched teeth.

Andrews sighed. "What did Mr. Yillen say when he first arrived?"

I didn't want to stay in this car any longer than I had to; I really did have to tell them something about what happened last night.

"Mr. Yillen asked if I was hurt, where I was hurt, and that he would take me to a safe house to clean up."

Vomit nearly followed the words.

Andrews nodded, his pencil scratching across the paper in front of him. He paused halfway through and pulled a manilla envelope out of the side door, handing it to me. Dreading rising already, I opened the envelope to find two pictures.

Daimyn loomed over my prone form, feet planted, one arm extended out behind him, a huge grey mass blurring away from his fingers. That had to be the undead thing that had attacked me. I looked ghostly, and I stared up at him like… well, now that look on my face had been captured for everyone to see. Lovely.

The subjects of the second photo were blurrier: Daimyn held me, my face in his neck and his chin resting on top of my head as he turned a corner into the shadow of an alley. He looked positively arctic.

"What did he say on the way to the safe house?"

I froze. Had I given away Daimyn's safe house? I had. Confirmed and everything. Wow, I was bloody stellar at this.

"He was quiet. I don't think he said a single word."

Andrews nodded again, pencil still scratching.

His questions continued. He asked about what happened inside the safe house, what Daimyn said, what he'd used on my injuries, what he'd said about the injuries. Dr. Manning tried to interject to look at my torso again, and it took a lot of effort not to bite his head off. I told them about the golden stone… which made my heart wrench terribly, and pushed me into my first attempt to hide something. A test.

"Then he continued his usual diatribe," I continued. "I'm an idiot for putting myself in danger, I've attracted bad attention, blah, blah, blah. He was convinced this meant there was some sort of hit out on me." I licked my lips and kept my voice even. "He wouldn't explain why he thought that."

I waited for his reaction. It took effort not to babble; babbling would give me away. Andrews shared a heartbeat glance with Dr. Manning.

I narrowed my eyes. "What?"

"Did Mr. Yillen share any thoughts on why you were being targeted?"

"No," I muttered. "For all I know, you set it up, since I'm so bloody expendable."

Andrews' circled something with his pencil.

"Well?" I pushed.

"Yes?"

I easily summoned anger. "What the hell does that *mean*? I'm a *target*? You obviously have thoughts."

Andrews hummed. "Why don't you share your own suspicions?"

I snorted. "So that's how this works? You leave me completely unprepared to face whatever the hell all of this is?"

Andrews inspected me for a long moment. "You are intelligent. It's not a big leap to understand Mr. Yillen's presence has brought danger to you."

I wrinkled my nose. "What?"

"I told you from the beginning, Daimyn Yillen is a danger to everyone around him. Those who get close to him usually end up dead."

I didn't have to try hard to conjure disbelief, either. "By a professional hit?"

"It appears we aren't the only ones who have realized how much power it would mean to have some… sway over Mr. Daimyn. They must have decided that was an unacceptable risk."

I stared, letting it give weight to his "reveal" and give me time to think. Daimyn and TASA had come to the same conclusion in regards to my being attacked. What the absolute crap kind of reality did I live in?

Andrews searched over my face for a second, and sighed softly. "It will be all right, Ms. Leynthall. We will pull you before it becomes too dire." He returned to his notes. "What else did you speak about?"

I would have to tell them some explanation for why we now spent more time together. I'd originally planned to act cagey, forcing them to "drag" out the info about working with Daimyn. Then they'd feel they won.

But another idea struck. I leaned back against the seat for the first time, crossing my arms, and sneered.

Andrews' eyebrows rose.

"I did what you wanted."

Maybe, if I went about it this way, it would seem like I cared less for Daimyn and more about the blackmailing.

"I convinced him that since he's supposed to be a protector or whatever, he needs to figure out who's targeting me. And the smartest way would be to take me with him."

Additionally, if I just acted like a general brat, I could make a smokescreen to obscure when I needed to hide things.

Andrews straightened. Dr. Manning leaned forward.

"And Mr. Yillen agreed to that?"

"Yes."

My stomach twisted at the light that Andrews barely suppressed in his eyes. "This is a huge step, considering his solitary nature, that he's allowing you closer. It speaks to his attachment to you that he agreed to this." He bent and began writing rapidly again. "Walk me through the conversation."

Thankfully, yesterday evening hadn't held much detail actually *about* Daimyn. That suited perfectly, and lay the foundation of how I needed to handle all 'reports' going forward: frame all interactions as dealing with the Mercators. Focus away from Daimyn and anything personal. When Andrews pushed, I'd insist he didn't trust me and avoided any questions I asked. Which would be mostly true, as I wouldn't be asking Daimyn personal things.

I hoped it would buy me time. I'd fight for every second I could before this inevitably was stolen from me too, but I knew this had an expiration date. That's just how things went.

"Anything else of note during your interactions?" Andrews asked.

Memories flashed in quick succession: the look on Daimyn's face when he pulled the hound off of me, the whisper of warmth across my forehead when he carried me into the safe house, him crouched at my feet to coax me into the shower, the strange easiness of walking next to him on Farfalla's streets…

"No," I said, hollow. I'd destroy all of those moments by the end of this.

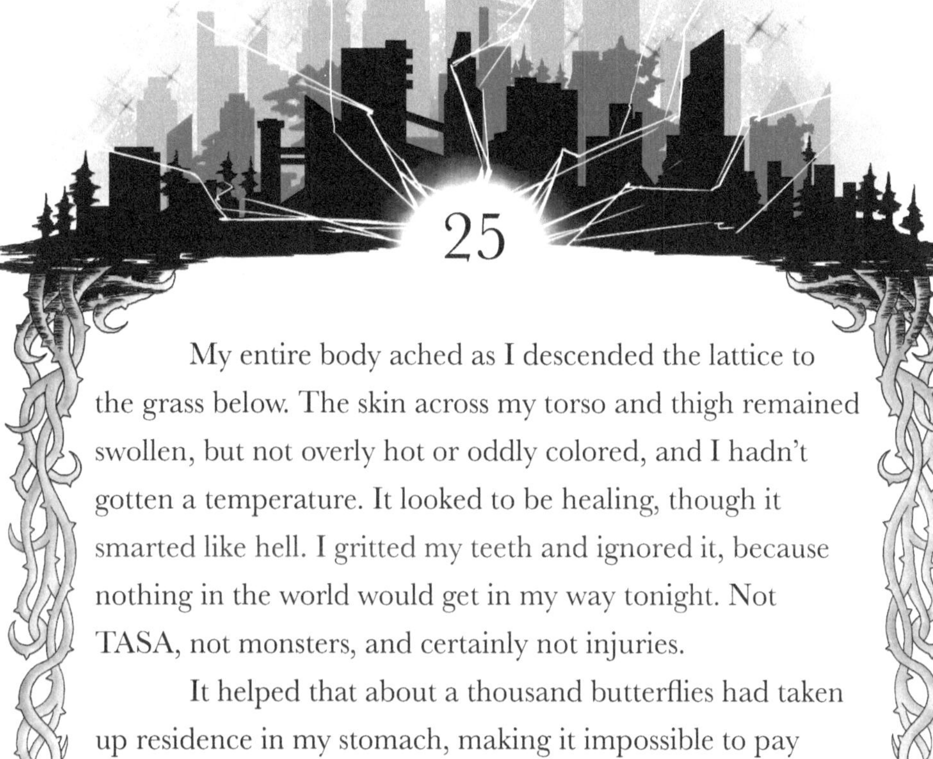

25

My entire body ached as I descended the lattice to the grass below. The skin across my torso and thigh remained swollen, but not overly hot or oddly colored, and I hadn't gotten a temperature. It looked to be healing, though it smarted like hell. I gritted my teeth and ignored it, because nothing in the world would get in my way tonight. Not TASA, not monsters, and certainly not injuries.

It helped that about a thousand butterflies had taken up residence in my stomach, making it impossible to pay attention to anything else. My distraction should have made it hard to sneak out, but I got past the guards so quickly it probably should have worried me. It didn't make sense I could do this so easily.

Daimyn and I had agreed to meet up at the entrance to the green where we'd encountered the shadow-snakes; I'd adamantly refused to meet right outside Leynthall grounds. I could make a ten minute walk, for sodding sake.

My neck prickled as I fast-walked through shadows and fog. Dread instinctively tried to sprout… then faltered in the face of curiosity.

Logically, I could believe Daimyn's insistence that the Divide had caused the symptoms of those inside St. Dymphna's, and that whoever watched me did so because of their interest in Daimyn. But that didn't change the gnawing uncertainty that I still had no answers about the whereabouts or reasoning of my sister's killer. I'd lived with the uncertainty for years, but now everything felt raw and ripped open again.

Well, it's not like you're about to speak to a supernatural guardian dude or something.

A lump formed in my throat as the thought made my heart skip.

I could ask Daimyn. Tell him everything.

Well, as much as he needed to know.

Indecision snarled my thoughts, and then I recognized the pathway into the green where Daimyn said he'd meet me. My steps faltered. All this angst-ing could be for nothing; I had no certainty he would show.

It's Schrödinger's mysterious gentleman… he's there and not there…

Snorting, I forced myself across the street. My footsteps dulled as I stepped onto the earthen path blanketed with darkness, and… I didn't even have to search. Daimyn leaned against a tree a few meters away, arms crossed. His gaze locked with mine, and my heart *leapt.*

Oh, mighty shitegibbons, that needed to stop right quick.

"How are you feeling?"

I cleared my throat to keep my voice steady. "A little sore, nothing terrible. How are the magical and deadly?"

"About usual."

Pushing off the tree, he strode forward until, with our combined movement, we stopped only a meter apart. His head canted to the side, cool dark eyes inspecting me.

"How is your temperature?"

"Totally normal. And it's a little swollen"— I patted my stomach gently—"but not hot or discolored."

"Good." He adjusted his stance. "If this is going to work, we need to set a few ground rules."

I tried to tamp down on the giddiness that he'd even shown up. "All right."

"Rule number one: if we are attacked and I tell you to run, or hide, or pretty much anything I order, you will go without protest. There will be times—"

"Not a chance," I drawled. "You could tell me to go home and never come out again."

"—*there will be times* that I will not have time to explain what's happening. If we encounter a situation where I am uncertain of my ability to protect your life, I need to know you will listen. I'm not used to having a shadow I need to protect."

I scowled.

"You're just going to have to swallow the idea I may know best in certain situations." He scanned my face. "And as tempting as it may be to order you home to 'never come out again,' that will only happen in the most dire of situations."

"What counts as dire?"

"When I am or I think I'll be overwhelmed. Which, lucky for you, doesn't happen very often."

He smirked at me, and I fought not to growl, rocking my weight back and forth. "If I think you're overusing it, or I *know* different, we're going to have a talk."

"I wouldn't expect anything less."

I squinted at the humor glittering in his eyes. "Fine. But no guarantees I won't complain the entire time."

Mirth *definitely* teased the corners of his mouth and eyes. I liked it, even if it was at my expense.

"Rule number two," he said. "Regarding your rampant curiosity: I have veto power over certain subjects."

"Things about you?" The words popped out without thinking.

"Maybe."

I gritted my teeth, instinctively annoyed, even as logically, this was good. I couldn't ask anything about him anyway because of TASA, and this would be a handy excuse.

"Fine. I understand. What's the third rule?"

His eyebrows winged upwards. "It's less of a rule and more of a warning. You've already said you accept the danger of being harmed, but I'm not sure you understand the risk *you* pose." He took a deep breath. "My…*job*… is to protect the vulnerable. There is a chance you will be exposed to a delicate situations while we are working together. I want to hear your vow of no ill intent."

I swallowed. *TASA, TASA, TASA…* how could TASA possibly think Daimyn dangerous, when protectiveness practically came off of him in waves?

"I have no interest in exploiting anything I learn," I said through an oddly tight throat. *Am I lying?* "About magic or anyone we meet." Was it really a lie when I meant it? And TASAs agreement had *only* to do with Daimyn. "The only way it's coming out of me is by force."

Daimyn's expression didn't ease. "Let's hope it never comes to that. I also reserve the right to create more rules as this progresses. I've never done this before and there may be some trial and error."

I narrowed my eyes at him again. "Then I reserve the right to refuse on the basis you are being overbearing and overprotective or may try to trap me with words."

"Trap you with—" His teeth snapped together audibly. "So untrusting. Whatever did I do to you?" Instead of anger, his voice came out with a vague humor that somehow worried me more.

"I just don't *know* you." *Even though I feel I do. Part of you at least,* came the alarming thought. "I promise I'll try not to be irrational."

His eyebrows shot up. "Take out the try, apply it to this as a whole, and we have a deal."

I rolled my eyes. "I promise *I'll try* not to be irrational when dealing with the dangerous and creepies that go bump in the night—and you—but make no specific promises."

He remained quiet for a beat. "That's probably the best I'm going to get."

Daimyn slowly extended his hand, like he didn't quite know how to go about this. I carefully reached out in return. His warm fingers closed over mine and we firmly shook. Glee made me light-headed, and dread made the ground feel like it was about to suck me under. *Please let all of this not end in disaster.*

Our hands released.

"So what are we doing now?" I asked, my voice coming out oddly tentative.

He gave a long-suffering sigh. "Follow me."

Turning on his heel, he headed out of the green. I darted after him. "Where are we going?"

"The library."

Not what I expected. "What?"

"If a Mercator has moved into town, I need to know where industrial ruins and graveyards intersect."

"Becaaauuuusssse—oh! Graveyards, for bodies to… raise?"

"It *is* the fuel for their art."

"And ruins because… "

His head tilted towards me, waiting.

"Good place to hide? Well, and hide walking bodies?"

"Now she's got it."

Daimyn didn't move to further speak, and I chewed on my lip as I remember a question that had been bouncing around in my head all day.

"I have a question about the Mercators and you—if you can answer."

Daimyn tilted his head towards me, one eyebrow arched.

I think this question is safe to ask. "You said someone had to hire the Mercators for the assassination. If they really don't like you—which you must think is significant since you brought it up—how do you know someone hired them and they're not just targeting me themselves?"

For several heartbeats, I heard only the sound of our footsteps and the faint breathing of the city.

"Their kind of magic requires a contract. There is a duality; their power both comes from and is bound by the agreement between the parties. The magnitude of the creature that attacked you was too powerful to be anything else."

How did that work? *Why* did that work? Who discovered that kind of amplification ability within constraints, and how had this practice developed like this?

I forced myself to stay relevant. "So you're saying we have two enemies of yours pairing up."

"If not more."

It didn't take long to make it to the library. Daimyn led me around the back of one of the smaller buildings, the trees and sculptures making ominous shadows across the ground. He stopped at a small door and crouched, fiddling with the lock briefly before the door swung open. I lifted my eyebrows.

"You gotta teach me how to do that."

He gestured for me to go in. With careful steps, I walked into darkness, making out the shape of maybe a hallway before Daimyn stepped behind me and shut the door, cutting off absolutely all light. Soft footsteps and the displacement of air swirled past me.

"Okay Mr. Supernatural," I said dryly. "I can't see."

"Ah yes, right."

His footsteps grew closer, as did a cloud of bubbly amusement. His warm hand wrapped around my elbow, and I let him pull my arm into the crook of his. Then he started forward, pulling me along. I scowled into the dark, trying not to stumble into a wall or object—or *him*. My toe caught on something, and his arm tightened to help me regain my balance.

I heard a soft rumble, almost a chuckle.

"Hey now," I warned.

"I said nothing," he said, a smile in his voice.

Daimyn took me through a door that sounded heavy as it closed, and down another long stretch of walking. He stopped, and I could make out vague movement, and then the creak of another door. He released me, moving past again.

A click, and light exploded into my eyeballs. "Ah! Warning!"

Daimyn chuckled again, moving into the small room I could barely see beyond watering eyes. Huge rolls of paper and giant laminated sheets filled every corner and shelf of the small room, and Daimyn made his way through it all, scanning them as he did.

"Here, grab these," he said, holding out three huge rolled up scrolls of paper from halfway across the room. I rolled my eyes but complied, walking *across* the room just to take them from him before turning and walking *back* to the big table in the center of the room. I watched him for a beat as he apparently ignored me while he searched through other scrolls, his mouth pursed as he obviously repressed a smile. Shaking my head, I turned my attention back to the rolled paper on the table.

Complex etchings formed into a layout of a city. It took me a second to recognize which one.

Farfalla. My eyes fell to the date.

"Whoa."

This map detailed Farfalla in the late 1800s. Shipyards, industrial mills, toxic waste disposal systems—all of them outlined in detail. Farfalla and most of the surrounding area had been mostly agricultural even during the height of industrialization, but during the panic of the Collapse, there'd been attempts to boost food cultivation with machines and chemicals. This looked to be an outline right after the initial surge. Strange how straight and unusually formed Farfalla's rivers looked, without the spiderwebbing of canals and bustling docks that now broke up the natural lines of the waterways. Faded colored lines depicted various tunnels, waste lines, and electrical systems. I followed familiar streets with my finger, noting roads that hadn't been built yet and buildings no longer in use, my skin prickling at the contact.

"Graveyards," I said out loud, identifying the symbols and patterns on this map.

The air grew heavy as Daimyn padded quietly up behind me. He leaned over my shoulder and I stilled at his proximity, his face really just right there next to my face. Heat soaked into the entire left side of my body. *What on earth is that Feeling coming off of him?*

Oh jeez, he'd shifted closer.

Nope, you ninny, that's you leaning towards him.

I immediately corrected myself.

"Those caverns near it would also be a good spot to hide," Daimyn said, jerking my brain back on subject.

He turned to the other maps on the table, sifting through them until he pulled out another laid it out on top. Tracing similar lines, he found the same spot on the map and grunted.

"There's a research facility built there now. Too much activity. The Mercator may pull bodies from that area, but they won't be hiding there."

"Mercators are reclusive?"

"To say the least."

I frowned. "Huh. Must be a lonely line of work."

Daimyn lifted his eyebrows. He looked about to speak, then shook his head and set the map down, pulling out another.

"There's an abandoned tunnel system here that doesn't show on modern maps." He tapped the new map with his finger, showing me the route the tunnels took. "See if you can find anything that lines up."

I started with the oldest maps we could find, noting graveyards and tunnels and even sites of battles or skirmishes, to my best recollection. City construction during the Industrial Age was *bizarre*. It didn't make any sort of sense. Why in the name of everything holy would you put a pollution-producing factory *next* to the water, the most precious resource on our planet? Then I turned to the newer maps. New developments gradually replaced the old, and it fascinated me to see how the city slowly grew over itself, to reconstruct the burying of history through history.

Within an hour, I found several Mercator hideout possibilities. Smirking and absolutely *not* skipping over to the other end of the table where Daimyn worked, I dropped my list next to him.

I'm useful, damn it.

Daimyn's mouth curled, brilliant gaze lifting to mine as he pulled my list towards him with the tips of his fingers. My stomach did this ridiculous flipping thing that needed to stop. His attention dropped to the paper, and he studied it for a moment, tapping the end of his pencil to his lips, before crossing out the first on my list.

"Cucoy recently took this over. That would be a lot of effort for the Mercator to take it from them." He drew a line through the next. "Outbreak of fungi. It'll break down the bodies too fast." He used a wiggling line to cross out the next. "Your father is actually renovating this tunnel to connect to a rail line headed into Spain. Too much traffic."

Oh. Shows me how much I knew about my supposed legacy.

Daimyn looped circles through the next on my list; I suppressed the urge to shift agitatedly. His lips quirked like he fought a smile.

"Previous Mercator hideout. It's possible, but doubtful. They don't like someone else's leftovers."

I bit back an exclamation as he crossed out the *next* on my list with several lines.

"Landslide buried this last year."

Daimyn's gaze lifted, not even bothering to hide the humor glinting there. He tapped the final area on my list with his pencil.

"And this one…?"

I braced myself.

"A solid possibility."

My eyes narrowed, and his smirk spread as dark eyes held mine unflinchingly.

"You enjoyed that," I muttered.

"You're the one who strutted over here." He almost looked… *playful*.

I sniffed, snatched up the paper, and returned to my side of the table. Something warm and comforting stuffed up behind my ribs, something that tugged up the corners of my mouth. I wanted to wrap myself in it. I definitely had not expected this when I'd pushed my way into becoming a burr in his side; Mr. Badass pouring over maps in the library. But it was *fun*.

Comfortable quiet settled over the room again, but I struggled to fully focus this time. A particular thought kept thrusting itself to the front of my consciousness.

Ask about my sister's killer.

My stomach twisted. I glanced at Daimyn, unable to help it. He bent over the map against, tracing out something on paper. My lips parted—and my mouth flooded with bitterness. I shut it.

He might not know anything. Or maybe I couldn't force the words out because if I didn't ask, there always existed the possibility of an answer to a question that had plagued me for half a decade.

I do not let fear control me.

I inhaled silently to speak, and my stomach summersaulted into gnawing butterflies. *Just open your mouth and speak!* I looked back down at the maps, not really seeing them at all now. *Come on you absolute—*

"Are you going to say whatever is on your mind," Daimyn's voice cut in as a low rumble. "Or continue to fidget over there?"

I blinked at he looked up without moving his head, eyes amused.

Sass sprung easily. "I'm intent upon helping you save me from distress, you know."

"You can't ask incessant questions and work at the same time? I thought that was your default."

I eyed him. "Maybe I don't know if you'll actually answer me."

One eyebrow arched. "Has that stopped you in the past?"

"I don't have anything to hold over your head this time," I said sweetly.

His head lifted. "Ah, so there is a specific question in mind. And it's *important*."

My weight rocked—*fidgeting*—and I made myself still, taking a deep breath. "I need your help—" My tongue froze. I glared hard at the table. "I'd like to ask you about something. And see if you can identify who… what…" I swallowed. "Who the creatures were that killed my sister."

Okay, it's out. My face felt numb.

Daimyn set aside the map he'd been inspecting. Lacing his fingers together, he turned all his attention to me. "Go on," he said, voice heavy.

My lips formed words as if from far away.

"When I first met them… when I first met *him*, he looked human. They can make themselves look different." I cleared my throat, waving a hand around. "Totally different. And they can… trap someone in their own minds, some kind of all-encompassing mindfuck. Torture someone, make the pain real. Though they can create beautiful things too."

I blinked slowly at the table, dizzy for a second. "When he stopped pretending to look human… well, there were at least three of them, though I think there were more in the whole group. Anyway, they stopped pretending to be human, and maybe this was a disguise too, they were tall and… willowy." I touched my cheek. "Sharp cheekbones. All of them had white-silvery hair, different skin tones, but all still… silvery. Metallic, almost. He had bright blue eyes."

Those, at least, had not changed in whatever form he took.

I hazarded a glance at Daimyn's grave expression. "And I guess I should say they could kill, too, with their… talents."

Daimyn's chest expanded tight under his shirt before he spoke. "The human name for them is Dokkalfar. Sometimes known as dark fae, though it's a bit of misnomer. A subset of fae creatures, they have a natural affinity for mental arts: illusions, shifting perception…" He trailed.

Probably because I'd started hyperventilating. *This? This is how I find out? Just like this?* 'Dokkalfar' meant nothing to me, did nothing to the hole in my being.

"Why would they want to take someone? Why would they want to torture someone?"

He shook his head once, slowly. "I don't know."

I looked anywhere but at him, needing to say *something* but not knowing what. "Everyone said they were ransomers." *Telling me over and over it had all been in my head.* "Everyone said I made it all up to cope with her death."

"They might have started as ransomers, but that is not what happened with you and your sister," Daimyn said quietly.

My eyebrows drew together tightly. "What are you talking about?"

"Cerin and his—"

I flinched violently at the name. Awareness throbbed through the room, Daimyn's gaze unblinkingly locked with my own.

"That group," he began again. "Was an extreme sect of the Dokkalfar peoples unsanctioned by their Senate, trying to gather funds in order to build another stronghold. They'd been working through the West with lower-scale ransoming schemes. And then something changed with you and your sister."

All my limbs turned numb. I could barely process what he'd just said to me. But the familiarity of his recital of these facts… a breathless uneasiness shifted the ground beneath my feet.

"How do you know this?" I whispered.

Daimyn smiled without humor. "We almost met before, you know. I didn't put it together until recently. But I was there. I found the facility where you were being held and cleared it out before alerting the human authorities to your location."

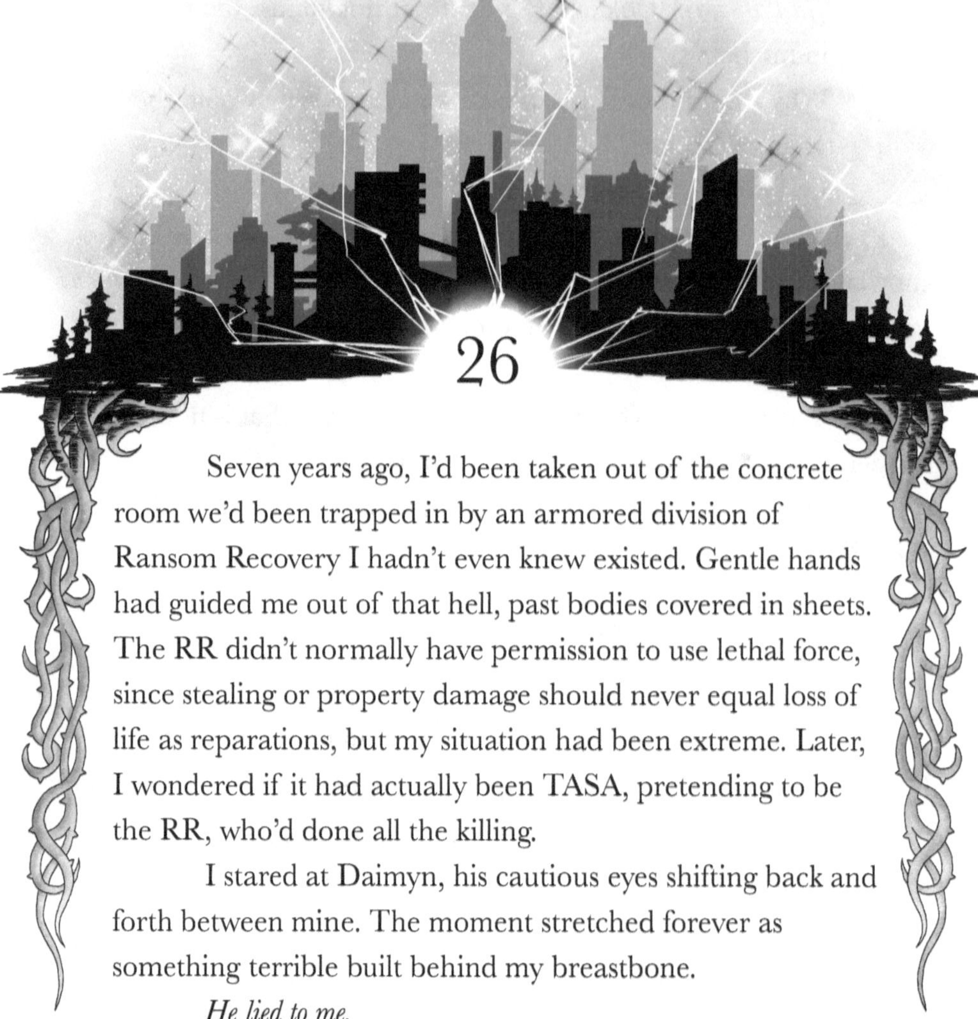

26

Seven years ago, I'd been taken out of the concrete room we'd been trapped in by an armored division of Ransom Recovery I hadn't even knew existed. Gentle hands had guided me out of that hell, past bodies covered in sheets. The RR didn't normally have permission to use lethal force, since stealing or property damage should never equal loss of life as reparations, but my situation had been extreme. Later, I wondered if it had actually been TASA, pretending to be the RR, who'd done all the killing.

I stared at Daimyn, his cautious eyes shifting back and forth between mine. The moment stretched forever as something terrible built behind my breastbone.

He lied to me.

"You knew I was looking for answers." I couldn't breathe. "You knew this *all along*? I asked you. Before, I asked— you *knew* I was looking—if you knew *this*—you *lied*—" If I could just *form a coherent sentence.*

A muscle ticked in Daimyn's jaw. "We only put this history together recently."

"You just happened to *forget* you rescued someone named Fairian Leynthall seven years ago?" My voice, loud and oppressive in the room.

Am I that forgettable?

Daimyn's eyes dropped. "Seven years ago, I was not… registering details of what I did. I did not remember the name of the girl I rescued."

What the hell?

Another question occurred to me before I could form something in response to what he'd said. "*When* did you figure it out? This *history* together?"

"A few days after the mediation with the serpentus umbra."

I stared without seeing a single thing. "And you disappeared."

And he obviously had no intentions of telling me.

"I didn't know—" He stopped. "I did not set out to keep it from you. I thought it might come up, now that we are working together. I did not know if it would hurt you; I did not want to bring it up until you asked yourself."

A disbelieving laugh broke out of me. "And if I'd never been attacked by that damned undead thing, then what? You *knew* I was looking for answers, you even *insisted* I had to have some kind of motivation, and you bloody *disappeared*."

Something flickered in his eyes too fast to read.

"You're right. I could have reached out to you. I'm not proud of my involvement seven years ago, so perhaps my intentions were more selfish than I'd like to claim." He shifted his weight. "But intentions rarely matter in the face of actualities, so I would like to say I am very sorry."

Another sound came out of me, really unintelligible at this point.

"Where are they now?—Since you know so much." My words moved like gravel through my throat. "Those dokkalfar?"

"Dead."

Heat twisted in my chest, threatening to tear out of my eyes. "I know he's not dead. I *saw* C-Cerin, after I was freed. I *Felt*—" I stopped. That would only incite questions of what I meant by 'Felt.' And the last time I'd told someone—when I'd told Cerin—he'd responded by torturing us and killing my sister.

Daimyn's eyes tightened. "He is also very dead."

"I *saw* him." The words ripped out of my throat in a snarl.

So many people, telling me over and over I made it all up.

"When did you see him?"

"What?"

"After you returned home, *when* did you see him?"

Much of the events of seven years ago had blurred together, and it took me a second to organize it correctly in time. "About a week after the… funeral. So maybe just under two weeks after. He stood on the street outside my bedroom window, at night."

Daimyn nodded, eyes thoughtful for a beat. "Then I caught up to him just under a month after that."

My heartbeat seemed to throb in every part of my body. There was no way that was true. For years afterwards I'd Felt hunted, studied, in danger. I'd felt those prickles on the back of my neck…

Prickles.

The blood drained from my face. Prickles like TASA evoked, prickles like the ones lately, which now I knew indicated someone watching, but not their identity. Technically I'd never *seen* Cerin since…

"What if he just made it seem like he was dead?" I demanded.

"Alteration magic doesn't work on me. Including illusions."

What on Earth—no, it didn't matter. I breathed deep to fling all my evidence… and stopped. Because the article that had made me think Cerin operated in Farfalla had been disproven. And the sensation of being watched, so similar to everything after Mari's death, had another reason entirely.

"You thought he was hunting you," Daimyn said, a question that wasn't a question. "Here, in Farfalla."

My stomach filled with rocks. "Yes," I spat. "I realize I am incapable of comprehending danger or reality correctly anymore."

A silence followed. I refused to cringe at it.

"Your comprehension abilities have never been in question," Daimyn said softly, and his tone lightened. "What you *do* with the situations you comprehend, however, is another matter. I would absolutely love to discuss where you've put your sense of self-preservation."

I stared at him for several long seconds, and just as the teasing in his expression faded to caution again, unsteady hilarity bubbled up my throat. I clapped a hand over my mouth after the ridiculous *giggle* that escaped. I shut my eyes, hiding and finding solace in the darkness of my eyelids.

"Fairian."

After a few grudging seconds, I opened my eyes. Daimyn rested his forearms against the table as he leaned towards me, very somber now. "Cerin cannot hurt you anymore. I promise." My heart lurched; it infuriated me that he still could still pin me here with his attention, radiating stability and safety. "The dokkalfar are not hunting you. Even if they were, they will not get to you. I will not allow it."

To my horror, my eyes began to burn, the edges of my vision blurring. "You don't even want me here. You made it clear you don't want anything to do with me." *Just like every other bloody person on this planet, as soon as they know me.*

His blink looked closer to a flinch. "Don't assume you know my desires. Either way, it's irrelevant now. Or have you forgotten your encounter with the death hound already?"

Yeah, he would be here while this situation got sorted—but after?

Daimyn still stared, that unselfconscious observing. Silence stretched, and I couldn't hold his gaze, staring down at the maps in front of me again; words wouldn't form in my head in a way that translated to my mouth.

"If you would like," Daimyn broke the quiet carefully. "I can make inquiries. To see if we can find out what happened, why they… did what they did to you."

My heart stopped, the answer instant and visceral. "No."

I did not want Daimyn anywhere near Cerin's reasons for taking Mari and I. Cerin had called me *special*; he did what he did after I told him about my Feelings and episodes, and I still had no idea why. Cerin was—had been—dangerous. Daimyn resided in a category all by himself. Until I understood what had made Cerin react like that to my bullshit abilities, I could not reveal it to anyone else. What if Daimyn reacted badly too?

"All right," Daimyn said quietly. "I will find another way to make amends to you, then."

I barely heard him. *Cerin was the only person who made me feel like I could be more than a freak daughter with a nebulous pedigree, and he had turned out to be a monster.*

My throat swelled until it hurt, and no amount of swallowing seemed to help.

"Cerin made us see awful things," I rasped, shocked at the words coming out of my mouth. "Some days I felt like terror was all that existed."

Something icy and predatory rose from my gut, a Feeling that couldn't be mistaken as originating from me even before it blipped out. I shut my eyes. Even as the foreign sensation practically drowned in sheer protectiveness, the intent and power behind the reaction tightened my stomach. Yes, Daimyn existed in another category of danger than Cerin.

"After she died," I said, and I wondered if I'd told another living soul about this. "After he killed her, he showed me… very beautiful things. I think in his fucked up way, he was trying to make me feel better."

My throat tightened until I couldn't speak. That had been the worst part, the most confusing. He showed me vivid, glittering landscapes while riding on the backs of glorious creatures, brought me elaborate dishes of food, my favorite treats, shared funny stories of his home and childhood. I understood now that's how cycles of abuse worked—the horror and then the placating, over and over—but having that logic didn't make living with it much better.

I squared my shoulders, lifted my chin, and opened my eyes. Daimyn watched me, and I couldn't tell anything from his expression. I didn't want to talk about this anymore, and flippancy came easy to hide in:

"Well, I suppose all of that is in the open now. Let's figure out where this death merchant is hiding."

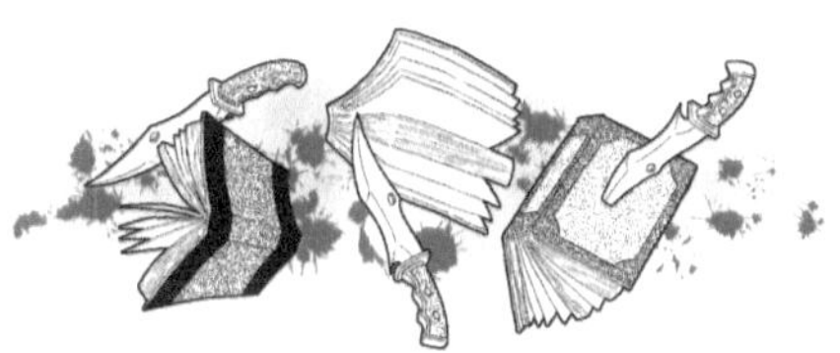

Betrayal tried to spark in my heart, the fact that he'd *kept* this from me. But somehow… I didn't let it. Maybe sleep deprivation had a hand in that, or the quiet gave me time to adjust to the reveal. Or maybe Daimyn's darting glances, the occasional flickers of something too calm for anxiety and too deep for nerves, reassured me that he hadn't intended harm.

Whatever the cause, the thought grew louder and louder: I didn't want to hold onto this anymore. Apparently, I had been holding onto Cerin long past his expiration date, and I didn't want the weight of any of that one second longer.

It bothered me Daimyn had been a part of that time in my past. Scratch that, I *hated* it. I just wanted to hold my sister in my memory and find incredible things, and it turned out that a thread of all that bullshit found me even now. But Cerin didn't get to poison my present. I didn't know what I would do about Daimyn's revelation—and the issue of his hiding it—but the last thing I wanted was to destroy whatever tentative partnership we had made.

With a deep breath, I looked up directly for the first time in… a long while. It took a second before dark jade flicked up. He turned motionless. I didn't know how to talk about all of this yet, sooo…

"Find anything else?" I asked hesitantly.

Caution threaded through the set of his shoulders. It did something to me, that my being upset affected him.

"Maybe another spot. Up towards the labs."

Awkwardness nipped at the air. I refused to break eye-contact though, and it drug on… way past socially accepted limits. He didn't seem bothered. Or to even notice. I wondered if he just didn't know, or didn't care, or if it was specific to me. I hadn't seen him interact with others enough to know if he brazenly watched them too.

And then a yawn nearly split my face open. It came from nowhere and before I could stop it.

"Bloody hell," I muttered, mortified. I rubbed my face briskly.

"Ah, so you're bored," he teased.

It seemed forced, but I took his opening and ran with it.

"How long do you expect *maps* to keep my attention?" I said scathingly. "Where are these dangerous creatures and attempts on my life you promised?"

Daimyn's eyebrows winged upwards, one slightly higher than the other. Then he shook his head, and started piling together papers on the table. "I think that's enough for tonight. We found a few potential places."

I jumped to my feet. "What are we going to do now!"

"Clean up, and then you're going to get some sleep."

My heart fell. "Never mind, let's stay here. I'm sure there's more to do with the maps."

Daimyn shot me a wry look. "Come on, Ms. Human needs her beauty sleep."

I blinked at the teasing, at the insinuation my humanness didn't apply to him. I still needed to get used to that.

We cleaned up all evidence of us being here and walked out, turning off lights and locking doors as we went. I didn't bother hiding my yawn as we walked back to the pazo, stretching and gazing up at the moon. It had taken on an eerie and beautiful green tinge around the edges. Our steps synched up, despite the height difference. Daimyn's eyes flicked over shadows, scanning everything around us with a weight that felt like a lighthouse without light. But his head was tilted towards me… as if I still captured part of his attention.

We reached Leynthall property, and slowed to a stop at the trees ringing the grounds. Exhaustion rubbed grit into my eyes and turned all my limbs heavy, but my heart clenched at the idea of just… walking away. I struggled for something to talk about even as my thoughts smeared in an exhausted mess, any subject at all.

Then Daimyn spoke as if carefully selecting his words: "Tomorrow, Regan and I will hunt down the Mercator, if they can be found."

My head whipped towards him, eyes narrowed.

"But we need to hunt down whoever hired them. I could use your help, specifically going through movement reports of some of my established enemies."

The rising frustration of him trying to leave me out stopped dead. Who were his established enemies? How did they have reports on movements? This sounded like a spy network.

My eyes narrowed. "You sure you just don't want me where the action will be?"

Daimyn's mouth tightened. "Mercator nests are guarded with their raised creations. We have no idea what we'll find there, if we do find them. The likelihood you'll get hurt is high. Your skills are better suited to this."

I knew it. I crossed my arms over my chest. "So I'll just stay safe like a good little girl," I said sweetly.

His arms braced across his chest with much more effective intimidation, which only exacerbated my irritation. "We each have a skillset, and using your abilities to our advantage only makes sense."

His all being rational made it really hard to argue.

"I'll sweeten the deal: I'll find any book on any magical subject you want."

Whooo boy. My brain staggered, the possibilities sprinting. By rote, my mind turned to Cerin. And with a sudden *snap* of weightlessness, I realized I didn't need to. It didn't have to be about him anymore; I could shed him like a skin. The lightness of the realization had me near-paralyzed.

I could request something on strigoi. Or performing magic itself, versus the creatures that lived it intrinsically. I could ask about the Divide, or those snake people we'd encountered, or fae, or maybe there were compendiums of magical history—

But. *But.*

It was obvious how much Daimyn wanted me *safe* while he went off and tangled with the dangerous and creepy. Furthermore, it was *not* safe for me to get access to any of Daimyn's information or information gathering capabilities; that sounded exactly like something TASA would want. I gritted my teeth.

"When will I ever get the chance to see something like this again?"

"Hopefully never," he retorted.

My fingers curled into my palms. "No—I want to be a part of this. *All* of it."

Bloody hell, our last fight only ended like an hour ago.

A deep rumble filled the air—out of him, I realized a second later, that sound like an honest-to-god growl. I blinked rapidly. He'd done that the other night and made the things sitting on the counter rattle. How did he do that? What did that mean? How did it work? If I put my ear against his chest would—

"Why?" he demanded.

I jerked back to the conversation. "*Because*," I shot back, and felt about five years old.

Daimyn stared at me, jaw flexing. Clustered feelings burst out of him, a tangle of sensations I didn't understand, all the more startling because, yet again, I got Feelings off of him.

"No. I will meet up with you afterwards and let you know what we find."

He turned and strode away. My jaw almost dropped.

"*Daimyn!*" I hissed, remembering at the last second not to shout.

He disappeared into the shadows.

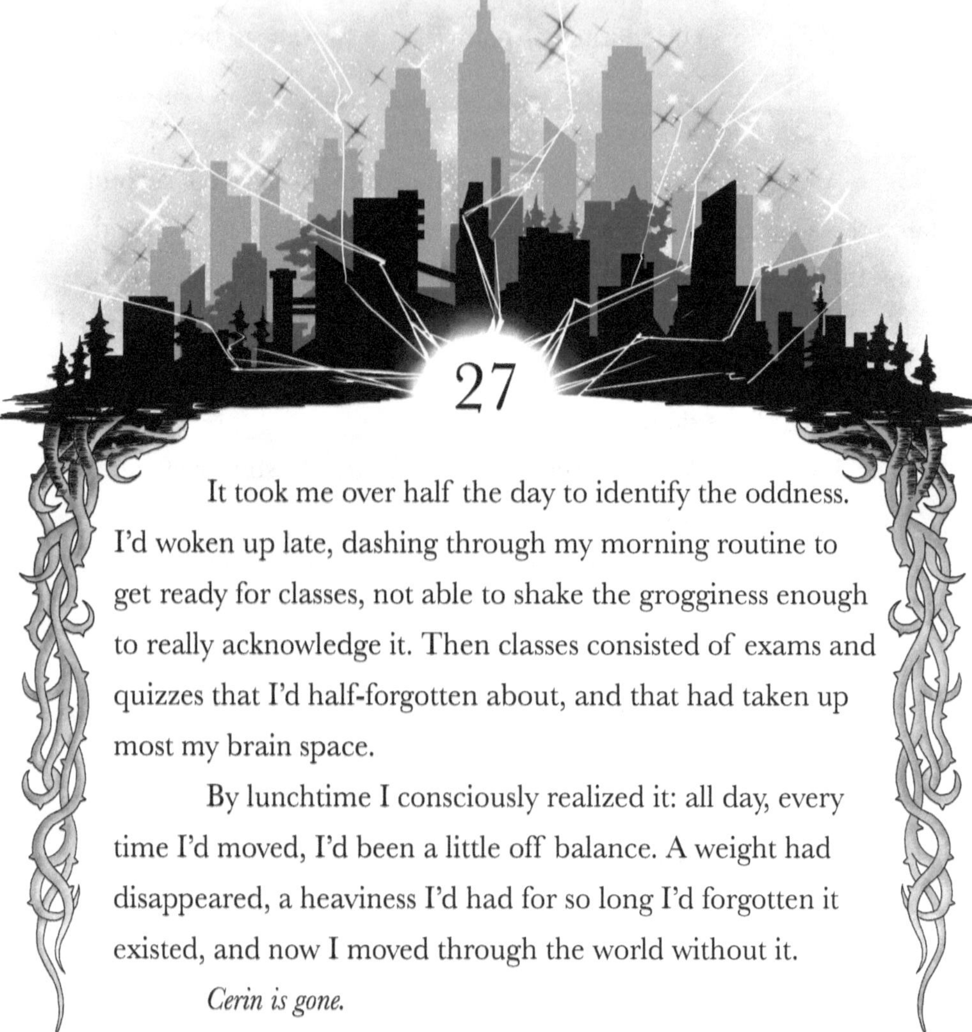

27

It took me over half the day to identify the oddness. I'd woken up late, dashing through my morning routine to get ready for classes, not able to shake the grogginess enough to really acknowledge it. Then classes consisted of exams and quizzes that I'd half-forgotten about, and that had taken up most my brain space.

By lunchtime I consciously realized it: all day, every time I'd moved, I'd been a little off balance. A weight had disappeared, a heaviness I'd had for so long I'd forgotten it existed, and now I moved through the world without it.

Cerin is gone.

Maybe I shouldn't just take Daimyn at his word, considering I'd known him all of a minute. But while I'd been sleeping my subconscious had apparently decided he spoke the truth, and my body adjusted accordingly. It left me feeling strangely… bereft almost. Anxiety kept habitually rising in bursts, then sputtering out as I remembered.

Oh, you've still got plenty else to worry about, my practical side announced cheerfully. *TASA for one, and then whoever is trying to murder you.*

Right. Always with the having to worry about danger. I scowled.

"I so failed French," Tiff mumbled from across from me.

My surroundings came back into focus, where Tiff and I sprawled across cafeteria table benches across where people's butts usually resided. The cavernous room had strangely little noise for the time of day, but I had the suspicion that students had bolted from campus the second their tests for the day finished. Exam Weeks apparently had a thriving culture of fuckoffery, the fuckoffery only getting steadily worse the farther in the semester.

"You didn't fail," I grouched.

"I don't have your affinity for languages." She mumbled something else about needing good grades.

"You're smart, Tiff. You got this."

She sighed and pillowed her arms under her head. "You used to care about this stuff too."

I nearly guffawed. *When was that? When I pretended not to be bored out of my mind?* "I have Tutor for the caring part of this equation."

Speaking of Tutor, he'd cancelled tonight's session to visit family or something. Gleeful restlessness seeped into my limbs. A whole afternoon to myself. I probably should take a nap, considering I had no plans to sleep tonight. Jerkface's precious keep-me-safe opinions notwithstanding.

Other tantalizing ideas tugged at me. In the past, Tiff and I had been able to sneak into Northampton's ES by working together. She'd even already suggested it after I'd told her about Sir Lightly's passing. The urgency of the Cerin issue may be gone, but that just meant I could research what I *actually* wanted.

I nibbled my lip. "Wanna ditch?"

She narrowed her eyes at me. "And do what?"

"Sneak into places we don't have permission."

Her signature evil smile teased her mouth. It faded a second later. "You haven't talked about… *him* in a while," she said slowly. "Is that why you want to go? Is there something… you found out?"

I had the urge to shout "he's dead!" and then cackle, but I didn't think that would score points for my sanity, or for her help.

"Yes, there might be something about arseface in there." I technically didn't lie: I could research Dokkalfar if I wanted. "Why can't we just go because we want to?"

Tiff eyed me for a long moment, and then with an exaggerated groan, pushed off of the cafeteria bench and sat up, tendrils of honey-gold hair sticking up in weird directions. "Le'go. We need a plan."

I didn't see asshole guard from last time as we scouted the entrance to the Exclusive Section. Only one librarian hovered at the desk by the entrance; a golden-haired, rosy-skinned, cherub-faced young man.

"We should check for windows," I said.

"We could also pull the fire alarm."

I considered it for half a second. "They'd probably lock it up or something… and take the keys. And then there'd be official attention." I didn't really know how Farfallan emergency services really worked, but if it mimicked anywhere else in Europe, we'd get in trouble.

A middle-aged ruddy-faced gentleman moved past us, headed down to the hall to the ES desk. Tiff and I made faces as he reached the desk and handed over what looked like a pass. I sighed heavily. Sure, that dude could get in when he wanted—

The receptionist shook his head as he spoke, blonde curls bouncing, and handed back the slip. The gentleman straightened, waving one hand. I couldn't quite make out what they were saying from this distance.

"Trouble, trouble, pudding in a puddle," Tiff sang quietly, citing an old half-remembered nursery rhyme.

The gentleman gesticulated sharply, some of his words making it down to us. "… right to be in there, there's no…" followed by something else I couldn't hear and: "…know who I am? This is… "

I snorted. Then blinked as two security guards marched past us towards the commotion. Tiff elbowed me as the guards approached the gesticulating gentleman. He jerked his arm out of the grip of one of the security guards when they tried to place a hand on his shoulder.

"Ooo boy," Tiff said.

After a few minutes of quiet, tense protest, the guards suddenly gripped him by both arms and started marching him away from the door to the ES. My eyebrows shot up. They really didn't kid around.

"Move along," one of the guards said to us as they marched him past, barely even glancing at us as they steered their quarry to the front doors of the library.

"—how *dare* you, mark my words—"

Tiff and I, not remotely heeding their order, stared on in interest as they marched him around the corner. Her elbow made contact with my ribs again. *Ow.*

"Fair-Fair. The door is unguarded."

My head jerked towards the ES door. The cherub-looking attendant had gone with the guards and unruly gentleman, leaving the hallway empty.

"Oh crap," I muttered, speeding towards the door before I could really decide a good plan of action. Tiff practically trod on my heels. I glanced over my shoulder; no one had returned yet. My heart pounded. We'd get caught any second now, this would get me into so much trouble—

My hand closed around the door handle. It turned. Heart in my throat, I pivoted on my heel as I opened it, watching the hall behind us as Tiff slipped past. I finished my pivot and stepped through, shutting the door behind us. Tiff and I stared at each other, breathing a little quickly.

"That's never going to happen again," I said.

Pure luck, in fact. *That's the second time I've gotten through doors with luck alone.*

Across from the door hung another map, like the one on the kiosk when first entering the library. But on this one, the greyed out "Exclusive Section" areas had the subjects filled in. My heart shivered in delight.

Northampton's Exclusive Section had been relegated to only a few small rooms, ordered neatly; there hadn't been enough per section that they *took up entire rooms by themselves.* The only other ES I'd been inside of was in Oxford, about two years ago, for only a few hours when I'd snuck away on a family trip there. I'd been on my WWII kick then, and I'd finally gotten an answer to the nebulous question of how the Allies were really able to defeat Hitler: magic. History books tried to explain it via the "Atom Bomb" or whatever, but in truth Allied forces had packed more than just guns and cannons. That, and how many Thule Society experiments had blown up in the Nazi's faces.

It had also been the first time I'd seen TASA's name in writing. I didn't know if the organization had been created before or after WWII, but it took on a significant role afterwards either way. I'd gotten a much better understanding of their meddling patterns, finally understanding why my leads on magic so often seemed to up and disappear.

"Where to first? History?" I asked.

Tiff rolled her eyes at my completely unsurprising interest, and made a 'let's go' gesture.

We walked, my heart skipping in delight. *I'm here I'm here I'm here.* An older gentlemen with spectacles, sandy skin, and dark hair passed us in the hall, his gaze lingering on us with an odd look. I forced the gigawatt grin off my face.

Chill. Don't be suspicious.

Tiff and I reached the history room and breath punched out of me. At least a dozen shelves spanned the room, standing a couple meters high, broken up by a few tables. How would I ever have enough time to get through everything? I needed another benefactor, to get access legitimately. I made a face, swallowing at the pang of grief and nearly writhing at the unfairness of it all.

Tiff started forward, her eyes round as she looked through the shelves. Her gaze caught something and she pulled out a book. I knew it's probable subject even before I walked closer to see: Humanitarian Efforts of the 21st Century. That fit with Tiff's usual interests.

Everyone knew the awful things Hitler had done to the Jewish and Romani people. And they also knew what many countries had done during the environmental crisis in the name of curbing excess, population control, and obedience. Attempts to save the planet started bloody and cruel. While most people acknowledged these things from our past, not many knew how bad it had been, or that it had ended a lot later than commonly said.

The point was: Tiff liked to know about this. I didn't know why. Learning about people doing terrible acts to other people didn't appeal to me. But she had a strong desire to know the truth, just as I did (though somehow she could turn the drive *off*). It was probably one of the things that made us friends.

I just couldn't talk to her about magic. The image Andrews had shown me of Tiff covered in blood, next to her dead boyfriend, flashed behind my eyes. I winced.

"You good here?" I asked, itching to move.

Tiff's gaze slid to me. "Yeah. Where are you off to?"

"Not entirely sure yet, going to see where it takes me."

Ignoring her stare, I darted off. My shoulders locked up as I strode down shelves, titles flinging themselves at me. Where did I even start? My brain felt like it had caught fire.

That relief of shedding Cerin's weight pulled oddly again. Maybe I could look up Dokkalfar to see if something could help explain Cerin's insistence on my "specialness." I made a face and mimed barfing to myself; I didn't want to look up Dokkalfar or try to hunt down *why* it all had happened, I wanted to live in the *now*.

Look up the Divide, my mind whispered. Its influence had been the thing to make me think Cerin had returned in the first place. *Make sure you understand it, so you don't make the same mistake again.*

Learning about the Divide had already been high on my research list. Plan solidifying, I tried to orient myself in the sea of bookshelves. The Society of Libraries, thankfully, had created a universal organization system that most libraries followed. But even once I'd figured out where I stood, it was difficult to actually comprehend titles as I walked along the shelves. Sometimes my inability to actually be calm deeply frustrated me.

Then a black book among the browns and greens caught my attention. A title finally registered.

Obsidian: A True History of the Divide.

I stopped so fast I almost fell over. My hand shot out, touching the frayed-looking binding as if to make sure it actually existed. I slowly pulled it from the shelf and sank to the floor, the book cradled in my lap. Thick, sizable, and worn, the writing had faded to a bronze sort of color. I barely breathed as I opened it to a random page, the paper feeling excruciatingly fragile.

A sketch of a wall hovering over water took up the two pages in front of me. A thrill crawled up my spine and over my ears and face. Sections of the wall had been drawn telescoped, blown up to show strange shapes and curling designs across the surface. The shapes did not belong to a language I knew of.

I flipped to the page before it, skimming quickly to get context. Someone had managed to get close, for long enough, to see these symbols carved into the… obsidian? The author said the Divide was made from meter-thick obsidian.

Without pulling my eyes away, I yanked my pack off one shoulder and fought with the zippers. Without the use of my eyes it took me longer to locate a notebook and pencil, but I couldn't look away if my life depended on it.

Ripping a page out of the notebook, I laid it over the diagram of the Divide and began to trace, as quickly and as accurately as possible. This probably broke a few laws, but I had a limited amount of time and had to take what I could.

I finished my tracing and quickly flipped to the introduction. The author quoted the first mentions of the Divide, starting in the 12th century, and laid out all the expeditions that had tried to get across and failed. I knew the basics, but the flushed out information thrilled me.

Pope Benedict XXII had taken credit for the Divide in his war against the 'unnatural and profane,' but little evidence existed that he'd actually had it built. I remembered again, Daimyn's explanation of the history of the use of the word 'demon.' Flipping through pages and speed-reading for my life, the author addressed speculations from other scholars of the Divide origin, but quickly disregard their research as flawed for this or that reason.

At the end of the chapter, he only wrote that we had no real idea who had constructed it. But he did believe evidence had been purposefully destroyed during the crusades against magic, when they drove magical creatures into the sea—

Wait, *what?*

I searched the rest of the book but found nothing related to the sea, even in the index. I looked up from the treasure in my hands and focused on the other books shelved where this one had been.

Ocean Fortress: Sea Travel in the Obsidian Age—I yanked that one out, a thinner, green book, and set it next to me.

What Split the Planet—that came next, another small book, this one light brown.

I flipped to the index of the first, looking for anything related to oceans or sea or crusades. Nothing.

Next book—*score*. I flipped quickly to the highlighted pages, skimming quickly. This author postulated that the Divide and the disappearance of 'demons'—what did it mean he used that word in an intellectual context?—occurred within a very short period of each other, if not simultaneously. He didn't give any evidence for his theory, only his musings.

But 'demons' haven't disappeared.

I flipped the book over to find the publication date. Over a century ago. I flipped to the first page of *A True Story* as well. Its release date was closer to 150 years ago. If these scholars believed magical creatures disappeared… did that mean they returned within the last century? Were these authors uninformed or lying?

Maybe should find something that highlighted Farfalla's history specifically.

"Hey," Tiff whispered right behind me.

I about jumped out of my skin, smacking the book shut on instinct. She frowned at me, eyes flicking down at the books and notes sprawled all about me.

"Bloody hell, don't sneak up on me," I groused at her, trying not to look suspicious. "I was deeply involved here. What's up?" I smiled cheerfully.

Tiff's minor hesitation *almost* had sweat breaking out across my body. "I'm heading to another section. Meet you back at the door in two hours? We should probably get back to campus and act like we didn't ditch."

"Sounds great," I said, absolutely smiling too much.

Tiff rolled her eyes at me and then trotted off. I exhaled quietly, scanning everything stacked around me. I don't think Tiff could have seen much, but I needed to be more careful. I put away a bunch of my notes and cleaned up the sprawl of books around me better.

While sorting, the index of one of the books caught my attention again:

Divide Burden

> *Dakar*
>
> *Farfalla*
>
> *W. Ireland*
>
> *E. Australia*
>
> *N. Russia*

I frowned, flipping until I came to the right pages. The author detailed Farfalla's "Divide Burden" as causing people's nightmares to come alive and hunt them down, and something inside of me relaxed. I'd believed Daimyn when he'd told me, but secondary confirmation always made me feel better.

I flipped to the page numbers of the other places listed, and my eyebrows slowly rose.

"*The area of Dakar, South along the coast, is characterized by outbreaks of possessions…*"

"*The people of Lebu and Sereer have a long history of dealing with spirits and exorcism…*"

"*In the areas of Portmagee, Dunquin, and Belmullet, Ireland, the ground itself opens up to swallow people whole. This phenomenon has also been recorded on the northern island of Scotland. Oddly enough, animal or magical flora and fauna do not seem to be targeted."*

"Despite denials by the crown, there is ample evidence fae and human openly work together for safety…"

Fascination pooling in my mouth, I flipped to the introductory paragraph for the section to get the author's take on all of this.

The Divide's proximity to land has a direct magical influence on coastal-living peoples. The affects have been well-documented throughout the years, though are rarely elaborated upon beyond emergency services and ivory tower debate. This author's aim to give a broad overview of this phenomenon, also known as Divide Burden, in an effort to add to common understanding and discourse.

The reason behind this phenomenon is not well understood. Theories range from the Divide's presence as an evil force, to it being a defense mechanism…

"Walls are built to defend what's on the other side," I whispered.

To my utmost frustration, the author did not go into further detail on that theory. I set the book down and turned to another, turning against to the index to look up 'burden' this time—

A flicker of unease had my head coming up. Sitting on the floor as I did, I had a view of part of the room through the gap between the top of the books and the higher shelf. Through it, I saw the slow, deliberate gait of someone wearing black dress pants that I'd seen all the guards around here wearing.

I stiffened and slowly put down the book. The individual meandered towards me, and through a gap higher up, I saw a flash of a face I recognized.

Asshole guard.

Shite. He knew my face, and that I didn't have a permit. I came to my feet as silently as possible. I didn't have enough time to clean up the evidence of my being here. I grabbed my backpack and my notes, hesitating with a pang at leaving the books on the floor.

They'll be fine.

Keeping an unfocused eye on AG, I slid along the shelves quietly to keep them between him and I. As he walked into the stacks, I turned and quick walked out of the room into the long connecting hallway. A prickle crept up my neck, and I increased my pace, biting my lip.

He's on to me.

Getting caught without a permit in the Exclusive Section came with a variety of penalties and fines, which I'd never really cared about in Northampton. But I had three new problems in Farfalla: they might revoke my Simple permit as a penalty (and then I wouldn't have access to *anything*); I did *not* want to get Tiff in trouble, especially with my mother's warnings; Farfalla's ES treasure trove was a much bigger loss than Northampton's.

I considered diving into another room, but that made me more easily cornered. Swearing quietly under my breath, I aimed for the door leading out instead. I had wanted to open a window for the possibility of sneaking back in later, but footsteps grew louder behind me.

Making sure my steps came down businesslike but calm, I turned to the hallway with the door leading out and did not look behind me. A second later I'd closed the door behind me, heart racing staccato, and the cherub-looking man behind the desk smiled at me distractedly.

"Good evening," I said pleasantly and with as little memorable inflection as possible, and strode away.

Almost there, almost there.

I'd just reached the end of the hall when I heard the door click open behind me. Turning the corner, I broke into a dash, putting shelves between me and the hallway and diving into the history room. I quick-walked along the edge, as much out of view as possible, and grabbed books at random.

I found a free desk and sat down, spreading around the books and flipping them open to random sections. As a final touch, I pulled off my jacket and hid it under the table, out of sight, and pulled up my hair. Then I pulled the books closer and diligently ran my eyes across the pages, though not a single word penetrated comprehension.

Probably overkill. But I'd stay here for a while just in case.

A few minutes later, when AG paused a few meters away, obviously taking me in, I deliberately did not look up at him. I barely breathed, until he finally turned and stalked off. I exhaled silently in relief.

Not overkill, then. Thank goodness for paranoia.

Relaxing back into the chair, I pulled out my PCD to check the time. An hour had passed since we'd gone in; Tiff would be there a while yet. Until then I'd write down everything I could remember I'd read.

Tiff found me about three-quarters of an hour later. "Did you find everything your heart desired?" she asked lightly.

I snorted, finishing up putting my notes away. "Like that's even possible. No, I almost got caught." I sniggered, able to be amused about it now.

"What?" Tiff demanded under her breath.

I waved a hand and explained the situation.

Tiff crossed her arms and frowned, but nodded. "Sorry you had to leave early."

"It's all good." I grinned. "I took excellent notes."

"What did you find?"

Ah crapsticks. She usually didn't ask outright. "Uh, yeah, let's talk about it on the way back. I want to get back to campus before we get in trouble."

"Sure," Tiff said after a beat.

I'd have to tell her something. Maybe I could say I'd figured out Cerin wasn't here; that would probably get her to drop it, *and* be reassuring. She had every right to ignore magic or anything related to it if she wanted, I just didn't want to deal with her lecturing me about it.

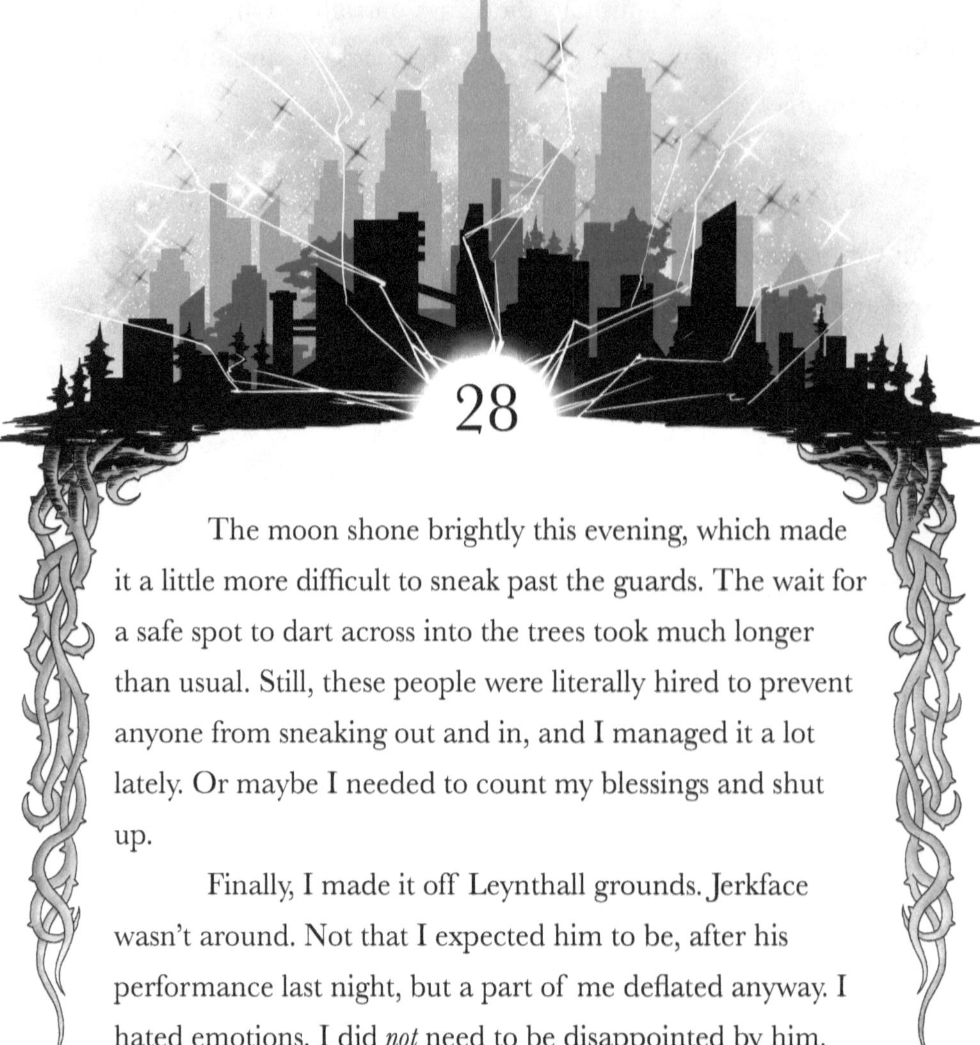

28

The moon shone brightly this evening, which made it a little more difficult to sneak past the guards. The wait for a safe spot to dart across into the trees took much longer than usual. Still, these people were literally hired to prevent anyone from sneaking out and in, and I managed it a lot lately. Or maybe I needed to count my blessings and shut up.

Finally, I made it off Leynthall grounds. Jerkface wasn't around. Not that I expected him to be, after his performance last night, but a part of me deflated anyway. I hated emotions. I did *not* need to be disappointed by him.

I didn't really know when Mr. I'll-Just-Keep-You Safe would arrive at any of the places we'd identified the night before—or maybe it had been really early morning at this point, whatever—so my plan consisted of flying by the seat of my pants. Obviously, I could not face a freaking monster-creating magician by myself. But I would not be left out of this. I'd find Mr. Save-the-Damsel and glue myself to him if I had to.

I winced at how desperate that sounded.

The closest possible Mercator hideout to me that we'd identified was an abandoned underground rail station that ran under an old cemetery that had gone out of use in the 1700s. The actual entrance to the railway—an old maintenance access point—was on the eastern edge of Farfalla. I'd start there and see what happened.

Because I was *trying* not to be a twit, I found Daimyn's contact number in the Population Survey Database as I strode towards my destination.

F. Leynthall: *Look, I found a self-preservation instinct. I'm letting you know I'm headed to the railway entrance to look for signs of death merchants.*

See? I could get smarter.

Chill crept into my bones and clung, the quiet around me seeming to grow its own consciousness the further I got from home. The scuff of each of my steps seemed to grow louder the more I walked; my footsteps were the only thing to break up the stillness.

I shook myself vigorously before I gave way to nerves. All of my missions had been solitary; this wasn't new. This even reminded me of the first time I'd snuck out on a magic-seeking mission, a week or so after Mari's death. I'd heard rumors about magical activity, and had needed to start somewhere. I'd found a 'secret society' that had been all talk and stomach-curdling cultish devotion. Their meeting had been raided, we'd all been arrested for 'obscene activities,' and I'd spent my first night in jail.

I made a face. That was probably the first time I'd met TASA, though I hadn't really known it at the time. I shoved that away, though it stuck like tar. No doubt they'd be following up soon to talk about my "interactions" with Daimyn.

What am I even doing? It's not like my presence is needed. It could not be more obvious how much I'm not needed here.

I shoved that ruthlessly away too.

Maintained streets slowly gave way to old dirt and gravel roads. Out here, the wild quickly reclaimed buildings that sat abandoned for decades. It both comforted and alarmed to see how quickly it all disappeared.

I slowed at the sight of an old metal sign tacked to an even older metal shack.

MA TEN NE AC ES

OF ICI L BUS NESS O LY.

Growing closer, I could see the peeling and worn paint, letters covered in dirt. The door had been chained shut. I stopped and heaved a deep breath, my ribs briefly compressed in the corset I'd worn as an additional measure of protection. Steel boning was no joke.

"Tell me."

I yelped, spinning towards the voice.

"Did you consider how your friends and family and fucking *me* would react, wondering what happened to you for the rest of our lives?"

Ohhh, he's pissed. Daimyn strode towards me from a few meters away like an oncoming avalanche. It made me want to erupt in giggles. Could I have normal reactions for once?

"I was planning," I said carefully. "On seeing if I could find you here. I was not planning on going inside and being eaten."

"And you decided to do this without protection, knowing there are those who stalk you."

"Hey, I alerted you!" I threw my arms out. "See? Growing as a person."

His eyebrows became hard slashes across his forehead. "Yes, thank you for the most basic attempt at helping me find your *body* later."

I scowled. "What did you think would happen? That I'd stay *home* and *safe* like a good little girl?"

Daimyn came to a halt a half-meter away, glaring down at me. I forced myself not to fidget or cross my arms defensively, instead just lifting my eyebrows as coolly as I could at him.

"Fairian," he murmured, and something about the way he said my name made me wary. "You don't have to fight so hard anymore. You are safe from him."

The hair on the back of my neck stood on end. "What is *that* supposed to mean?"

Daimyn shifted before becoming impossibly still again. "I understand you have been driven for a long time." The strange gentleness in his voice made *all* the hair on my body stand on end. "But you have your answer now, don't you? You're no longer in danger from him, and there is no need to be this reckless. I can—"

I cut him off as I finally understood the enraging, erroneous conclusion he'd come to. "You think that's why I've been—you think this is about *him*?"

"All your recklessness makes sense if you've been operating under the assumption he still hunted for you—"

"My recklessness *doesn't* make sense, okay?" The words sounded too loud, like I shouted, but I hadn't. "Don't tell me what it's from. Do *not* tell me that *my* decisions are due to *his* bullshit."

I'm shaking. Damn it. Daimyn's sharp gaze hunted over every centimeter of my face.

"This is *mine*." My entire being vibrated with offense and hurt. "Do *not* tell me it's because of him."

I didn't care if Cerin had made my magic-seeking worse, I didn't care that psychologists could have a field day over this. I'd made this *mine*.

I don't know what Daimyn saw on my face, but his predatory-stillness softened. Before I could try to interpret what that meant, he gave a single, abrupt nod, and looked over my shoulder.

"All right. I will not bring it up again."

I blinked at his sudden surrender.

"There was no sign of a Mercator at the mill or the graveyards up by the research facility," he continued. "Regan is headed for the old mines to the North. Let's see what the tunnels have to show us."

He strode past me towards the shack. I'd barely registered his words before a terrible shriek of metal split the air. I swiveled around to see him drop broken chains from the door to the ground. Daimyn yanked, and the door swung open, one hinge snapping clean off so the door hung awkwardly on its frame. He frowned at it, and then disappeared inside the shack.

Another groaning shriek of metal followed a second later.

I swallowed hard, off balance from his anticlimactic acceptance of what I'd said when I'd been ready to fight about it. *Did he even believe me, or just decide not to argue about it?* Warily, I walked over to see Daimyn crouch and pull open a round metal door set in the ground. Cold, stale air filtered up into my face, smelling of mold. Darkness enveloped everything below.

Daimyn rifled through his coat and then handed me a small black object. A torch.

"Now, what are the rules from yesterday?"

I blinked slowly at him. "Don't hurt anyone, you have veto power over some subjects, and definitely throw myself at any danger we encounter."

Daimyn slowly turned to look at me. "That is definitely not what I said."

I tapped my lips. "Oh sorry. Was it, poke at everything I find to see what happens…?"

His eyebrows lifted, expression unamused.

"Or was it—"

"Fairian."

Why did he have to say my name like that?

"You don't have to act like a brat to get my attention."

My lips parted, abruptly off balance *yet again*.

One corner of his mouth curling upwards, Daimyn stepped forward over the hole and disappeared feet first. I sucked in a breath, lurching forward a step as a muffled thud came from below. Mr. Badass apparently didn't worry about things like being able to see where his feet landed.

"I have a good feeling about this one." His disembodied voice came back up at me. "It seems like a place a Mercator might take up residence."

"Ha-ha, I found it," I said on reflex.

You don't have to act like a brat to get my attention.

My stomach flipped. Shaking it off, I clicked on my torch, walked to the edge, and peered into the hole. An old rusty metal ladder extended down about 3 meters or so. Daimyn's torch clicked, and a beam of light panned over uneven ground; he stood on a narrow ledge, probably a maintenance walkway, that ran alongside the deeper depression where the railroad tracks lay.

"You coming?" he asked without looking, and something more than those words lay in his question.

"Yes," I said simply, answering all he asked, and held the torch in my teeth as I grabbed the rusty metal rods of the ladder and climbed down.

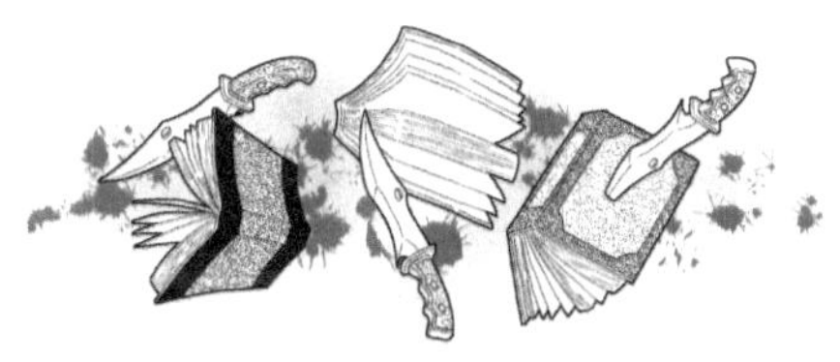

The stone ceiling of the underground tunnel arched high above us as we traveled down the walkway next to the tracks. Weird stuff I couldn't identify lined—or grew from—the cracks of the stone. A skin-crawling sense of sentience filled this whole place. I agreed with Daimyn; this place practically oozed something happening.

The darkness seemed to reach out like hands, the little I could see of the walls seeming to shift in the corner of my vision where the torchlight lost its power. Another shiver ran up my spine, and I kept my breathing even.

"How will we know if we hit the lair?" My voice echoed down the tunnel and bounced off the walls.

"You'll know," came the reply.

Helpful.

The floor sloped downwards, and I glanced at the ceiling uneasily. The weight of the earth up there felt nearly tangible, and the mass of it only increased the further we went. *Now is not the time to think about that.*

"I'm going to walk over here," I decided, and then jumped down into the depression where the tracks ran. The light from Daimyn's torch slowed, then kept pace with me. I balanced on one of the steel rail tracks as I walked, trying to distract myself. The tunnel felt even bigger from here, towering above my head. Contrarily, my claustrophobia only increased.

This really, really reminded me of things I really, really didn't want to dwell on. Cerin had trapped us in darkness for hours as we heard *things*, saw glimpses of horrors we couldn't identify. It's why I chose to fall in love with the night. Otherwise it would have swallowed me whole.

I glanced over at Daimyn, or more accurately, towards his torch light. The darkness, the turn of my thoughts, his presence—a question rose that had lingered in the back of my skull since yesterday.

"Why aren't you proud of your involvement seven years ago?"

The soft sound of his footsteps slowed. I winced, realizing how out of the blue that sounded. I couldn't see anything of him to try to discern what he thought. The quiet stretched and I scowled, annoyed at the lack of answer and uneasy at the disturbing image my mind supplied of Daimyn not actually existing over there anymore, just that beam of light keeping pace with me.

"Are you not supposed to rescue foolish heiresses or something?" I joked.

"No, nothing like that," Daimyn said. "I simply did not need to handle the situation in the way I… I didn't need to kill them. I understand you do not—should not—have sympathy, but they were young and foolish, and I could have done many other things besides end their lives."

I swallowed. "Why did you? Kill them?"

His answer took even longer this time. "I was not myself."

I opened my mouth and then stopped as Andrews' words came back full force: *That family is often ruled by a darker nature.* I shut my mouth, heart hammering. I shouldn't ask more, not with TASA hovering.

My stomach flipped with bile-inducing intensity. I almost disregarded it as my body's reaction to the direction of my thoughts, but Daimyn's light halted. A cold gust of air rushed across the back of my neck, pebbling my skin and freezing the air in my lungs.

Between one second and the next, Daimyn appeared next to me. Howling broke out down the tunnel. The sound itself transformed into a living thing, raging towards us, straining against the stone walls. It morphed, echoing from everywhere, engulfing, no original point of the horror, just the dark screaming.

The two lights blurred across my vision, grey smearing into jagged shapes. Blood thudded in my ears. My mind turned static, scrambling along nothing, *absolutely nothing, nothing was real, I had to remember nothing was real—*

"Remember how I told you I would occasionally order you to run?"

I gulped for breath. Daimyn hadn't been there, in that place Cerin had made. I clung to that discordant fact like a lifeline.

"Yes," I husked.

"Time to run."

Panic swelled like a gathering tsunami. All my limbs had turned numb and useless.

"Fairian, *go.* Gain some distance."

I couldn't run, because when we ran, the ground moved and grew razors, the blades slipping into our feet and—

Daimyn cursed. His flashlight clicked off, and he disappeared into the gloom of the tunnel like he'd never even been here.

My heart gave up and died.

The howls turned high and eager, the excited yelps of finding prey. My skin tried to shudder off my body, and screaming picked up in my head. A heavy thud followed a gust of air over my right ear, a smack sounding afterwards. A keening cry of pain abruptly cut off. The howls turned murderous, snarls and growls filling the space until it threatened to burst. I couldn't see. I couldn't *see.* Slowly, so slowly, I lifted my torch, towards the sounds.

A black coat, snapping as Daimyn moved so fast he blurred. Light, glinting off metal that cleaved through distorted grey limbs, teeth, flashing claws and sickening twisted faces.

My chest heaved in deep, controlled cycles; I'd forced myself into the calming pattern out of habit.

The key to your mind is through your body.

That was right, that was right. I knew panic, I knew fear. It did not control me. I gripped the handle of the knife on my hip. I was here, now—Mari was gone, she was dead, there was nothing I could do to save her. And Daimyn, he couldn't be hurt.

It would be okay.

Impact. My back slammed into the ground before it registered something hit my chest. Sharp pain shocked across my body. I gagged—on the smell, the weight on my lungs. My jacket and shirt jerked, hard. My arm came up on instinct to defend my face, and pressure and piercing pain slammed down on my forearm.

The crushing weight thrashed back and forth, jerking against my forearm and shifting its weight across my ribcage. I writhed, couldn't dislodge the weight on top of me. With a heave of effort I bucked my whole body, and it fought for balance, claws raking across the boning of the corset.

I knew this, being trapped in the dark and helpless. I hadn't been able to fight then.

My next breath drew in fire and ignited in my chest.

I'm not so helpless anymore.

My fingers found the handle of my knife. I couldn't see, but *there* —I drove the knife upwards. My arm jarred from the impact. Pressure released from my forearm as the thing on top of me let out a gurgling shriek. I sliced again before I lost its location in the dark, my blade skittering on something hard. It ripped away from me with a gulping croak and yanked my knife along with it.

Weight toppled off of me. I lunged backwards, away, rage's gift of strength turning to ash. Grey limbs and the edge of black coat flashed in front of the light of my fallen torch.

Daimyn bellowed my name. For not the first time, I realized.

I flinched instinctively, waiting in bile-inducing anticipation for the next attack, eyes wide open and unseeing. But even as I moved away from the noise, I headed farther into the darkness.

…have to get the torch…

It took all my willpower to stop and roll forward into a crouch. It took even more to stay still and suck in gulping breaths. *I will face fear. I will not let it control me.*

Daimyn roared my name again. A sickening crunch followed.

"Yes," I husked.

"*Are you hur—*" He broke off with an aggravated bark of sound, followed by whistling metal.

My knees practically knocked together as I rose to my feet, then shifted forward, centimeter-by-centimeter, towards my torch.

"I'm okay," I whispered. "I'm okay."

Finally I reached the light, snatching it up off the ground and directing it at Daimyn's voice. He had something grey and multi-limbed in a headlock under his arm, and furiously hacked at another one with a sword. I swept the light over the walls, searching for others. I flinched at every new space revealed.

The only others lay unmoving at Daimyn's feet. They were all different: different sizes, some with long limbs and others with short stubby appendages or multiple ones in weird places. A few with two heads and several rows of teeth.

The final one struggled in Daimyn's grip, pinned under one of his arms. As I watched, Daimyn grabbed and twisted its head with a sickening crack, then literally pulled its head off its body. Tendons and pieces of it fell to the floor.

Hrk.

Daimyn whipped towards me. "Are you all right?"

I jerked back and he halted. I hadn't meant to flinch; I hadn't even consciously realized he'd advanced towards me.

"I think I killed one." My voice came out thin. *Damn it.*

Daimyn's attention fell to the ground, and I kept my light on him as he walked over and kicked over one of the bodies. Something glinted. He reached down and pulled it out before palming it up towards the light: my knife.

"Hit straight in the heart," he murmured, his head tilting. "It's the only way to kill them, besides fire or complete dismemberment. You have incredible luck."

"It's skill, don't you doubt it." Falling back on my ability to bullshit came with a flood of relief. It probably would've been much more impressive if I hadn't been shaking, sending the light from my torch quivering.

"Are you injured?" He slowly walked up to me and I didn't flinch this time. He held out my knife and I took it with my right arm, immediately regretting it as it throbbed with hot, dull pain. I winced, and Daimyn's fingers slid around my wrist, pulling me towards him. With a click, he shone his light on my arm, turning it back and forth. *How did he know?*

Daimyn grunted, furrowed eyebrows visible even from the faint light. "I don't like that it broke skin again. We need to address this, and I don't have the healing stone with me."

"After we find the Mercator," I said firmly. Well. As firmly as I could.

The tail end of his sigh gusted faintly over my cheek. "Let me at least wrap it."

"With what?"

"Roll up your sleeve."

I couldn't get my jacket up past my elbow, so I took my arm out of it and pulled up my sleeve. Daimyn put the torch in his teeth as he rustled around in his coat, withdrawing a small bundle. He untied it, revealing long strips of cloth which he proceeded to wrap around my arm. *Where did he hide all this stuff?* Within seconds, he'd tightly bandaged my arm, tucked the ends in, rewrapped his bundle, and shoved it back into the recesses of his coat.

"Huh," I said, twisting my arm back and forth.

"You don't have anything to prove, you know," he said quietly.

Yes I do. To myself. "We need to find this thing. Let's go."

My personal nightmares were coming to life in this dark, and I would not allow my terror to drag anyone down. I resolutely wobble-marched forward. A few endless seconds later I inhaled quietly in relief as Daimyn's footsteps picked up and reached my side.

Our beams of light bobbed down the tunnel in companionable silence.

29

I finally stopped shaking by the time the tunnel opened up into a terminal of some sort. I'd *almost* managed to stop flinching at every unidentified noise, too. My arm throbbed like hell, but somehow that helped me focus. It was pain. Real pain. Not nightmare pain, pretend pain like Cerin had fed our brains as a drug.

Daimyn swept his light back and forth over the room, the beam catching on swirls of dust and cobwebs that… did not look right. I couldn't put a finger on why. There wasn't a lot of light down here, but even considering that the grey seemed starker than normal, like the color had been bled from the area. A broken down rail car leaned off to one side, its windows smashed and frame bent oddly. Other machines and stacks of boxes sat out along the edges of the room. I expected to smell dust and mustiness but instead my shoulders tensed as a familiar sicky-sweetness teased my nostrils.

Am I imagining that smell?

I pointed my torch beam upwards, guided by an urge I didn't even think about—and froze.

Something huge hung from the ceiling. Something not a machine. My brain couldn't make sense of it, wouldn't put it in any coherent order. I made an involuntary noise.

Daimyn shot me a look and followed my gaze. His whistle echoed through the cavern. "Haven't seen one of those in a while."

"What… is it?"

"At the moment, just a hunk of dead flesh."

"I think our dear death master left," echoed a voice from across the platform.

I nearly leapt out of my skin with a muffled squeak. Daimyn directed his light across the terminal, and Regan's form materialized out of the darkness. Well, didn't he just look like a super badass. I scowled, heart thundering. Regan wore a similar get-up as Daimyn, striding across the room like he owned the place, each of his steps sending up clouds of dust that seemed to move too slowly.

"There are only two ways out, the way you came and the way I came," Regan said, his voice echoing. "Hullo, Fairian! How's your first taste of the hunting nightlife?"

"I killed a few already," I shot back.

Thankfully, Daimyn didn't correct me on my numbers.

Regan chuckled. "You look pale as the dead. Don't worry, it'll all be over soon."

Daimyn leaned over and spoke in my ear. "Stay here. Please. I hear something." He strode forward before I could respond, disturbing the dust on the floor and sending up more of those clouds of swirling grey that moved as if the air was too thick for it to settle down again. For once, I decided to listen to Daimyn and stayed put. Maybe because of the please. Either way, I did *not* want to be underneath the giant whatever-it-was hanging there.

I panned my light across the terminal, curiosity pricking at me over the odd shapes. I stopped over what looked like a coal-powered locomotive with lifted eyebrows. Now *there* was an old piece of technology. I'd seen one in a museum once when my father had been on one of his educational sprees—

Chills spread up my spine a second before a whispering hush spread through the terminal. Daimyn and Regan both halted as one. I hunkered down closer to the wall, then rolled my eyes at myself. Hello, my torch beam broadcasted my position to everyone in the vicinity.

Wind buffeted the room with a giant *WOMPH* of air. Dust stripped from surfaces into opaque clouds that stung my face. I lifted my light, and got uncomfortably close to understanding why people peed themselves with fear. The huge thing hanging from the ceiling had spread gigantic wings, and with no further fanfare, slammed down on top of both Daimyn and Regan.

My hand clamped over my mouth.

The creature resembled something between an elephant and a huge bird. One eye swelled out of its socket, cloudy and bulging, while the other looked like it had exploded at some point, a hollow shell of something oozing dark fluid. Grey strips of flesh hung off its body, pale flashes of bone showing through.

The creature jerked up as if struck from below; it shuffled its wings and settled back down again.

A figure strode out of seemingly nowhere, quickly skimming around the commotion in the center of the room, headed straight towards me. With no obvious presented gender, they were as pale as bleached bone. Dressed in grey, tattering clothing, but the fabric moved slow, almost like it was underwater. Drawing closer, I could see their irises looked like they'd been leeched of color until they blended in with the surrounding eye, making their pupils the only color.

I swallowed hard.

They smiled widely with a mouth of perfectly straight, white teeth. "Hello."

My heart drummed in my chest, but my feet knew what to do, lightly shifting across the ground into a better stance. I fought my thoughts into line. *Undead. Mortis Mercator work with undead. Was it iron that hurt undead?* My hand closed over my iron knife at my hip.

Please let iron work.

The monster in the middle of the room abruptly jerked upwards, careened, and slammed onto its side. Expletives bounced off the walls. I didn't dare look away from the creature in front of me.

"It never stops being cute how much the alive fight so hard," they mused.

Then lunged at me. I jerked out of the way on instinct and sliced upwards—

My blade slid through them like they consisted of air.

A hand slammed into my throat, and my skull cracked against the wall. Stars danced across my vision, chaotic swirls of nonsense. The abyss of their eyes bored into me, invasive, pressure directly on my brain. My heart beat like a hummingbird in my chest. The bones in my neck creaked as clammy fingers closed, slowly, ever so slowly. I couldn't draw in a single molecule of air. My hands scrambled against *nothing.* My fingers passed through them like they were air, a ghost.

"Look at you," they crooned. Their other hand lifted, and stroked one bony fingertip down the side of my face. I jerked. *Wait— they touched me.* I grabbed at their fingers, and only scratched my cheek with my nails. They leaned closer, bringing the sickly sweet smell of rotting fruit. "I suppose I can't fault him for getting attached. But you must understand, it's very dangerous for old ones to be given something to care about. This really is for the best."

I bucked, slamming my feet into the ground and thrusting myself up the wall a bare centimeter. A gasp of air slipped through my throat before they retightened their grip.

Silver, I thought with shocking calm. *It's silver that has an effect on the undead.*

"Maybe I'll keep you as a pet. Wouldn't that just send him to the edge…"

Remember, because werewolf lore has them originating from the undead, which is why silver supposedly hurts them too.

Pressure pulsed through my face and head as neither blood nor air could pass through my neck. My arm tingled worryingly as it closed over the handle of my silver knife. I could barely feel my fingers as I stabbed upwards as hard as I could into the armpit of their arm holding my neck.

The pressure on my throat released as they jerked away from me with a shriek. My inhale wheezed, hideously loud. I staggered to the side, one knee collapsing briefly before I lurched upright again. The creature hissed at me—honest to god like a cat—and I stumbled into a guard position facing them. *Halle-freaking-lujah* I'd kept ahold of my silver knife. I snickered, head swimming.

"Not so helpless now, am I?" My voice rasped. It hurt to swallow. It also hurt to breathe, but I sucked in oxygen double-time.

The creature straightened. "It's adorable when they have claws."

They took a step towards me, and then a large black blur slammed them into the wall. Daimyn had them off the ground against the stone of the tunnel, his forearm against their neck. A familiar red-glowing blade rose up in his other hand, the tip pressing against the creature's chest.

Oh thank god, he's okay—wait, how come he could touch the strangle-happy arsehole? Each of my breaths hitched, as if my throat didn't quite want to let air through. Some numb part of me found that fascinating.

The entire cavern shuddered. I glanced; Regan bounced like a bloody ping-pong ball off the *walls*, slashing and striking each time he passed the giant creature, the glint of something metal in his hand sending sparks of light through the grey. The creature had its mouth open like it wanted to scream, but no noise emerged as it lashed out, crashing into old equipment and the terminal walls as it tried to spin fast enough to face Regan.

"You had your chance." Daimyn's quiet voice drew me back to him. "Now it's my turn. Who hired you?"

The grey creature laughed, a sound like nails on a chalkboard. "What are you going to do, kill me?"

Daimyn flicked his wrist. A gash appeared down the creature's side, through clothes and flesh. The—Mercator?—flinched and sneered. I heard sizzling.

"This doesn't have to be painful."

Everything inside me stilled at the chill in Daimyn's voice.

"Do you honestly think… there is anything you could do to me… that would convince me to help you?"

A shudder shook the whole place. The monster thing had collapsed. Regan lithely jumped on top of it and then started hacking through its chest with what looked like an ax. My stomach lurched.

Daimyn let out an exhale that sounded tired. "Shall we change your mind?" He lowered the glowing dagger to their abdomen, and the Mercator flinched, arching away.

Then Daimyn paused. And swiftly looked over his shoulder at me, like he'd just remembered my presence there. I blinked at the suddenness of his attention.

The Mercator began to laugh, a terrible clattering shriek. "Yes, go on, Deathless. Torture me in front of your new mortal snack."

The muscles around Daimyn's eyes tightened. I wondered if this had been the real reason Daimyn hadn't wanted me on this adventure.

"Fuck." Daimyn turned back to the Mercator and sank the dagger into their chest before I could blink.

The creature hissed. "It's futile; she's marked for death—"

They froze, twitched once, and… collapsed inwards. Daimyn took a step back as the Mercator crumbled into nothingness.

Why do I keep encountering the undead magical creatures? I mean, really. Where are the dragons and unicorns?

Daimyn sheathed the dagger, then turned cautiously towards me.

"So are Mercators like actually undead?" I blurted, because I absolutely needed to say something. "Or do they change into that, or another species, or…?"

"Not actually undead. But their craft does change them."

"Oh," I said lightly.

Regan approached. He wiped at his face and clothes, sloughing off the sticky, grey goo that covered him from head to foot. He stopped about a meter away and grinned at me. A wave of sickly sweet odor came with him, hitting the back of my throat.

I covered my nose with my sleeve. "Oh my god."

"Hey, more gratitude here please." Regan turned, eyed his brother, then the pile of ash on the floor. "Ah, nothing to be found there, then?"

"No," Daimyn said, his tone inviting no discussion.

To my left, behind Regan, a belch sounded, followed by gurgling. We all spun to look. The huge monster thing Regan had killed bubbled, seeming to melt into the ground. A wave of stench, twice as bad as everything up until now, walloped me in the face. I didn't think that was even possible: my eyes stung and watered profusely as I clamped my hand over my mouth and nose, seriously trying not to vomit.

The collapsed monster of grey ooze rippled. I furiously blinked watering eyes to make sure I wasn't seeing things.

"Uh oh," Regan said in a singsong voice. "It's one of those."

Daimyn sighed heavily. His hand curled around my elbow and I almost jumped. Jeez he was warm. Or maybe I'd gotten that cold.

"We need to go."

A low moan gasped through the terminal. My head whipped back around. Yep, my original thought proved right: little creatures currently grew out of the big creature. Before my eyes, the giant elephant bird thing melted into smaller elephant bird things, and they scrambled towards us, jaws gaping as their flesh jerked and quivered, seeming to have problems staying in shape.

"Um."

The amount of creatures lumbering towards us didn't quite seem to equal the mass of the giant elephant bird thing. Was the goo replicating itself? And since when did they get to crawl on walls? Also, what was the point of eye sockets if they had no eyes? Several of the nearest ones lunged, certain pieces of their body flying faster towards us than others. I yelped, dancing backwards, finally regaining my ability to move.

Daimyn nearly pulled me off my feet as he dragged me back down the tunnel. We beat a hasty retreat, our steps loud as we crashed across the gravel. It unnerved me to hear three sets of racing feet but not see them, Regan and Daimyn ghosts of shadow on either side of me. My torchlight beat chaotic patterns against the ancient walls. It dawned on me that what I'd previously assumed was moss was definitely *not* moss. Unless moss was lumpy and grey.

I tripped, almost falling on my face, but recovered even before a hand gripped my shoulder to steady me. I kept on going, keeping my breaths slow and deep and trying to watch my step.

The noises behind us softened as we gained distance.

"We can slow down." Daimyn's voice materialized out of the gloom, not sounding the least bit out of breath.

I slowed to a fast-walk. The sounds definitely came farther away and muffled.

"They can't move very fast. Their usual tactic is to surround someone and overwhelm with numbers," Daimyn said.

I shined my flashlight down where we had come, not seeing anything down the dark, seeming endless tunnel. The walls seemed to warp in the corners of my vision, constricting inwards—

Nope, none of that now. I cleared my throat hard. "Do we need to… unalive them so they don't hurt someone?"

Regan coughed, and his words shook with laughter. "'Unalive them'?"

"They'll decompose in a few hours without their animator," Daimyn said, amused.

"Helpful."

My heart slowly resumed a normal beat, though hilarity kept bubbling up my throat. I clamped my teeth over the surges. There was no telling what might come out of my mouth at the moment.

When we reached the part of the tunnel where the— necromantic minions?—had first attacked, the bodies left had… melted. As if all the bones holding up their frames had disappeared, leaving behind piles of malformed flesh. Something that looked almost like blood oozed out and spread across the whole floor.

"Yeesh." We all moved up onto the maintenance walkway so we didn't walk through that. Regan led the way, and my back hummed with Daimyn's attention behind me.

Cool air brushed over my cheeks, and a second later I spotted the steel ladder Daimyn and I had originally climbed down. I snapped out of the strange hypnosis that walking through the endless monotonous darkness had lulled me into. A blinding burst of energy filled my limbs.

Regan gestured for me to go up first, and I didn't need to be told twice, scrambling up into the metal shack and outside into the rich, dark green sky. The stars glinted, barely visible behind wispy clouds, and the wind felt indescribable. I inhaled salty-sweet air over and over again and resisted the urge to shake myself like a dog coming out of a river. Everything down there had been so grey. The colors of the night seemed ten times more vibrant after everything in the tunnel.

Daimyn and Regan emerged.

"Man, I never want to do that again," Regan said.

My lips parted to agree, but stopped as I noticed Daimyn's scrutiny. I didn't want him to have any more ammunition to argue with me about my attendance here.

"It's going to get worse," Daimyn said to me, confirming my suspicions.

"Though I will say that was at the top of the gross scale," Regan said cheerfully, and flicked some goo off of his shoulder.

I just breathed and grinned. "Can't get rid of me that easily."

Regan barked out a laugh.

Daimyn gave a long-suffering sigh, but his eyes crinkled at the corners. "I'd like to take a look at your arm. Then I'll take you home."

"I can tend to it," I insisted. Mostly for myself.

Regan turned to his brother incredulously. "You took her into the scary train station wounded?"

"Did you think I could convince her otherwise?" Daimyn muttered, and I smirked. Regan grinned very slowly and gave his brother a look I didn't understand.

Daimyn wrinkled his nose. "Go bathe. And burn those clothes."

Regan laughed, spun on his heel, and trotted off down the road with a cheerful backwards wave.

Daimyn pinned me with his gaze. "Safe house."

30

"How many safe houses do you *have*?" I asked as Daimyn led me into another smaller and much less well-kept residential dwelling. *And I'm basically handing TASA each one. Awesome.*

"Officially, three."

He flipped on lights to reveal a sparely furnished set of rooms with absolutely no décor. I didn't get much of an impression of the floor plan as Daimyn headed straight to the kitchen, located farther back in the house than the other one.

With a huge yawn, I eased into one of the two chairs around a small table.

Daimyn shed his coat, weapons harness, and sword. All of his equipment added a surprising amount of bulk; he was actually built lithe, even with those broad shoulders. The fabric of his shirt clung to the indentation of his spine, then to flex of muscles spanning his shoulders as he reached up into the cabinet, and—

I lunged to my feet. "You're hurt!"

Daimyn blinked at me, and then looked down at himself. When he reached up, stretching the fabric of his shirt, it revealed the myriad of tears and punctures across the fabric, and now I could see that the fabric was off-colored in

317

large swaths, particularly on his left side where his shirt seemed stuck to his skin. *Of course*, that giant thing had landed on him—

Daimyn made a dismissive gesture with his hand, setting the box on the counter. "I'm fine."

"That's blood, isn't it?" I took a few quick steps towards him, hands flexing as I'd never had to dress someone else's wounds before.

Daimyn began pulling out items out of the box. "I promise, it's all right."

"Don't be macho," I snapped, hesitating to touch him. My heart dropped as I noticed the dark smear coming up from his shoulder to his neck.

"Take off your jacket and the bandaging," he continued. "I want to look at that bite."

"Daimyn, I'm serious."

He stilled for a moment. Then turned towards me, expression guarded, and pulled up the hem of his shirt, exposing his side and part of his back. My hands automatically hovered over whatever injury…

Lean muscle stretched over ribs and abdomen, unbroken dusky skin covered in flaking and half-dried blood. The hem of his pants looked off-colored too. But no injury. I leaned over to look further at his back—there should've been bruising or *something*—but nothing looking wrong there either.

My eyes lifted to his. One side of his mouth quirked up.

"I heal really fast."

"You could've just said that," I muttered.

He let go of his shirt, which fell down awkwardly, half-shredded and clinging to him. "Your insistence told me you needed to see it to believe it."

Daimyn turned to the first-aid kit again. His shirt hadn't fallen down all the way and left a strip of skin visible at his waist. I could see a muscle that dented beside his hip before it headed down the front—

Okay, what the hell, brain?

"Sit, sit. Bandaging and jacket," Daimyn insisted.

I wiggled out of my jacket and picked apart his careful knot in the bandaging, unwrapping it as he walked over with disinfectant pads. Daimyn frowned as he inspected the holes in my forearm; five punctures littered my skin in total. Some nasty now-totally-dead creature had been missing one out of its pairs of teeth when it bit me.

"So where's my friend the golden stone?" I asked.

"Recharging," he said, and began wiping the disinfectant across my arm. I sucked in my lips at the stinging burn.

"Arm-guards," he muttered.

"I *was* thinking about a nighttime wardrobe involving some protection," I said, latching onto that idea.

His lips quirked. "Leather is good as a start." His swiping motions slowed. "Maybe I'll take you armor shopping."

My eyebrows shot to my hairline.

Daimyn cleared his throat. "Speaking of injuries, how is your side?"

"Fine," I said, uninterested in that line of conversation. "Armor shopping?"

His gaze lifted to mine, something building in his expression—except then his eyes dipped below my chin, and all humor dropped from his face.

"Fuck," he whispered, his hands suddenly hovering on either side of my neck.

It took me a second to understand. *Right.* I'd been near-strangled tonight. I tipped my head back so he could look. Deja vu hit as I made my throat vulnerable to him. "That bad?"

Daimyn made a soft, aggrieved noise, and his fingers brushed featherlight down my skin. "Is it tender?"

"Now that I'm thinking about it."

A thundercloud grew between his brows. "The stone should be functional tomorrow night. Until then, you might want to wear something to cover this. The bruises are already purple, and obviously from fingers."

I winced.

"I should have known the Mercator would go for you given the chance," he muttered. "I'm sorry." Something—his thumb?—brushed along my jaw towards my ear, and heat crept up my face.

I swallowed. "You're not omniscient."

Daimyn's cold, sharp gaze perused over my throat like he could somehow change what he saw through glare alone. His fingers skimmed along sensitive skin, his touch firmer as he tested the muscle along the side of my neck, spending particular attention along the bones of my throat. My insides quivered oddly.

"You're really bothered by this," I said before I'd really planned out the thought.

His gaze flicked up to mine. Then he eased back, hands dropping, and now I regretted speaking and breaking his focus.

"That's about all I can do at this point."

He stood and leaned a hip against the table nearest him, arms crossed as he watched me. It suddenly took *all* my concentration not to stare at his skin revealed from the half-destroyed cloth of his shirt. *Ugh.*

"You're sure you're okay? I can't do anything?" I asked quickly.

Daimyn smiled faintly, dark eyes roaming my face. "I'm sure."

I got to my feet with a dramatic breath. "Well, as the disadvantaged member of this partnership, I am miffed to discover yet another thing you don't need me for."

I wanted to ask him how long it took to heal, what he could heal from, why he could heal like that—but I didn't. Because TASA.

"Partnership, huh," Daimyn said, and a new kind of smile flirted over his mouth.

I narrowed my eyes at him, trying to ignore how much I liked this look on his face. "*Yes*. Don't argue I bite."

His smile grew, curling up at the corners and revealing just the tips of his teeth as his eyes crinkled at the corners. My blood fizzed, ridiculously proud I'd provoked that.

It didn't take long to clean up. We headed back towards the Leynthall pazo while I stifled yawns and blinked dry eyes, and despite actually looking forward to my bed, I made a face as we reached the dwelling. How long would it take before I stopped feeling like this would disappear right out of my hands?

We halted just outside the ring of trees, and Daimyn stuffed his hands in his pockets and tilted his head. "Ready to stay inside and stay safe yet?"

I glared, nearly offended he'd even asked… then registered the teasing. I stuck my tongue at him. "Never, you arse. What are we doing tomorrow?"

I blinked hard as I *swore* I saw relief flicker across his expression.

"Provided you *sleep* and *rest*—" he said with mock-sternness.

"Yes, yes, yes." I flapped a hand at him.

"—I have another idea on how we might find who hired the Mercator. But I need to check if it's even an option."

I arched an eyebrow in question.

He smirked. "Go to bed, Fairian."

I wrinkled my nose. "*You* go to bed."

"I don't need to sleep," he said, blinking lazily.

I huffed and rolled my eyes skyward. "Of course you don't."

31

Crankiness filled the daylight hours of the next day. I fell asleep in the back of class twice, and was content sleeping there except Tiff kept kicking me awake in the classes we had together. Which made me crankier. Thank god it was Friday.

"Nice scarf, by the way," Tiff said as we ducked into the car to head home. "If I didn't know better, I'd think you were trying to hide hickeys."

I guffawed and very deliberately did not adjust the deep green scarf wound around my neck.

Tiff broke into a huge yawn. "God, I'm tired too. Maybe we're getting sick."

"Or need a vacation."

Despite my latest marks coming back excellent, Tutor acted like I would fail the next round of quizzes. But I was on my best behavior, and not just because of the agreement with my mother for Saturdays at the library. Spending time with Daimyn in the evenings… made everything better. It was amazing what a little something to look forward to did to the psyche.

That night, I jogged into the city, but kept my pace slow once I neared my destination, trying not to look like a ninny running to find him. When I turned the corner, his dark eyes already tracked me from where he leaned against the wall.

He pushed off and stalked up to me, familiar gold light filtering through his fingers. I couldn't really describe the look on his face, only that it made a near-painful giddiness bloom in my gut. His fingertips brushed my chin, gentle, and I tilted my head back, caught by that simple touch. I barely registered the tingling that spread across my throat as he passed the stone over it, the light in his eyes oddly… feral. My stomach filled with the most ri-di-cu-lous case of butterflies.

An alien tendril of *something* curled in my chest, there and gone. *Thank you, Feelings, I already know he has a strong reaction to the bruises on my neck.*

Daimyn's hands dropped away, his shoulders relaxing as he gave a short nod. "Better. We'll be information gathering this evening," he said evenly, slipping the stone into his coat. "Though our destination should be interesting enough for you not to complain."

I automatically smiled with annoying brightness, but didn't speak. I didn't trust what might come out of my mouth and he obviously wanted to just move along from this whole thing.

"Let's hope that the people best at finding secrets don't particularly hate me today."

Half an hour later, Daimyn knocked on an intricately carved door set in the wall of a nondescript alley. I was still trying to interpret the look on Daimyn's face when the door opened… and there stood someone I'd only read about.

Tiny. Slender frame. Big eyes. Greenish-skin. Though none of my books gave justice to their cute button nose and impossibly long eyelashes. *Goblin*, I almost blurted, beating down wonder with an ACT NORMAL stick.

The others did not share my mood. The goblin's eyes narrowed on Daimyn in a decidedly unfriendly way. Daimyn's simply looked neutral.

"Good evening," he said quietly. He did that thing again, shoulders curled, where he tried to seem less… intense. "We're here to see Shahar."

"Is he expecting you?"

"No."

The goblin shifted. After a second, they nodded, and stepped back with the door open to usher us in. Okayyyy, hello palpable and oppressive tension. We stepped inside a small, gloomy foyer that smelled like growing things and something sweet. I made sure to meet the goblin's gaze as I passed and smile. They only scanned me up and down, face stony.

Eek. Maybe not then.

The goblin shut the door. "I will take you the back way. We're busy today, and the less people who know you were here the better." Big eyes narrowed on me. "Especially with her."

I blinked. The goblin turned and made their way over to a shadowed doorway on the right side of the room. Daimyn paused when he reached it, gaze flicking to me. My shoulders tightened; if he tried to tell me to stay behind—

"Please stay close," Daimyn murmured. "Don't leave my sight."

I blinked and nodded, and he ducked through the doorway. It just brushed the top of my head as I entered. At my feet a narrow, shadowed staircase led down. Neither Daimyn nor the goblin said a word as they descended, each of their steps creaking on what sounded like wood, and bright light coming from the bottom of the stairs shone around Daimyn's form.

With a deep breath, I made my way down the steps, tapping each with a toe before committing to it. The pervading silence made the creaking sound like thunderclaps. My nose itched, growing worse the farther down I moved. I rubbed it vigorously, which didn't do a thing. Daimyn reached the landing at the bottom of the staircase, haloed in bright light, and his head twisted back towards me. The goblin stepped through the doorway and… I couldn't see beyond, my eyes watering and stinging after the darkness of the staircase.

Daimyn turned and lifted his hand towards me, palm up. "Just in case."

I had no idea what he meant, but my hand just skipped right past higher brain function and my fingers slid between his without a second thought. He interlaced our fingers tightly, and my stomach quivered. Then he turned and stepped through the doorway. I took a step… and stiffened as all the hair on my body stood on end. Before I could decide if that meant *danger* or just *really weird*, Daimyn pulled, and I let him drag me through.

It took several moments for my eyes to adjust. We stood in a gigantic room filled with desks, and my jaw loosened at the size of the place. Monitors, electronics, and stacks of paper teetered precariously everywhere. People darted from place to place, and two goblins near us caught sight of us and froze.

Daimyn tugged on my hand and led me down the center of the room, which was fairly clear of items and people. Most everyone here looked to be a goblin, but there were also humans—or people who looked humanoid, I corrected myself belatedly. The far wall was almost entirely windows. Beyond the windows, there were dozens of people waiting in line behind well-dressed goblins sitting at large, ornate desks.

Where on earth am I?

Daimyn turned left. The goblin gestured at another doorway, and Daimyn pulled me into a different room, much smaller than the one with all the activity. It looked almost like an old-time parlor, with ornate couches and lamps, a bookshelf taking up most of one wall.

The door shut, leaving Daimyn and I alone.

"Uh," I said. I tried to put together coherent questions but he still held my hand and my whole limb seemed to tingle.

Daimyn smiled. "I'm impressed you haven't asked a hundred questions by now."

"Yeah, way to throw a girl in a situation without any forewarning. Where did the goblin go? Wait—first, where the hell are we?"

Should I let his hand go? Was I supposed to hang on? Was he waiting for me to let go first? Was my hand getting sweaty?

"We are in one of the foremost goblin strongholds, run by the Goldenapple family, the best miners of secrets for many generations."

"Goblin spies!" I gasped, delighted. I very carefully held his hand with the same pressure, not squeezing or loosening at all, because I had no idea how he'd interpret it. "Also, they're beautiful and cute, what is wrong with my books that they didn't say that?"

One eyebrow lifted. "What books are you reading?"

I wrinkled my nose. "Probably the wrong ones. Why are we in this room?"

"I assume Zuchi is informing Shahar we're here and getting approval before she'll actually takes us to him."

"Why doesn't she like you?"

Daimyn stayed quiet for a long moment, long enough for me to wonder if I shouldn't have asked.

"I did a great dishonor to their family," he said. "I imagine they won't forget in their lifetimes."

"What did you do?"

Another door—how many doors *were* there—flung open. The same goblin as before entered. Zuchi?

"Shahar has time now. But not much," she said stiffly. Her eyes flicked down to our intertwined hands. Heat crept up my neck. I'd just started getting used to the pressure and warmth of his skin.

"Thank you." Daimyn followed her as she led us out of the parlor into a long, narrow hallway. We wouldn't be able to walk side by side. *Ah crapsticks. Do I let go of his hand? Hold on and walk behind?* Daimyn made direct eye contact, ran his thumb over my wrist, and released me. I about swallowed my tongue.

I didn't have time to analyze. Zuchi had practically left us behind, and we fast-walked past door after door before the goblin opened up one at the very end. Daimyn seemed to brace himself before entering. I followed on his heels.

A grey-haired goblin with coppery-green skin sat behind a huge dark mahogany desk, and watched us through intricate spectacles as we walked in. It still smelled like growing things in here, but now faintly smokey.

"Thank you, Zuchi," the goblin said, and Zuchi disappeared out *another* door and shut it before I could thank her too.

Two chairs sat in front of the desk, several shelves lined the wall with various items, and some kind of contraption crouched in the corner I couldn't even begin to identify. The color scheme reflected the first room we'd entered; rich reds and browns and blues.

The older goblin laced his fingers together and stared at Daimyn under heavy brows. The size of the desk he sat behind put his head at the same height as Daimyn's, and it was oddly intimidating.

"Shahar," Daimyn said, inclining his head.

"Deathless," he responded. I twitched at the name, now the second time I'd heard it.

"What brings you here?"

"Information."

"Ah. Business then. Is your reasoning true?"

"Protection of an innocent. The highest goal there is."

Shahar's mouth firmed. I didn't get the impression that made him happy. His eyes flicked to me. "I cannot deny your reasoning."

Daimyn's chin tilted down.

"What do you have to trade?"

"Firstly, I want assurances. If I do not have enough for both assurances and information, I will take assurances."

Shahar tilted a hand to continue.

"I realize what bringing her"—Daimyn tilted his head towards me—"may seem to confirm. I want that information unsold. This is what I have to offer."

Daimyn reached out and placed something on the desk. His hand pulled back to reveal a shimmering, opalescent stone.

Shahar picked it up. "This secret is valuable to you."

"Yes."

I darted a look at Daimyn's face. I could tell nothing from it.

"It looks unfilled," Shahar said, brow furrowing as he inspected it in his palm.

"It is. For whatever you feel best."

Shahar slowly set the stone down with a tiny click. "That is enough. The secret will be lost. Now what is the information you require?"

"Someone is targeting Fairian Leynthall. The Mortis Mercator is already defeated, but I need to know who made the request."

Shahar's gaze drifted and rested on me. I swallowed convulsively without meaning to.

A quick, light knock came from the door to the right, and it swung open. Another goblin with richer-green coloring and delicate features came in and then froze.

"Oh, I apologize—" The goblin's eyes went wide. "*Daimyn?*"

Before I could blink, the goblin raced across the room. Daimyn knelt so abruptly his knees thudded against the wooden floor, and the goblin threw their arms around Daimyn's neck. He embraced them in return.

"Chaya, it is very good to see you."

I almost startled at the emotion in his voice.

Shahar's face set in stone, his jaw clenched as he watched Daimyn and the goblin… girl? Embrace each other. *Oh boy, so much I don't understand here.* And that wasn't even getting to the weirdest bargaining conversation I'd heard in my life. I fidgeted and made myself stop.

The girl—Chaya?—withdrew, beaming up at Daimyn.

"Are you well?"

"I am very well," Chaya said. Her gaze lifted over his shoulder to me. Her grin, if possible, grew broader. "And this must be Fairian."

I struggled to keep my face under control. I needed to figure out how to react to all these people just knowing me. Yes, lots of people knew my *name*, but this was different.

"Hi. I see you've heard of me," I said dryly.

"We're a family that makes our way by secrets, are you surprised?" She looked positively impish as she made her way towards me, hand extended. At least I knew what that gesture meant. I reached out to take her hand and then immediately panicked, wondering if I should kneel or bend over or—

Chaya shook my hand firmly, making no attempt to hide her inspection of me. A faint huff came from Shahar's direction.

"My dear," Shahar said, his exasperation layered with fondness. "We are in the middle of business."

"Ah, business, that must be why you didn't inform me he was here," she said, spinning towards Shahar. "Well, carry on, I won't interrupt." She settled herself in a chair just off to the side of the huge desk.

Shahar stared down at the goblin girl for several long moments before he seemed to let it go, lifting his attention back to Daimyn.

"Information on who is targeting your… young friend, yes?" Shahar said.

"Oh, of course," Chaya said quietly. Shahar shot her a look. She mimed zipping her lips, and I almost laughed out loud.

"Yes. I need to know who hired the Mortis Mercators," Daimyn responded.

"Those awful people," Chaya muttered, then sucked her lips between her teeth as Shahar turned towards her again. She caught me looking at her and winked.

Shahar folded his hands again, and sat back in his chair, not speaking. Chaya and Daimyn simply looked patient as the silence stretched longer and longer. I forced myself to stop fidgeting.

"I do not currently have the information you seek, so I will have to find it," Shahar said, and I nearly exhaled in relief. He tapped the stone Daimyn had given him with one finger. "You knew the value of this. It will pay for half, along with your assurances. The rest of it in information."

"What information are you looking for?"

"It's not from you I want information."

For a confused second, I looked at Chaya. A beat later I realized Shahar watched me.

"Oh," I blurted.

"No," Daimyn said sharply.

I scowled at him, but he didn't even glance in my direction. Shahar simply watched me patiently. I repressed a surge of hilarity— what on earth could I have that he wanted?

"What do you want to know?" I asked slowly.

"You and your sister were kidnapped by a rogue Dokkalfar," Shahar said. "I want to know what happened while you were captives."

All the air left my lungs, and I forgot how to inhale again.

"*No*," Daimyn said again, and his strange, almost submissive demeanor evaporated. I thought the tension had been thick before; now the very air seemed vibrate in warning. "She is not a part of these dealings."

I made myself breathe. It was just a story. I'd told it before. The instant I was free, in fact, to Ransom Retrieval and law enforcement and my initial therapist. After a while I stopped telling it. Because it did nothing but drive people away and make me doubt my own self.

"She is the *subject* of these dealings, of course she's involved. If you didn't want her involved, then you shouldn't have brought her here," Shahar said. "You knew the interest this would provoke."

I hadn't told anyone what had happened for years. I'd learned to be quiet.

Chaya interjected: "Grandfather, look at her, this is a painful price—"

"And gathering this information will be expensive and dangerous."

But why would anyone even want to know what happened while Mari and I were captives?

"This is not her burden to pay," Daimyn said shortly. "I will do whatever you require."

"Yes, because your services worked so well last time."

"Grand-da!"

"That is *my* burden. Not hers. Shahar, there are many things you could ask of me in this situation," Daimyn said, low and deliberate.

"Why?" I asked, voice emerging too quietly. *Ugh.* I cleared my throat and tried again. "Why would you want that… information?"

The room quieted as three pairs of eyes turned to me.

Shahar spread his hands. "My currency is secrets. And that is a secret only you know. In my world it makes it very valuable."

"But I told people," I said. "They didn't believe me, but I told people."

"There are reports and information to be found here and there, but it is too filtered—intentionally and otherwise—to be worth much."

I blinked at the insinuation he'd already looked into this.

"How would that… even help you. Cerin is dead. What happened—" I cleared my throat. "I can't imagine how it would be valuable." Another thought blind-sided me: "Unless you have someone already interested in this information."

Shahar sighed, eyeing me. "It's bad form to ask about other deals. But I understand you're new. No, I do not have a buyer for the information. Your secret is interesting because no one knows it, and because of your connection to *him*." Shahar's gaze flicked to Daimyn. "Will it be directly valuable? That's for me to decide. Some bargains are gambles, but having a head start at gaining information, with the… *development* between you two, could be worth something."

Daimyn turned towards me, stepping close and blocking my view of Shahar. His eyebrows furrowed together tightly.

"You don't need to do this."

I blinked at his fervency. "I know that." My voice came out calm —much more in control than I thought. Shrugging came oddly easy, and the grin that followed too. "It's just a story. It's not like I haven't told it before. If he wants to know something so silly, have at it."

Daimyn studied me for a long moment. "I don't trust where the information might go."

"Are you saying don't do it?"

"I am saying you should feel not one iota of pressure to agree to this. He will see reason and accept other payment."

A grunt sounded behind Daimyn. I bit my lip, studying the strip of Daimyn's harness peeking out underneath his coat. *I want to be helpful*. But more than that, the idea my 'secret' had value latched onto my diaphragm. I'd had to fight to make anyone listen to me before. I'd never had someone seek out my story. Maybe pure recklessness drove me, but still, I…

I leaned to the side and met Shahar's gaze. "Fine. One story of tragedy and trauma coming up."

Daimyn didn't say a word, dark eyes watching me.

"Excellent," Shahar said, as if he knew that would be the decision all along. "Chaya, I know you'd like to catch up with our guest." The slightest emphasis on *guest* made me lift an eyebrow. "Why don't you and Daimyn talk in the meeting room?"

"I will be here, Shahar." Daimyn's voice broached no argument.

"It's not much of my secret if everyone else knows as well, is it?"

Tense silence followed. Daimyn had said not to leave his eyesight…

"For the Gods' sake," Shahar said. "What on earth would I get out of hurting the girl?"

"He won't hurt her," Chaya said quietly.

Daimyn shifted, something about Chaya's reassurance seeming to get through to him. He looked at me, mouth tight and turned down at the corners.

"It's okay," I said again before he could even ask. Then smiled brightly. "I'll scream bloody murder if someone decides to kill me. Go, catch up."

Daimyn made a soft sound, I suspected the beginning of a growl he swallowed. With a last glance conveying deep dislike, he exited the room, Chaya on his heels. She winked at me again and shut the door behind them.

Silence snaked through the air.

Shahar and I studied each other in strange accordance. *This guy, this guy here, he knows things,* a lot *of things.* Right now my information and access to magic all came through Daimyn, but I had no idea how long he'd put up with me, especially when this adventure ended.

"Would you be willing to make deals with me in the future?" I kept my voice calm. "For information?"

Shahar's eyebrows lifted. "Of course. That is my business."

"I'm new obviously, so is there… are there particular things you want? Or need? That I could bring to trade?"

Somehow I doubted they had internships.

"It depends. How close are you really to the Deathless?"

I clenched my teeth. "If you're asking me to sell secrets about him, I won't," I said shortly. Christ, I already had that problem.

"Pity." But the humor in his eyes made me relax. "Take a seat, Fairian." He pushed away from the desk, and then disappeared behind it. He reappeared on the ground to the side of the desk, and walked over to the rows of shelves along one wall.

I shuffled over to one of the chairs and sat down, rubbing my hands down my thighs. "Okay." I cleared my throat. "So I just… tell you the story?"

Shahar turned and gave me a gentle smile. "Sometimes that's how it works. For this, we will be doing things a little differently." He reached up and pulled down a small chest from one of the higher shelves. "How much do you know about mental magicks?"

My heart skipped a beat. "Not a lot."

Shahar walked back over to me, setting the chest on the small table in front of me before flipping it open. He reached inside with obvious care and withdrew something, holding it out to me.

"Do you know what this is?" In his hand rested a clear crystal cluster. It filled his palm, a frozen explosion of jagged points.

"… Quartz?"

Shahar chuckled. "Well, yes. But for our purposes, we will use it to copy your memories."

I swallowed. "And that will do… what, exactly?"

"It means someone will be able to view your memory by watching and experiencing it. It is a truer way of getting a story—as true as memory can be, anyway."

Shahar set the crystal in my hands. The warmth from his hand had bled into it, and it glinted with each tiny shift in position, a thousand refractions of light. He pulled over the other chair and set it in front of me, sitting down and leaning forward to cup his hands under my own.

"I'll do the hard part," Shahar said. "All you need to do is tell the story. Tell me everything you remember. Picture it in your mind, as best as you can. It's alright if it's not linear; memories rarely are. We'll fill it in as we go along."

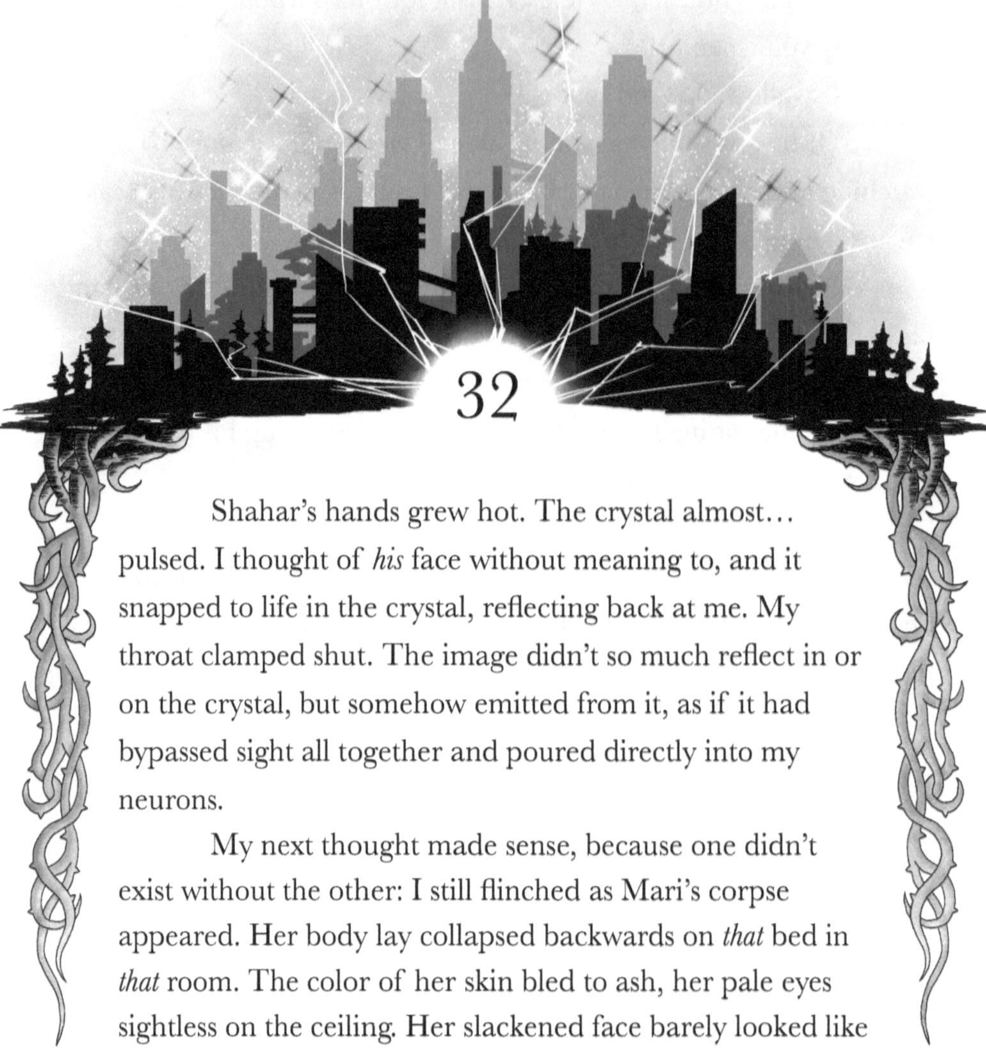

32

Shahar's hands grew hot. The crystal almost… pulsed. I thought of *his* face without meaning to, and it snapped to life in the crystal, reflecting back at me. My throat clamped shut. The image didn't so much reflect in or on the crystal, but somehow emitted from it, as if it had bypassed sight all together and poured directly into my neurons.

My next thought made sense, because one didn't exist without the other: I still flinched as Mari's corpse appeared. Her body lay collapsed backwards on *that* bed in *that* room. The color of her skin bled to ash, her pale eyes sightless on the ceiling. Her slackened face barely looked like her. It had shocked me, how much being *alive* gave form to the physical. Or maybe it was just because *she didn't Feel right.*

"No." I almost fell on top of her, shaking her. "Mari? Mari!" My head whipped to Cerin, words ripping out of my throat like gravel. "Let go of her!"

Let go, however he snared our minds and made us strangers in our own bodies.

Pity shone in his eyes, but it was the shock that made me believe him. "I already have."

336

I shook her, harder. Her head lolled around on her neck.

"Why isn't she back!" I shrieked, as if… if I screamed I could change the answer to the question.

"She dove into it," Cerin said quietly, sounding so achingly sad. "I'm sorry, I didn't understand until too late."

"I TOLD YOU TO STOP!" My throat tore from the violence of those words.

"I know."

She wasn't breathing. I suffocated on the air in this room. This wasn't happening. It wasn't.

"Mariposa…" Her name was barely a gasp.

"Ms. Fairian. Fairian."

If I could just go back, if I could change it so she'd never followed me. It was my fault, if she just hadn't followed me. If I'd just never told Cerin my stupid secret if I had been smarter and not so desperate for anyone, just anyone to like me as—

"Fairian, recenter. Focus on my voice. That is in the past; you are here with me now."

I gasped for breath as my heart ruptured over and over. Tears poured from my eyes faster than I could blink them free. My body— my older, different body—shook with repressed sobs. My teeth ached with how tightly I clamped my jaw shut.

With willpower I didn't know I had, I wrenched my hands out from under the crystal. Shahar barely caught it before it hit the floor. I wrapped my arms around my middle, bending over to suck air between my knees.

"I apologize, Fairian, I should have reacted quicker to prevent that."

After several seconds of no sound in the room beyond my shuddering breathing, I managed to bite back swearwords and croak out something intelligible.

"Why didn't you warn me?"

"You took to that unusually quickly," Shahar said, sounding troubled. "Most find it takes much longer to get even halfway into a memory deeply."

It had been like I was *there* again, for the first time. But time and context took shape now; the hole in my heart was old, and I knew how to handle its emptiness. With a deep breath, I managed to pull my arms away from my torso and grip my knees, straightening.

"Sorry."

"I can't imagine what for."

All right, sure, whatever. I swallowed through a dry throat and glanced at the crystal still in his hands. "Is it going to be like that again?"

"No." He studied me. "I will hazard a guess that it will be more intense for you than most, but I will keep you from falling into it, now that I know."

Shahar offered the crystal. *Ugh.* Warily, I took it, and he cupped my hands again.

"You don't need to go quite so deep. If you need to, look at me or away instead. Usually watching the crystal is needed for the connection but… maybe not so much with you."

I stared down at the multifaceted stone, panic a sick twist in my gut at how utterly I'd just *lost* myself. Ironic, considering what I'd reveal. Everything seemed to be conspiring to make me face my past lately.

"That's what Cerin did," I whispered. "Only we didn't consent to it."

"What did he do?" Shahar asked gently.

"Made us think—made us *believe* and *feel*—like we were someplace else entirely. We forgot everything. Time. Place. Our own bodies."

Under the crystal's glinting surface, sharp shapes and oozing forms seethed. My lips turned numb. Familiar bone-rattling terror closed around my heart like a frozen, clawed fist. I looked up at Shahar, forcing myself to see him, forcing deep and controlled breaths.

He held my gaze calmly, but I didn't miss the groove forming between his brows.

"The first time," I said, carefully making each word. "Right after we were taken, when we woke up. Mari and I were completely unprepared. I'd never experienced pain like that."

Cerin rolled his shoulders, pacing back and forth in front of us. No, not pacing. Gliding. He even moved differently—light and floating as he walked. It wasn't just his face and body that had so utterly changed from how I'd come to know over the past few months.

Mari edged herself in front of me. "Why are we here?"

"Because we needed a controlled environment to conduct a few tests." His smile and eyes held ice as he looked at her.

I swallowed heavily. Mari and Cerin had never liked each other. Wonder why, said a faint, sarcastic voice in my head. Mari had always had a much better radar for people than I did.

"What kind of tests?"

Cerin's eyes flicked to mine, and a different kind of smile lit his face. Mari tried to block his view, but it was too late: I recognized that smile, part-warmth-part-excited. The one that made me feel interesting *instead of just a freak. The one that had grown so bright when I'd told him about my episodes.*

I swallowed, horror burgeoning under my skin. That wasn't why he'd taken us, was it?

The concrete walls of the small room around us rippled. Rippled, like water. My breathing stopped. Cerin disappeared in a blink. The door was gone, the bed, the smaller door to the bathroom—

The walls bulged and expanded all around us, gaining mass in large, gulping movements, the ceiling shooting upwards into infinity as the edges seemed to blur and dim until I could barely make out anything around us. Mari's hand bit into mine, her shoulder pressed against me.

We stood in a place swathed in darkness, the walls built of nothingness, the only source of light blinding down upon us.

Things moved in the dark, things I couldn't quite glimpse but provoked an instinctive terror so deep it boiled out from my very bones. We bolted. There was no other option, no room for anything else.

The ground moved under our bare feet, roiling like the oceans, and then changed. Fire split across my sole. I slammed into the ground, the same slicing fire lit up my hands, a wail shrieking out of me. I tried to move, the primal terror yanking on my very bones, but every time I put too much weight on anything…

The ground. The ground. Razor blades covered the ground, embedded in the floor, their edges tilted upwards at the perfect angle to slice deep.

Blood pooled between my fingers, my knees and feet split with pain. Mari collapsed next to me, gasping half-sobs. Blood ran down her legs, stained her nightgown. I tried to move, I tried to shift across the ground, avoiding the sharp points. Nothing I did helped. My knees became a mess of flesh; I could see the tendons of my hands beneath ravaged skin of my palms.

A snuffling started up behind us. Mari let out a broken sob and I stopped breathing. Those things had caught up. We scrambled to our feet; another razor blade imbedded into my heel. I screamed, the sound like nothing I'd ever heard before, animal and broken. I collapsed back down. I couldn't stand. I couldn't do it.

"You have to get up, you have to," Mari panted.

My brain wheeled unmoored in the dark. "I can't…"

Mari stared at me for an endless second before her attention abruptly dropped to the gown she wore. Her hands clenched in the fabric of her gown, and with a terrific heave, she tore the stitching on one of her sleeves. She did it again; she had to do it three more times before she tore off the whole thing.

"Give me your foot—" She reached out for it, yanking it onto her lap and tying the torn off sleeve around it. I gasped with pain, my entire leg shaking as pressure made it worse.

But I understood. We tore strips from our gowns and bandaged our feet for some protection against the ground.

And then the sharp edges underneath shifted again. I yelped, my hands slamming down on instinct to lift myself up. Fresh fire split my palms. But the ground continued to shift, the blades turning. I stared at the ground and realized… the blades had flattened down to make smooth ground again.

I struggled backwards out of the memory, that *place*, biting my lip hard to create real pain.

"Agh." My mind stretched like taffy. The images in the crystal flared vividly; it hurt how clearly I could see them when they weren't really *there* at all.

"When we ran… the razorblades showed up again. We had to walk, no matter what." I managed to focus on Shahar's face as images flashed inside my head and eyes and that crystal, jerking me out of my body with each pulse. "And the things in the dark got worse… it was unbelievable, that kind of terror, when we couldn't even tell *why*."

"How long were you there?" Shahar asked quietly.

"I have no idea. He eventually brought us back."

Everything wavered. Like we were looking at our surroundings through water. My stomach rolled, my equilibrium spinning as directions twisted wrong… and then, we stood in the concrete room. Cerin leaned by the white door, like nothing had changed from hours and hours and hours ago.

Mari dropped to her hands and knees, retching violently. I stared at him, the sharp angles of his new face, the world shifting back and forth uneasily as I swayed. The pain in my feet and hands gave a lurching ache and disappeared. I looked down, lifting my hands. Unmarred palms met my gaze, my gown still pale and clean. No blood-soaked bandages anywhere.

My voice came out small and childlike. "What did you do? Why?"

Cerin's eyes brightened. "Now that is the question, isn't it?"

"This went on for days," I said, making my voice as bland as possible. "Always that same place, just terror and pain."

I looked off to the side, trying to sidestep the spun-glass spider webbing that fought to constrict across my thoughts. After a second of staring at the very real wall, reality settled and I turned back to Shahar. Kindness reflected back at me through his eyes. I appreciated he didn't make grand apologetic statements or emotional gestures. He was just steadily there.

"She was fine at first," I said, and then my throat clamped shut.

Mari paced back and forth across the room. "Hallucinations this complex should be impossible to control—shared hallucinations should be impossible. This can't be just drugs. There's got to be something he's doing."

She scanned the room with newfound fervor. She walked to the corners, stood on the bed to run her fingers along the seam of where the ceiling met the wall. Then Mari paced in front of me, jerking on my arms, holding them out and inspecting my forearms and the creases of my elbow.

"My love, do you have any marks? Any marks where they might be giving us something. Check me too. Are they on my back?"

I did as she asked, even as it felt like rocks had filled my stomach.

"There's nothing…" I whispered. "There's nothing."

"They've got to be somewhere. To create hallucinations this explicit, it has to be tailored, right?" Her fevered, glassy eyes wouldn't meet mine. For a second I wondered if she was drugged. "They must have scientists, to be so complex…"

"I don't think it's drugs—"

"It has to be, nothing else makes sense."

My spine stiffened. "That can't be the only answer—"

"We have to be smart and figure this out, not fall prey to whatever they want us to believe." She snapped her fingers. "Airborne, it has to be airborne, maybe under the door?" She crossed the room, crouching in front of the door and peering underneath.

I swallowed against the thing trying to boil out of my stomach. "Mari…"

She popped up from the floor. Her lip trembled for the barest instance before she bit it. "Somehow, when he enters here, he's doing something…"

"MARI!" My voice thundered through the room and shocked me. "This isn't normal, stop saying it's normal!"

Her chin lifted, defiance lighting in her expression. Something snapped deep in my chest.

"It's MAGIC!" I stabbed my finger at the door. "Those are DEMONS."

The catharsis of shouting it filled me with weightless terror and breathless light.

Mari burst into tears.

"You know, she wasn't even supposed to be there? With me?" My voice was a croak. "I'd snuck outside to see him. He wanted to meet me. It was right after…"

Alarm slashed through the cloying fog of the crystal. Shahar wanted my memories from when I'd been kidnapped, but he didn't get more than that. It all started when I'd told Cerin about my episodes and Feelings, but I didn't want a record of explaining my freakish little abilities on this crystal thing.

"She wasn't supposed to be there," I repeated lamely. "She followed me out when I'd gone. So he took her too. It was my fault he took her." I swallowed. "My fault that she died."

Mari's pale face was a mockery of itself. No expression lifted her features, the blankness there filling my chest with ice. Even her breathing was so still I had to strain to see it.

It was doing something to her. This—this thing that Cerin did, it was bleeding her dry, leaching away all of her will and personality.

"Mari?" I whispered.

Her head moved on a swivel like a machine, blank eyes showing no recognition for a long, terrifying moment.

"I don't think they're coming to save us," she said. "I thought he'd come. But grandmother was wrong… she was wrong…"

"You're not making sense," I choked. *"What…?"*

I cleared my throat and fought down the crushing ache in my chest. Good thing I didn't need to tell this story linearly, because that had been near the end.

"Did it keep going like that?" Shahar said quietly. "Always that same place? And this… hurt her, but not you."

I swallowed and shook my head. "No. Something else happened."

"What was it?"

"I got out."

Mari pressed up against my back. The tremors of her shaking body became mine, my shudders hers. If we ran, the razors would come. The logic of it didn't stop the wordless screaming that boiled up from my very DNA. Not heeding the instinct made me want to tear out of myself, to scream endlessly.

The terror never left, here. It was only afterwards it took its proper place in reality.

This isn't real.

Something moved in the dark. Another wave of fear tried to swallow me; I gritted my teeth and locked my knees. I swayed, vision warping. Mari's hand bit into my own. A massive shadow raced over us, feeling like death ghosted through our souls. My knees nearly buckled.

This isn't real. *I whispered it that time.*

"Stay with me, baby sister," Mari husked. *"We'll get through this again. You'll see."*

I shook my head. "No, it's not that. This just… isn't real." My voice sounded odd and detached. My stomach and chest lurched, trying to tear me into the blinding terror. Oddly enough, that only made my mind more calm, my thoughts separating out from my body. In a detached way, I wondered if this was what losing your mind felt like.

"It isn't real," I said again. My eyes cast over the darkness, watching the things move in the nothingness. Things I couldn't see nor make out. Because they never came out of the shadows, even when it made sense for them to.

"What do you mean?"

It wasn't real…

A form flickered; not in the nothingness, somehow comprised of it. My body sagged in terror as my mind seemed to lurch even further away, ignoring the things churning in the dark, the beat of wings, Mari's half-shriek.

Cerin wavered into view, not far from us. In fact, exactly the distance away from us when we'd last seen him. Then I couldn't unsee it. The shapes and lines of the concrete room seemed to superimpose around us, more impressions than anything, something I didn't quite see with actual vision. Cerin's pale, pale eyes watched me.

As my gaze connected with his, he straightened.

"It's not real." My voice came out loud; Mari jumped, twisted towards me. A hysterical laugh burst out of me. "It's not REAL!"

I moved. Not in this place, but where I actually stood in that concrete room. My foot came down—and the dark around me snapped out of existence. Concrete room, white door, Cerin leaning against the wall.

Triumph tasted like lightning.

A smile of pure joy overtook Cerin's face.

"I knew it." He leapt across the room and had my face in his hands. "I knew you had it in you, I knew it! I knew you were special."

He pressed his lips to my forehead, over and over, and I froze. His interest and affection for me had always been overwhelming, lancing to a bruised spot in the center of my soul. Despite everything, I still succumbed for a second. If Mari hadn't been right next to me I might have lost myself for longer. I shoved him away, stumbling back as tears filled my eyes.

He didn't look put out; he just watched me with that smile splitting his face. I glanced at Mari to see her reaction, mortified.

Mari stood there with unfocused eyes and muscles twitching in her face.
"Mari…?"

"Only you realized it for what it was," Cerin said.

"What?" I whispered, and a whole new horror overtook my being. "Put me back there! Don't leave her alone!"

"I don't understand why it was so different," I whispered. "I even told her how to get out, how to see it for what it was, and she was just… stuck."

"She did not have your affinity for mental magic," Shahar said.

Terror choked me. *Special. He called me special.* I wanted to fling the crystal into the wall and shatter it into a million pieces, but my limbs had turned numb and unresponsive.

"Then what happened?" Shahar asked. I swallowed, hard, and focused on his question with all of my being. *Just keep going.*

"It started hurting her."

Mari made a noise, and swayed where she stood. Cerin frowned. Her head tilted back, spine curving backwards in a slow arc, her knees bending. She collapsed like a puppet with its strings cut, her head cracking against the floor. Before I could move she jolted, then shook, her limbs flailing in erratic, violent movements. I tried to grab her; one of her arms smacked into my nose, and my eyes watered.

"Help her!" I shrieked at Cerin. "You're the one doing this! Stop it!"

"I've already stopped," he replied, a crease between his eyebrows.

My head jerked back to Mari, still spasming in my arms. My heart practically stopped: blood was trickling out of her mouth and nose.

"Stop it stop it…" I gasped. "Make it stop."

Heat trickled from my eyes and I quickly wiped it away with my shoulder.

"Once she'd regained her strength, Cerin kept sending her to the same place as before. She couldn't break out of it."

"It's worse without you there," she croaked.

My eyes burned. "Why?"

"I don't know. It's just worse. Everything is worse. The things that come out of the dark…" Her pupils swelled with fear. "What they do…"

"I'm sorry. I'm so sorry."

"It's not your fault… I just thought… they'd find us by now… "

"What happened with you? You just had to watch?" Shahar asked.

I blinked a few times, taking a second to understand his words.

"No. Cerin had other illusions for me." I scoffed a laugh. "I actually woke up in a hospital with my parents there, as if I'd been rescued. I don't know how long I was there in real time, but it felt like weeks. He was even more delighted when I figured out that wasn't real too. I don't… I still don't entirely understand. It wasn't always terror he wanted, sometimes… other things. It all felt very orchestrated, though, like tests. The 'tests' of his grew more complex, the mind games progressively weirder. We tried to escape…"

I let out a snort.

"Actually, I don't know if that was real or not. It seems like a real memory, but everything was so weird around then, I'm not entirely sure."

A long hallway stretched both right and left. Right led to a flight of stairs. Mari bolted for them. My scalp prickled, the skin pulling painfully towards my back, my gasps burning in my lungs. The plan had gone so horribly wrong we were so stupid the plan was stupid we were going to be caught—

We reached the bottom of the stairs, and my vision rippled. Dread burned up my throat. The hallway stretched, growing longer and darker, the staircase moving miles away. Mari shrieked.

No! It's not real! Just keep going, you know it's not real!

My legs collapsed under me, face slamming into the steps, tasting blood and iron pain. Whimpering, I struggled to my feet, keeping my eyes shut to keep from seeing what I knew was a lie.

My legs wouldn't seem to get under me… flopping the wrong way…

Bile rose heavily, my eyes open and staring before I'd even realized I'd done it. My legs twisted, folded under me, collapsed like an accordion. My mouth opened, but no sound came out. A convulsive shock ripped through me, as if I'd slammed into something, and my legs twisted even further.

That's when the pain hit.

"I think it was real, the first part anyway," I said, fighting to speak as the crystal seemed to amplify the memory into reality again. My legs ached, and I rubbed them together to make a different sensation, a real one. "Because after that Mari was so much worse. I tried to tell her… "

"Mari, he's going to let us go someday, I promise!"

"You don't know that."

"You said before it was just an elaborate game, that we'll be ransomed back, that—"

"You never believed that. We don't know why he took us, and if we were going to be rescued, it would have happened by now."

My throat clamped closed. "But I think I know why—"

I shied away from what happened next, talking to focus *away.* "I tried to provoke her sometimes, to ignite anything besides her despair, but it didn't… it just seemed to drain the last of her away."

Bits of memory burst within the crystal, despite me trying not to see it.

"—I told him about my Episodes—"

"You told him what?"

My heart beat thin and fast.

"So it's your fault. It's YOUR fault! If you'd just kept your mouth shut and gone to the doctors like mother told you—"

"I almost got Cerin to stop," I said loudly, and my mind stretched painfully before popping free of the memory. "But it was too late."

Shahar watched me with steady eyes.

Something in her eyes chilled me to the very core. Then one corner of her mouth lifted up. Despite the fact it was a break from her vacant staring, it filled me with dread.

"Let's get it over with then," she said.

"No," I seethed. "Stop."

I clenched my fists and stepped between Mari and Cerin, trying to be a human shield, but Mari had already fell heavily backwards onto the bed, eyes fluttering shut. She had gotten so thin. She looked like a ghost lying there.

"STOP!" I screamed, and ran right at Cerin, trying to shock him. I hit at him once, then faltered; I'd never hit anyone in my life and didn't know how.

Cerin frowned and crossed his arms over his chest, turning fully towards me. "It's already begun." He shifted his weight. "But I am willing to concede that my efforts seem fruitless on your sister. I've made this one easier. If she doesn't take this time, it will be the last."

"Make it stop now," I spat at him.

"I'll stop this instant if you can tell me why you're here," he said.

My breath stilled, pulse thudding in my ears. I didn't know, I didn't understand what he was even doing! "You keep telling me I'm special," I whispered. He'd done it from nearly our first meeting. "Is that why you're doing this to us? Because I'm…?"

I couldn't say it. I didn't feel 'special.' I felt toxic.

Cerin took a breath as if to speak—then jolted, his attention snapping over my shoulder. His nostrils flared. I turned, dread rising like choking smoke.

Mari's lips were blue, her color ashen, worse than before. All the hair on my body stood up. Her motionless speared dread through me. And she didn't… Feel right.

"No." I almost fell on top of her, shaking her. "Mari? Mari!" My head whipped to Cerin, words ripping out of my throat like gravel. "Let go of her!"

"Ugh," I said, pulling away with tears streaming down my face again. "Sorry."

"It is completely fine," Shahar murmured.

I shook my head, limbs and eyes heavy. The desperate desire for hot tea and a place to lie down slammed into me. *Focus.*

"After that, after they took her body, he was gentler with me." My face twisted into a sneer. "Showed me all sorts of pretty things he… made up, I guess, though he said some were real places."

Walking through forests so old and so green it had to be a fantasy. Riding unicorns through prairie grasses that rippled all colors of the rainbow. Sitting at the top of a mountain so still that the peace made tears stream down my face. Spelunking through caves made of pure gemstone, with phosphorescent pools that held small creatures I couldn't even dream of.

I skipped over how much I'd hated myself. How I wanted to die, refused to eat, but couldn't stop myself when Cerin brought dishes of tasty foods. I didn't dwell on the games he played to pull me out of myself, the comfort he gave that confused me so much, and how he seemed to know that my curiosity would spark my will to live. I hated myself for living. For somehow being able to live, when I didn't know why.

Those images flashed in the crystal anyway.

"And soon after, I was found."

Armored Ransom Recovery agents breaking through the door of that concrete room. Bodies under sheets as I walked away from all of it. I was convinced for days… weeks… that it was all another illusion.

I swallowed against the pain in my throat, trying to steady my shaking hands.

"I'm not sure all of me truly believes I left," I whispered.

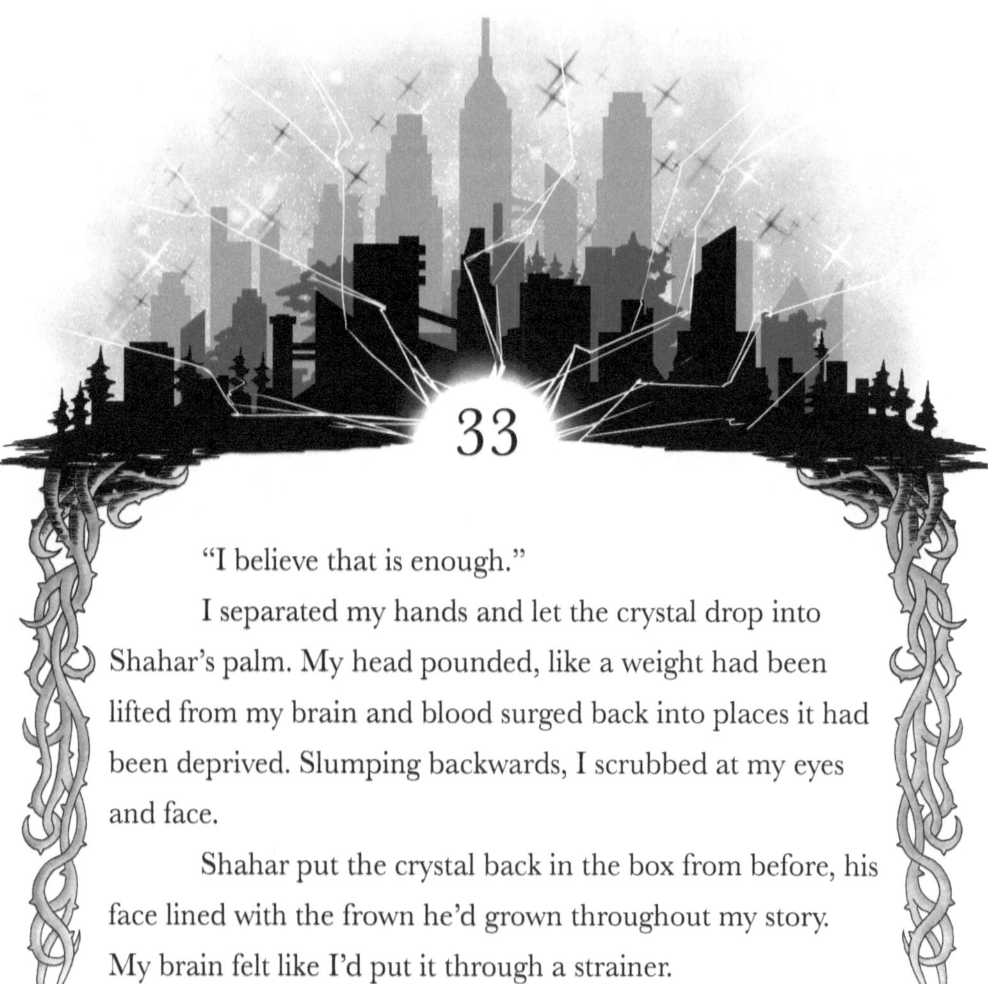

33

"I believe that is enough."

I separated my hands and let the crystal drop into Shahar's palm. My head pounded, like a weight had been lifted from my brain and blood surged back into places it had been deprived. Slumping backwards, I scrubbed at my eyes and face.

Shahar put the crystal back in the box from before, his face lined with the frown he'd grown throughout my story. My brain felt like I'd put it through a strainer.

"When you do find something to trade that might interest me, come back," Shahar said, his voice almost reluctant. "I have information that would interest you."

I stilled. There was no way this was a coincidence, that he had "info" for me minutes after that memory I'd just given him.

I managed to make my voice cheerful, though it rasped through my throat. "How do you feel about charity? In case you haven't heard, I'm the new kid on the block and in trouble."

The door swung open and Daimyn entered. He halted in his tracks as he scanned me, Chaya peeking out from behind him at waist-level. I smiled brightly, trying to put on the picture of ease. His eyes narrowed on my face, and I grew very conscious of my puffy-feeling eyes.

Shahar sniffed and shuffled some papers on his desk. "The deal is made. I should have an update for you within a week. Now, are we done?"

Damn it, damn it. I didn't want to push Shahar for what he might have, not with an audience. How could I figure out what Shahar wanted and then get back here?

"Yes," Daimyn said. "Thank you."

"Then thank you for your business." Shahar looked back to the papers on his desk, dismissing our presence.

My brain growled in frustration. *Don't make a scene.* I got awkwardly to my feet, unsure about the etiquette for politely leaving. "Uhm. Thank you too, as well."

Shahar lifted an eyebrow but didn't look up. Resisting the urge to stomp my feet, I headed for the door Daimyn held open for me. Chaya smiled on the other side. Maybe I could pry her for information. Daimyn ushered me out, shutting the door with a distinct click.

What did Shahar know? What did he see in my memories?

"How come everyone wants a price for being helpful," I muttered.

Daimyn cocked his head, eyes holding a question.

"What," I muttered.

His eyebrows lifted. But before I could respond, his lips quirked and he started off down the hall. "Let's get out of here."

With a silent huff, I followed, and Chaya did too. She caught my eye and smirked. "Hello again."

"Right—hi," I said awkwardly. "Uhm. Did you… have a good time catching up?"

"We did," Chaya said. "I hope my grandfather wasn't too much of a bear. He can be quite grumpy."

"Oh, he was nice, really. The crystal memory thing was interesting."

"He used memory crystals?" Daimyn interjected.

"Uh. Yeah. Is that bad?"

"No." He didn't elaborate, and I couldn't see his face to get a read on him.

We headed down the same hallway as before, and back into the huge cavernous room with desks and monitors and cabinets and piles of paper. As we passed, people stilled, and it felt like every eye in the place turned to us, covertly and not so covertly. One goblin got up and walked away. Another glared openly.

I eyeballed Chaya, who cheerfully scampered along beside us.

"Soooo how come you're the only one here who isn't glaring."

"Oh, my family views the world through the ass-end of our traditions and thinks I don't have my own brain," Chaya said loudly. Several heads turned towards her with a frown.

Oh, I like her. But what did that even mean? I tried to put it all together—her apparent emotional closeness with Daimyn, traditionalism, the self-righteous glaring…

"Oh… so you two like… hooked up?"

Daimyn missed a step.

Chaya burst out in a delighted laugh. "Is that what you thought?"

Heat flushed up to my ears. "I don't know!"

Daimyn halted right outside the doorway we'd come in and gestured for us to go first. Practically cackling now, Chaya disappeared into the darkened staircase. I met his gaze before I thought better of it, and he lifted an eyebrow at me, eyes probing.

Face burning, I strode past him and didn't acknowledge his silent question. My nose took up that terrible itching as I stepped through the doorway. I scrubbed at my face, then my foot hit the bottom step of the stairs and I nearly ate the steps. Why was this stairwell so freaking dark? I blinked rapidly, trying to get my eyes to adjust.

"Tell you what," Chaya's disembodied voice said. "You come back, and we'll trade Daimyn stories."

"I feel that is a distinctly bad idea," Daimyn said behind me.

"No one asked you," I retorted, starting up the steps carefully. "And yes," I said to Chaya, barely able to make out her outline at the top of the stairs. "I would love that, actually." Not only because of her connection to *this* giant pile of tantalizing secrets. "This guy is going to kick me to the curb once this is all over anyway." I hitched my thumb over my shoulder, and shoved down the unacceptable pang those words evoked. I understood this tentative partnership had an end date, for multiple reasons. "So I'll have some free time."

The sound of Daimyn's steps behind me slowed.

"Is he now," Chaya said.

I reached the top of the steps and froze. Because Chaya stood on a cobblestone path surrounded by trees and manicured bushes, which was absolutely nothing like the room we'd entered into when we'd arrived here.

"Uhhh." I turned and walked backwards a few steps to look at what we'd come out of. Daimyn emerged. We'd come out of a garden shed?

"Didn't we come up the same stairway we went in? It looked like the same stairway."

Chaya blinked at me.

"The staircase is a portal," Daimyn said. "The entrance is never in the same physical place for long. It's for defense."

"A portal," I said mildly. "Well of course it is. What else would it be?"

Daimyn watched me with amusement.

"Shut up," I muttered.

He smiled wider and turned his attention back to Chaya. "Chaya, it was lovely to see you again. You should return before anyone gets particularly upset."

She sniffed. "I can handle it. It was very good to see you." Her eyes cut to me. "And to meet you."

"Likewise," I said quickly. "Uh. Let me know when you… have time or something. Wait, how do I contact you?" I glanced at the garden shed. "Especially if you keep *moving*."

Chaya laughed, a tinkling sound of joy. "I'll teach you how to find our whereabouts. Meanwhile—" She reached into her pocket and pulled out a folded piece of paper. "Write me a letter, and paste this on it. The mail carrier will find me." She winked.

Inscribed on the page was the outline of an apple with a little leaf on top, with a symbol inside that I couldn't make heads or tails of.

Just paste it to the letter?

"Huh. Magical stamps."

Chaya sidled back towards the garden shed. "Bye, Daimyn," she said softly, and disappeared without a glance back.

Daimyn's stared at the doorway for a beat before turning back to me.

"Soooooo," I began.

"Once we hear from Shahar," he said. "We can figure out a plan."

"And Chaya and you?"

"Not my story to tell," he returned promptly. "But I am glad to see her doing so well. Thriving, really." His head tilted, looking more at my shoulder than my actual face. "Are you all right?"

I blinked. "What do you mean?"

His chin tilted down. "I don't know what exactly happened with the Dokkalfar, but I understand the memory is not pleasant— "

"Oh," I blurted as I understood. Then wished I hadn't as Daimyn shut up.

My heart felt tender, my eyes puffy, and my limbs too heavy, now that I thought about it. I licked my lips and tried to figure out what to tell him.

"I'm truly fine. I promise."

I thought I'd stop there, but Daimyn kept watching me, and more words spilled out.

"It was surreal and definitely reopening old wounds. But…" Pieces started connecting in my head. "For so long, that 'secret' has been dirty, something to lie about, or pretend never happened. The idea it was somehow valuable to someone…" A short laugh burst out and caught in my throat at the end. "I feel kinda cheap, 'selling' it off like that, and at the same time, it's freeing." I stared hard at his collarbone. "Does that even make sense?"

"Yes." He shifted his weight. "I imagine you have had many people attempt to make you doubt your experiences and feelings. Having that treated as important sounds cathartic."

Okay. Maybe he did understand. I cleared my throat, trying to get past the tightness there. "Yeah."

Daimyn inspected me. "We're done for tonight. Let's get rest."

I made a face. "You mean *I* need rest, Sir I-don't-need-sleep."

A slow smile spread across his face. "Tomorrow, we'll see what else we can dig up in other places. And work on making noise to distract from Shahar's info-gathering." His eyes narrowed. "Yes, you can be involved, as long as we can keep your exposure nonexistent."

I sniffed. I had no idea what that meant, but I thrilled to find out. "It's good you have my help, because I am excellent at making noise."

He snorted and shook his head.

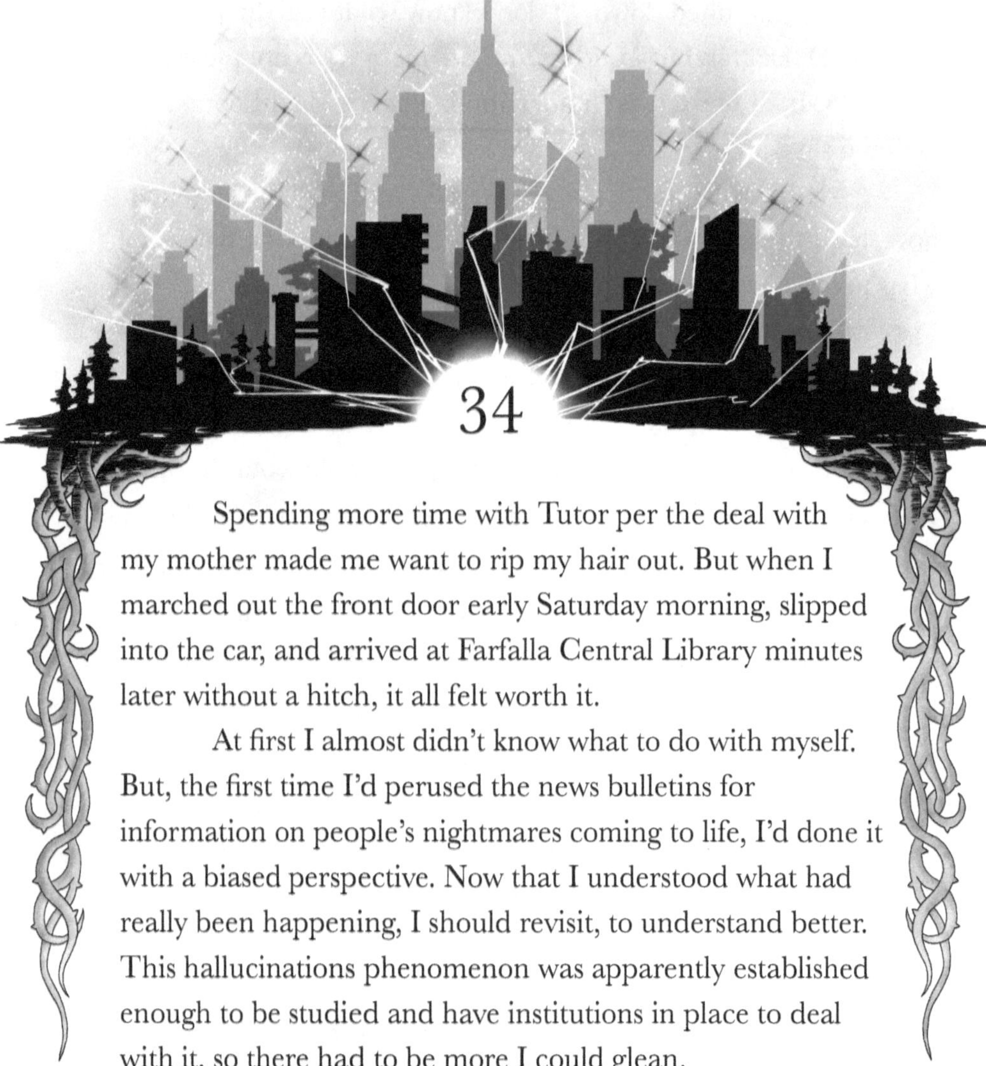

34

Spending more time with Tutor per the deal with my mother made me want to rip my hair out. But when I marched out the front door early Saturday morning, slipped into the car, and arrived at Farfalla Central Library minutes later without a hitch, it all felt worth it.

At first I almost didn't know what to do with myself. But, the first time I'd perused the news bulletins for information on people's nightmares coming to life, I'd done it with a biased perspective. Now that I understood what had really been happening, I should revisit, to understand better. This hallucinations phenomenon was apparently established enough to be studied and have institutions in place to deal with it, so there had to be more I could glean.

After looking over reports for an hour, the pattern I'd seen before still glared out at me: these "Nightmare" attacks increased dramatically about seven years ago. Before that, only a few incidents a year had been detailed. There'd been several dozen cases this year so far. But I already knew all of that.

Inspiration sparked. I'd never looked farther back than a decade or so, but the library had preserved articles going back centuries.

I would have balked halfway through at the tediousness of the task if I hadn't been so fixated. An hour later, I sat back in the chair, triumphant. A little under a 100 years ago, for 9 years, an increasing number of people fell ill with a "mind sickness." Then it tapered off, only one or two people a year mentioned. That is, until seven years ago, when it started up again.

This "Nightmare" thing… it came in waves. A shiver spread down my spine.

Was this phenomenon in reaction to something? Based on the position of the stars? Did someone control it? I drummed my fingers against the table until I realized how loud it was and stopped.

I needed a better idea of Farfallan history, a framework for to put all this into context. Heaving myself to my feet, I stuffed all my notes into my bag and headed out of the current affairs room. The history room lay at the back of the grand complex of the library; I cut through new publications and some sort of literature section, weaving through shelves, rounding a corner—

And came to an abrupt halt at the sight of a broad-shouldered gentleman with his back to me. Two books rested in the crook of his elbow while he scanned another open book held in the other hand. He turned a page, and the sight of his hands confirmed it. Why in the name of everything holy did I recognize his *hands*?

I stared and couldn't seem to make myself move. Despite the ripple of indescribable strength that teased the edges of my mind, dressed as neither Badass Guardian nor Upperclass Gentleman, something about him struck me as… vulnerable. Or maybe lost.

Lonely?

My whole body tilted towards him; I jerked back through force of will and stumbled. Making a face at myself, I froze, but he didn't seem to have noticed.

Still staring, I chewed on my lip. Would he want me to say hello, or would that be an annoyance considering I'd already barged into other aspects of his life?

What is he reading?

Should I go over there, considering TASA's unhealthy interest in everything about him? I could argue the justification of meeting up to solve my attempted-murder, even if my presence wasn't strictly necessary. But a social visit… could reveal many things. Other things.

My heart sank.

Walk away. Turn, and walk.

Daimyn's head came up. I stopped breathing as his head turned, his profile not quite fully to me. For a thundering heartbeat he didn't move. Then he turned back, re-shelved one of the books he'd been flipping through, and walked further into the shelves, disappearing from view.

My insides pulled as if compelled, and my legs committed mutiny. I'd crossed the half dozen meters or so of distance before I could stop them. Not that it made a bit of difference; Daimyn had disappeared from the aisle. I wrestled down inappropriate and entirely too intense disappointment, and locked my knees to prevent any further bright ideas my body might have.

Stawwwp you useless ninny.

My eyes slid to the shelf where Daimyn had put a book away. Tip-toeing forward, I tried to recall the book's thickness and color, turning my head sideways to read titles to get an idea of subject…

This all looked like poetry.

I rolled my eyes, grinning. *Why did emotional prose and brooding just* fit?

Subtle movement between the gaps in the books, on the other side of the shelf, made me freeze. My heart skipped. The angle of his jaw came into view in a gap between a series of shorter books and the shelf above it. I barely breathed. He shifted again, and his eyes came into view to catch mine. The corners crinkled, then he leaned out of view again.

Heat flooded my face. My weight shifted back and forth. I heard him slide a book off the shelf. The air seemed to buzz with attention and anticipation.

This is ridiculous.

I *am ridiculous.*

"So, how's your family?" *Smooth.* I kind of wanted to smack myself.

"Doing well. And yours?"

I grimaced at the amusement in those four words. The rumble of his voice made my insides writhe around and now I *really* wanted to smack myself.

"Oh, dandy. My father is expanding his glorious empire, and mother is up to her usual machinations."

"And you?" His voice drifted further down the shelf. "What has captured your attention today?"

I took a few steps down the aisle, following the sound of his voice. My chest squeezed as I thought about the answer to his question—because I summoned lies by rote, and then realized that I could actually tell him the truth. My throat closed at the prospect. I looked around quickly to make sure we were out of earshot.

"Did you know that the Nightmares the Divide causes—it comes in waves?" I blurted in a low voice.

After a beat he responded. "Flux," he murmured. "We call them Flux situations."

My eyes widened. A faint scuffing sound continued down the aisle, and I slid my finger along the spines of the books while I kept pace, staring at them without seeing.

"Oh?" I said, hoping the questioning sound would prompt him to continue.

He hummed in response, and didn't say more.

I made a face. *Okay fine, Mr. Reticent.* "Do all the… do all the places that experience Divide Burden experience Flux Situations at the same time?"

I tried to sound like I knew what I talked about, even as the words I'd read but never spoken felt strange and oddly-shaped in my mouth.

"Not always as one." Daimyn's voice came through the shelves, soft and amused. "But yes. Up and down the coast, incidents have been increasing."

Nightmares coming alive. People being possessed. The ground opening up.

"Is there a way to stop it?"

He huffed, that almost-laugh I'd heard from our very first meeting. I frowned at the memory of that weariness, peering through the gaps between books to try to see his face. I caught a glimpse of downcast eyes.

"No. The symptoms can be managed, however."

"You help manage this?" I asked tentatively.

"I do what I can."

I chewed on my lip. Then Daimyn surprised me by speaking again.

"Magic is not inherently evil, something that warps just because it exists, as many want to believe. It's just powerful… and easily manipulated into both good and evil things." A pause. "You'll need to instill that lesson deep if you plan to stick around. It takes a great and powerful person to find the balance, and not be pulled to the extremes."

My heart lifted at his mention of me 'sticking around.'

The shelf ended. It startled me, despite the fact that I could clearly see the end of the aisle and it didn't magically move when I reached it. I hadn't mentally prepared for the lack of barrier, instead fully confronted with all his sheer physicality.

Daimyn smiled the instant my gaze met his. "Hi."

"Hi," I whispered back.

He leaned into the corner of the shelf, starting up his unabashed staring again. I cleared my throat and fidgeted, immediately making myself stop. My gaze fell to the books he carried in the crook of one elbow, and I gestured towards them with my chin.

"And you? What are you up to today?"

Daimyn wordlessly offered them to me. I accepted them both, one thin and one thick. The thin one had worn edges and a soft cover, something about the bloodlines of horses.

"For my father," Daimyn said.

Painful curiosity seized me. I didn't know really anything about Daimyn's father, not even what he looked like. I wanted to ask more, but remembered to stop before I did. Bloody TASA.

I should go. I should make excuses and go.

Instead, I turned my attention to the next book. It looked brand new, still stiff. By the cover, it had to be something about technology.

"For my brother."

Further reading revealed it had something to do with high-level communication wavelength technology.

"He planning some kind of server takedown?" I asked mildly.

"Not today," Daimyn said in the same tone.

I grinned, then handed the books back. "Nothing for you?"

"I hadn't gotten there yet."

It took everything in me to swallow down all the questions piling in my throat. "Well. I should… I won't take up more of your time," I forced out. "I'm sure you have better things to—"

"I don't," he interrupted. "Unless this is your polite way of saying you do?"

My mouth opened. Shut. "No," I whispered.

You utter fool.

I led Daimyn through the library towards where I'd been the past few hours, something light bubbling in my chest. My secluded spot in one corner of the current affairs room hadn't gained any occupants, and I dropped into a chair. Daimyn slid into the one across from me.

For a moment, silence reigned. I didn't know what to do with him. Or myself.

"Well, I suppose I should look into all the people that might be targeting me," I said. Not that I knew where to start.

"You must have other interests beyond magic."

I lifted my eyebrows. What happened to Mr. You're Going To Die If We Don't Figure This Out? Daimyn just smirked at me. Okay, we were doing this. Whatever this was…

"Well, this won't shock you at all, but I do love studying mythology and folklore. The stuff that manages to make it through regulation, anyway," I muttered.

Daimyn's head cocked, eyes distant for a second. "I think I saw something in new publications."

Rising to his feet, he strode off, leaving his jacket and books behind. I blinked after him for a minute, and hadn't really had time to wrap my head around this turn of events before he returned, a huge crisp book in hand.

"I'm not sure how I feel about this translator, he tends to take too many liberties…"

I scanned the author-translator's name.

"As opposed to what, relying on translations stuck in the past and not understanding languages don't always translate truthfully when it comes to meaning and form and generally swayed by the current political bias?" I asked, very sweetly.

Daimyn hummed, his eyes lighting up. I grinned, unable to help it.

"I need something, I'll be back." He waved a hand. "Again."

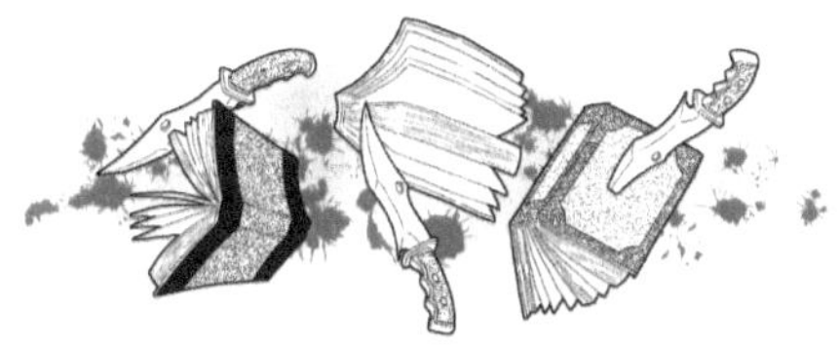

It turned out that Daimyn had another superpower: making time fly. We started talking about mythology and literature and folklore and philosophy and errors in translations, and somehow the sun now touched the horizon, sending curtains of green-gold across the floor of the library. I ignored it, even as the indicator of time passing pressed painfully against my skull.

Our latest debate had me staring at Daimyn in disbelief.

"Oh my god. You're a hopeless romantic."

Daimyn's head tilted, vivid green watching me under heavy lashes. "Why, because I enjoy tales of good triumphing over evil?"

The library table looked like a paper explosion. Various translations of different myths and tales splayed open and piled on top of each other, ranging in translator and time period. Daimyn knew his stuff, to my utmost delight. But I got to lord my language fluency over his head. He apparently knew Welsh and Russian, which struck me as an odd combination, but I didn't know them, so. I couldn't remember the last time I had this much fun bickering intellectually with someone. Never mind it had now devolved into me making fun of him.

"You're a softie," I said, getting into the shite-giving. "Mr. Badass of the night, a big ol' mush ball who wants all the bows at the end and the villain to become good and—"

"Okay, okay, okay," he said, sitting back against the seat heavily.

I leaned forward across the table towards him and cupped a hand around one side of my mouth like I would tell a secret. "Don't worry, I won't tell anyone."

Daimyn swiftly leaned forward, his face a scant few centimeters from my own, eyes locked on mine. "When I find your hidden romantic, I'll be sure to give you the same kindness you show me."

I swallowed. "You're wrong. I'm a cold, cold bitch."

Something fritzed out in my brain with his face this close, and before I could stop it, I poked him in the nose.

His eyes narrowed. The twitch of his shoulder didn't give me enough warning before warm fingers wrapped around my own, firmly pinning my pointer finger down, trapped between two of his. Before I could react, he nipped my knuckle with a flash of teeth.

"It's not nice to poke."

I stared at his mouth. *Did he just… bite me?* Also, what was up with his teeth? My fingers tingled. All of them. My brain bolted for the hills, immediately fixed on recalling if I'd ever seen him smile wide enough to see his teeth or if this was the first time I'd seen that both his upper and lower canines—

Daimyn blinked, humor disappearing. "I wasn't very normal just now, was I?"

"Normal is overrated," I said instantly.

Daimyn released me and leaned back, palms pressed into the edge of the table. "I apologize."

I blinked at his overly-neutral expression, my hand slowly floating down to rest on the table. "Well I did poke you." I didn't even have time to feel mortified over that, between tingling fingers and staring at him.

Daimyn watched me from the corner of his eye, under his eyelashes, like he tried to inspect me without actually looking at me.

I jumped when my PCD buzzed against the table, shattering the strange and delightful awkwardness. I glared at it, already guessing the sender, and sighed.

"That was heavy," Daimyn said, the words almost a question.

I gritted my teeth and opened the message to confirm. It would not be good to ignore my mother the very first time I had a Saturday to myself. "It's my summons home."

"May I walk you back?"

My gaze snapped to his. "You're not sick of me yet?"

"Engrained gentleman habits. I can't let you walk by yourself in the fading light." His voice changed to mock-horror. "It's *dangerous* out there."

He winked. I made a face at him. *Okay, we're just going to move on from the nipping me thing. That's fine. Sure. Whatever.*

We returned the books we'd pulled from the shelves to a librarian, and headed towards the exit.

"I'll meet you out front, I need to use the restroom," Daimyn said.

Well at least he has to pee like the rest of us mere mortals.

For a second I contemplated just leaving him here, just to see what he'd do. But that sounded like a lot of effort for something that really didn't offend me, and I couldn't even pretend to myself I wanted to leave him. I'd spent almost the entire day with this guy and I hadn't grown even a little bit sick of his presence. How annoying.

I leaned against one of the stone columns at the library entrance and watched people scurrying about. The horizon had started taking on hues of pink and red amongst the rays of green-gold, and I smiled at it. When had I last just stopped to enjoy a sunset? I huffed a laugh. *When was the last time I felt content enough in my own body to stop and enjoy* anything *peaceful?*

Someone grew close, smoking a cigarette. I glanced, irritated at the invasion of my personal bubble… and my stomach tightened up into my throat.

Lieutenant Andrews looked different in civilian clothes, too.

"This is good progress," he said, gesturing back towards the library. "Spending the day with you shows attachment."

I couldn't make my tongue work.

"We expect a full report tomorrow. Come to this address whenever you're able to get away."

He held out a card. I couldn't make myself move to take it.

"The lovely Tiffany seems to be doing well," Andrews said. "I even understand she's making friends in the right circles."

I flinched. My numb fingers wrapped around the thick paper.

Andrews put out his cigarette in a nearby tray and headed down the library steps. At the bottom, he turned a corner and disappeared, as if he'd never been there. Goodbye peace, welcome back restlessness trying to eat me alive. Could I have one goddamn day? Just one?

Pressure touched my arm. I jumped, spinning around.

Daimyn frowned, eyes searching over my face. "Everything all right?"

I have to tell him.

The thought came like a sonic blast. Today changed things. If I waited any longer it would be too far, too long, too gone. It would come out somehow in the worst way, and I wouldn't be able to explain it right, or…

"Yes," I said, fighting to keep my voice even. "Shall we?"

Daimyn's studied me as we walked down the steps. I avoided his gaze, which probably only made it worse. I was not being subtle. He quietly kept pace at my side as we turned and headed down the sidewalk, his gaze on the sky instead of me, but his head tilted in my direction, as if waiting. He didn't say a word, gave me space without question, while his attention still rested on me.

My eyes stung, and I blinked rapidly, trying not to let him see. When I told him about TASA, it would be bad. I would lose all of that attention, wouldn't I?

Maybe I don't have to tell him quite yet.

And how long would I use that excuse? Until he started trusting me for real, telling me things that could do harm to him in the wrong hands? In *my* wrong hands considering what I had to do with the information?

It was only a few hours until I'd see him again. I could wait until then, form what I needed to say.

No. If I started delaying, I wouldn't stop. My stomach wanted to eat itself to get away from this situation.

We reached the street in front of the Leynthall pazo entirely too quickly. *I'm not ready.* My face flushed; my clothes stuck uncomfortably to my skin. Daimyn slowed, not seeming in any particular hurry to part ways. Everything had become much worse because what had happened today had done something and god I was going to throw up.

We drifted to a stop just outside the trees that ringed the grounds. Daimyn rocked back on his heels, then looked at me. I froze his expression, one I'd never seen on him before, soft and almost… vulnerable.

"I appreciate you spending time with me today. It helped."

My eyebrows drew together slowly. "Helped?"

One side of his mouth kicked up in a tired kind of humor. "Here's something for you: I lose parts of myself if I fail to protect someone."

I blinked. "Come again?"

"If I'm… triggered to protect someone, and I fail to do so, I lose bits of myself. I guess you could call it my humanity." He took a breath. "Early this morning, after you left—well. I didn't get there in time." He gripped the back of his neck with one hand. "You asked once if I was forced into this job. My family is—"

"You can't tell me this." The strangled words burned as they burst out of me, as it finally registered what was happening: Daimyn had told me a secret of his own volition.

I had to come clean *now*. Panic surged, encased my chest.

In a snap second, his intensity sharpened, softness gone. "What's wrong?"

I viscerally mourned the loss of his vulnerability, his trust.

How do I say this how do I say this how do I say this—

"There's—I have to tell you… " I swallowed. "TASA, they have…"

Everything in Daimyn's expression shut down. My words stuttered to a halt. *He made that leap too fast.* This wasn't the first time something like this had happened to him.

"They have pictures of Tiff," I blurted, words crowding my throat all at once. "There's magic and she's covered in blood, and a body—she got caught up in something, I don't know all the details, but it looks *bad*, really bad. I don't think she meant it and she lost someone—Tiff's my best friend. They s-said they'd made the photos public if I didn't…" I lost all air in my lungs, had to heave to get any oxygen. "If I didn't tell them things about you. I've been avoiding them as much as I c-can and misleading—I haven't told them anything important. I—"

Daimyn stared at me without expression. Nausea rose with a vengeance.

"You can't tell me anything important." I tried to keep my voice steady. "Please don't tell me secrets—I won't give you up. I promise I won't. But you have to understand."

Daimyn gaze slid away, unfocused and bland. "I see. And what have you told them so far?"

I sucked in a breath, trying to relieve my starving lungs. *You have to breathe.* "That… you're strong. Fast. Things like that. They want to know what you are, how to control you—"

"That's why you pushed for the partnership," Daimyn murmured, understanding dawning in his voice.

"What? No! Absolutely not, that's not why—that was what *I* wanted—"

He pressed his fingers between his eyes. "Fuck, I took you to Goldenapple."

My heart dropped to my toes. "I haven't told them about that." My voice rose loud, wavered. *Though will I have to, tomorrow?* "I've hidden things. And—and I don't ask about you." I cringed at how that sounded. "I don't want to hurt you."

He chuckled a bitter, ugly noise. Unlike a real laugh, this didn't sound rusty, like he hadn't made it in a while. "Gods, I'm a fool. I couldn't figure out how you found me, *why* you looked for me… of course, if you had TASA tracking my movements."

I stared in bewilderment. "What are you talking about?"

He smiled wide, a baring of teeth. Distantly, I realized I'd been right earlier: all four of his canines were long and sharp-looking.

"I could never figure out how you knew where I was the night of mediation with the Denashkesh," Daimyn said, voice filled with a vague amusement.

I froze. That had been the night of the dark moon, when I'd Felt him. My throat convulsed in a swallow. Daimyn took in my expression and looked away with a shake of his head.

"Do me a favor and don't lie to my—"

"I'm not!" My chest crumpled inwards. "TASA showed up *after* that. It wasn't until *after*. It was—it was the next day. Then they showed up with the pictures."

His expression didn't change; I wondered if he'd even registered my words. Trees shushed nearby, making his preternatural stillness all the more stark. He'd never felt so distant, even at the very beginning, as complete strangers. How could I tell him about my episodes? Especially now.

The last person I told about my Episodes killed my sister because of it.

Telling him my secret wouldn't fix anything anyway.

"You want an in to the magical world," Daimyn began blandly. "You've made yourself invaluable to TASA with your association with me, and I assume given you resources. This sounds like the perfect scenario for you. Why are you telling me this?"

My stomach cramped. "You think I'm going to work for my blackmailers?"

"Ah. It's the way they went about it, then."

Acid burned in my gut, my eyes stinging. "Fuck off. That's not—"

Flat eyes flicked over to meet my own and knocked the tiny bit of air I'd managed to recover right out of me. "I must apologize for the position you've been placed in."

The difference in his voice between now, and just minutes ago, filled my insides with splinters of ice. *Ah yes. Back to reality.* This *is my life. I don't get nighttime adventures and flirting in the library, that's not for me.*

"Now that I understand the situation, I will handle it."

Daimyn turned and strode away. I flinched, breath hitching. *This went wrong so fast.*

I knew, with a slow dawning certainty, what his words meant. If he removed himself from the picture, I could not gather information for TASA. If I had no info for TASA, I would not be valuable, and they would leave me alone.

Tiff would be safe.

He would be safe.

And he would be gone.

35

That evening at supper, my parents excitedly chatted about their developing relationship with a Galician family they'd met via the Farfallan Council. It sounded like my father had found a friend as well as a possible business partner. I paid attention to every boring detail with an attentiveness that made my brain come out my ears, desperate for any distraction.

It turned bad so quickly.

"Their son is very bright, and so handsome," my mother said. "He had such a long conversation with your father and is very interested in the transportation business." She looked at me carefully. "And in you, my dear."

Comprehension dawned. No. *No.* This conversation was turning bad now, too.

"We've arranged for you two to meet, and see how well you get along," my mother said, as if that settled it.

Everything I'd just eaten turned rotten in my stomach. Both my parents watched me, my father more surreptitiously. The expectation had always been that I would marry and start creating the next Leynthall generation as quickly as was proper. We were new money; we needed to establish ourselves. The plan didn't even need to be spoken out loud.

I'd thought being in college protected me for longer. But I could see already how my mother would arrange it. The courtship would last over my final year in school. The wedding could take place early summer. By this time next year, I could be carrying the next generation of Leynthalls.

Bile rose in a flood, and I swallowed again and again. I opened my mouth to say… something. Something deflective or snarky or belligerent or…

"May I be excused?"

My mother blinked, and my father put down his fork.

"You've barely touched your food," my mother said.

"I'm not feeling well this evening."

"You do look pale," she said worriedly.

"May I go?" I asked, desperately trying to sound normal.

"Of course, darling."

I lurched out of my seat and out of the dining room. My vision swam. I tripped on the stairs headed to the second floor, bashing my elbow on the railing. I hated the hurt sound that came out of me. *Just get to the bedroom. Just get there.*

"Ms. Fairian, are you——?"

I rushed down the hall, past the startled guard, and threw open my bedroom door. Tiff sat on the floor next to my bed. Relief welled up; I wasn't *alone*.

"Tiff—my parents—"

I stopped. My secret chest sat in the center of the room, lid open wide. The contents spread across the floor. All my secret, wonderful, *vulnerable* books lay next to Tiff's knee, sprawled open almost obscenely; my notes and research on the Divide laid out in an arc in front of her.

Intense, sudden vulnerability washed over me. Dominoes fell, set in motion too long ago for me to stop them, and I didn't know where the next one would hit.

Tiff's head slowly lifted. "I thought you were researching your sister's murderer."

"What? I am. I *was*. I figured out—"

"What is *this*?" Her finger stabbed into the sketch I'd made of the designs on the Divide.

My insides shriveled.

Tiff rose off the floor. "What do you think you're doing? Do you have a death wish?"

I tried to summon the ability to get through this conversation. *Tiff, covered in blood, horror in her eyes as she held a mangled corpse.* "Look, I understand this scares you, but—"

"No—*no*—don't you dare patronize." She stabbed her finger at me. "You don't have a bloody clue what you're doing while you act all high and mighty, like you're somehow *better* than everyone for sticking your nose where it doesn't belong."

A sobbing laugh came out of me as I flung my arms wide. "Tiff. What the hell. None of this is new to you!"

"Looking out for danger is one thing. That's just keeping you *safe*." She heaved for breath. "This? *This?* You're going to get yourself killed! How do you not understand this? *This* killed your sister!"

I flinched.

"It nearly killed *you*!"

She snatched one of the books off the ground and threw it. It hit the wall with a bang and flung open. The binding split as it crashed to the ground, sections of fragile pages ripping free.

"*Tiff!*"

"Obviously you don't give a shit about what I have to say," Tiff said. "But I'm starting to understand why your parents act the way they do. You need a bloody straitjacket."

"Tiff—"

She strode past me in a cloud of rage and fear that clawed at my skin and face. My door slammed a second later. I flinched, pressing a hand against my stomach. For a long moment, I became nothing and stared at the wall, just trying not to exist.

"This day can seriously go to hell," I whispered.

I walked to my secret—not so secret—book, carefully picking up all the pages, trying to put them in order without ripping or damaging them further. It took several minutes to carefully put them back and assess everything. My vision blurred. By the time I was done, the world swam, and I couldn't clear my eyes for longer than a second.

My breath hiccoughed as I returned to my research sprawled across the floor, carefully sorting paper as best as I could, trying not to get saltwater on everything. The rest of my books looked okay. My stupid eyes would not stop *running*.

Once everything had been returned to their place, I shut the lid of the chest, locking it up again and carefully pushing it under the bed with as little noise as possible.

Ah. There's the key to the chest lock.

I must have left it in the open.

She didn't know what she'd find in here, it's not her fault.

I need a new hiding place for the chest.

With my room back in order, I locked my door and… a stabbing pain in my chest as I realized I would not be climbing out my window tonight.

I could just go out there anyway and…

I found myself under the covers, knees to chest, blankets wrapped like a vise around my chest and head. It would be okay tomorrow. It would all look better tomorrow. I would figure it out tomorrow.

A sob burst out of me. The sound sharpened everything into clarity so painful it shattered.

She's supposed to be here.

She'd been sophisticated and educated and smart and charming and *cared* about things like business strategy and people's birthdays. *She* would never have been blackmailed, entirely too clever for that. *She* wouldn't have hurt Daimyn or drove Tiff off with her unnatural interests. *She* was and always would be the true Leynthall heir, the one destined to take our family forward, and she was dead, seven years rotting in the ground.

Everything, *everything* would be so much better if it had been me who'd died instead.

36

It took an hour to compress everything inside of me to a manageable size. Brittle determination had me rising from the bed, dressing, and heading out my window. Tiff wouldn't calm down and listen until at least the morning. But I had to fix something, because so many things were unfixable. If Daimyn wouldn't accept apology or discussion, fine, but no one could say I didn't try.

I have his PCD number. I could just message him.

Not that he would answer. He might even know how to avoid me if I said something.

Just give it up. You knew it was too good to be true.

The moon hung bright enough to lightly outline everything around me. I checked all of the spots Daimyn had met me before, but each remained vacant. I wandered streets, hating myself for my aimlessness, struggling to put my thoughts in any sort of order. At least movement brought some kind of peace.

I cut through a small street with dozens of balconies and windows crammed with silver-light-coated flowers and ferns and vegetable plants. Each one of my breaths emerged as fog. I'd traveled far enough from any channels or rivers that silence thickened the air; I'd gotten used to the trickle and rush of water, and quiet pervaded all space.

I shivered as a chill spread down my spine. And at the end of the street, a shadow moved. I slowed, right as a scuff sounded behind me. My head turned, a figure materializing out from under one of the balconies with a hood obscuring any detail of their face. Out of the corner of my eye, a hulking figure moved to block the end of the street.

That chill hadn't been from cold.

It hit me, as alarm cleared the fog from my head, how many times Daimyn had warned me about being alone in the streets of Farfalla. Worse, I'd just assumed he'd be out here somewhere and just avoiding me—but he might not be so preoccupied with my livelihood anymore. My hand closed around my dagger.

The figure from under the balcony lunged. Heart skittering, I slashed upwards—

Pain exploded in my wrist, fingers instantly numb. My knife pinged shrilly as it hit the ground. A hand clapped over my mouth from behind, an arm wrapped around my neck. I twisted, slammed my heel backwards. Whoever held me jolted, but didn't let go. I slammed my elbow back, again and again, and it made no difference.

The hulking figure appeared on my right, grabbed my wrist in a vise, pulling it straight and twisting my palm up. I shouted, muffled behind the hand over my mouth.

Why do I keep putting myself in fucked situations? Why?

The hooded one in front of me pried my fingers open and shoved a knife in my palm. *What?* Hulk on my right reached around, and pulled something from a large bag at their side. A small form struggled.

It looked like a baby deer… but tiny wings frantically fluttered on their back.

That's a peryton.

Wonder barely had time to spark before horror overtook. Hood clamped their fingers around my hand holding the knife, and twisted it towards the small creature. I shrieked, understanding their intent without understanding *why*, flexing my fingers away from the knife, yanking my arm—my whole self—backwards. Pain drilled through my fingers and wrist. My demands for an explanation turned garbled behind the hand over my mouth.

Hood forced the knife in my hand against the peryton's throat. Then drew it sharply away.

The small body jerked. Silvery-red blood sprayed out in an arc. I screamed horror into the night.

It didn't last long.

Or maybe my mind just skipped forward, unable to process.

The small peryton drooped from Hulk's hands.

Hood released me, and the knife slipped from my grip. The sharp clang barely registered over the hoarse sounds grinding out of my throat; I couldn't seem to stop whimpering. Hulk set the peryton's body on the ground.

I should have held onto the blade and started stabbing them all.

Too late now.

"That should do it," said Hood, masculine voice sounding breathless, excited. "Let's get out of here."

Hulk turned, keeping me pinned painfully to him with an arm across my chest and a hand clamped over my mouth, pawing through a bag at their side with their other hand. He pulled out a circular ring of metal, and Hood pulled it into two halves with a click. I writhed away, every muscle heavy as stone, as they fit the cold metal around my neck.

Click.

My mind... for the first time I could ever remember in my life... turned silent.

~ PART THREE ~

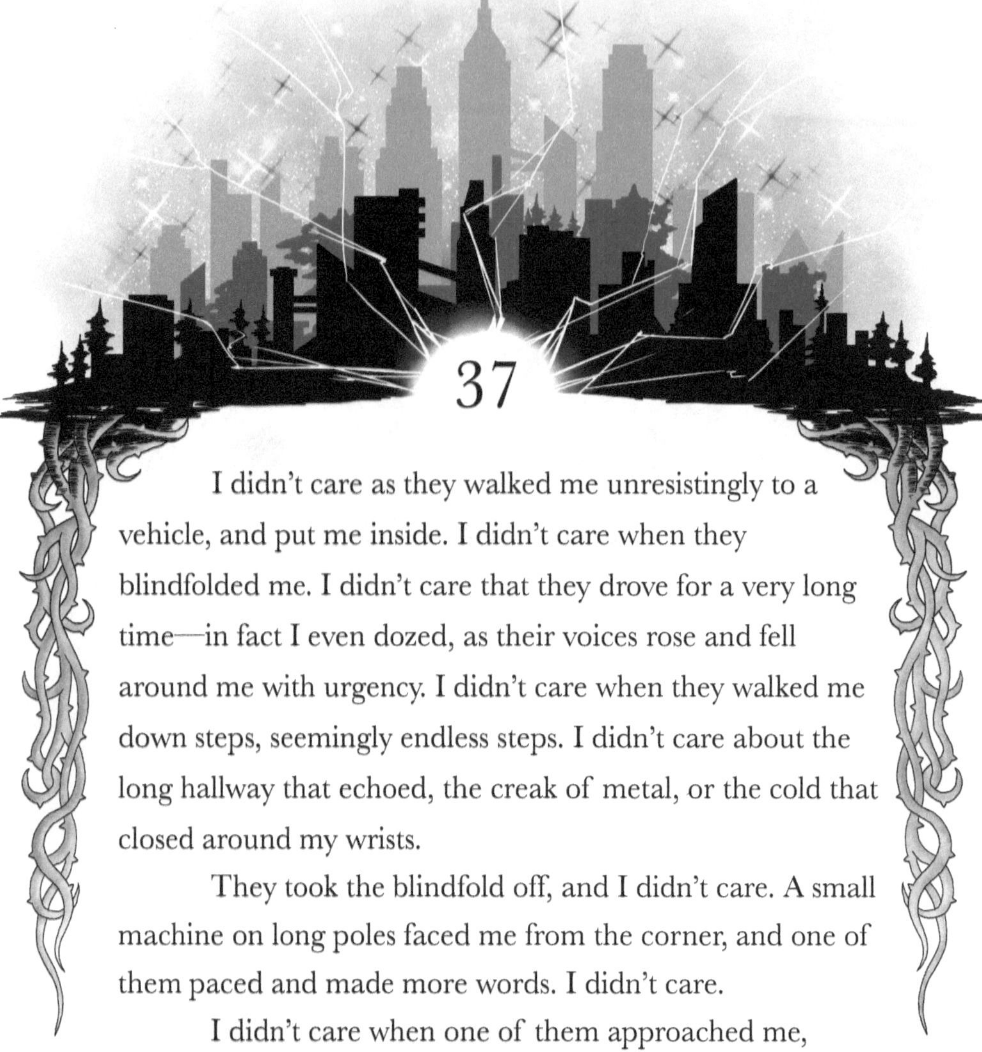

37

I didn't care as they walked me unresistingly to a vehicle, and put me inside. I didn't care when they blindfolded me. I didn't care that they drove for a very long time—in fact I even dozed, as their voices rose and fell around me with urgency. I didn't care when they walked me down steps, seemingly endless steps. I didn't care about the long hallway that echoed, the creak of metal, or the cold that closed around my wrists.

They took the blindfold off, and I didn't care. A small machine on long poles faced me from the corner, and one of them paced and made more words. I didn't care.

I didn't care when one of them approached me, when they pulled on the metal around my throat and it released with a click—

Thought screamed into my skull. The back of my neck and scalp buzzed like hornets had caught under my skin. The room around me was small, the walls and ceiling uneven stone, some small stalactites, but the ground was curiously smooth. A door made of bars blocked the exit, almost like a jail cell. Three people stood in here. The one nearest me, masculine with short-cropped pale hair and a twisted face finished pulling the metal collar off me.

A broad-shouldered, feminine figure leaned in the doorway across from me, looking attentive with no discernible emotion.

A smaller figure, slender, slipped out the room with the machine they'd all been focused on earlier—a recording camera?

It smelled like stone and brine. Based on the number of hazily-remembered descending steps, we were underground. Something heavy and cold encased my wrists. The only light came from torches of some kind, across from what looked like the only exit out of here.

All of this I interpreted out of the corners of my vision, because I did not dare look away from the strigoi in front of me. The last time I'd faced down one they'd tried to eat my neck. This one looked decidedly more coherent. He also looked like he waited for my reaction, a grin quivering on thin lips.

My heart pounded, insistent that I wake up, that I go back, that all of this was a dream, an error in comprehension. *You done fucked up now.*

Killing the peryton had been too specific, the kidnapping too orchestrated—this was planned.

They hadn't hurt me while I'd been listless, so the plan wasn't my death—for now.

This odd room, the recording camera—they had *specific* intentions.

They didn't bother to hide their faces—they weren't planning to let me leave alive; or, optimistically, they thought they couldn't be hunted down if I got out of here and described them.

While that metal thing had been around my neck, they'd been talking, but I'd been unable to comprehend the words. It could have been in another language for all I knew.

Kidnapping 101 told me to be careful and give them what they wanted, because everyone involved wanted me alive and unharmed in the end. But everything, from making me kill the peryton to not hiding their faces to the alarm buzzing across my skin, told me this wasn't a ransoming.

I could provoke them to get information, or give them no reaction and see what happened. Dread and grief rose and made the decision for me.

"So? What reaction are you hoping for?" My voice came out as a rasp.

The strigoi slow-blinked, expression still riveted. "I'm not sure. I'm simply painfully curious to find out what finally made Deathless slip."

Familiarity pinged at his voice. This one had been the hooded figure, the one to draw my hand and knife across the little peryton's throat. I breathed through the inferno that ignited in my chest, fighting the confines of flesh, raging to wreak destruction. I memorized his features, so I'd be able to recognize him again, no matter what happened.

Deathless, he'd said. He was talking about Daimyn. Well, duh. As Daimyn said before, he was my only real connection to the magical world.

"So you changed your mind about killing me, then."

The strigoi blinked and then gave a started laugh. "You're much too useful to me alive. Death is not in the plan, little consort."

This wasn't the same person that hired the Mortis Mercator.

"Mostly," he added belatedly, his smile growing.

I snorted. "I'm not sure what you mean by consort, but I'll tell you right now, I won't make a good one."

The strigoi threw back his head and laughed. "I'm not in the market even if I went for sweets like you. Though stealing you from him *would* be satisfying."

Confusion drew my eyebrows together. *What?*

Then I got it.

"Oh wow," I said, and couldn't keep the heat from my voice any longer. "You're under the misconception I somehow matter to him. You *are* a fool."

I couldn't say his name. Words spilled out of me before I thought through their wisdom.

"I'm a TASA pawn, you nitwit. I was gathering information for them." I smiled widely, baring all my teeth. "And guess what? He just found out—and you can guess what that did to his opinion of me. So if you're looking for leverage, you're out of luck."

Amusement drained from the strigoi's expression, his eyebrows lifting. Strangely, the feminine figure leaning in the doorway smiled. The strigoi hummed and looked me up and down, and without another word, turned and left the room. The woman followed without pause, swinging the metal door shut with a hideous shriek.

I was shackled to the goddamn floor. The weight on my wrists were manacles, attached to chains, attached to the ground. There was barely enough length to cross my arms while sitting. The only light came from a fire torch across from the door, which made me feel like I'd been transported back to the middle ages. I worked at the chains in the dim and fading light, searching for any weaknesses. They fit snug to my skin. I'd heard somewhere you could get out of shackles by breaking your thumb… but I didn't know the first thing about how to do it. I didn't even know if I *could* do it.

How did I keep getting myself into these situations where I was helpless? Was I really that incompetent? That pathetic?

The torch slowly ran out of fuel, dimming as shadows overtook my cell, until darkness swallowed everything. Sound became sharper in the lack of light. A constant hush pervaded this place, something that didn't quite form but carried presence, broken up by a shuffle, a scurry maybe, or a whisper. Something dripped, far off. The air hung heavy, almost stale, but every once in a while a puff of breeze reached me. It was cold. And smelled like salt.

With some rearranging, I could lie down on the floor. Boredom came quickly. I rarely had the chance to just sit with my own thoughts, to allow my mind to spin and unfurl. At first, it was almost peaceful to just breathe in the dark. Though I worried how easily I fell into neutral, back to that waiting, waiting, *waiting* for something to happen. At least this time I could see the danger.

Time ticked on…

At some point I realized that I'd lost all my special knives. One I'd lost in the river with the kelpie, and my kidnappers had apparently relieved me of the others. The realization hit like a punch, jerking me out of neutral and over a screaming void of everything I could not feel right now.

My reaction was silly. It had taken time and money to get the knives commissioned out of alternate materials, but I could do it again. When I got out of here. If I got out of here.

Excepting that, I remained perfectly calm.

I dozed, too cold to really sleep well. I wondered if the sun was up yet. If my disappearance had been noticed yet. I fitfully shifted in and out of consciousness, shivering on the stone. My parents would put out the call to Ransom Recovery, since that would be the first assumption for my absence. How long would it take before they realized this wasn't a ransoming?

My mind felt thin. I was terribly thirsty.

Boredom turned on me, as it always did. Nothingness surrounded me. No sound, no movement, no stimulation, nothing but stale air my nose got used to. Breathing became my only companion, until I couldn't stop focusing on it, until I felt like I was going to freak out if I kept breathing.

Time dragged on and on until I started counting minutes because it felt like I was losing time.

How long would it take for my disappearance to reach Daimyn? Would he care? He'd obviously stopped watching over me like he had been before. But… he had been telling me, before I interrupted, something about losing his humanity if he didn't save people.

Would he *have* to try to save me?

Hunger turned into my second companion. It became critical as seconds turned to minutes turned to hours turned to… I didn't even bloody know. My mouth was dry, my throat hurt, my head ached.

I started to doubt everything. Were my memories even reality? Or perhaps this was the truest reality, and everything that had come before had been my imagination. Maybe I was the only one alive, and I'd imagined everyone else in the world. When I talked myself out of that, my mind made up new scenarios. Maybe my kidnappers had left, or been driven off. Maybe they'd forgotten about me.

My stomach stopped hurting at some point, but hollowness left me shaky. My lips dried and cracked, and I couldn't stop licking them, which only made it worse. I sat up and stood and laid back down, then did it again. I wanted to pace so badly I had to keep from screaming. It took all my willpower to stop pulling against the chains on my wrists, which stung where I'd rubbed skin raw.

My thoughts were killing me. Sitting in the dark was going to bleed my brain right out of my skull. Ransomers at least would give you something to do if you asked nicely. Cerin had too: there was plenty of screaming to be done trying to escape terror coming to life right in front of you.

38

The back of my skull buzzed. I inhaled sharply, my eyes coming open. Through the bars of the door, distant light faintly outlined the hallway… and slowly grew more distinct. Adrenaline kicked hard. I got to my feet quickly, too quickly apparently, as vertigo rushed over me.

Footsteps followed the light as it filled the room.

Anticipation shot through me, swirling with determination. It disappeared abruptly. I'd barely recognized the Feeling as not-mine when anxiety hit, too hungry to be my own. Then my fingers went numb for a second. Then my throat closed, in a kind of weary anger. It steadied me, the stream of insight into these people—even if I didn't completely understand what the Feelings meant.

The strigoi man and the woman—who I didn't think was strigoi—strode into view. Without looking at me, the woman strode to the recording camera that I'd forgotten about, still set up in the corner. Her outline almost blurred, like smoke.

She turned on the camera, and a red light flicked on. "Whenever you're ready."

The strigoi sauntered over to me. I glared, leaning away when he stuck his damn face in mine.

"You wanna back up there, friend?" My voice came out as a croak.

"Recording in two… one…" the woman behind the camera said.

The red light began blinking. Unease quickened my heartbeat.

"Good morning, Deathless!" the strigoi said, voice exhilarated in a way reminiscent of old-time showpeople. "Or perhaps it'll be evening when you get this. I hope not, because this time, there's a ticking clock. Maybe you don't think we're serious, or maybe your little friend here is right and you really don't care."

I swallowed, realized I stared into the camera, and jerked my gaze away.

The strigoi put his arm across my shoulders. "Warning your intended target was—"

I yanked away from him, the chains jerking my wrists painfully. "Touch me again and I'll bite your face off."

Delight lit up his expression as he leaned in close. "Did you know—"

I lunged with my head lowered, slamming the top of my head right into his face. Pain splintered down my spine, like I'd just head-butted a wall. My knee abruptly met the ground as my vision blurred. I opened one eye to see him stumbling away from me, a hand pressed to his nose.

Good. But ow.

"Serves you right," the woman behind the camera said. "Stop trying to be cute. I'm restarting the tape."

She fiddled with the camera, the red light turning solid again. The strigoi took his place next to me again, more cautiously this time. Annoyingly, he looked interested more than put out.

"You're on in two… one…"

The man swiveled towards the camera. "Deathless, good morning. Or is it evening by now? Let's hope you receive this soon, or—"

"So do you have like a script or something," I cut him off, voice loud. "Because this is going to get tedious if we have to keep repeating it."

The muscle under the strigoi's eye twitched, and he turned towards me slowly. I fought back a smile and not a small amount of trepidation. Ah yes, messing with his theatrics surely caused a reaction.

"Just gag her," the woman said, waving a hand.

With a jerk, he pulled a scarf from around his neck and came towards me, knuckles tight around the cloth.

"No you bloody don—"

Three minutes later cotton filled my mouth. Literally. I glared, breathing hard through my nose, my eyes watering from my hair caught painfully in the scarf tied around my head. It tasted awful. Like brine and sweat. I tried not to gag. My jaw started to ache from the tight band.

"Two… one…" the woman said.

The man turned towards the camera with that same showman energy as before. "Deathless! Here we are again…"

He repeated himself for the third time, though got farther into the plan and demands. Rocks filled my stomach the longer he spoke. The implication of the strigoi's words seemed to take a long time to register, far beyond what it should have.

These people were instructing Daimyn to assassinate someone, or they would start hurting me.

I pressed my cheek—and thus the gag—against my shoulder and rubbed, trying to pull it down. Goddammit if I would be caught on camera just sitting here docile. I couldn't lift my chained hands above my waist, so I bent over, managing to get a finger underneath the fabric.

The strigoi seized my hair and pulled me forcibly back to my feet, derailing my attempt to get the gag off.

"I will admit, I rather forgot how fragile humans are," Strigoi continued conversationally. "Did you know they'll die after a week without water? What is this, closing out day three?"

Had it really been that long?

"It seems to me that not only must you fulfill my tasks so I don't hurt her, you must also be on your best behavior so I'll give her water. And perhaps food, depending on how long you want to drag this out."

He jerked the scarf off me, which yanked hair from my scalp. "Now you can speak, pretty thing. Anything you'd like to add?"

"You're both arsewits," I said, trying to sound bored while my eyes watered.

Not the most impressive of comebacks. But the stones in my gut gained mass and weight, and my bravado faltered. Obviously, Daimyn needed to tell these wankers to piss right off. But I had no idea what that would mean for me.

Daimyn could simply ignore all of this and he'd be no worse for wear. I mean, I believed he would… I don't know, try to find me. I thought he would. But I didn't know that. Not in my heart of hearts.

"You're doing this for nothing," I said, voice faltering.

"She seems to think you don't care," the strigoi crooned to the camera. "Are you going to prove her right?"

I swallowed. *He has to prove me right.*

"Now, you have 24 hours. Your full instructions are enclosed. And just to be sure you understand our seriousness…"

The strigoi yanked me back until my wrists caught on the manacles, forcing my arms out straight.

The back of my skull buzzed in alarm.

He gripped my arm on either side of my elbow, leaning over it. Pressure, then pain sliced deep. Air exploded out of my lungs as I jerked back. But I got absolutely nowhere. The chains, duh—and pulling on his hold was like trying to pull the entire stone wall.

Suction. His mouth sealed to the inside of my elbow, his fangs in my flesh. With a furious sound, I slammed forward into him. He braced, and barely shifted from my hit, teeth sinking deeper. I winced, writhing. I couldn't get a good angle that wouldn't slam my eye-socket into the back of his head. I couldn't push him off. I couldn't throw him off. I couldn't run away.

Was my only option really only to sit here and endure it?

I stared at the ceiling, a horrible fragility taking seed in my heart. All the muscles in my body trembled. Panic subsided wearily, and in its wake, my skin seemed to thin to near-nothingness. I swallowed, throat clicking.

I had to do… something. I would not be used as some sort of force to hurt people. Even if all I could do was endure it. Daimyn had to know that, but just in case…

My gaze drifted down to the dead eye of the recording camera. I fought my voice steady. "I told you from the beginning I accept the consequences."

Pressure came off my elbow. The area throbbed against the cold air.

"It's all right," I husked to the dead metal. "It's all okay."

The strigoi stood fluidly, his arm sliding around me with his hand over my mouth. I grimaced; who knows where his hands had been.

He pulled me back hard into his shoulder, pinning my head there. "She speaks. 'It's all right,' dear Deathless." He pulled my head to the side, farther, even farther, until it hurt, and my neck stretched out, obscenely exposed. "Well. I think you and I both know it won't be 'all right.' Not if you don't do what I say."

A long pause followed. Then a click, and the strigoi released me, exhaling in a whoosh.

"Wow, that was intense," he said, stepping away. He wiped at the corner of his mouth, inspecting his finger briefly. My elbow throbbed, a trickle of wet running down my forearm.

His eyes flicked to me, pondering me with a new light. "You're probably too young and human to understand this, but you're lucky to be here in this time of change. This is a monumental moment."

"Don't be so dramatic," the woman said, pulling a tape out of the camera. "We don't even know if it's going to work."

"Why do you hate him?" I asked, as evenly as possible. As per usual, I was the person with the littlest information in the room. I had only the barest clue of Daimyn's identity.

The strigoi pursed his lips to the side, eyes thoughtful. "I don't hate him. Though many of us do. That whole family… they're arrogant, overpowered tyrants." Despite his claim, poison rose in his words. "They shouldn't even exist, yet they pass judgement, as if they're some sort of authority. They've shaped our society for so long, who knows what heights we'd reach without their meddling."

The strigoi focused back on me, his gaze decidedly cooler. "Well. It's time to take back power."

"I'm not special to him," I insisted. "This won't make him do anything."

The strigoi pursed his lips to the side. "Even if you're not, he was never one who could stand suffering. That in itself might just put him over." He spun towards the woman. "Why haven't we tried just using a random person before?"

"Because you're not old enough to remember his rampages," the woman muttered.

Curiosity burned. Instead I swung my attention to her and kept on subject. "You have to see this isn't going to work."

She didn't seem particularly convinced by this plan, either.

Fire seemed to crackle under her skin, blooming in her eyes. "Do you think we'll just let you go if you convince us you're not valuable? If this doesn't work, *he's* going to make you a meal and *I'm* going to enjoy it. I'm not one of the ones that are nice to your kind."

Ah. Well. Crapsticks.

She looked me up and down. "Your insistence that you don't matter only makes me think you really *are* a hold over him. Be good, and this doesn't have to be too painful."

Then they left. Darkness closed around me. Again.

39

I'd been right. Daimyn did not, in fact, comply with their demands.

"… think you're quite clever, figuring out my business holdings, hmm?" The strigoi asked, his voice tight.

From the sounds of it, the strigoi had wanted Daimyn to take out the head of a rival business or something—and Daimyn had done something disastrous to the strigoi's business instead.

I smirked. *Cheeky bastard.*

Pressure exploded across the side of my face, jerking me off my feet and right into the ground. Pain came a second later in a thick, sickening wave. My wrists throbbed where the chains had jerked me to a halt.

"She might think you're cute, but I don't."

Fear does not control me. I am calm. I will get through this. I am calm and will get through this, I am—I tried to move my jaw, and a whimper escaped my throat.

The strigoi man seized my hair and forced me to my feet; thankfully he had enough of a grip that it wasn't overly painful. I still gasped, my jaw screaming at the movement. I elbowed him, the strike glancing off his ribs; it was like elbowing cement.

With a snarl, he wrenched my head to the side. Pain stabbed into my neck.

Unprepared to prevent my reaction, I shrieked and thrashed. The vulnerability of being bit in the elbow and the vulnerability of being bit in the neck was incomparable. Sound ground past my teeth, another cry I tried not to give power. That fragile seed in my chest cracked wider and dug in with roots.

I am really, truly alone.

He released me, and I staggered. Warmth slid down my throat. I couldn't reach my neck standing up, so I dropped to my knees, scrambling on instinct to put as much pressure as I could over the puncture. The strigoi towered over me.

"The punishments will only get worse, doubly so if you continue with your little reactionary temper tantrums," he said, licking his lips and wiping at his face. "It's no hardship on *my* part, she's actually quite tasty. There's something… almost *fizzy*…"

Liquid warmth oozed between my fingers. My heart raced, which probably didn't help. A bizarre giggle rose in my throat. *Come full circle. Bit by a stirgoi, meet Daimyn. Partner with Daimyn, get killed by a strigoi.*

The woman behind the camera dashed forward.

"You idiot, you hit the jugular!"

"Of course I hit her jugular what—" The strigoi looked down at me, and his expression went slack.

The woman skidded to a halt in front of me, ripping off her over-shirt and pressing it against my throat. I thought about fighting them for a long, long moment. If I fought, with a fast heart rate and enough time, I wouldn't be a pawn in their game anymore. Daimyn wouldn't have to make choices about whether to let them hurt me or to hurt others.

I hesitated too long. Or maybe I just couldn't make myself really want to die—that familiarity hurt, I'd worked *so* hard to kill those feelings. They managed to bandage my throat and use some sort of coagulant to stop the bleeding.

After that, I laid on the floor with the world slowly spinning around me. I shivered, too hot, then too cold. I'd stopped being able to sweat a while ago I think, but my skin felt sticky and gross. I drifted for hours without realizing what I was doing. I hated it—I hated myself for not knowing what to do. My whole damned life: just waiting to be rescued or something to happen or sod it all.

At least I wouldn't be used to hurt other people. I clung to that comfort.

The entire room jerked on its foundations. The room hadn't *literally* moved, but it certainly Felt like it. Something… odd was happening all around me. I saw things that weren't quite… physical. But I did a great job of not acknowledging what was happening, even as I stared at the bizarre shapes shifting around me in the dark.

A wave of rage broke all of those shapes apart. Somehow I knew it came from the strigoi even without any light.

Metal shrieked, the sound of the barred door slamming open. A hand clamped down on my arm and yanked me upwards, pain blooming in my shoulder as he jerked me to my feet. Light finally spilled into the room; the woman carried the bright lamp, setting it up near the recorder. The strigoi holding me up seethed. Maybe the shadows from the lamp cast tricks, but his cheekbones seemed to pierce through his skin, his bones even more stark.

The woman eyed him, hovering by the recorder without touching it. "Remember what we talked about."

He wrapped his fist in my hair and forced me to face the camera. "My memory is fine."

After a pause, the woman turned to the camera and the light began to blink. I forced my quivering face muscles into a grin, my chuckle more like a wheeze. "S'not working, is it?"

"You brought this on yourself," he snapped.

For a second I thought he spoke to me, and my heart lurched at the truth of it. I really wasn't a smart person. I didn't go about things the right away. I blundered around and pretended I knew, and—

The strigoi gripped the collar of my shirt and yanked down, tearing the fabric open.

Another kind of horror swelled on my tongue, a new kind of way to be afraid freezing my mind.

He clapped a hand down, over my heart. A… pulse left his hand, a sickening churning followed in its wake. My skin crawled— and every one of my muscles seized. I would have hit the ground, but the strigoi's bruising grip on my arm kept me vertical. I wished he would drop me; his hold really hurt.

A sickening itching welled up underneath his palm; it shoved between my muscle and skin, between tendon and joint, foreign and icy-hot. Weakness gushed through me, my head flopping forward with a strangled sound.

I winced. *Shut up. I will be stoic, damn it.* At least my boob wasn't hanging out of my shirt. At least the stirgoi hadn't… ripped the rest of my clothes off, for another reason. *There we go, think positive!*

"I'm going to assume you know about my family's blood curses, but if you don't, here's the summary: in 12 hours she'll hemorrhage to death. "

My eyebrows hitched upwards. Lovely.

"The only way she can survive is if *I* decide to push it off for a while longer."

Well then.

"You know what I want. You have a whole list of my demands. This is the last chance to see her alive otherwise."

So, I had 12 hours left to live. *What should I do with 12 hours, sitting alone in the dark?* I nearly laughed.

I carefully didn't look at the camera, afraid of my expression, despite my bravado. Then the woman stopped the recording, and I wondered if that had been a terrible decision. If that was the last correspondence I'd ever have… I should have done something. Said farewell. Apologized. Asked him to watch over Tiffany.

Grief welled out of my very soul. There was so much I still wanted to do. Starting with stabbing this guy through the brain and then maybe running away from home, find my grandmother, find someone who'd teach me to actually enjoy kissing—god, maybe even sex—sail to the Divide and see it for myself…

The strigoi let go of me. I barely managed to avoid breaking my face on the stone floor by falling heavily to my knees, then onto my butt. My captors left without another glance. I struggled to stay upright. A shudder worked its way across my skin, a foreign crawl that brought bile up my throat.

Such a waste. What even is the point of me? I'd just closed the hellish chapter of my life after Cerin. I'd thought there would be more than this. That my life would be *more* now. Daimyn had warned me, but this…

Daimyn…

Despair swelled until my ribs strained to hold it. He had made his choice. The right choice, of course. I just wished I could see the sky one more time. The Farfallan sky I'd quietly fallen in love with, that felt like what I'd been looking for my entire life.

Maybe, if such a thing as heaven did exist, my resting place would shimmer black jade with thousands of stars.

40

The singing started low. At first I thought I dreamed it, or maybe hovered in a memory. But I blinked in the pitch black, shivering while my flesh itched in waves. I was definitely awake. Maybe my captors wanted to comfort me before death. Ha.

I strained to listen… and it took a while to realize I didn't actually *hear* anything. Not with my ears, anyway. The singing came from the same place as those shapes in the dark, that grew more numerous the more I watched.

Familiarity tugged at me. I strained to place it. Sourceless melody twisted softly from nowhere and everywhere, not echoing in the room but somehow still formed by the shapes around me I couldn't see, until…

Then it dawned. The images and sounds just whispered, a bare taste of what I'd experienced before, but I knew it—because this happened every dark moon. Only a million times worse. The dark moon brought a hurricane of sensation. This was… this reminded me of lulling waves, lapping at my brainstem.

I gave up any pretense of ignoring the hallucinations and concentrated. Like it had been waiting for me to really pay attention, it all grew louder and more complex. Until it wasn't just sound and shapes, but light as well. Threads of light casting shadows with seemingly no pattern or organization.

Come look, it coaxed. Perhaps I'd finally snapped, or this blood curse thing had infected my brain, but there wasn't much else to do anyway.

I knew my captors returned long before torchlight touched the gloom or footsteps reached my ears. The music-light threads around me shifted and spun into new patterns and humming anticipation. They approached, the sensations around them much more complex than anything else I'd been watching. It disoriented me, nausea twisting in my stomach.

Well. More nausea.

I remained sitting as they approached, only because I didn't know if I laid down if I'd get up again. I grinned widely at my captors as their physical selves arrived. The interaction of the music-light-thread-nonsense and physical material immediately fascinated me. Unsteady giddiness filled my veins like champagne.

My female captor's form danced with flame and smoke, her flesh a restraining cage around the inferno at her center.

Well. Anyway. That wasn't important at the moment.

"How much time I got left?" I croaked.

The strigoi strode over and offered me a cylindrical container.

Liquid sloshed. The strange music around me said *water*. Thirst seized my throat in a painful wrench; I snatched it from his hands, my lips latched around the nozzle at its top. I sucked too hard, and water hit the back of my throat. I immediately choked—and forced myself to swallow through it. Coughing and swallowing, I sucked down water faster than I'd done anything else in my life, spluttering half of it down my front in the process.

The strigoi placed his hand on my back, over my left shoulder blade, and muttered something. The horrible tightness around my chest eased.

Oh god… the relief of that itching and the cool water sliding down my throat nearly brought me to tears.

"Water and 24 more hours," the strigoi said.

What? I stared at the blinking red light on the front of the camera. When had they started recording?

"As requested, your little friend has water. I'm in such a good mood after your behavior that I think I'll even give her more later. Keep it up, and she may just survive this."

I hadn't realized, too overwhelmed by the chaos of the music-light around me: the sensations emanating from my captors shone bright, swirling with nervous glee.

"What did you do?" I asked, my voice barely a sound. *Daimyn, what did you do?*

The strigoi walked over the camera, leaning down with his hands on his knees so he looked directly into the lens.

"There are more instructions in the box."

The woman flicked off the camera. They both looked at each other. A shaky, triumphant smile stretched the woman's face.

"She was right," the strigoi said.

"It's working," the woman breathed back.

My chest crunched, the water canteen slipping from my grasp to clang against the floor. *No.*

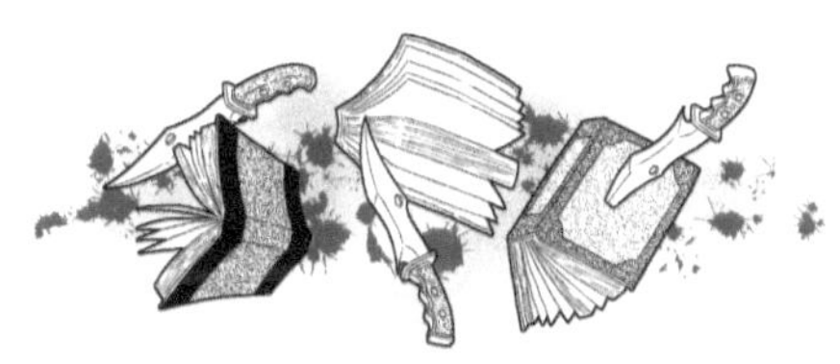

The next time they came to record, a slender boy—who Felt like wildfire and supernovas—fed me rice and vegetables. Yes, *fed* me, as in I wasn't even allowed the utensils. My stomach rebelled at the feeling of solids for the first time in—a week?—and I exercised real willpower to keep it down.

The strigoi bit me that time too. His teeth sank into the ball of my shoulder, and it hurt. He didn't drink anything; I think they knew I didn't have much to spare.

"Every time you pull stunts like *that*, my displeasure will be written in her flesh," he snarled, lips stained with my blood.

Whatever Daimyn was doing, he wasn't being a completely compliant little assassin.

It occurred to me sometime later that my captors had backed themselves into a corner. My health was bad—they had to give me at least water or I would decline rapidly, no matter what Daimyn did. The strigoi also had to keep pushing back the icy itching in my veins, or I'd expire. Both things they had to give up to keep this game going. They might think they did it based on Daimyn's actions, but would they really destroy their way to influence him after they'd had a taste of manipulating him?

Which meant: to even play their game they had to give up moves. It seemed like such a small thing, but for some reason it felt monumental. Something unseen built in this game they played. Some subtle pulling I couldn't quite make out, but feel—and well, I was Feeling all sorts of weird things right now, wasn't I?

On the plus side, the space around me no longer remained stagnant and boring. I don't know how I had ever been bored. Material space became meaningless in a way I'd never thought about before. It wasn't the end of one material and the start of the next… it was the way the two met. It was the gap where molecules resisted touching each other that made the order of the universe. Somehow, when I focused on interactions instead of substance… there were impressions of what happened beyond the walls of the room. Thicker threads grew obvious to me, seemingly pulled by things beyond my immediate vicinity, denser collections sliding through lighter space, sending ripples across everything.

It was so easy to become lost in watching the not-music and light-weavings slowly roll and sigh. And the more I drifted, the further I saw. Something beautiful and indescribable rested at the end of all of this, gently tugging, far away. I couldn't quite see, and couldn't figure out what it was.

There was something beautiful…

"Helloooooo—hey!"

Pain glanced across my face. I blinked up into the strigoi's face, cheek stinging. *Oh shit—I didn't even know they entered the room*, was the first thought purely my own in a long time.

"Good, you're alive," he said. "Playing dead with me isn't going to get you anywhere."

He pulled me upright, and my head swam. Underneath my skin, something crawled, and I swallowed heavily and repeatedly to keep the contents of my stomach down. I wanted to disassociate from this place again, fling myself back into the fascinating things beyond this room.

My head cleared the longer I focused on the strigoi talking and gesticulating, bringing both relief and trepidation. I couldn't lose myself like that—it'd be a real problem if I lost track of everything. If I didn't get a hold of myself, I would fade away.

The follow-up thought didn't hit until after my captors had left again: *Maybe that wasn't such a bad thing.*

Daimyn found me in my dreams. I knew they were dreams because the threads of him weren't attached to anything around me. His mouth moved, but emitted no sound. His fingers wrapped around my thin limbs, trying to get me up, trying to get me out. His urgency drowned me, making it impossible to breathe. As much as he tried, he couldn't break the bindings on me. He ripped at them, bruising skin and muscles, but they wouldn't budge.

What did you do, Daimyn? What did they make you do?

Some timeless stretch of space later, the slender boy came back.

—heart beating fast, the slow creep of something coming out of the shadows behind you—

—and undid my manacles.

I stared dumbly at the door after he left. He'd left a lamp on the floor too, casting a golden glow across the room, cocooned in shadows. They'd never left me with light that stayed on before. Was this one of their comforts for Daimyn's 'good behavior'? Did they think I was afraid of the dark?

I struggled to my feet, my wrists stinging and cold without the heavy weight of metal. My equilibrium did a somersault and I almost ate the floor, legs shaking under me as I got to my feet. I'd lost muscle mass over the past however-long I'd been here.

Urgency beat in my heart. I was a pawn in this game between them, but I'd been literally unchained from my place on the board. A bizarre certainty rose that Daimyn wordlessly communicated to me that my status as a pawn was a ruse. The strigoi thought I was harmless; obviously, they weren't even here, and I was about as strong as a wet piece of paper right now. I didn't know how long this freedom would last, and I wouldn't be able to make very many moves. But I wasn't completely stuck.

Circling the small room, I ran my hands over the rough walls, familiarizing myself with the entire space, looking for anything useful. I could break off little pieces of rock. It was something, though not immediately helpful.

Back to the stone age, I chortled.

As I circled my enclosure, I made sure to address the recording camera still set up in the corner by meticulously smashing it to pieces.

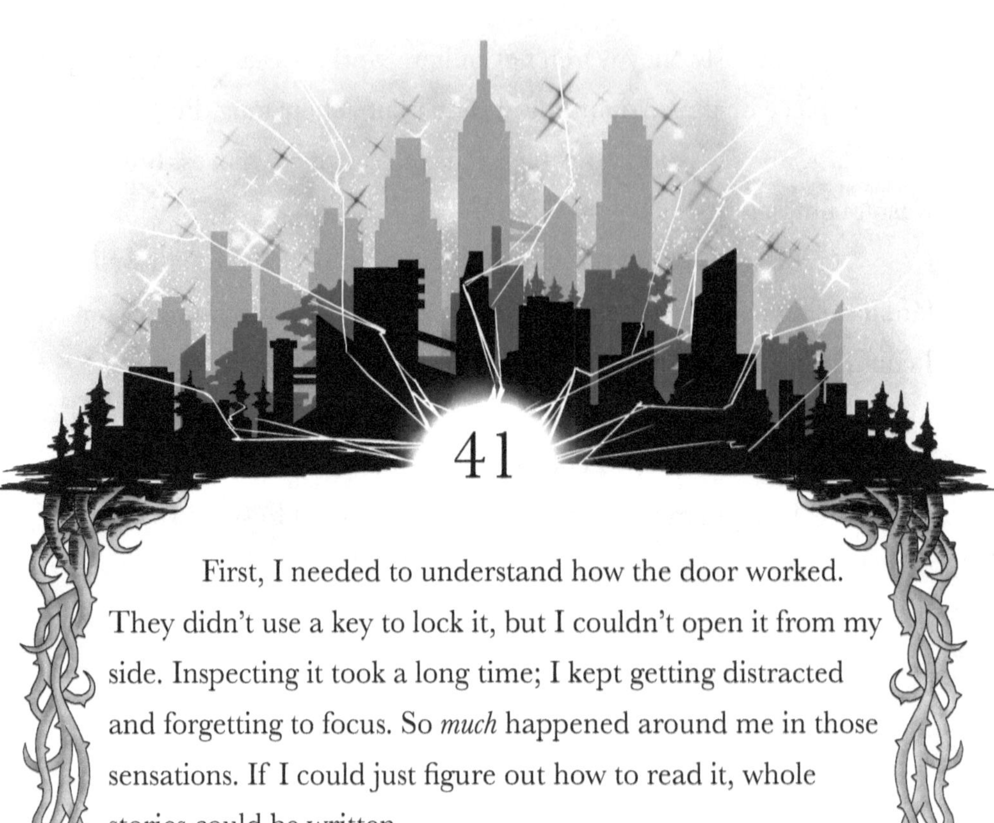

41

First, I needed to understand how the door worked. They didn't use a key to lock it, but I couldn't open it from my side. Inspecting it took a long time; I kept getting distracted and forgetting to focus. So *much* happened around me in those sensations. If I could just figure out how to read it, whole stories could be written…

Standing for any decent length of time also didn't work. This would be a problem.

Eventually, I understood the mechanism for the door. It was a cogwheel; a toothed chain wrapped around two cogs. When the wheel outside the door turned, it turned the cog, which pulled the chain, which pulled the other cog, that pulled a metal bar out of the wall, attached to the door, that allowed the door to swing free. I could just touch the chain by reaching through the door.

The great thing about chains? They got bound up when you stuffed things in them.

Step one was making the door inoperable, though only once it was open. But my captors wouldn't just leave the door open and me unshackled.

So step two would be to make sure I wasn't actually stuck—they'd only leave if they *thought* I was secure. So they either needed to think the door worked or the shackles worked.

I inspected the shackles. Lost some time staring into space until I recovered myself staring at the shattered camera. Crap, that would make them mad. It might even make them put me back in shackles.

While the manacles were rusty and worn from age and probably the salty-wet air, I knew—since I'd already tried—that I wouldn't be able to break them off of me. I smashed one repeatedly against the floor, using my entire weight, and managed to bend one of the hinges. That was exciting, so I bent it beyond its ability to close.

I paused over smashing the next one. If they had no way of securing me, they'd maybe assign a guard, or find another way to lock me in this room. One shackle instead of two was one more free limb. And my wrists were small… if I just had a little more room…

My whole body ached as I tried to bend the second one carefully, just a little, just enough.

Then I stumbled to the door and pressed bits of stone into the chain that operated the locking mechanism. I put the pieces far enough along the chain that they'd be able to open the door, but then, if my luck held, it would get bound up from there.

Then time ran out, the prickling on the back of my neck announcing their approach.

The woman spun the wheel to open the door, and a slight crunch sounded at the end of the spin. My heart leapt. The woman frowned as if she'd heard it too—but their attentions caught on the mess I'd made with the camera. The strigoi man stared at in disbelief.

The woman laughed. "Well, should have seen that coming."

With a scowl, the strigoi dragged me back to the manacles in the center of the room, and locked one around my wrist. My stomach lurched. *Was it looser?* I think it was.

The other one wouldn't close… and with an aggravated noise, he bent the metal back into place.

My mouth dried. I hadn't taken his strength into account.

"I'll get a new damn camera, *you* get me something to eat," the strigoi snarked. "This whole willpower test is great for my character and all, but I am sooo not…" I lost the rest of his sentence as he stalked up the stairs.

The woman smirked and swung the door shut. She turned the wheel, which made a horrible grinding noise. My heart leapt again. She frowned, and yanked. Metal shrieked hideously, followed by an unmistakable snap. A thundercloud forming on her face, she spun the wheel, the chain obviously clanging around freely inside the mechanism.

The woman stared at me, face devoid of expression. Focusing on material reality became hard again. I took advantage of that, drifting away so she couldn't try to read anything from me…

When I came back to myself, she was gone.

I didn't have much time. The manacles were, thank god, looser than they were before. Even if I had to peel my skin to get them off, this was my chance. I spat what little moisture I had in my mouth onto my wrists, trying to create any kind of grease to get them off me. It was gross, and painful, and took way too long to get the first one off.

Whimpers caught in my throat. My eyes stung from the pain, but I was too dehydrated to cry. I was also too dehydrated to give up spit for my next wrist too, but that couldn't be helped. My eyes and throat and whole body hurt, as I pulled, and twisted, and pushed…

Clang. The second one hit the ground.

My legs shook as I got to my feet. I wanted to tuck my wrists under my arms, but anything touching them was blindingly painful.

I pulled open the door… and my stomach flipped like I'd just stepped off a cliff. I stared at my feet, which refused to move.

My mouth filled with metal as I managed to shuffle one step, two… then panic thundered into my heart, taking over all the atrium and ventricles. I shut my eyes and took a deep breath. I knew this kind of panic, but it wasn't like I could tell myself I was safe and breathe until it stopped.

FAIRIAN, MOVE YOUR GODDAMN ARSE.

Trembling from head to foot, I looked right, where my captors usually headed after their fun little sessions, up a flight of stairs. I didn't want to follow and run into them. Not when I didn't know where they were. So to the left it was.

Move your leg. One step. Gooooooo.

It's like I'd forgotten how to make myself just *do* something.

Goddamn it, not this, not now! You have the chance to free yourself! You can literally change your own narrative. This time will be different. You just have to DO it!

My eyes burned.

And then the back of my neck prickled.

Times up, you dolt.

Adrenaline finally broke me free.

The hallway to the left continued on into darkness. I tried to run —and one of my knees buckled. I fast walked instead, and my legs only threatened to give out every few steps. The darkness swallowed me, soothing me, even though that was probably irrational, because my captors most likely operated in the dark better than I did. I felt along the walls to guide me, nervous to Look in my other way, when I lost track of myself. The itching in my veins shivered with warning.

A gust of air brushed over my face—colder, saltier, fresher. The ocean lay ahead. I could hear it, and Feel it. I almost whimpered.

The wall underneath my fingertips disappeared. I turned to look, and across a large cavern I could barely make out, across a stretch of water only visible because it occasionally glinted with movement in the dark, I could see the night sky.

I stood next to a sea cave, the ocean pouring in. Beyond the cave, I heard waves crash, but in here, the water shushed gently in and out.

Behind me, not far enough away for comfort, urgency and anger lit the air.

They know.

The tunnel continued on past this sea cave, going who knows where, but my legs shook with fatigue. I stumbled out across the cavern floor made of stone and sand, and my toes caught on uneven parts as I struggled to walk correctly. The air felt heavenly, even if it was freezing. My soft steps, my ragged breathing, sounded distressingly loud.

My shoes met water. I wouldn't be able to swim, and definitely not faster than my pursuers. But maybe I could hide underneath the water.

I lurched towards the far end of the cave, where sea met the stone wall and farthest from where I'd come in. My knees buckled a meter from it. *Whelp, here's where I'm at.*

On my hands and knees, I turned, facing away so I could back into the water feet first. Ice closed around my ankles, knees, thighs—

My captors closed in, so close, too close.

I dropped onto my front, ice closing over my hips and up my torso. The cold stole my breath. Which was the only reason I didn't scream as salt-water hit my ravaged wrists.

Shuddering with cold and pain, salt-water poured over my back and shoulders, up my neck. Water surged from behind and underneath me, and for a second, I hung weightless as the tide pushed me back up the embankment. I scrambled for the solid floor below me, found an edge of stone, and pushed backwards. I took a deep breath. Ice closed over my head.

I lost all sight at the same time. The room, the location of my captors, my ability to watch those threads change to reality around them —all gone. The sea shoved me up the embankment. A pause, and then it retreated, threatening to drag me farther out. I clawed at the stone ledge, holding on with my nails. I had to stay under. I had to stay under until they were gone.

I didn't know where my captors were, what they were doing. I didn't know if they were coming closer. I was afraid to try to look harder, afraid that if I paid too much attention, I'd drift and forget and try to breathe. It took all of me just to hang on with my fingernails and hold my breath.

Please only see water, please only see water, there's only water here, there's only water…

Nostalgia struck. As a child, playing hiding games, I'd always squeeze my eyes tight and pretend I could become my hiding space. Hide-and-seek became my least favorite game, because barely anyone ever found me. Not even Mari. I'd stopped doing it after my mother started taking me to a doctor for my episodes. I'd forgotten that.

With a child's plea, I did it again.

There's only water here… only water… I am water…

My own threads, the ones that weaved into my own being, were usually much harder to see compared to everything else. But under the water, where the world became muted, differentiating Me was not so difficult. Behind my eyelids, the complicated music and light stitching that made up my outermost edges seemed to shift. To change. Mimicking the waves.

I couldn't be elated, because something else became obvious: I could see the foreign thing lurking in my veins. The itching writhed like an egg sac in my blood, ready to break open.

Nothing I could do about that now. My lungs felt fit to burst. Panic tingled in my limbs. When I thought I could stand it no longer, I held my breath for ten seconds more. Then with the next surge of water, I let go, and it pushed me up the bank. My head broke the surface, and I used every ounce of willpower to inhale quietly instead of heave for breath.

The tide dragged me immediately back into the water. The wall to my left collided with my side, and I grabbed onto it so I didn't get sucked away, fitting my fingers into whatever crevices I could find.

My eyes creaked open, though I didn't need sight to know: the cavern was vacant. I didn't know their precise locations beyond *away*, but I was alone.

Urgency beat at me, but I rested trembling muscles, half floating and half lying in the water. The parts of me outside the water became chillier than the submerged parts of me. I couldn't remember how long a body could be in certain temperatures before going into hyperthermia. It was cold—but it was also fall, just coming out of summer. The ocean would be at one of its warmest periods. Despite how cold it seemed, I had to have some time.

Without really making the decision, I used the wall to get to my feet and made my way into deeper water. The waves, despite being gentle, sent me toppling. I had no idea what I would do when I reached stronger currents.

It grew gradually deeper, and narrower. I pulled myself along, still holding onto the wall for guidance and support. My arms and legs trembled, my body shaking. If I stopped now, I would go under. So I clung, and breathed, and fixed my eyes on my destination.

I made my way out of the cave, and the sky opened up around me.

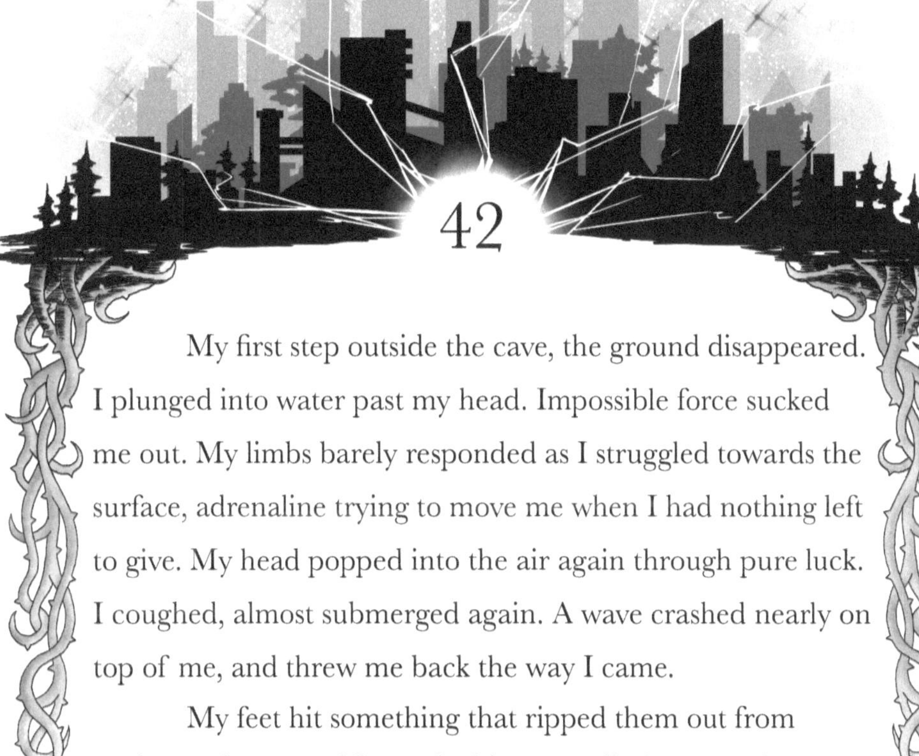

42

My first step outside the cave, the ground disappeared. I plunged into water past my head. Impossible force sucked me out. My limbs barely responded as I struggled towards the surface, adrenaline trying to move me when I had nothing left to give. My head popped into the air again through pure luck. I coughed, almost submerged again. A wave crashed nearly on top of me, and threw me back the way I came.

My feet hit something that ripped them out from underneath me, and I smacked into a wall, the roar of waves filling my ears. I clawed at the stone, gasping and struggling to get to my feet as the water threatened to pull me away again. Sand lay under me. The waves surging against the rock really only came waist high, but I had no strength left, every part of me shaking with fatigue. I looked up the rock wall… and up and up. I stood at the bottom of a cliff. The entrance to the sea cave I'd come out of lay to my left.

To my right, a tower of jagged stone rose out of the water and met the top of the cliff, the gap large enough to drive a small ship through. Farther down, stood another—and beyond it, another. As far as I could see, natural stone arches towered above my head and met the top of the cliff face.

It was beautiful. And distinctive. But I had no idea where I was. The only thing I knew: the sky was black and blue, so I wasn't in Farfalla.

My knees gave out. I crashed down, spluttering on salt. A boulder sat a couple meters away, resolute and immovable. With the last of my strength I stumbled over and flopped on top of it, just trying to stay anchored in one place. With most of my body out of the water, the tide had much less pull.

Relief turned me limp. *I did it. I made it out.*

This time it was different.

My eyes opened; I'd fallen unconscious. Blessed darkness still cloaked the world, and the water level around me had lowered, a sandy bank revealed. Helpful, but also not. Hiding in the water had gotten me here. I didn't know where or how my captors would be searching, but sand made footprints, and there weren't many places to hide. Climbing the cliff face was out of the question. There was no way in hell I was strong enough.

I eased down the side of the boulder, so it was between me and the sea cave, my butt hitting the sand. Those stone arches spanned the sky in front of me, protective and cathedral-like. The waves surged in to cover my hips and thighs, provoking a shiver. I stared out at the waves, numb and tired; the ocean did something strange to the music-light around it, though I couldn't quite put a finger on it.

I tried to get up, and I immediately collapsed again. My second attempt brought no better results. I swallowed, and it hurt.

Maybe I needed to throw myself back in the ocean; I could survive for a couple hours before hypothermia set in. I'd get out of here. I wouldn't be used to hurt people.

Or I wouldn't survive. I could walk into the ocean, and my body would be found wherever the currents took me. The only people who would really mourn me were my parents and Tiff. They'd be okay, though. Maybe they'd rely on each other. Maybe they'd name her the heir of Leynthall Industries—that was a beautiful idea. She was smart and talented, and it would make her unstoppable.

I smiled, and my eyes stung, too dehydrated to actually cry.

I need to get up.

Exhaustion sucked everything out of me. I'd gotten myself out, but to what end? There was no way I was making it any farther. I'd done it… I'd made it out myself… but it wasn't enough.

I need help.

The crashing waves drowned out the sound of my snort. Help was nowhere to be found. What was I going to do, send a PCD message? Maybe a carrier pigeon? Maybe while we were dreaming, I could send my thoughts directly into someone's brain. That'd be fun.

No, I was alone. Alone, and not strong enough to make it further.

I'm so tired of being alone.

My lungs hitched. It took me a second to realize I tried to sob, but it wouldn't escape my chest. My ribs contracted tighter and tighter, until everything hurt. My breathing gasped, audible over the waves.

I covered my mouth to stop the noise. Who knew when my captors would come back, or how well they could hear. I couldn't make noise, or they'd know I was here. I couldn't make a sound, or I'd be caught.

This cramming myself down, smaller and smaller. I was sick of that too.

My chest fractured, fragility a noxious weed tunneling between each rib, my breaths like shards of glass in my lungs. I squeezed my eyes shut, my throat hurting so damn badly. How could this be the end of me? *I'm not done yet.* A cry strangled itself in my throat, shattering emptiness battling with blistering fury.

The weavings that connected me to the world, spread around me like a rainbow web, vibrated red-hot—changed in furious despair, altered in rage.

That fact stopped me dead.

I had no communication device, no carrier pigeons, and I couldn't send my thoughts to someone's mind. But these singing weavings making up the world connected everything together, and they changed in reaction to me. I was also pretty sure I'd *made* something change back in the sea cave. If I could locate someone I knew… if I could alter something, communicate somehow…

It felt like the desperate grasping of a dying person—ha, well, that was exactly correct. The fact that I'd gotten myself out wasn't enough. I thought I'd changed; I thought I'd come so far. I thought I'd become a stronger person. Yet here I was, needing help and ceding control, ceding my own strength.

My own thoughts lashed out at me. *Do you think Tiff is weak, using the privilege of your family to forward herself? Do you think Daimyn was weak when you helped him communicate with the shadow-snake-people? Do you see either of them as lesser people?*

Yikes, I was quite biting when I talked to myself.

You're running out of time.

Another thought made my shoulders relax. If my survival depended on my choice to reach out and *ask*, then that made it under my control, didn't it? I'd just forgotten how to ask. I'd stopped asking a long, long time ago.

With a deep breath… I focused on the kaleidoscope around me. I hadn't experimented much with *following* those threads spinning around me. But I had to get somewhere *not here* to find anyone.

Here goes nothing.

I regretted it within 30 seconds.

I'd become a minnow that jumped from a fishbowl to the middle of the ocean. A force so massive it reordered the universe pulled me off course, made me blind to everything but it. Details grew lost in the pull of its current, until I spun hopelessly upside-down. I could barely keep a single thought in my head.

I vastly overestimated my understanding of this. I didn't even know where my own head existed anymore.

A world of difference existed between watching what happened around me and actually *following* what happened around me. Following threads was dreadfully painful, because they constantly changed, and I didn't have a specific direction. There *were* no directions. Staying on course stretched my mind to thin taffy. But if I stopped focusing, I would fall into an abyss I'd never get out of.

I hadn't realized before that even during the worst of my Episodes, I still held a thread of who I was. Right now, it seemed plausible my mind would drown and lose itself all together. Terror held my focus by the thinnest thread.

I gave up the pretense I wasn't looking for Daimyn. For one, there was no room for pretense in this place. And two, I would have to pull some magic shite, and who else would actually listen?

The only reason I found him in the hellish maelstrom was because the way he Felt. I could not mistake the shockwave like the birth of a star that finally gave me a point of focus. Relief nearly broke me as I fought forward.

Intensity vibrated from him, different than the burning beacon of his identity. It took me a second to place it: bone-deep, unsettled rage. It was unlike and alien to anything I'd ever encountered, but something about it was so pure I wanted to bask in its warmth.

Getting closer only me small and raw and vulnerable. I wondered if he even cared. If he would even come to find me, if I managed to communicate. Something must have happened back in Farfalla for him to be so angry; maybe he didn't have the time.

Nevertheless, I pulled together what shreds of confidence I had, and reached out and touched him. Nothing about him paused or reacted or showed any sign he acknowledged me.

I tried to push. Not even a ripple of reaction, in him or any of the weaving threads around us. Frustration swelled up inside of me—

None of the threads around me responded like they had before.

Great. Just great. Daimyn stood right here in front of me and it didn't even matter. I was a ghost. I couldn't… *interact* with him. I didn't even know how to start trying. Strength drained out of me, my focus fraying, like a stuttering film reel. I wouldn't be able to hold myself here much longer.

Despair hit like a wrecking ball. The only thing I could do to keep it from pulling me under was turn it into rage. So I leapt on him.

You will see me! You will acknowledge me! You will—

He halted, everything about him stilling into predatory silence so familiar I sobbed. Pride died in the face of exhaustion. *It's me. It's me. Please.* I tried to touch him, to feel him, but nothing in this place acted material, all of it unrelated to physicality. I wanted to cling to him. *I can't hold on!*

And then Daimyn turned and ran away from me.

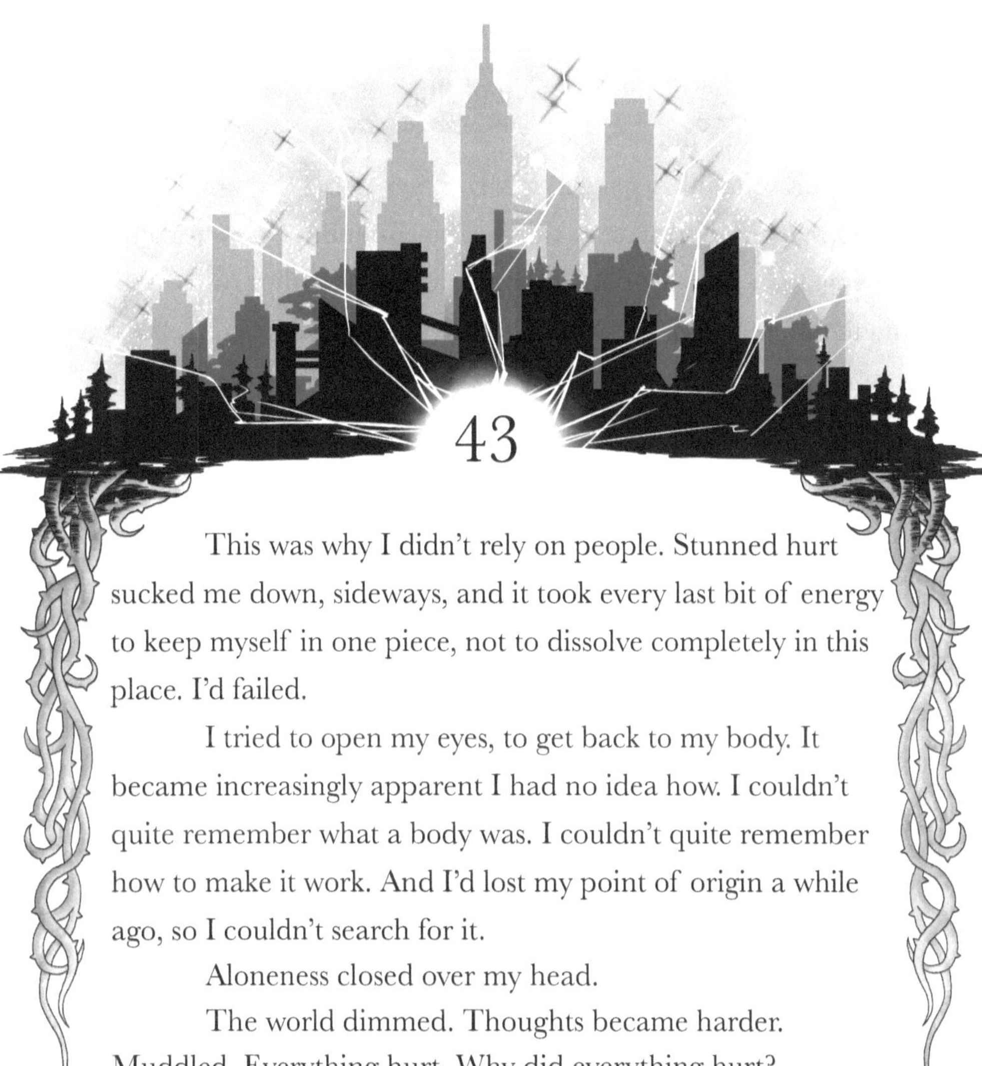

43

This was why I didn't rely on people. Stunned hurt sucked me down, sideways, and it took every last bit of energy to keep myself in one piece, not to dissolve completely in this place. I'd failed.

I tried to open my eyes, to get back to my body. It became increasingly apparent I had no idea how. I couldn't quite remember what a body was. I couldn't quite remember how to make it work. And I'd lost my point of origin a while ago, so I couldn't search for it.

Aloneness closed over my head.

The world dimmed. Thoughts became harder. Muddled. Everything hurt. Why did everything hurt?

And then, suddenly: warmth, so much warmth, surrounding me like a wall of fire, familiarity making me react on instinct, driving me closer. My head rang with tearing pain. *Help*.

In the overwhelm, someone else materialized. They tasted of gold and lightning, unfamiliar, and I shied away, but not fast enough. Claws of crystal caught me, and slammed me to the earth.

Connected. Grounded. In one piece. I sagged into their hold, pain whiplashing over me, the pain of finally letting go after gripping something so hard muscles froze.

This unfamiliar person, this complex nerve cluster of sensations, focused so sharply on me, the vibrations of their form changing, then pausing, then changing again, as if they were tuning a radio to different stations. They became clearer and clearer, almost a real presence—

Then I forgot about them.

Because now I remembered the supernova lit with intensity and the color of Farfalla's night sky—and something about him nearly turned solid.

I leapt… and Daimyn's face was in my hands. I mean, not literally. But something about him opened in my palms even as he struggled to wrap around me. He rippled; the sensation of a voice far, far away that I couldn't hear or reach. I'd dreamt this; him being voiceless, trying to pull me to him.

Unlike the lightning-gold person, he didn't tune himself differently. I don't think he could. But he understood my presence now, and that bone-deep rage seethed higher as he fought to touch me or speak in a way I could hear.

Oh. Maybe the anger is about me.

Then the other person vibrated anew, and brushed against me. I jolted in surprise. Daimyn's threads surged with aggression as I lost my tentative connection with him.

—where—

The voice wasn't audible, more the sensation of a voice, but I understood the shivering question all the same. Right. I had to tell them where I was, and I had to do it right now.

I focused on lightning-gold, the pressure in my head growing exponentially worse. No vocal cords existed here, and I didn't know how to create particular sounds anyway. But I'd always been a pretty visual person, and the natural stone arches on the beach with my body were distinct. It had to be enough to figure out my location. It had to be enough.

Holding a picture of the beach in my mind hurt, which hopefully meant something. Before I lost the image, I—*painted it in the air?*—and slammed it towards them both. The last of my strength went with it.

It bounced off Daimyn completely. But the other caught it, and recognition flared through the weavings around them. They understood.

Relief. I collapsed like drenched fabric sucked downriver.

Those crystal claws snatched me back from the abyss again.

—you're exhausted—

They—*she*—grew clearer. Then she paused, a buzzing between her and Daimyn. Part of her reached into Daimyn's chest—my alarm halted at the willingness radiating from him—and pulled out a little ball of warmth. It shone dark and beautiful; it breathed fire and spread wings that blocked out the sky; it sang a song so lonely my heart broke. She gently pulled it through her hands, and set it in my abdomen.

It shocked me, like I'd stuck my finger in a power outlet of oxygen. Euphoria pounded in my veins and mind and heart, colors turning vivid, the ground settling under my feet. I'd been struggling worse than I'd even understood.

I had only a second to comprehend it. The world began to dim again, much faster than before. Alarm twisted her nearly out of tune with me.

—Go back, go back NOW*—*

She touched the center of me, and something jerked, as if a hook had taken hold. Like a caught fish, a line yanked, and I hurtled down.

I slammed back into my body and wished I hadn't. Heaving for breath, coughing and hacking through what felt like a mountain sitting on my chest, I honestly wondered if I'd died while I'd been gone. My entire body shook, as if my mind, after having forgotten my body, had to shock me over and over to make sure I still functioned. Nausea lurched in tune with the world spinning around. It was like the aftermath of my episodes, but worse. Much worse.

It's bad I was gone that long. Oh, it's bad.

My chest heaved for a long time. Everything hurt. *If I make it out of this alive, I am sleeping for a month, eating my weight in cannoli and gin, and not moving the entire time.*

The weight on my chest slowly eased, but my breathing didn't become normal, hitching and too fast. The sky lightened, the held breath before the sun broached the horizon. I'd never liked sunrises. This one filled me with particular dread, as if when I lost the darkness, I'd be losing the last of my defense too.

Behind me, beyond the sea cave, inside the cliff, flickers of that chilling focus and anxiety still darted. My captors still looked for me. Really, it was a miracle they hadn't found me already.

Warmth spread down my upper lip from my nose. Startled, I wiped at it, and my fingers came away bright red.

"Oh."

The ocean swallowed the tiny hurt sound. I knew instantly what was happening. In the time I'd been away, the foreign thing in my flesh had enough time to hatch. It had been too long since the strigoi had done whatever he did to prevent its growth. I stared at the blood on my fingertips for a long time, tasting it on my cracked lips and vaguely wondering how blood got so bright.

I stared at the upcoming dawn, my heartbeat lurching and uncomfortable.

At least I changed my story. Maybe I hadn't been able to get myself totally free. Maybe I didn't have the power to completely rescue myself. But this time I'd gotten myself out of hell on my own two legs, and if this was the end, the sky would be over my head.

It wasn't the sky I yearned for, but that was okay. The stone arches were neat.

The horizon brightened as my vision dimmed. *I should lie down.* If I hemorrhaged from inside out, my heart needed to be even with the rest of my body to give me the most time before my organs shut down. It would at least keep blood supplied to my brain longer than sitting upright would. I crawled as close to the cliff face as I could, away from the waves, worried about the tide coming back in and drowning me if I was unconscious.

Then I realized that worry was silly, because I'd be dead long before the tide returned.

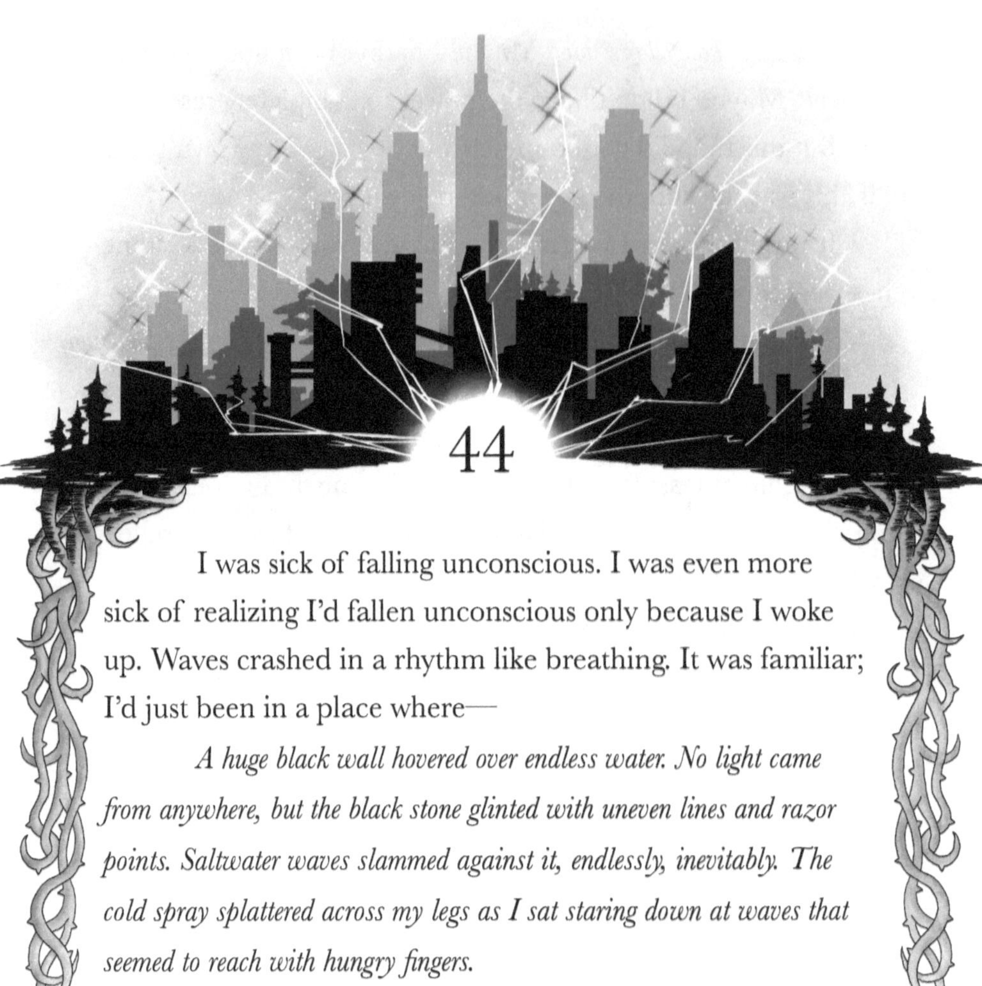

44

I was sick of falling unconscious. I was even more sick of realizing I'd fallen unconscious only because I woke up. Waves crashed in a rhythm like breathing. It was familiar; I'd just been in a place where—

A huge black wall hovered over endless water. No light came from anywhere, but the black stone glinted with uneven lines and razor points. Saltwater waves slammed against it, endlessly, inevitably. The cold spray splattered across my legs as I sat staring down at waves that seemed to reach with hungry fingers.

Lilting words spilled from his lips as grief bled from his heart. Heartbeats raced in tandem.

There were no heartbeats in this place.

She sat next to me. "You can't stay here."

I waved a hand around me towards the endless black-blue ocean. "Where am I going to go?"

His grief suffocated. He remembered holding death in his arms; he remembered it more than anything else. Death and loneliness had worn grooves in his tale, grooves deep enough to lose himself.

"He's trying to save you."

"I know." A pinprick of heat flared along the inside of my elbow, the only warmth in this place. "I think it's only because he has to."

"I'm not so sure about that." A pause. "You could save him too, you know."

Hope had long since turned to ash. He couldn't hope anymore or he would try to unmake the world in despair.

"Aren't you supposed to be convincing me to live for myself? That there's more to live for or whatever?"

"Okay." She patted the black wall beneath our butts. "Why did you come here, of all places? Don't you want to know why it's here?" She grinned widely. "Don't you want to know everything? Things like, oh I don't know, maybe where the dragons went?" She tilted her head to the side, squinting off in the distance. "Well. Most of them, anyway."

I was freezing—

—my whole body boiled: heat flared, incinerating the horrible itching that had taken up residence under my skin. That heat burrowed deeper, into tendons and sinew and bones, hunting, ferocious, revivifying.

"I already did this. I already had to put myself together after hell. I'm too tired to do it again."

"It's called PTSD, baby girl. It's the gift that keeps on giving."

Another surge of heat. Fire was too tame a name for it; it was microscopic and galactic, a cosmic creature hunting through the infinitesimally small space between my molecules.

"It hurt so much, and in the end it meant nothing."

"You've got to stop trying to do this alone."

The creature didn't only sift through me, but crouched over me, his silent growl vibrating the world into submission. It made the gentleness with which he held me seem impossible. One of his hands smoothed over my hair.

"Promise me you won't chase death anymore." My vision skipped, like a film reel with missing pieces, and she grinned, a mischievous sparkle dancing around me. *"You can chase Deathless."* Skipping again, her eyes cold like they'd never been in life. *"Just not death."*

My head and neck rested in his lap, the rest of me spread forward across the damp sand. He whispered something I couldn't quite catch, something my conscious mind struggled towards, fraying the connection to that black wall.

"Promise me you will."

My chest didn't hurt, for the first time in days. My heart beat steadily, a comforting rhythm against my ribs, pulsing against the edges of my body and reminding me of my shape.

"Promise me."

My eyes opened, and anything else from that conversation on the black wall evaporated. The world focused like a tilt-a-whirl coming to a stop. He froze, staring down at me. Dawn filled the sky, and for once, I didn't mind the coming of the light: half his face bathed in it, his cheekbones cut into sharp contrast. It reflected across one eye, green lit up vivid dark emerald, the other black as Farfallan night. He looked haggard and heartbreakingly young all at once.

I struggled to smile, to do something that would ease the grief frozen mid step in his heart. It was intimately apparent as his heartbeat sped. A thin tube ran from his throat, near-black in the shadow of his body, coiled haphazardly across me. I think the tube ended in my inner elbow, which explained the pinprick of pain there, but I couldn't look away from him.

Daimyn's stillness broke as he swallowed. One of his hands spread along the side of my face, and I almost groaned at the blazing warmth. Once I regained the ability to move I was going to crawl into the magnetic heat he carried around like his own personal panacea—

"Tell me your name." The shaky order came out in English. I realized he'd been speaking something else until now. "Do you know what your name is?"

He's worried about brain damage.

I tried to answer him—and immediately started coughing, my throat as dry as the Sahara. The upper half of my body was abruptly lifted upright, the solid warmth of his chest bracing against my back, and a water canteen appeared before my face. My hands shook and my head spun, but dark, delicate fingers held mine in place as I managed to get the container to my mouth.

"Good," muttered a feminine voice. "I was not prepared for death drama today."

Once I started gulping, I couldn't stop. Daimyn's arms slid around me, his heart beating hard against my back. There and gone in a blink: *wings folding around me.*

I protested as the water canteen pulled away, but couldn't do much else as the world threatened to spin.

"Easy, let's not have you barf," said that voice.

She had a point. My stomach roiled, and I fought to focus my eyes. A strangely ageless femme crouched in front of me—probably the most enchanting person I'd ever seen. She had the face of an Egyptian queen, her hair a cloud of perfect black spirals held back from her face by a wide blue headband. Her eyes resembled moonstones, her skin like rich umber, and she was dressed in a deep blue dress with a silver chest-plate that managed to be flattering instead of just bulky. There was something about her, unrelated to her appearance, like she glowed on a spectrum I couldn't see.

Lightning-gold. Her magic tasted like lightning and gold.

"We need to get her out of here," she said, eying me but not addressing me. "Hypothermia and all."

The texture of the air around Daimyn's head changed, almost like a soundless murmuring. It ended just as quickly as it arrived. I frowned. *What…?*

"Regan has the car ready," Daimyn said.

"You carry, I'll watch the flow of life juice," the enchanting woman said—I would call her Enchantress, I decided. "Let's get the hell out of here."

I blinked hard, trying to put everything in a comprehensible order. Daimyn slid to the side, his arms coming behind my back and under my knees. My weight settled into his arms as he lifted me off the cold sand. Enchantress held the tube connecting us, carefully rearranging it, checking the places where it inserted into my arm and his neck and smoothing down tape to hold it in place.

A tube… that ran from… *there was a tube running from Daimyn's veins to mine.* His own literal blood ran into me right now. The humming under my skin gave another hunting surge, from my marrow to the tips of my limbs, and then settled, satisfied. I no longer itched like insects hatched under my skin.

"… Blood transfusion?" I mumbled, struggling to come up with the words for the rest of my question.

"I panicked," Daimyn said, as if that explained anything.

He readjusted me in his arms, tucking my head into his shoulder—and when I pressed my forehead against the bubbling warmth of his neck, it spilled all the way down my spine. All my breath left involuntarily, tension sliding right out of me. All I could feel was relief; relief that my body wasn't hostile anymore, relief that I knew, without a doubt, that I was safe.

Daimyn took off in a fast-walk down the beach. I didn't care where he took me. I could be like this for a while, surrounded by his heat and his scent, something I didn't have the brain space to identify but made me think of tea and wildfires.

I opened my eyes, watching the cliff-face pass by. A crumpled heap of clothing lay a little ways down—

No. Not clothing. It was the strigoi man, sprawled on the sand like he'd been thrown. Well. Most of him.

Where's his head?

Reality crept through me with darts of awareness. I stared at the section of beach I could see beyond Daimyn's throat, and my soupy state of half-recognition drained away. Something like a scorch mark scarred along part of the cliff face… and that was another crumpled heap of not-clothing.

He came for me.

He did bad things so they wouldn't hurt me.

He let them hurt me.

I remembered the way we'd left things. It didn't fit with to the way he held me now, urgency pounding out of his very heart. I didn't understand. What had changed?

What had they made him do?

Why had he done it?

I licked my lips and fought the heavy muscles of my mouth and throat into line to speak. "What did they make you do?"

Another two strides, and then he murmured into my hair. "No."

"No?" I had to think through that one. "You're not going to tell me what he made you do? To keep me alive?"

"How would that information benefit you?"

"You answered a question with a question, that doesn't count," I whispered. I fisted the collar of his coat with weak fingers, my eyes burning. His arms tightened in response.

Enchantress' voice came from somewhere on Daimyn's other side: "This is your way up, Mr. Broody."

A tiny path cut sideways in the face of a cliff, rising sharply from the beach to the top of the wall. Daimyn started up it with lunging steps, the path really too narrow for him to be carrying me like this. My stomach swooped, and I clawed at his coat for stability.

His arms tightened, binding me against him. "It's all right. I've got you."

I relaxed, one muscle at a time.

We reached the top of the cliff, and everything opened up to a wide, flat space broken up by boulders and patches of long coastal grass. A car sat wedged between two huge rocks, as close to the edge as it could get. In front of it, Regan strode towards us.

"Darling Fairian, I was afraid I'd have to spend the next decade consoling my brother over your death," he said, his usual mocking cheerfulness overlaid with genuine relief. Daimyn grunted in response. My stomach tightened further, confusion vibrating in warning.

"The car should be sweltering inside by now," he continued.

"You need out of these damp clothes," Daimyn said, pressing his cheek against my forehead. "Can you change by yourself?"

I swallowed heavily. "Yeah."

I'd be damned if anyone saw me naked in this state.

The air shifted again, that textured-air-murmuring appearing around Daimyn's and then Regan's head. *What in the name of…* Regan spun and strode to the boot of the car, rummaging around the contents.

Enchantress walked over and pulled up the tape on my arm that held the transfusion tube in place.

"Are you sure that's enough?" Daimyn asked. "It won't hurt me to keep going."

"She's conscious and coherent, and we don't know what your blood is doing to her."

Their exchange held echoes of an argument.

Enchantress pulled the line from my arm and logic reared its head. Daimyn wasn't even human—how was I not seizing in reaction to his blood? He tilted his chin up as Enchantress pulled the other end of the tube out of his neck. A line of bright red slid down his throat.

"Thank you," Daimyn said quietly, readjusting me in his arms.

Enchantress met my gaze, and she smiled, something both sharp and warm as she wound up the tubing. "It's not everyday I get to assist in a greater act of blood magic in the wee hours of the morning."

I got the distinct impression she said it for my benefit. My eyebrows furrowed. Even that hurt.

"A blood transfusion is an act of magic?" I managed, my voice a tad stronger than a rasp.

"For *him* it is," Enchantress said, then turned and strode towards the car.

Daimyn hesitated, and then followed at a slower pace. "Ignore that, she's exaggerating." He paused, as if realizing that wouldn't be enough of an answer for me. "My blood acts human. And it has no antigens for any specific blood type. It's also packed with magic, particularly the kind that affects the physical body, like healing. I didn't believe you would make it to a hospital. I panicked."

My ribs constricted tightly into themselves. That didn't sound like an action of someone just doing their magical-guardian-whatever job. Giving me his life-blood, *literally*, that was—that was—

Regan held up a bundle of dark cloth he lifted from the boot, and then opened the door to the back seat. He was right: heat blasted out of the vehicle. Daimyn gingerly set me onto the seat, his arms slowly withdrawing, pulling his heat and comfort with him. He placed the bundle Regan had found next to me. The last of his touch disappeared, something inside of me snapped, and he gently shut the door.

Everyone turned their backs, giving me privacy to change. Surreality infested the quiet in the gloom of the car. I could barely hear the ocean anymore, and my ears rang with the lack of it. Enchantress said something I couldn't quite make out, and Regan answered. I unfolded the bundle of clothing they'd give me, because I was supposed to be doing something with these. The soft grey pants and shirt were a copy of the clothes Daimyn had given me after the death hound tried to eviscerate me, the ones currently buried in the back of my closet. How many of these did they have?

My arms trembled with fatigue as I stripped off my damp and salt-encrusted clothes. My elbow banged into the door, and I got stuck briefly while taking down my pants. The week(s?) of no bathing and fear-sweating became distressingly apparent. I glanced at the turned backs of the three of them around me before I took off my underthings, unable to look at the difference in how my bones stood up under my skin. Being completely bare in this foreign place was awful, but I couldn't stand the idea of my underthings touching me anymore.

Redressed, I still stank of salt and fear, but the clothes were soft. My breathing wouldn't calm, acid boiling in my stomach.

It's fine. It's fine. Everything is fine. It's over now.

But I'd said that before, and obviously it had been an utter lie.

I fought for the door handle and shoved the door open, which smacked into Daimyn as I gave no warning. I flung the clothes out onto the ground. He crouched as if to grab them—

"Leave them," I said.

His vivid gaze seared through me. "I'm not going to leave your clothes here as evidence. But I will put them in the back, out of view."

Chilly air filtered in from the outside and the understanding in his expression hit like a punch. Irrational, unsteady heat flared in my chest. *Don't you pretend to understand you don't know anything—*

Daimyn retrieved my clothes, shut the door, and walked to the boot of the car. My underthings were in there, probably in full view. Great. Just great.

It felt like all my insides had been scraped raw—were being scraped raw, over and over again, and nothing I could do would stop it, I had to stop it, I couldn't stop it.

The front passenger seat door opened; Enchantress slid into it with a sigh. The car rocked gently with the added weight. The driver's side door opened next, Regan taking that seat and rocking the car again. The door to the seat next to me opened—

"Why did you do it?" I demanded as soon as Daimyn's head came into view.

He stilled as he sat, one foot still on the ground outside.

"Why did you listen to them?" I insisted again.

He pulled himself the rest of the way inside and shut the door carefully. "To clarify, you're asking why I took action to halt your torture?" He sounded so bloody *reasonable*.

"You didn't at first," I shot back, and I wished I would shut up.

Someone muttered something from the front seat. Regan put the car into drive and the machine crept forward. My stomach gave a sickening lurch. All of us swayed back and forth, then rocked violently, as car wheels hit rocks and holes in the uneven ground. I braced my hands against the seat underneath me and the back of the driver's seat in front of me, struggling to stop the car from flinging me back and forth.

Daimyn turned towards me, his eyes focused on my shoulder more than my actual face. "I thought I'd find you quickly, that I could get us through this without me hurting anyone. I know it's not enough, but I am so incredibly sorry."

"Not *that*," I snapped. "There was no reason for you to *start* listening. There was *no* reason for you to do horrible things for me. I told you I accepted the consequences. Dying was *fine*." My voice cracked.

He blinked once. "Maybe I decided *I* would not accept the consequences."

I wanted to scream at him and his bloody calm tone and none of the things I wanted to scream made sense. "You said you lose parts of yourself when someone dies." My voice beat back at me, too loud. "Is that why you did it?"

He finally met my eyes. "You think this is about *my curse*?"

Curse?

My head thunked against the door as the car jerked again. I couldn't keep myself from smacking into things, my arms shaking with the effort of holding myself in place. Daimyn reached towards me, then withdrew, dropping his hand to grip the seat. Our postures mimicked each other; facing one another, gripping our seats below us, back braced against our respective car doors.

"I wasn't triggered to help you," he said, his voice dropping soft and low. "I couldn't even *find* you."

Enchantress sighed in aggravation from the passenger seat. "Hey, I'm here to specifically avoid drama, don't make me listen to this."

The heat in my gut latched onto the new outlet. "I'm sorry, who the hell *are* you?"

Enchantress turned slowly to look at me, unimpressed eyebrows raised.

"Fairian, this is Sebille," Daimyn said easily. "She has spent a lot of time and effort helping me find you."

The car jerked over another bump, and then its travel abruptly smoothed out, picking up speed as it continued down what felt like an actual road.

I shut my eyes. *I'm being a bitch. Count to ten, just count to*—

"Have you had a panic attack before?" Sebille said. "I think she's having a panic attack."

"I know," Daimyn murmured, just as I near-shouted: "Of course I'm having a bloody panic attack why else would—" Mercifully, my voice broke, and I wrangled control of my vocal cords.

"Regan," Daimyn said in an exceptionally polite tone. "Would you turn on some music that might entertain our guest?"

Regan immediately turned on the radio, and Sebille leaned forward to argue with him over the station. The noise of the radio—each station cut off abruptly as they changed channels—and their deliberate bickering pressed down on me, grating, my heart beating too hard.

Something nudged my hand, and I startled, eyes popping open. Daimyn held out a canteen of water. I realized then he'd been holding it since he'd gotten into the car.

That awful fragile thing that had rooted and grown jerked, trying to crack my chest open. Unsteady fury twisted into something else, and my skin felt too thin, my bones too brittle. I took the canteen from him with trembling fingers, and it took several minutes to get the sodding cap off the sodding container and get it to my sodding mouth. The taste surprised me—salty and sweet at once, and I could almost hear my cells screaming in relief.

I drank the whole thing and it barely satisfied me.

"Do you want more?"

I did. But I shook my head.

"Do you think you can stomach any food?" he continued. "We'll stop for empanadas at this great place I know, unless you want something else."

His dark eyes searched over my face. I thought I'd gotten used to his intensity, the way his focus made things the center of the universe. But too much had changed; or maybe the way he watched had changed, as if I were precious, as if I meant something.

I couldn't look at him. The idea of being touched made me homicidal, and yet I wanted to be held by him on a level that reached despair. I stared sightlessly out the window at the landscape rushing by, everything unmoored, words refusing to form in my throat. My knees folded to my chest and a shudder worked down my whole body.

Daimyn's stillness broke as he leaned forward, struggling with something. He took off his coat, pulling out from behind and under him, then shook it out and moved as if to cover me with it.

"*Don't.*" The word ripped out of me. I couldn't stand his kindness for another second.

The air turned brittle. He lowered his coat onto the seat between us.

"It's there if you'd like it," he said softly. Then he turned away and stared out his window. Aloneness swelled up to choke me, feeding that crippling fragility in my heart.

45

It would take over two hours to drive back to Farfalla. Because I stayed conscious and coherent, we decided to drive straight to a doctor the Yillens knew instead of stopping by a local emergency hospital first. And when I say decided, I mean that Regan announced we would stop by a local ER to check me out, and I demanded we continue on to Farfalla. And when I say demanded, I mean that my voice shook as I asked if we could please just go home. That freaking murmuring appeared around Regan and Daimyn's head, in tandem and then alternating—what the hell *was* that?—and then Regan drove on.

The landscape sped past. The sight of cars and other people scalded, even as few as there were this early. The complex weavings of threads spun all around me, though muted, as if physical reality brought down a veil over the worst of it. I was grateful for that veil. My head throbbed from even just this, and with everything Daimyn and Regan put out I'd probably be unable to see at all.

Daimyn's head rested on the back of his seat, eyes shut, tension faintly lining his face. He wasn't sleeping. I think he did it to eliminate any accidental awkward eye-contact or movement. Silence had consumed the car except the tiny sound of the radio that grated more than soothed.

Frustration choked me. Everything about this was just—just *wrong*. My arms ached with how tightly they held my knees to my chest. I'd been here before, a long car ride home after a horrible thing happened—shouldn't this be easier? Shouldn't I be less paralyzed? I was too tired for this, he was too tired for this.

Life is too bloody short for this—this—

"You didn't bring me out last time," I whispered, barely a sound. But I'd managed to force something coherent past my lips, even if I wasn't quite sure why I'd said it. I stared at the back of the seat in front of me, so I could see Daimyn out of the corner of my eye without actually looking at him.

"What do you mean?" he answered immediately, without moving.

"When Cerin took me." I swallowed, heard my throat click. "You didn't come get me, you had the authorities bring me out."

Then I understood why I'd brought this up. Because if Daimyn had rescued me out of obligation or responsibility, he could have done it in other ways, like he'd done seven years ago. Not show up himself and transfuse his freaking blood into me.

"Does that mean you forgive me?" I didn't know why I said that either, but as soon as I did my eyes stung.

Daimyn lifted his head and looked at me, the weavings around him contracting tightly like they were being stuffed into a very small space that didn't fit them.

"There's nothing to forgive," he said in an aggravatingly even voice.

My panic attack must've not been over, because his calm made me want to bite him. Fighting myself, I finally, *finally*, turned and looked at him. He studied me, head low and shoulders curled, like he did when trying to seem less threatening. That made me want to bite him too, especially in combination with the openness I Felt all around him, as if some sort of restraint he'd always had with me before was gone, and he—he—

"It doesn't make sense for you to care about me," I accused. "I've been entirely a nuisance."

Wow. I can't just have a conversation, I have to be hostile while I'm at it.

He blinked once. "Are you questioning the honesty of my feelings, or wishing I didn't have them?"

I nearly recoiled, feeling the slap of those words like I should.

Daimyn shut his eyes. "Forgive me, Fairian. That wasn't fair."

Why couldn't he just be angry with me for being awful to him? He'd just rescued me and I acted like a bitch.

Sebille sighed from the front seat. I swallowed down further words, my chest tightening with a far off feeling of unease. I knew I was not running on all cylinders, and we *were* forcing everyone to listen to this. It would be embarrassing later, when I could think clearly.

But I had to do something to fix this. Right now. No doubt returning to Farfalla would be chaotic and there'd be no chance to talk and then time would pass and uncertainty and awkwardness would stain everything. Though opening my mouth had turned everything sour in the first place—before that it'd been the simple profound relief of being held by him, that razor edge between *the terror is over* and *now I have to drag myself out of THIS hole of trauma.*

Daimyn watched me with smooth features, gripping the seat below him as if he worked to keep his hands in place. Or himself in place. *It doesn't make sense for him to care.* I swallowed. Oh, sod it all, if I was going to be ravaged and neurotic, I might as well go full out and be vulnerable too.

"Will you hold me?" Voice hostile, my heart held it's tattered edges together as that fragility gave a vicious yank.

Daimyn froze for a heartbeat before relief crashed into the air all around him, his exhale silent but obvious. He reached for me. I already clambered over the seat, my eyes now burning at his reaction. As soon as he touched me, the humming under my skin that chanted safe, safe, safe ratcheted up in intensity.

That's all I need, another way to be hyper-aware of him.

We spent a few minutes of awkward rearrangement where I curled back into a ball against his chest. I think I accidentally clocked his chin with my head. Then I found myself in a thankfully familiar position: face pressed into his neck, shoulder to his heart. My knees still pressed to my chest even though my hips ached. Daimyn shifted, his thighs flexing underneath my butt and feet. Fabric wrapped around me; he'd pulled his coat from the center seat and did his best to personify the meaning of *wrap*.

I made a face. "I feel like a mummy."

"You feel like an icicle," Daimyn muttered. His arms came around me and it happened again, that Feeling of *wings folding around me.*

One second numbness formed a barrier between his skin and mine, stuffed my head with cotton. In the next, his closeness turned agonizing. All my insides were exposed, and his slightest twitch would torture. The beat of his heart against my shoulder threatened to form bruises. The warm skin of his neck against my face started to burn. The scent of him—

Nope, that was my own smell.

"I stink," I whispered, mindful of Regan and Sebille and also so Daimyn wouldn't hear the quiver in my voice. "Sorry."

Daimyn snorted, as if the thought were ridiculous, and soft skin and heat brushed my forehead—his lips. I took the deepest breath I could.

In the semi-privacy of the backseat of the car, we found time to adjust, to learn the shape of touching each other. Disbelief flared as my conscious mind remembered who he was to me—*how is it possible he held me like this, that the sheer pleasure humming out of him I recognized in my very bones?* Yet his warmth sank into me with the steady slowness of permanence, and my muscles finally gave up their death grip on my bones. With each of my breaths he had the power to hurt me, and with each of his breaths I learned he could be trusted. Our edges melted and fit against each other; our bodies had no interest in subterfuge.

But in the quiet, or maybe because of the quiet safety, my thoughts had time to grow loud. It crept back, slowly but surely, until I couldn't stay quiet anymore.

"They made me kill a peryton," I whispered.

Daimyn's hand slid to the back of my head, his fingers tangling in the knots of my hair.

"They took my hand and forced a knife in it and—" My entire body spasmed to contain whatever horrible thing tried to birth itself from my gut, which really hurt, and short-circuited a full-on sob. Which was relieving, really. I'd been irrational enough in the past hour, thank you very much.

"I think they did it so I couldn't find you," Daimyn murmured against my forehead. "The details can get complicated… but your hand on the knife that killed an innocent, I think it disconnected my ability to locate and defend when you were threatened. How they knew to do that, we will need to find out."

The explanation made me ravenous. He had to know how much it meant that an answer even existed, and that he shared it. The last time I'd told the truth of trauma I'd been shut down and dismissed.

With a jolt, I remembered: "They weren't the ones who hired the Mortis Mercator." I lifted my head to meet his eyes. "Did Shahar figure out who hired the Mercators?"

"No," Daimyn said, very deliberately and very quietly. "Whoever they are covered their tracks exceedingly well." His arms tightened. "But there is some evidence they funded this kidnapping."

I blinked. "So they're really into other people doing their dirty work, but something changed in their plan."

"It seems that way."

This close, his eyes looked to hold specks of silver, like infinitesimal stars.

"And they're still out there."

"Yes."

"Oh," I said, but I couldn't contemplate the implications of that right now.

Instead I lowered my head back down. After a beat, Daimyn's hand tentatively lifted, stroking once over my hair, his fingers catching on salty tangles. My throat began to ache with the questions that burned to be asked, and my heart thudded heavily against my ribs as I realized… I could ask them.

"What's a blood curse? What's it doing to me?" I spoke in a near-whisper so we didn't bother the other two. I didn't think I could handle anyone else in this conversation.

Daimyn's fingers threaded through my hair, carefully detangling the mess as he went. "The transfusion should have taken care of that, but we will do tests to be sure." He shifted, somehow merging himself further into me. "'Curse' is really a misnomer. Strigoi carry around particular…" He paused. "We'll call them diseases, that they can control. They can't usually affect large groups of people, but individuals are easily influenced if they know how."

Provoked by his answers and his touch, words became easy. They tumbled out of me, sometimes scrambled in the hurry to get out of my mouth. I told him about the collar thing that they'd put on me—*nasty mental magic taking away higher-function thought, it wouldn't have worked indefinitely,* he said—and the recording camera—*they received 8 videos of me*—and details about my kidnappers, one I recognized as a strigoi and then the woman made of fire—*sounded like a Jinn.*

When I told him about interfering with the taping sessions so they had to redo them, Regan snickered from the driver's seat.

"What's funny?" Sebille asked.

"You said you didn't want to know about their drama," Regan replied.

She huffed.

Too tired to care that Regan could hear us, details spilled out of me in no particular order or coherence with the relief of cutting open an abscess. Daimyn listened, his hand continuing their slow, steady movements. The calmness almost deceived me, but I Felt the slow tightening of something dangerous, deep in his chest, both a promise and a threat.

I mumbled through my escape to the outside, and faltered when I reached the point where I'd… shown them my location. I couldn't continue the plot by just skipping over it, and if I explained this strange supernatural bit, that opened up a lot more questions. Would he ask, if I didn't say anything? Would I tell him—even the parts I skipped over? Would he know what it meant?

Would he see the same thing Cerin had?

I hadn't thought there would be another way I'd have to be vulnerable. It must be possible to be intoxicated by trusting someone, because I wanted to do it. I wanted to tell him everything.

Daimyn's chest rose in a deep breath. "Did you really think that I wouldn't come for you? Or was that a line you fed them?"

I blinked, jarred by the new subject. Then I remembered the strigoi's taunting in the beginning. I didn't know how to answer. Because yes, a big part of me had believed it, but with him cradling me like this, it seemed borderline offensive to say it out loud.

His hand stilled, pressing firmly against the back of my skull as he held me to him. "I know I left upset that day, but I need you to understand I did not abandon you."

My heart gave a vicious lurch that seemed to destabilize something vital in my ribcage.

"After you told me about TASA, I left to deal with them directly. Regan was monitoring from a distance. I should have realized you would pull a stunt like leaving your house, your safety, in the dark, without alerting anyone, even though you *knew*, Fairian, you *knew* you were a target…" His voice dropped lower. "You cannot give our enemies openings like that. You cannot do that again."

Yeah. I'm super great at decision-making.

My fingers curled into the fabric of his shirt, and my voice came as a bare whisper: "I had to apologize."

His fingers tightened, and his voice came out with that deceptive and disconcerting vague amusement. "Did it occur to you we are both in possession of devices that easily transmit messages?"

I fought an inexplicable smile as my fingers traced the collar of his shirt like they had a mind of their own, skimming the heat of his skin. "What happened next? While I was gone?"

My parents had assumed a ransomer had taken me and had prepared accordingly, Daimyn said. He had *hoped* that was the case… but knew he was deluding himself even before the video showed up. It appeared on the Yillen doorstep about 24 hours after the time they thought I'd been taken. That one had been filmed while I still had the collar on.

"I thought if I could be quiet enough, I could prevent altering your life forever," Daimyn said. "Any action of mine outside the norm brought the risk of more attention. So I skulked about trying to find information on where you'd be taken."

Underneath my fingertips, his throat moved in a swallow. I followed the movement, entranced by touching him.

"Then what happened?"

"Then they hurt you."

"And you were angry?" As if I were a child, needing to confirm all his emotions.

His chest rose in a slow, deliberate movement. I found the hollow at the base of his throat, the beat of his heart rising against my fingers.

"I was angry," he confirmed. It fascinated me how calm those words were, while the air around us practically shuddered. "But I couldn't comply. If I proved that I would do as they asked to keep you safe…"

I followed his collarbone with my fingertips all the way out to his shoulder. That was less nice, because I had to stop touching his skin due to his shirt.

"Yet I still could not find a single whisper of where you were."

His fingers, still working through the tangles of my hair, tugged on a particularly bad knot, and I winced.

"I am so sorry, Fairian." His voice was a rasp of sound. "There are not enough apologies in the world."

Maybe it made me masochistic, but I held no betrayal in my heart.

"But… you eventually did what they asked. You did… you had to…" I licked my lips. The pieces of everything over the past days, weeks, months started clicking together into a picture that couldn't be real. "By complying with their demands, you proved that they could control you. Using me. That's what you did, isn't it?"

"Yes."

My hand curled into a fist against his chest. "But… that sounds bad. That sounds *really* bad."

"It will have consequences."

"Why would you do that?"

"Why do you think?"

Goddamn question to answer a question. "This can't have been the first time someone tried to manipulate you this way."

He finished working his fingers through that knot in my hair and took his sweet damn time responding.

"I have earned the reputation of being ruthless for a reason. Creating a way to control one of us, to manipulate our actions, could be catastrophic to supernatural power dynamics. It is much safer to turn our backs on one life than allow the possibility of one of us being used for an agenda to harm many others."

I stared forward, unblinking. "Then what the hell happened with me."

"Something else, obviously," he said mildly.

I scowled. Murmuring shot across the car from Regan's direction. It nearly made me jump; I'd forgotten about the others in the vehicle.

Daimyn huffed. "Fine. Here's the truth: I knew as soon as the first video arrived that I should *let you go*." The last words caught in his chest with a guttural reverberation that made all the hair on my body stand on end. My breath caught even as my whole body pressed closer. His fury felt just as purifying in person as it had before.

"I deluded myself into thinking I could do it, I could find you with no one the wiser. And when that fucking leech made everything critical, I knew what I was *supposed* to do. Despite knowing it would result in your death. Despite the notion making me want to rip everything apart. I absolutely could not be selfish and do everything to keep you."

Sebille groaned from the front seat. "Lord save me from courting…" Her last word I couldn't make out.

Oops. We'd gotten loud.

Daimyn cleared his throat, and his words came out clear and polite. "My apologies, Sebille."

Regan leaned forward and turned up the radio. Amusement made little eddies in the air around him. *That is so weird.* Disregarding their presences again, I slid my hand up Daimyn's neck to the base of his head while also trying to process what "do everything to keep you" did to my insides.

"But you didn't do what you were supposed to do," I murmured, determined to get us back on track.

Daimyn lowered his mouth to my ear, and the heat of his breath caressed my skin with every word. "No, I didn't. I made a decision instead."

I shivered. "What did you decide?"

"I decided, until you tell me otherwise, I will not let you go. Not to the bastards who took you, not to death, and not to the thousand next who move against us."

I fought to swallow correctly, dizzy disbelief assaulting me. "Why."

"You know the answer to that." Was he *nuzzling* my ear? "You seemed quite upset about the fact earlier."

My fingers clenched in his hair and I shut my eyes. Under normal circumstances I would have been a stunned deer in the headlights, but exhaustion destroyed my pretense. "Tell me anyway."

He was definitely nuzzling my ear.

"Maybe I also need some reassurances first." His voice dipped into teasing, but none of the rest of him said playful. "Considering the last I knew, you were trying to sell my secrets to TASA."

I stiffened, my eyes popping open. *God, we still have that to get through.* "That's not what—" I struggled to organize my thoughts, trying to wiggle my head out from under his chin so I could look at him. "Daimyn, I'm sorry."

His grip on me tightened, preventing me from moving. "It's not *your* fault. You were handling a difficult situation in the way you knew how."

I stopped fighting and squeezed my eyes shut. "I should have told you earlier, or—"

He jostled me gently. "Stop it. That's not what I want."

My stomach and heart crammed up my throat. I was pretty sure he wanted *reassurances* in the same way I wanted *reassurances*: the need to know where the other person stood after this hellscape situation. Which created a stomach-hollowing level of nerves, but was somehow also reassur*ing*.

What could I say that would be honest and somehow explain… everything?

"When I first met you…" Nope, that was corny. "When I'm around you…" When I'm around him *what*? I turn into a nitwit? "I have never trusted any—" That just sounded melodramatic.

With his cheek pressed against the top of my head, his spreading grin telegraphed against my scalp. "I like this. Keep going."

I huffed. "You like what, my inability to complete full sentences?"

"Have I made you *speechless*?"

I groaned and crammed my face into his shoulder. He chuckled, readjusting his arms around me, and the air seemed to soften and warm.

"You've got to stop trying to do this alone," the sister in my dying mind said.

"Until you tell me otherwise, I will not let you go," the Daimyn of now said.

I knew I didn't understand the full extent of what all of this meant, the repercussions it would have. Still. I took a deep breath to speak, and his attention rested heavily as he waited.

The fragile thing that had taken over my chest blared a warning, wrenching at my insides, threatening to tear me wide open. But I leaned into the protectiveness Daimyn had wrapped me in, the night-dark blanket I saw every time I closed my eyes.

A shocking amount of ferocity filled the words that came out of me. "I'm not letting you go either."

Deep within his chest, a rumble ignited. This one was different than the others I'd heard. A hum of soft bliss resonated into the very depths of my heart.

I dozed the rest of the way to Farfalla. Well, except for a few moments in the middle somewhere.

"Are you *purring* right now?" *Sebille*. She sounded scandalized and delighted.

Said-purring hiccoughed, severely interrupting my nap. Complaints grumbled out of me. "Don't stop."

A laugh quickly turned into a cough. *Regan*. My eyes creaked open. Outside the window, the sky was already more green than blue. *Home*. We were almost home.

Daimyn's purr picked up again with decidedly more volume. *I should ask how he does that*. Sighing, I snuggled into him, and drifted back to sleep.

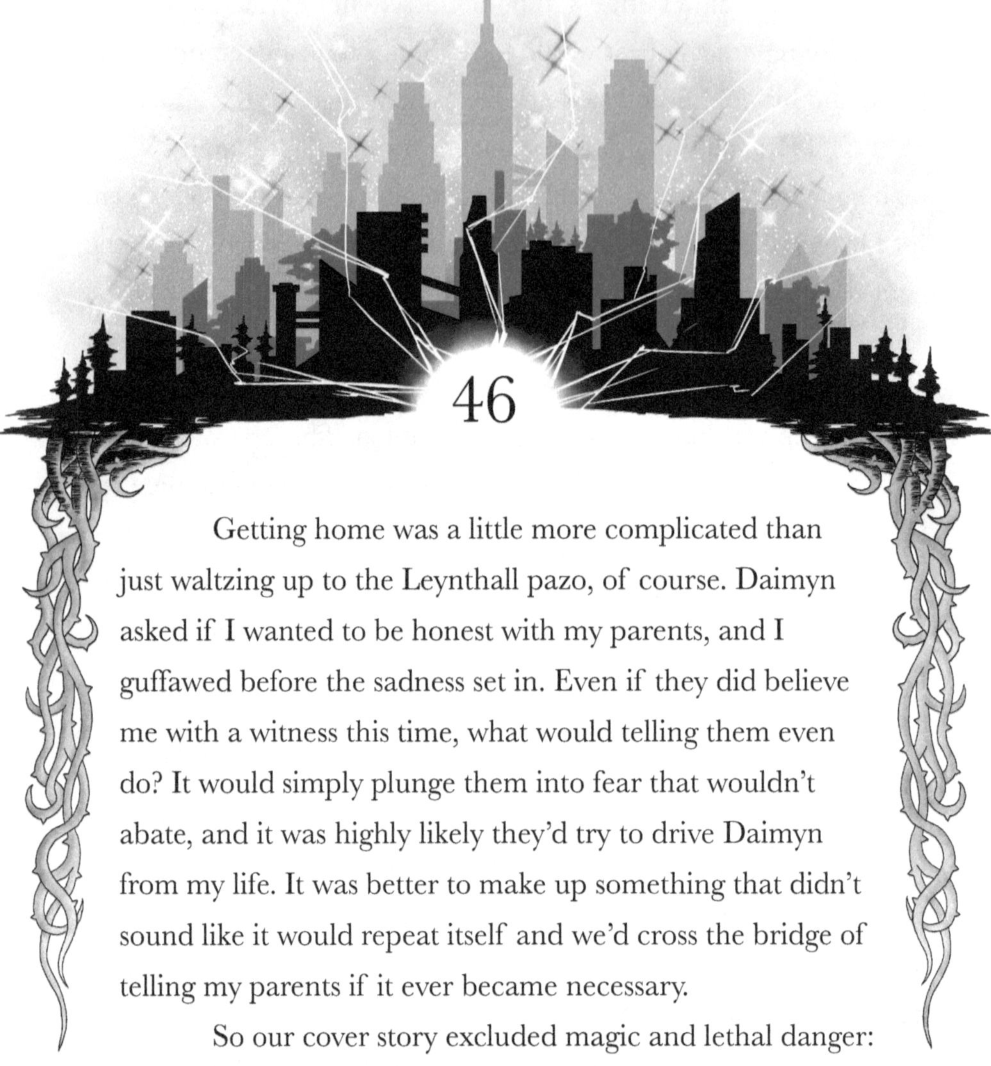

46

Getting home was a little more complicated than just waltzing up to the Leynthall pazo, of course. Daimyn asked if I wanted to be honest with my parents, and I guffawed before the sadness set in. Even if they did believe me with a witness this time, what would telling them even do? It would simply plunge them into fear that wouldn't abate, and it was highly likely they'd try to drive Daimyn from my life. It was better to make up something that didn't sound like it would repeat itself and we'd cross the bridge of telling my parents if it ever became necessary.

So our cover story excluded magic and lethal danger: amateur ransomers had taken me, but I'd escaped and gotten lost in the woods. After stumbling around for a week and a half, a concerned stranger found me and took me to a hospital in Farfalla. It would explain my weakness from dehydration and starvation, and Daimyn used the golden stone to heal the appearance of the strigoi's bites. He'd tried to heal as much as he could of the raw skin on my wrists, but the stone couldn't completely erase it.

My legs trembled as I got out of the vehicle in front of the hospital, but the electrolytes and the nap had me at least stronger than wet paper.

Daimyn looked like he'd swallowed something bitter, his gaze fixed on me and tracking every twitch.

"I will not be far," he lectured for the fifth time. "I will listen and watch and make sure you are safe."

I nodded, trying not to smile at how his hands gripped the car like he needed to physically keep himself in place again, then turned to walk into the hospital.

My mother burst into tears as soon as she rounded the doorway into the hospital room they'd put me in. Real ones that heaved her entire body and made her face bloom an unattractive red and splotchy. I found myself sobbing into her chest as she held me in a vise, my father gingerly sitting next to me on the hospital bed as his entire body shook, head bowing low over our clasped hands.

Tiff arrived a few hours later. She'd probably been told the story I'd already managed to relay to my parents, but she didn't say a word. She simply climbed into bed with me, hideous purple bags under her eyes and her face white as a sheet, and wrapped herself around me like a cocoon. Both of us slept the afternoon away.

By that evening, after fluids and liquid nutrition and whatever else they gave me in those IV bags, the hospital released me. They said that there was not a lot to do but rest, recuperate, and heal.

Through all of it, a steady warm hum wrapped around me, unseen and undoubtedly present.

The police and Ransom Recovery took my statement the next day as seemingly half the household hovered over me. I kept it simple, trying to joke and play myself off as a fool for escaping and getting so very, very lost. They'd seemed mollified. Though Tiff and my mother had peculiar expressions afterwards. It hadn't escaped my notice that our security team seemed to have doubled overnight, that Abigail and Tiffany literally never left me alone. My father had already told me he was interviewing candidates for my own personal guard.

It gave me a new appreciation for the consequences of my reckless actions.

Daimyn, to my utter surprise, called on me as Polite Society Yillen only a couple days later. Tiff and my mother's eyebrows seemed glued to their hairlines as they watched Daimyn tease me about survival skills and asked superfluous questions about my health. Superfluous, because he already knew the state of my health inside and out. He and Regan had been taking my vitals and running tests daily to make sure his blood wasn't doing bad things to me.

I messaged him soon as he left.

F. Leynthall: *What was that?*

D. Yillen: *What, you don't want your family to know about me?*

D. Yillen: *That was a joke. Establishing a baseline acquaintance and trust with your family will probably be helpful in the future.*

To Daimyn, that apparently meant visiting every couple days. Which did not construe a "baseline acquaintance" to my mother or Tiff, who now had *ideas.* Somehow I never got around to asking him to stop.

Clara Sylvan and her family visited, too. And I had to sit through visits from a few others that my parents had befriended in the couple months we'd been here. Those visits made my brain want to melt, so at least some things never changed.

The visit I should have been expecting came a week after my return to Farfalla.

47

I jolted out of a doze by a quiet knock on the door.

"Ms. Fairian?" Mr. Greaving said, opening the door. "Are you receiving?"

I lurched upright.

Tiff, lounging across from me, snickered. "Wow, it's only been like 24 hours since the last visit."

I made a face at the insinuation in her voice, privately smug that *no*, he'd been in my room like 14 hours ago, sitting on my windowsill and talking to me until I fell asleep. Not that she needed to know *any* of that. I scanned my outfit, blinking rapidly and trying to drag my mental state into the land of the living. There didn't appear to be food on me, and my clothes were presentable enough: long wrap tunic and leggings. *Good enough.*

"Yes," I called out, then cleared my throat of grogginess. "I'm available."

"There is a gentleman here from Ransom Recovery."

I stilled. The temperature in the room seemed to plummet as every eye turned towards me.

"Did he say why?"

455

"He did not elaborate beyond saying he needed further information for your ongoing protection."

Suspicion prickled at me. It deepened to anxiety as I registered something else: the lack of Daimyn's presence. My new and improved overwhelm of Feelings had not dissipated, and Daimyn and Regan were unmistakable to be around. I'd fallen asleep with the Feeling not unlike a hurricane had parked itself on my head. The absence of it, after days, made space eerily empty.

"I've put him in the drawing room," Mr. Greaving added.

I slid my feet to the floor and stood, pulling my PCD out of my pocket and noting a new message from Daimyn.

"What is a description of the gentleman in question?" I asked.

D. Yillen: *I need to grab something, will be back shortly.*

"I recognize him from months ago, miss Fairian. Blonde and light blue eyes."

A chill spread down my spine. It could not be a coincidence he showed up in Daimyn's absence.

"Darling, do you want company?" my mother's voice came softly.

Yes. But I didn't want my family anywhere near Lieutenant Andrews. I briefly considered having Mr. Greaving send him away, but he'd certainly just return, and probably with more threats. Andrews had no doubt arrived with a purpose and I needed information on his plans.

"No," I said. "It's all right. It'll be quick, I'm sure."

I stared at the closed door to the sitting room in front of me and took deep and even breaths. While I understood the anxiety, I really wished my stomach would stop tying itself into knots. It would make thinking easier. I traced the shape of my PCD with my fingers, hesitating over the send button for the message cued there. I might have asked for help in the midst of dying, but that didn't make it any easier to do it now.

I gritted my teeth. I'd been blissfully ignoring the issue of balancing my autonomy with the realities of my situation now in regards to Daimyn, and apparently that time had come to an end.

How pathetic is it that I can't even handle one blackmailing dude?

On the other hand, it is *because of Daimyn I'm in this situation, so it would make sense to rely on his assistance.*

I didn't tell him about Andrews before and see how well that went.

And that whisper came back to me. *"You don't have to do this alone anymore."*

Swallowing, I hit send to the message to Daimyn and Regan.

F. Leynthall: *Lieutenant Andrews from TASA is here. He's the one who blackmailed me before. I'm going to talk to him to find out what he wants.*

With one last deep breath, fixing a sarcastic curve to my lips, I shoved open the doors and strode inside. Andrews turned towards me, standing behind the flowery lounge. A tray of tea and biscuits sat on the low table between the lounge and opposite couch.

"Lieutenant Andrews, what a pleasant surprise," I said with saccharine-sweetness. "Do sit."

I moved to the couch opposite him, busying myself with preparing tea. His gaze rested heavily on me, and warning prickled along the back of my neck. I suddenly wished I'd thought to grab a knife, or some kind of defensive weapon.

Relax, they're not going to kill their source of information, I thought bitterly.

That didn't mean they wouldn't try other things.

"Ms. Leynthall, it is good to see you," he said, and even if he sounded genuine, I had to bite back a nasty word at what he called me.

I hummed vaguely in response to his statement. "Tea?"

"No, thank you," he said, easing down on the lounge. "I might take a biscuit, though," he said almost like a joke.

I finished with my tea and prepared two biscuits on a plate for him, handing it over and bizarrely determined not to let any part of me touch him. He took the plate awkwardly, sitting on the very edge of the lounge as if resting his full weight might break it. It *did* look deceivingly delicate. I didn't try very hard to hide my smirk at his discomfort.

The clock ticked on the wall, grating my ears as I took a sip of tea and made a face. This new blend was bitter. Maybe it was a Galician thing. Cafe con leche was more the style.

"What can I do for you?" I asked after several moments, aggravated that he didn't just get to the point. "If you're looking for information, I'm not sure what I can give you."

Andrews set the plate with biscuits down on the low table after taking one bite. I affixed the patronizing smile to my face.

He met my gaze grimly. "I wonder if you truly realize what he has done to you."

Irritation swallowed me whole, and before I thought better of the idea I opened my eyes wide and clutched my chest with a theatrical gasp. "Oh no! What has he done?" Then I let my face fall flat and stared at him.

A muscle ticked in Andrews' jaw. "That creature won't even remember you in a few years, but this will haunt you for your entire life."

Not remember me? What did that mean?

Don't rise to the bait.

Which all reminded me: Daimyn and I needed to have a private heart-to-heart because I needed to *not* be the person with the least amount of information about him in the room.

"I don't really have time for dramatics," I said. "What do you want?"

Another long silence. Meant to intimidate or make me uncomfortable? I sipped tea and realized with a small amount of horror that my hands trembled. *This is* not *anxiety, just lingering weakness from being held captive.*

"His actions have signaled open season on you," Andrews said, low. "Everyone will see the opportunity to influence him, now that he's confirmed it will work."

I waved a hand around. "I know that already."

"I think you don't have the slightest clue what kind of hell will rain down on you." Andrews leaned forward. "You realize that everything will change. You won't be able to walk down the street without fore-planning. Your relationships will always be suspect, and never your own. Your choices will depend on whether he allows it. Your—"

"Your point?" I bit out, instantly regretting I'd been provoked into a response.

Andrews nodded, as if whatever he'd seen on my face confirmed something. "We can protect you from this, before it's too late. In a much better way than he can."

I snorted, nearly upsetting my tea. "You're the one who keeps going on about how powerful he is. How would *your* protection somehow be better than someone who clearly scares the shite out of you?"

"Because we may be able to give you a normal life."

I snorted. "I have never desired a normal life."

"Perhaps, but you desire autonomy, the ability to choose, to be able to learn and grow at your own leisure. Do you truly want this dangerous spotlight he's placed you in?"

I inhaled slowly, pissed that he hadn't completely missed the mark. I'd drank almost all my tea already; the nervous gesture betrayed me. *Damn it.*

My chin lifted, my stomach tightening. "And what—if I don't comply, it's back to threatening to ruin Tiff's life?"

Andrews eyebrows drew together in confusion. Then he let out a bitter laugh. "Your paramour has neglected to tell you we are no longer in possession of pictures of Tiffany Collins."

What?

"This is not about holding anything over your head. This is a genuine offer, Ms. Leynthall. No more games. So I ask you again— what is it you truly want?"

That's not my goddamn name.

I couldn't think of what he'd accomplish by lying about not having the pictures of Tiff—which meant it was probably the truth. Relief and bitter delight drove the words from my mouth. "Mostly for you to take a long walk over a tall cliff, but I doubt I'll get my wish."

Andrews' jaw clenched, and his gaze dropped to the low table between us. The ticking clock grew ominously loud again, and I twitched as he abruptly rose to his feet.

"I am sincerely sorry. I wish you would let us help you. Though it is not your fault, you have become a great threat."

Tension crawled up my spine. My brain wanted to blank in panic as I pressed instinctively back against the couch. *I'm entirely too unprepared for this.* My **PCD** buzzed against my thigh, and I couldn't help but think he was too late.

To my utter bewilderment, Andrews simply turned and strode for the door of the sitting room. My mouth parted in confusion, feeling vaguely like I might throw up.

Andrews reached the door—and it swung open all by itself. Andrews froze, then rapidly retreated as Daimyn stepped into the room with a familiar, deceptive, and faintly amused smile. My lungs collapsed in relief. I caught a glimpse of Mr. Greaving's concerned face right before Daimyn smoothly turned, shut the door, and swiveled to face me.

"Are you all right?" His soft words slipped past all the prickly attitude I'd donned.

I nodded quickly as a lump formed in my throat. *He came.*

How had I not Felt him approach? But I'd been distracted, and Daimyn Felt like a hurricane encased behind glass; subdued and muted in a way I didn't believe for an instant, a blizzard straining to crack the pane.

Those dark, sharp eyes slid to Andrews. "Agent," Daimyn said with vague amusement. "It's about time we met in person."

Andrews paled, chin lifted and hands tightly fisted at his sides.

"Deathless," he responded, his voice *almost* making it to neutral. Resignation crept over his face as his hands flexed open.

My stomach cramped, as if protesting the relief that had dumped into it. Daimyn hummed, taking slow steps further into the room, inspecting the spread on the low table in front of me.

"Biscuits are good," I blurted. "Tea is a little bitter though." *Helpful, Fairian. Just helpful.*

Daimyn glanced at me with real amusement crinkling the corners of his eyes. Just as quickly, they turned cold and slid back to Andrews, lips still curled in a slight smile.

"It seems I wasn't clear in regards to the rules for *interactions* with Ms. Fairian."

SEE! Someone could use my name right.

Andrews' throat moved as he swallowed, his attention darting to me and back. His fear seemed to infect everything around him, seeping through the room and sending nausea twisting through me. Grimacing, I pressed a hand to my abdomen.

"What are the rules, agent?" Daimyn asked, low and arctic.

My skin prickled. *Andrews really just came here to spout doom and gloom, without a single thing to hold over my head?*

"I understand the guidelines you outlined in London and—"

"What are the *precise rules, agent?*" A guttural rattle snagged in his chest even as his expression remained perfectly the same. Why did that hair raising sound comfort me so much?

Andrews glanced at me, then winced as if he hadn't meant to.

He really planned to just walk out of here without doing something? Dread rose inside of me.

"Prior approval," the TASA agent finally said. "Anything construed as a threat will—"

"Did he threaten you, Fairian?"

I grimaced. "Not really. But no more blackmail, huh? That would have been a nice head's up."

Nausea surged, and I pressed the back of my hand to my mouth. *This can't be just Andrews' fear, can it? Of course I would barf all over the floor during this very tense encounter. Of course.*

"Ah, right, I'd forgotten to—" Daimyn cut himself off. "What's wrong?"

I looked up to see him scanning me. "I don't know," I gulped, and with acknowledgement it all seemed to get so much worse, acid bubbling up my esophagus.

Daimyn stiffened and slowly looked back at Andrews. Andrews, who paled further, something flinching across his expression. Then I Felt it: guilt.

All heat drained from my face.

"Did he touch you?" Daimyn demanded. "Give you anything?"

"No, I made sure—"

Then my attention zeroed in on the table. And the tray.

Each word came with dawning, rasping horror: "The tea was already here—"

Daimyn snatched up the teacup closest to me and lifted it to his nose, inhaling.

"—when I arrived," I finished uselessly.

Daimyn stilled, his predatory motionless blanketing the whole room, even as his eyes flared with understanding. For the first time since he entered, that vague amusement fell, his features twisting into something downright feral.

Andrews darted for the window, his forearms rising up as if he meant to protect his head diving through it. He'd barely made it two steps when Daimyn *appeared*. Daimyn hooked his arm around Andrews' neck, taking his feet out from under him and slamming the TASA agent onto the floor on his back. I flinched, the thud reverberating.

Daimyn knocked Andrews' strikes aside like flies as he pinned his arms down and drove a knee into his chest.

"*What did you give her?*"

My eyes widened as dishes and silverware on the low table rattled, the pictures on the walls of the room shivering in distress. Andrews made a choked sound. Daimyn's fingers spanned Andrews' neck as he wrapped one hand around his jaw, pressing down.

"You would have brought an antidote, something to counteract it in the hope she would leave with you."

My stomach twisted viciously, and I let out an involuntary sound. I pressed a hand against my mouth, the room blurring a little. Daimyn glanced again, then flipped Andrews onto his front while yanking his wrists behind his back with one hand, his other hand rifling through Andrews pockets.

Several endless moment clicked by without Daimyn finding anything, and misery rose.

"What if it's… in a car or…"

"You're reacting too fast. He would have kept it on him."

Despite the confidence in his voice, I Felt his bite of uncertainty. He drove his hand under Andrews' body, and the agent twisted wildly, as if protecting something. Daimyn grabbed Andrews' hair and slammed his face into the floor; Andrews stopped fighting, his expression dazed.

Daimyn rifled through his clothes again, and his hand jerked up with a small vial. My heart leapt.

"Is that…?"

Daimyn suddenly crouched in front of me. "Drink."

"Are you sure?" I husked.

"No time to confirm."

I reached out to take it, and my arm abruptly dropped into my lap. I stared, the limb barely moving as I tried again. I met Daimyn's gaze as panic surged up to my eyeballs. A muscle flexed in his jaw as he smoothly snapped off the cap. He brought the glass to my lips, his other hand resting on the back of my head to hold me steady as I tipped my chin up, and the most awful taste filled my mouth. I almost spat it out.

After a second of it thoroughly coating my tongue, I realized I couldn't make myself swallow.

It won't be strigoi that kill me, it'll be my inability to drink.

A hysterical giggle rose. Abruptly, *finally*, my throat seized, and I choked down the liquid, all of my strength dedicated to just *drinking the damn antidote.*

Everything seemed to drain out of me at once, and the world tilted. Daimyn cradled my head with one hand, the other on my waist, as he slowed my collapse and lowered me sideways onto the couch. His lips faintly moved as if he whispered, but I couldn't hear over the ringing in my ears. I tried to clutch at him in panic, continuing to swallow over and over in case any bit of the liquid was left. Then my throat stopped responding to my brain's commands.

It's too late.

Daimyn's purr abruptly roared to life, furious in its attempt to comfort. It cut through the ringing, the panic screaming in my head, my wheezing breathing as my ribs struggled to move. I stared into the wild dark green of his eyes and thought at least I'd die with this view instead of the one before, the blue sky I *didn't* love with my whole heart.

Not being able to breathe would not be a quick death. I'd have to feel each second of suffocation, and I tried to steel myself. I focused on him with everything in me, each of my breaths slowing and…

Getting easier?

My lungs began to fill deeper with each breath, the hammering of my heart easing a fraction. Daimyn's face blurred as saltwater gathered but I refused to blink in case this really was the end and I missed even a fraction of a second.

Several heartbeats later, my muscles responded as I shifted my shoulder so my elbow could take some of my weight from Daimyn's hand. I balled my hand in a fist, swallowed, and shifted my cheek against his palm.

"I think it's working," I whispered.

His eyes shut for a beat longer than a blink as his purr quieted but richened, and his thumb caressed back and forth across my brow.

A few minutes later I realized Andrews had disappeared.

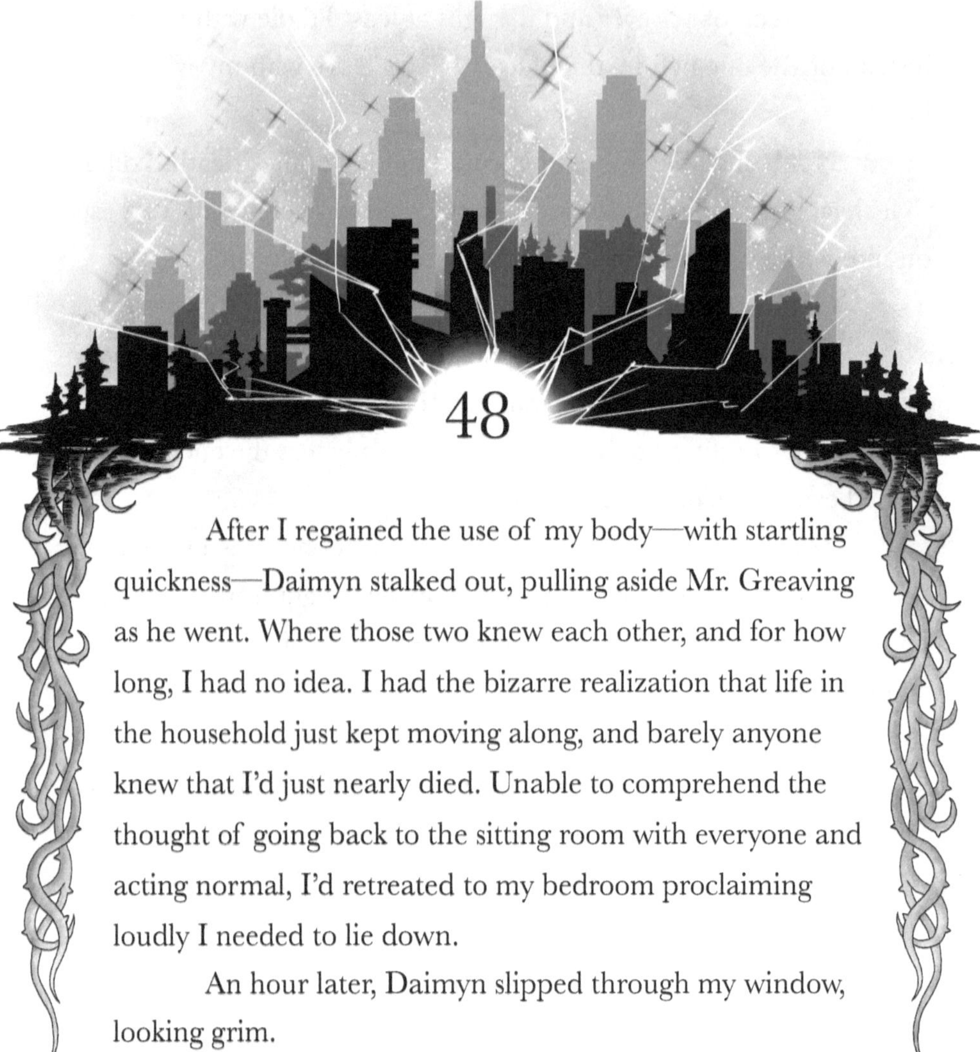

48

After I regained the use of my body—with startling quickness—Daimyn stalked out, pulling aside Mr. Greaving as he went. Where those two knew each other, and for how long, I had no idea. I had the bizarre realization that life in the household just kept moving along, and barely anyone knew that I'd just nearly died. Unable to comprehend the thought of going back to the sitting room with everyone and acting normal, I'd retreated to my bedroom proclaiming loudly I needed to lie down.

An hour later, Daimyn slipped through my window, looking grim.

"Well, that seemed like a big escalation," I said cheerfully from my position in bed. "For TASA," I added, as if the subject hadn't been obvious.

"I must apologize," Daimyn responded, his formal tone only further highlighting the bitter guilt clinging to him. "I did not think they would make that leap, and not so quickly."

I flapped my hand at his apology. "Stop. Why the leap, though? Why would they try to kill an 'asset'?"

"It seems they decided to eliminate the wildcard, now that you are common knowledge and they've struggled to control you."

Why do I get the feeling there's more to it than that?

"Because of what you did to get me back," I said slowly.

"That may contribute, yes."

I scowled when he didn't further elaborate, ignoring my subtle poking just as well as he ignored my outright questions about what exactly he'd done while I'd been kidnapped. He'd firmly stuck to his decision not to tell me anything.

Daimyn muttered something under his breath.

I blinked. "What?"

"I only left to get you presents."

That's what I'd thought he'd said.

"Oh," I said, delight already creeping into my voice. "Why?"

Daimyn grimaced. "The fact that you ask that makes this even worse," he muttered. "I initially set out for these because I want you to have them." His weight shifted. "Though they have become an apology now as well."

I frowned. "You don't need to apologize for sodding TASA and—"

"Not that. I have to leave Farfalla for a while. Though that will be delayed now for obvious reasons."

My heart sank a startling amount. "What? Why?"

"Let me also preface this by saying Regan will be keeping you safe. I promise."

I blew a raspberry in response to that, and parts of myself stuck in the fog of recovery snapped back into place. *I'm not helpless, for god's sake.* I crossed my arms over my chest. "All right, fine. More world saving duties, I imagine?"

"Sebille has asked for my help." His jaw tensed for a beat. "I owe her, and we need allies. This is a chance to build trust with Sebille and her family. They are powerful, and have a lot of influence."

I made a face. "Do you owe her because she helped find me?" *Nevermind I found you, but I wouldn't have been able to communicate, so—yeah. We owe her.*

He nodded once.

We hadn't talked about how they'd discovered my location. I wondered if he thought Sebille had reached me, not the other way around. Neither of them had said anything about it. Though, her offhand words as she departed after our one and only meeting had imprinted in my skull:

"Hey, I know it was a dire emergency and all, but next time you do"—she waved a hand—*"whatever that was you did to show us your location, make sure you anchor yourself. That was dangerous, doing it like that."*

Too bad I didn't have a clue what she meant.

I sniffed haughtily and tried to bury the rawness in my chest. "So the presents are buying off my goodwill. I see how it is."

Daimyn made an aggravated huff, but one side of his mouth pulled upwards into a crooked smile. "May I approach?"

I blinked, then realized he meant since I sat in bed, and also belatedly realized he hadn't moved from the window into the room at all.

Heheh, just a man in my room. Sure.

"Oh. Of course." I waved a hand, opening my mouth to say something like *you don't have to ask* or *I'm not afraid you're going to jump me* or something else that undoubtedly wouldn't help anything. I snapped my mouth shut instead.

Daimyn soundlessly approached, hesitating only a bare second before he sat on the edge of the bed. I sat up straighter, scooting up to make sure he had enough room, then worried the movement made it seem like I'd moved away from him.

Good grief.

Daimyn dug through a satchel strung across his body that I hadn't registered before. After a second he pulled a thick, dark blue book out of the bag and offered it to me. *Book!* My brain bleated. *From him, it has to be about magic.* I barely breathed as I accepted it. The cover was well-handled but newer, the edges of the pages softened but even.

"For anyone else I would call this homework," he said dryly. "That is a compendium of some of the best methods of defense against various types of creatures and magical situations. It doesn't have everything, but it does address the basics. I want you to have a working understanding of it all by the time I return."

My spine went straight, any affront at his order fading at the prospect of what might be inside. Then his words registered.

"Wait. By the time you return—how long are you going to be gone?"

"A few weeks. A month at most." He hesitated. "I think."

I narrowed my eyes, forcing myself to *not feel sad.*

He smiled slowly and lopsided. "Why? Will you miss me?"

I sniffed dismissively. "I just want you for your information goods, you know that."

His smile widened, exposing long canines. It made him look rather wicked. "I don't believe you."

Daimyn watched me, unmoving and exuding expectant patience. This was not the first time he'd done this; I knew what he wanted. And now heat crept up my neck to join the ridiculous party that was my body's reaction to him.

"Fine," I said austerely, waving a hand. "I will miss the hell out of you." *Aaaand that's all the vulnerable truth I have in me for today!*

His eyes turned soft without losing intensity. "Good." And without returning the sentiment—what a brat—he pulled another book out of his bag. "Your second present."

It immediately distracted me. This one was thin, and the cover looked to be made of a dark wood of some kind, worn smooth on the edges. His expression grew cautious as he handed it over.

"That is the only written collection of information my family has found on dokkalfar."

Weight dropped into my stomach.

His voice gentled. "I don't know if there will be answers to what happened with you and your sister, but I thought you might find something of comfort inside."

I swallowed and stared at the completely benign cover like it might spit poison. How did I feel about this? Did I even want to know? Did it even matter? Did—

"Also," Daimyn said, voice careful. "There is a letter inside. Regan found it, and I think you should have it. My memory is a little fuzzy on the issue—at some point I will need to explain that to you— but I believe it is the reason our paths crossed the first time."

I frowned at him, sliding my fingers underneath the wooden cover to feel the folded paper just inside. Andrews had mentioned something about Daimyn's memory, hadn't he?

"Third present."

Daimyn pulled another item from his satchel, with two hands this time and more carefully than with the others. I made myself focus on it: dark cloth, wrapped around something rectangular—book shaped again. He hesitated, studying me for a weight-filled second, then offered it to me with both hands.

"You may only keep this until I return, so I recommend translating quickly. The information inside, however, is yours."

I put the other two books down to accept it. It was surprisingly light, the cloth dense but soft. With another glance at his odd expression, I unwrapped it. This book looked far older than the others. The binding lined up unevenly and the spine looked broken in sections, barely held together with makeshift ties. The age-yellowed pages were wrinkled and torn along the edges, and the paper material looked varied. The cover seemed in slightly better shape, but a dark stain covered the lower half. My fingertips tingled. Worn, faded writing peeked out from one of the edges. It almost looked like archaic Latin…

"This is one of my father's first journals—back when he was human. It details the beginning of our history. That explains who we are, and why."

My eyes shot to his. Chills spread down my spine, and the journal doubled in mass.

"That… this sounds…" *Dangerous. It sounds dangerous for me to have.* I had the unsettling certainty I didn't fully understand the gravity of what he'd given me. My heart swelled and then sank at his trust. "Daimyn… you can't give this to me." I looked down at the journal, forcing my fingers not to curl possessively around the pages. "What if TASA gets more blackmail? What if someone *else* threatens me?"

He waved a hand dismissively. "Let me worry about that."

Oh, sure, just like that. I wouldn't worry. Sure.

"This sounds exactly like something TASA would want. How much could this information hurt you?"

Daimyn's head tilted to the side, his smile soft. "Fairian, you have my permission—no, you have my *request*—to share this information in a situation where you would need to reveal it to protect your health or life."

I nearly squirmed, narrowing my eyes on him. "Why are you giving this to me?"

One shoulder lifted in a shrug, his gaze lowering. "I withheld something important from you. Now I am giving something important. In the spirit of Shahar—this is a secret very few know."

I stared at him in confusion. Then I remembered: his promise, after I found out he'd known about Cerin, that he would make up for withholding the information from me. My mouth wordlessly hung open at the notion that he might still *owe* me.

"If you don't want it—"

"Of course I *want* it," I blurted, hunching protectively over it. I wanted it so much my stomach cramped.

He smiled lopsidedly. "Good. Be careful with it. There are a few preservation enchantments on it, but it's about three-thousand years old."

I stared at him as my head exploded. One questioned formed crystal clear in front of the chaos.

"If he's that old," I said very calmly. "How old does that make you?"

I suddenly recalled how Andrews had said they'd been trying to approach Daimyn for "decades."

Daimyn gave me an odd smile. "We're not entirely sure when we were born. My father apparently couldn't arse himself to put dates on anything."

I blinked. Blinked again. "But you're older than…" I scanned his face. How old did I think he was? "Twenty-five."

Daimyn winced. "I am *physically* older than twenty-five."

My eyes narrowed at his emphasis. "But not—what? Mentally? Emotionally?" I said wryly.

"Yes."

I double-blinked. Maybe I was trying to get more oxygen to my brain via my eyelashes. "What?"

Daimyn shifted, then opened his mouth to speak, though nothing came out for a few more seconds. "It's a bit of a longer explanation. That's why I want you to read the journal. What we are… is complicated. Part of that complication is that we don't…"

My eyebrows rose. I don't think I'd ever seen him at a loss for words.

"We lose time. *Lots* of time. It's better when we're awake, after we're more engaged, which lately only occurred after…" His gaze darted to me and away. "The point I'm trying to make is that I am younger than my age would suggest." He rubbed the back of his neck. "Though maybe that's not better."

Still mostly confused, I grinned like a snot. "How much younger? Younger than me? Does that mean I get to boss you around?"

He snorted. "You can try."

I stuck my tongue out at him. Deadpan, he stuck his right back out in return. I laughed out loud.

"I haven't had to explain this for a while," Daimyn said begrudgingly. "Read the journal. When I am back, I'll answer any and all of your questions."

When he is back. That killed my humor. I cleared my throat, annoyed with myself. I was a rational adult who was absolutely *not* going to mope over his departure.

Daimyn studied my face for a beat before his words came soft. "I would send Regan if I could."

"Maybe *I* should go," I said haughtily, ignoring that he obviously saw my bullshite emotions. "It's really my debt, anyway."

Daimyn smiled like he thought I'd said something cute. "This is for me to handle."

I made a face. *Speaking of debts.* "I'm going to owe you quite a lot by the end of this."

His eyebrows pulled down. "You don't owe me anything."

"Uh-huh."

Silence thickened the air for a beat.

"Fairian, I would like it if we did not have the kind of partnership where we had to speak of debts."

I nearly snickered at his precise formality, but the look on his face snuffed out that urge. *This really matters to him.*

"All right," I said quietly. "But didn't you just hand me your father's journal in the desire to make up for something?"

He shook his head once. "That was about amends. Not repayment."

Oh boy. What did he think owing someone was? What counted as amends or payment, and where could the line possibly be drawn philosophically, let alone practically?

But I let it go. Because it dawned on me, based on everything I knew about him so far, that he might not have many relationships not based on transactions of power. Did Daimyn have actual friends? People who he could count on, and counted upon him in return? People who... didn't speak of debts?

I held his dark, vivid gaze. "All right. No debts between us."

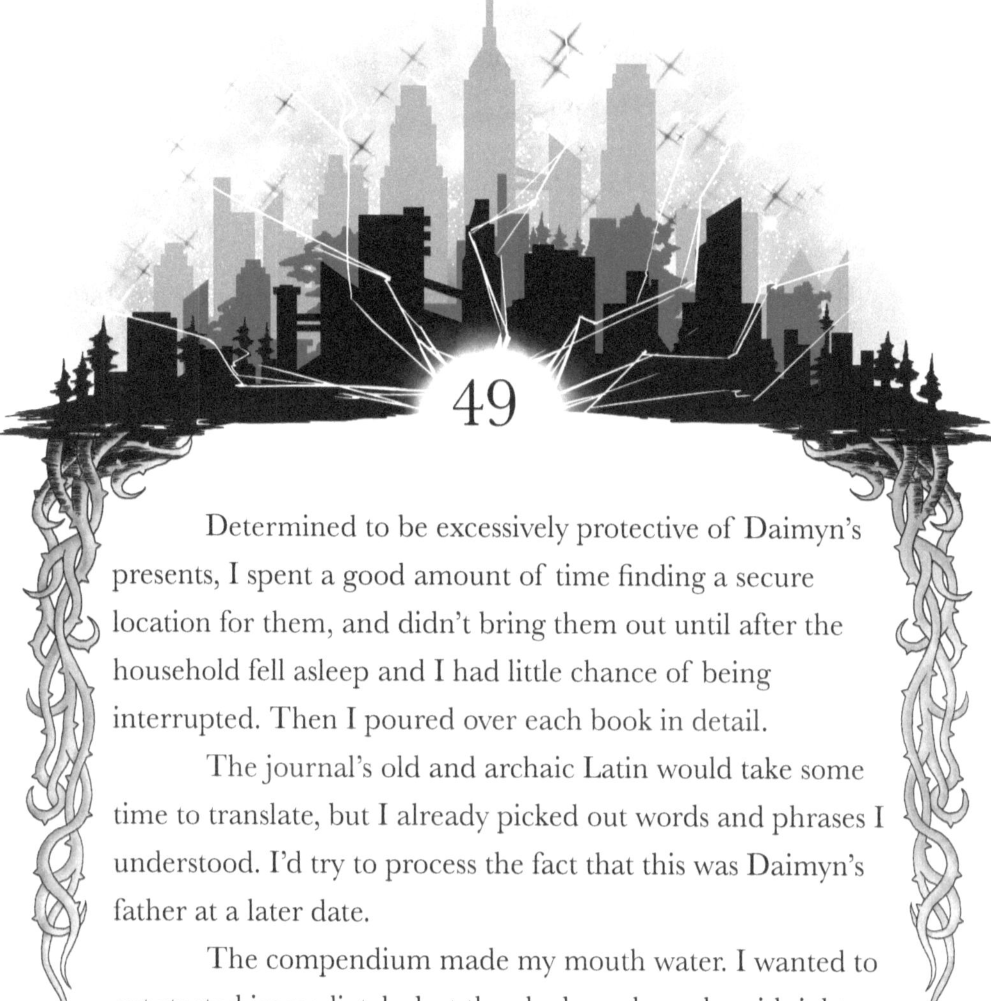

49

Determined to be excessively protective of Daimyn's presents, I spent a good amount of time finding a secure location for them, and didn't bring them out until after the household fell asleep and I had little chance of being interrupted. Then I poured over each book in detail.

The journal's old and archaic Latin would take some time to translate, but I already picked out words and phrases I understood. I'd try to process the fact that this was Daimyn's father at a later date.

The compendium made my mouth water. I wanted to get started immediately, but the clock read nearly midnight, and I'd promised myself I'd make a habit of actually sleeping. I'd start tomorrow.

Finally, I reluctantly turned to the dokkalfar book. With a deep breath, I flipped open the cover with one finger. Inside rested a folded letter, just like he'd said. The paper looked slightly aged, and 'Deathless' scrawled along the front in handwriting that…

All the blood drained from my face. I don't know how long I stared at it without moving. Mind static, I unfolded the letter, and the scrawl down the page was familiar to me as my own heart. My eyes fell to the very bottom of the page.

Her signature rested there.

Ms. Leynthall

Disbelief froze the air in my lungs. But there was nothing to do but start reading from the top.

Deathless,

My grandmother told me your story only once, but she impressed upon me the great importance of it. She spoke of your defense of the innocent, how you keep in check those whose power would otherwise consume the vulnerable. She told me what to do if ever I needed that kind of strength. So you can guess why I am contacting you. I don't know who else to turn to.

A man called Cerin Branwenn has…

My eyes shut. After a few endless moments, I opened them again and continued.

… called Cerin Branwenn has entered our lives, a few months ago now. On the surface he behaves perfectly well, a radiant and charming gentleman. Everyone is caught by him. But I have watched as he set his sights on my baby sister, as he draws her closer, and as he relishes in the power over her. Conventional means of keeping him away from her have failed. She is starting to isolate herself from us. I know why she is enchanted by him, and I am afraid she will not willingly leave his grip.

He's magickal, but I know not more than that. I wish I could point to a clear example of the danger; I wish I could say 'oh yes, he has a habit of eating young girls and plans to do so next Saturday at nine.' My grandmother's stories make me hope you will understand what I cannot articulate. I am hoping—praying—that you will understand the truth about this in a way I cannot.

Something has changed lately in the way he looks at her, treats her. You must understand—my sister is a light that the world does not deserve, and she does not yet know how to keep out those who would steal it from her. So I call upon your honor to defend her against those who would abuse her. I would be happy to be wrong, to be called out on any prejudice to magick that I am blind to be holding, to be proven as a dramatic and overly-concerned older sister. Please prove me wrong.

The words blurred, then cleared, as heat streaked down my face.

But please hurry.
Sincerely,
Ms. Leynthall

I turned the paper with trembling fingers to look at the date. It had been sent three days before Mari and I were taken. Three days before I'd met Cerin in that sodding garden, starry-eyed by his attentions and the idea that he might love me for being a freak, oblivious to Mari following me. Oblivious to the fact that I led my sister to her death.

Mari and I had gotten into so many fights about Cerin's attention. I wondered after which argument she'd wrote this. After I told her she was just jealous? Or when I said she couldn't stand the idea of someone wanting me over her? Or was it the argument where I screamed she just couldn't stand the idea that someone liked me without wanting to change me?

I stared down at the letter. This letter, which looked to have brought Daimyn to Northampton seven years ago. *Mari was the reason...*

Tears scalded down my cheeks. I couldn't breathe, or breathed too much.

Mari the reason Daimyn had gone to Northampton and found me. Mari was the reason I wasn't in the hands of a tyrant torturing me. Or dead.

If she hadn't sent this letter, would I have ever been found at all? Chills erupted across my whole body. Would I still be stuck there, if she hadn't sent this?

After Cerin, after Mari's death and the following cover-ups of magic, a gaping chasm had opened up between me and everyone else. I could talk to no one. My understanding of the world, myself—gone. The loneliness had been crippling. But if this letter had sent Daimyn to me, put him on the path of hunting down those who hurt me... I hadn't been alone.

Mari had made sure of that.

Through whatever bizarre quirk of fate, I'd found Daimyn again. I didn't like Daimyn's connection to my past any more than the last time I'd found out, but as I stared down at the soft paper, the deep creases of the fold, my sister's signature at the bottom... I smiled through tears. So what if the magic I'd found connected back to the horrible parts of my past. That just meant I was connected to it, too. Mari was connected to it, too. I was a sum of *all* my parts, and *my* choices had taken me here.

I set down the letter and looked at the rest of Daimyn's presents, touching each in turn. The symbolism of each dawned on me, and my throat closed, my fingers tingling.

My past. His past. A step towards the future.

For seven years, I'd been looking for magic. To prove it was real, to prove the world was bigger than everyone said… to prove that it wasn't all nightmares. All the while not entirely sure why it was so vital that I did. Maybe I'd really been searching to prove that what had changed in me didn't have to be only pain. It could be gentle touches and whispered secrets. It could be making a different choice this time. It could be trust.

I could both be changed and *not* be a reflection of the horror I'd survived.

Outside my window, the velvet darkness of the Farfallan sky gently embraced the world. All around me the city subtly shifted as it breathed and dreamed. Something soft nestled into my heart, something so unfamiliar it took me a long moment to recognize it. *Peace.* For this moment, contentment filled me. I had no illusions that it wouldn't be difficult going forward.

But this time, I didn't have to be alone.

A note to you, dear reader

Thank you for reading Jagged Emerald City, the first in the Obsidian Divide series. I really hope you enjoyed the beginning of Fairian's journey!

This book has been a long time coming. It actually started with me at 15 years old writing interactions between two characters as I tried to figure out my concept of romance. (I didn't kiss actual people to figure things out, I wrote stories about kissing people.) By the time I hit 20, Fairian and Daimyn started blossoming into the people you read today, and I intentionally developed the world where Farfalla exists. By my mid-late twenties, this story started it's final evolution into what you read here.

I think all debut authors probably say this in some form or another, but this book came right out of my soul. Not only did it grow with me, but—and I didn't realize it until nearly the end—I was working through a lot of my own trauma while putting Fairian through hell. Her struggles with PTSD, anxiety, and depression will continue to show up in the series, and I hope to do them justice for everyone struggling to be heard or seen.

Before you leave—and you've probably heard this before—if you have a second to leave JEC a review on Amazon, Goodreads, B&N, or wherever your heart desires, it would mean the world to me.

Author careers live or die on these things, and your thoughts make all the difference!

Additionally, I have a present for you: would you be interested in reading the first few chapters of Book 2 for free? You can find them here!

Also, if you'd like see what I'm currently up to and glimpse what's next in the series (and more!), you can find me at my website (rkbrainerd.com) using this code here:

Or if you're more interested in seeing daily updates, teasers, and my life as a writer, you can check out my Instagram:

Thank you again, and I hope to see you for book 2!

Acknowledgements

(Does anyone actually read these? Well anyway, here we go.)

As with any labor of love, this book has been influenced and helped by a lot of sources throughout the years. To count just a few:

To mom and dad—thanks for raising me to be someone who could accomplish this, cheering me on, and generally, you know, being my parents.

Elle—you were one of the first who helped me believe I could.

A shoutout to Mary Rosenblum, the first person to take me seriously—which made me start to take my own self seriously.

To the man I thought was my soulmate, thank you for your years of encouragement, time, and support.

Erika and Nicole and Kai: thanks for being amazing writer buddies.

Finally, last but not least, thank you to Will and Andy and the whole D&D group, who are a constant source of encouragement, humor, and inspiration.

About the author

R. K. Brainerd resides in the rainy Pacific Northwest and has been living in her own little world and writing it down since she was itty bitty. She's obsessed with anything related to dragons, myth and magic, environmentalism, and political/social justice. She believes that through the lens of science-fiction and fantasy we can understand our world better. (And if not, then we can have a fantastic time exploring imagination.)

She grew up devouring speculative fiction, so naturally gravitates towards this in her writing. Probably because of all this speculative fiction, social commentary of some element always finds itself somewhere in her stories. It also explains why she went and got a degree in politics.

It doesn't, however, explain why romance ends up in her writing too—that's purely her romantic soul.